Echoes in Time

Cover by: GetCovers

ISBN: 978-1-9162306-8-2

Echoes in Time

AMANDA M FLEET

Also by Amanda M Fleet

Out of Time

Writing as Amanda Fleet

The Wrong Kind of Clouds

Lies That Poison

The Guardians of The Realm Series

Aegyir Rises
Aeron Returns
War
Invasion
Chaos

For everyone who has believed in me, especially when I didn't believe in myself

1

"What am I doing here?"

Georgia halted a few steps from the doors to The Happy Badger pub, and sucked in a long breath. She would rather be at home, curled up with a good book, than have to make entertaining small talk for the next couple of hours on yet another blind-date. Should she just go home? That wasn't really fair to the poor guy. She should at least give him a chance. Who knew? Maybe this one might be The One?

Except she thought she'd met The One before, and he turned out not to be The One. At. All.

She checked the picture on her phone again. At least Mark was easy on the eye.

Squaring her shoulders, she yanked open the door and scanned the room, spotting Mark already at a table across the other side of the pub. She plastered a bright smile to her face, then made her way between the tables towards him. The local pub was busy for a weeknight and it took her a couple of minutes to negotiate the route.

"Hi! Sorry, am I late?" she said, peeling off her jacket and sitting opposite him.

"No, no. I was early."

He grinned at her, but it didn't settle her nerves. This was the tenth date that her flatmate, Becky, had set up for her over the past two years, and all of the others had been disastrous, one way or another.

On paper, Mark should have been a catch. Tall and lean, with a mop of straight, dark hair, and plenty of smile-lines around his eyes, he worked in a small firm in York, managing their marketing. Georgia had seen some of their campaigns on social media and found them quirky and amusing. She wondered why he was single, then caught herself. *She* was single. It didn't mean he was weird, any more than it meant she was.

"Can I get you a drink?" Mark asked.

"Um, thanks. Just a glass of white wine?" She smiled again, feeling awkward.

Mark nodded and hurried over to the bar. Georgia read over the menu, still feeling like this was a big mistake. At least The Happy Badger did good meals, so she'd be well fed, if nothing else.

"So, you work with Becky?" said Mark, sliding two glasses of wine on to the table and making her look up from the laminated card. "Do you also do the physics-thing?"

"Geophysics? No. I deal with any finds that come up in a dig."

Both Becky and Georgia worked for a commercial archaeology firm, Dig For It. Becky was one of the geophysicists who surveyed the site before any digging took place; Georgia was a finds manager, responsible for collecting any excavated artefacts, cleaning them, identifying them, and cataloguing them.

"My mum used to love that TV program. You know, the one where they always had just three days to discover whether someone like Henry VIII had had a house there, or if the lost Roman Legion might be found in a muddy field."

Her heart sank. The TV program he was referring to had been both a blessing and a curse for archaeologists. A blessing because it had put archaeology in people's minds and showed them what it could do; a curse because it had made out that archaeology was all exciting discoveries and a race against time, when quite often it was neither.

"And you work in marketing," she said brightly, wanting to deflect him away from the TV show. "Becky showed me one of your campaigns. The one with the knitted sheep in it. It was hilarious."

Mark's shoulders softened, and the smile-lines around his eyes deepened. "Thanks. I really enjoyed doing that. My mum knitted the sheep for me. They have wires in them so that they can be posed. The stop-motion took *hours*, so I'm glad you liked it."

"Did you do the stop-motion?"

He laughed, shaking his head. "No. We hired a firm to do it for us. But I wrote the scripts. Told them what we needed." He tilted his chin towards the menu, still in Georgia's hand. "Do you know what you want?"

"Um, sure. I'll have the lasagne, please."

Mark said he would have the same and scurried away to put the order in. Georgia people-watched for a moment. Chatter flowed gently around her, and everyone else in the pub seemed to be having a great night.

"Becky told me you worked in Orkney together. What was that like?" Mark asked when he returned.

Her heart sank. How to answer him? It had been the best year of her life and also the worst.

"The archaeology was amazing," she said, sticking to the safest topic. "And Orkney is beautiful, especially in the summer. Though the midges can be awful."

"What did you find? What were you working on?" He rested his chin on his palm, his eyes on hers.

She fiddled with the edge of her glass. "A Viking settlement. It was amazing. So many finds! Orkney was central to the Vikings. We think of it as miles away, and far from anything now, but for the Viking world, it was right in the middle of everything."

They chatted throughout the meal – about Orkney, about the Vikings, about his work – and the evening passed quickly. He was easy to talk to and seemed genuinely interested in her and her work, but he wasn't setting her pulse racing. No one had since that summer in Orkney.

"Do you have any brothers or sisters?" Mark asked, as they were finishing dessert.

Georgia toyed with the last bit of apple-pie in her dish. "Er. No." Her heart lurched, then settled. "You?"

"No, I'm an only child, too. I always wanted a sibling. Someone to play with when I was a kid."

She dipped her head. She had had a brilliant sister. She just didn't have a sister now. Desperately, she hunted for a different topic to talk about, landing on a recent period-drama adaptation that had won plaudits. Thankfully, Mark had watched it as avidly as she had.

At the end of the meal, Georgia insisted on splitting the bill with him.

"No, it's fine. I'm more than happy to get this," he protested.

She shook her head, unpleasant memories of an earlier date springing up. The man had insisted on paying and then been under the impression that he'd 'bought' her for the night. He'd gone home disappointed, but it had shaken Georgia and she'd vowed never to be in the same situation again.

The bill settled, Mark offered to walk her home. She glanced out of the window. If it had been light, she would have preferred to walk home alone. That way, she could avoid the inevitable awkwardness when they reached her place. She didn't really want to see him again. She definitely didn't want him to kiss her. But it was dark, and the route home passed a couple of areas she didn't like.

"Thank you. That would be kind of you."

She shrugged her jacket back on and the two of them set off, Mark describing a new campaign he was working on that followed on from the stop-motion sheep. She tuned out, her mind rehearsing how to let him down gently if he asked to see her again. Maybe he'd feel the same way, though, and it wouldn't be an issue.

At her door, Mark bunched his lips, tilting his head to one side. "I really enjoyed this evening. Did you want to do something another night? Go to the cinema?" He shrugged. "Whatever."

She swallowed, uncomfortable, her rehearsed words vanishing. "Um…"

His face fell. "That's a no, right?"

She breathed out steadily. "I had a lovely evening. Thank you. But…" She glanced away, mustering her words.

"That's okay. Good night."

He shoved his hands into his jacket pockets, blew out a long breath, then nodded curtly to her. She smiled weakly, awkwardness prickling her skin, relieved when he walked away. She sighed heavily, then let herself into the flat.

It was dark inside, apart from the hall light. Becky was an early-to-bed-early-to-rise person. Despite the hour, she'd already be asleep, ready to tackle the day at six in the morning. Georgia kicked off her shoes and headed to bed. Hanging on the wardrobe door was the work shirt she'd meant to iron before she went out. She groaned. It would have to wait. She wasn't about to do battle with the temperamental ironing board at this time of night and risk losing a finger.

She put her phone on to charge, then flopped down on the bed, her mind churning. Was she ever going to find someone who she wanted to have a second date with, never mind potentially settle down with? She fingered her brow. At this rate, she was heading for 'childless spinster with too many cats'.

"Maybe you need to set your sights a little lower," she muttered to herself. "Mark was the least weird of all the dates you've had!"

He'd actually been perfectly lovely, she had to concede.

If only he hadn't asked about Orkney and reminded her of what she'd once had, and lost.

2

Anders finished ironing his shirt and slipped it on a coat hanger, before looping a tie around it and hanging it all on the hook on the back of his bedroom door. His heart raced as he thought about the following day, and he clicked his tongue.

"Come on! It's just the two teams getting to know one another. Simple introductions. It will be a couple of dozen people at most. And they'll be a friendly crowd. You'll all be working together. Quit getting so worked up!"

But the thought still made his palms sweat and his belly fill with rocks. He hated speaking in public, however small the group and however informal the meeting. He'd hoped he would have got better at all of that by now, but he hadn't.

He'd headed up plenty of archaeological digs, but he'd always known all of the people he'd be working with. This would be his first dig with any outside company involved. The university was technically in charge, but the actual dig was being split between staff from the archaeology team at the university, and a company called Dig For It.

Part of him would have preferred that it was only the university involved, but to be fair to the company, they'd done the preliminary work that had led to this new project. A farmer had applied for planning permission for a couple of his fields, and Dig For It had been employed to do the initial site survey to check for historical importance. To the farmer's dismay, the survey had unearthed several key artefacts, including a Viking-era brooch. Dig For It had confirmed that the site could be of significant importance, and the local planning authority had decided that it needed thorough investigation to determine its extent, including a full excavation if necessary. The LPA had also decided that it should be a joint excavation, though the university would be in charge. He really hoped that Dig For It wasn't going to have their noses out of joint over that.

Despite his nerves over the meeting the next day, Anders was excited about the excavation. From an early age, the era of the Vikings in Britain had fascinated him. Half-Norwegian and half-British, he'd learned the history from both sides. It had been a turbulent time when the Vikings shifted from being raiders to settling in Britain. In Scandinavia, a new regime, coupled with a growing population, meant that there had been a significant exodus of people to Britain to make a new life. There hadn't exactly been land going spare, so every Viking settler meant an Anglo-Saxon being displaced because their land had been handed over to an invader. Over time, the two populations had become more integrated, but it didn't take a great leap of imagination to feel that the early years would have been bitter.

He rubbed his palm over his chin, still missing his beard, even though it was now two years since his father had looked him up and down, unimpressed, and suggested, not altogether tactfully, that he didn't make the right impression.

"If you're ever going to get anywhere *in academia, you'd better smarten up, Anders. You look like you've been dragged through a hedge backwards."* The words were etched into Anders's brain.

That same week, he'd shaved, got a haircut his father would approve of, and invested in smart trousers, crisp cotton shirts, two jackets, and a selection of ties.

He hated all of it.

His phone rang, and he peered at the screen. His spirits sank even further.

"Hi, Pappa. How are you?"

He tweaked his shirt to straighten it on the hanger, then strolled through to the lounge, wondering why his father was calling.

"Anders. Yes, I'm well. Thank you. But we speak Norwegian, please."

Anders sank down on a chair and stretched his legs out. His mother was English; his father Norwegian. They'd divorced when he was a child, and he'd spent most of his life flitting from one country to the other and back again, leaving him feeling as if he belonged nowhere.

"Of course," he said, switching to Norwegian.

"How is the new job?"

Anders scraped a hand through his hair. "It's going okay, thanks. The university team are meeting up with the commercial group tomorrow, ahead of the dig starting."

A light snort sounded on the other end of the line. "These things are much better when an academic is in charge."

"An academic *is* in charge, Pappa. I'm leading the dig. Remember?"

"You know what I mean. Much better to *only* have academics involved." His father huffed again. "I still don't know why you took the job. Though maybe the woman will not come back. Women do tend to prioritise babies over careers."

"I think you might find that some jobs don't make it easy to have both," he murmured.

"Pah. Most women have no ambition other than to have children."

He closed his eyes, already tired of the discussion. His father had some obnoxious beliefs, and very little in the way of a filter to keep his thoughts in his head.

"You should have stayed in Norway," his father continued. "Tried for a permanent position rather than yet another temporary one. I had tenure by the time I was your age."

Anders wished he'd had a pound for every time he'd been told this. He bit back his retort. Academia was a very different beast these days. Getting a permanent post at his age would have involved him being a prodigy, not just knowing the right people, which is what his father had done.

"Yes, well, it might only be temporary, but it's a step up."

"I suppose. Though *acting* head of department always sounds… weak. After the work you did in Orkney, you should be a head of department by now, not just covering for someone while she has a baby."

Anders wiggled his toes, keeping his thoughts unsaid. Being head of a department, even if only *acting* head, was a big step up. His mother had been delighted for him. He couldn't even imagine what he would have to do for his father to be delighted. He hadn't been impressed when he'd landed his last job, even though it had been a significant promotion for someone his age. All he'd focused on was that it was only a two-year post.

His father started into a long account of a conference he had been the keynote speaker at, moaning about everything, from the size of the lecture halls, to the accommodation he'd been put up in, and all points in between. Anders zoned out, his brain running back over the year in Orkney. He wished his father hadn't mentioned it. That had been one of the best summers of his life, but also the worst.

I wonder what she's doing now? She's probably married with kids.

He forced himself not to think about it. He'd lost count of the number of times he'd considered looking her up online to see what she was doing. He never had. He didn't know which would hurt more: finding out she was still single, or finding out she was married with kids.

He tuned back in to the conversation with his father, who was finally winding to a close.

"Well, I'm glad to hear the new job is going well for you. I will keep an eye out for anything that might suit you and let you know."

"Thanks, Pappa."

"Though you will have to actually *publish* a bit more if you ever want to be considered an expert in anything other than drinking coffee. You're wasting your life. And the brains you were born with. Sometimes, I'm embarrassed that we share the same name."

Anders ground his teeth. Pappa was *definitely* an expert in his field. How could Anders forget? His father reminded him of the fact in every conversation.

"Talk to you soon. Bye." He ended the call before he got even more annoyed.

Maybe the dig would find something momentous. Something important enough that even his father would sit up and notice.

3

The following morning, hammering on the bedroom door woke Georgia with a start.

"Hey! Are you getting up today, or what?" hollered Becky through the door.

Georgia frowned, rubbing the sleep out of her eyes, and picked up her phone. 0% charge. She groaned. The charging symbol wasn't even showing, and she peered over the side of the bed. Had she forgotten to plug it in?

No. It was connected.

"Oh, and the power's off," added Becky.

That explained that then.

"What time is it?" Georgia asked.

"Uh. Ten to eight."

"What?"

She threw the covers back and scrambled out of bed, stubbed her toe, then hopped around, swearing under her breath.

"Why didn't you wake me earlier?" she yelled.

She flung the bedroom door open to find Becky smirking, holding out a steaming mug to her.

"Sorry. At least the stove is gas, so we have coffee. Have a good night last night? Did you bring Mark home?" Becky peered around her into her bedroom.

"Nice enough. But no. Thanks for the coffee."

Becky cocked her head. "So, super-Mark wasn't so super?"

Georgia pulled a face at her. "He was perfectly lovely. But no. He didn't light my fire."

No one had lit any fires in her for two years, and she was beginning to think they were quenched beyond salvage.

Becky stuck her tongue into her cheek. "I'd offer to make you some breakfast, but we only have bread in, and I can't be bothered to get the grill going to make toast."

"I'll get something on the way in." She stared at her best friend. "How in God's holy name do you look so good when the shower doesn't work?"

Becky ran a hand through her buzz cut. "It's a gift. Get a move on. *Your* hair's going to need a bit more time than mine."

Georgia hurried to the bathroom. At least there was *some* hot water. Well, lukewarm water. She washed swiftly, then stared at her hair. Curly didn't come close to describing it. 'Curly' was a word used when someone's hair fell in soft, bouncy, *attractive* curls. Georgia's hair spiralled into corkscrews that defied gravity. On mornings like this, she wished she'd done what Becky had during lock-down, and just run some clippers over it. Becky had never looked back. Sighing, Georgia tried to tame the spirals with some de-tangler and her fingers, to little avail. Defeated, she grabbed an elastic hairband, scraped her hair back and snapped the band around it, then dashed back to her bedroom.

Back in her bedroom, she groaned at the shirt hanging on the outside of the wardrobe. The front of it looked vaguely presentable, but the sleeves and the back were a labyrinth of creases. She'd just have to put a jacket on over the top, because she had nothing else clean to wear.

She dressed, then joined Becky at the door to their flat. Despite the androgynous haircut and boyish figure, Becky looked gloriously feminine in a smart, knee-length dress and cropped cardigan. Georgia smoothed a hand over her front and checked the mirror in the hallway, scowling at her make-up-free face.

"I look terrible," she muttered, grabbing her bag. Her eyelashes were so pale they could disappear into invisibility without at least a *bit* of mascara.

"You look *fine*," countered Becky. "Come on. We're going to be late. And you hate being late even more than you hate your hair!"

Georgia took a final look at her reflection, her heart sinking. The power would have to go off today of all days. The very day when she had that meeting with the university group and wanted to impress. She shook her head. The building where she and Becky worked was always boiling, so as well as her hair looking like a bird's nest, she was going to be sweating like a pig under her jacket.

Could the day get much worse?

* * *

Georgia balanced her mug of coffee on her notebook and slipped into the seminar room through the rear door. Her nose wrinkled at the dusty smell in the room and she scanned the set-up, shaking her head. The room had been repurposed from another space and had a terrible layout at the best of times. The screen for the projector was mounted on the wrong wall for a start, meaning that half of the room could barely see it, and if the sun shone, *no one* could see the screen unless the blackout blinds were fully down, at which point you couldn't see your notes.

For today's meeting, the chairs had been rearranged into a haphazard semi-circle, with the screen to their side and their backs to the window. Who had thought *that* was a good layout? Sun poured in through the windows, making the room hotter than a greenhouse, and her shirt stuck to her back. Any other day, she'd have taken her jacket off, but not today when she'd be meeting the university team. The various members of the Dig For It team had already arrived and clustered together to one side. Georgia joined them, leaving a space for Becky, who had popped to the loo on her way to the meeting.

"I don't know why we can't just do the excavation ourselves," grumbled an older man, Steve, with straggly greying hair and a permanently dishevelled look.

Georgia juggled her drink and her notebook, desperate not to spill coffee down her front, to go with the crumpled look. "Because we don't have the resources to *do* the full dig."

She didn't really care that they wouldn't be in charge. An excavation was an excavation, and her least favourite aspect was all the writing and paperwork that went on after the dig had finished, and most of that would fall to the university team.

The woman next to her, Shona, shuffled in her seat. "At least the uni peeps are coming over to us, rather than making us go over to them."

"Be thankful for small mercies," grumbled Steve.

The rest of the Dig For It team said nothing. Steve was part of the geophysics team, along with Becky. The dig team comprised Bob, a quiet man about the same age as Steve, Denise, a permanently frazzled woman with small kids at home, and Shona, a middle-aged woman who Georgia got on well with. Scott, a sensible man in his late forties, completed the group. They all knew one another well, and made a tight-knit team, making Georgia wonder how well they would gel with the university bunch.

A commotion at the main door to the room drew her attention. Three people poked their head around the door, murmured their hellos, then took up seats on the opposite side of the room from them, chatting together, curious eyes flicking over the Dig For It team. Georgia frowned. Just three in the university team? Maybe there would be student volunteers who would be involved but who weren't coming to the meeting. She eyed the three newcomers, wondering which of them would be heading up the dig. She didn't recognise any of them. There were two men and a woman, all in their late twenties or early thirties, she'd guess. One of the guys had red hair and a fair complexion, the other had dark hair and a deep tan. The woman had shoulder-length blonde hair and kept glancing towards the door as if expecting someone else to arrive. Georgia followed her gaze.

Stacy, a plump woman in her late forties and the head of Dig For It, stood in the doorway, chatting to someone still in the corridor outside. Georgia sipped her coffee, flinching at the temperature, wondering why Stacy was so giggly and flirtatious towards whoever she was talking to. The person in the corridor moved slightly, and she could see part of the back of his head and his shoulders.

A flicker of familiarity tickled her brain. The man had thick hair that in some lights would be described as light brown and in others dark blond. It was cut fairly short, though if he allowed it to grow longer, it would be wavy, bordering on curly. A smart jacket sat on broad shoulders, but Georgia couldn't see the man's face. She shuffled through memories, but couldn't place who he might be. She didn't know anyone in the university department; well, no one that young, anyway.

Becky slid into the seat next to her, plonking a mug of coffee on to the flip-up writing surface attached to the chair. It was useless to her for writing on as she was left-handed, and the tables were fixed and exclusively on the right. Something she had moaned about on many an occasion.

"We haven't started yet, have we?" she whispered, balancing her notebook on her knee, her gaze darting around the room.

"No. Stacy's still chatting with someone in the corridor, and I assume it's whoever's leading the dig. Do you know who it is?"

Becky shook her head. "I didn't see them properly and I don't think they were named in the stuff that got sent through." She leafed through her notebook. "No. They weren't."

"It must be the chap in a jacket that Stacy's talking to," said Georgia, bobbing and weaving a little in her seat to get a better look at him. "There's something about him that's *really* familiar, but I can't place him. Mind you, I can't see him properly. Can you?"

"No."

Georgia pulled out the sheaf of notes that had been sent over, sorting them out. Most of the documents she was utterly familiar with as they were from the original work done by Dig For It, but she wanted to at least have the map of the site to hand. In the doorway, Stacy giggled again, pressing her hand to her ample bosom, then moved to stand at the raised desk at the right-hand side at the front. The light hum of chatter died away, and she smiled brightly. The man she'd been talking to in the corridor joined her, his head dipped, pressing his lips together.

Georgia stared at him, her mouth drying as she recognised him.

"Good morning, everyone," said Stacy. "Let's make a start. Let me introduce you to the academic lead on the project, the acting head of department, Dr Anders Mortensen."

Anders. Here? Georgia's heart missed several beats, and she put her coffee down before she spilled it.

She tried to sink into oblivion, slumping down in her chair as Dr Anders Mortensen raised his head, but she couldn't stop herself from staring at him. No wonder he'd seemed familiar, though the man at the front appeared significantly tidier now than he had in Orkney. The Anders she'd known there had had mad wavy hair, a scruffy beard, wore cargo pants, and always looked like he'd just rolled out of bed. He usually had. Out of *her* bed. *This* Anders Mortensen wore a crisp white shirt, smart trousers, and a jacket. Gone were the wild waves that used to tumble over his brow. Instead, his light brown hair was cut in a short-back-and-sides that accentuated his bone structure. The word that sprang to Georgia's mind was 'corporate'.

He smiled widely at the assembled group, and her heart lurched again. His sky-blue eyes swept the room, and despite her trying to hide, he clocked her instantly. His smile faltered and his eyes widened, and then almost instantly, the broad smile was back, only this time, it looked forced.

"Good morning, everyone," he said.

Becky sat up straighter and elbowed her in the ribs. "Hey, isn't that *your* Anders?"

She swallowed. "He hasn't been *my* Anders for two years."

4

Anders swallowed, gathering himself. Since when had Georgie worked in Yorkshire? Two years ago, she'd been up in Orkney. With him. After that, she'd been in Cumbria. When had she moved here?

The sweat on his hands made the papers he held soften. He straightened his back, trying not to look at her, wishing that his heart rate would settle.

Don't let my voice wobble. Don't let anyone see how nervous I am.

He cleared his throat, his mouth dry. "Good morning, everyone. Thank you for coming to this meeting. I know Dig For It has been involved in several excavations in the area over the years, and I'm delighted at this collaboration between the university and you. I wanted to get us all together in one room before the dig starts; let you at least meet one another."

He shrugged, trying to be lighthearted, but two of the Dig For It team were scowling at him. One was Georgie. The other was an older man with long hair. A bead of sweat ran down Anders's back between his shoulder blades, and he turned to Stacy, wishing he was anywhere else but this stifling room.

"Stacy, perhaps you could introduce the Dig For It team members? And then I can introduce the uni team."

She bounced to her feet, beaming at him. "Oh, yes, of course!" She turned to the group huddling to one side. "We have two of our geophysicists on the team. Those are Becky and Steve."

He knew Becky. She'd been in Orkney. Steve was the long-haired man who still hadn't stopped scowling. Both of them gave small, embarrassed waves.

"Then the dig team are Shona, Denise, Scott, and Bob."

In turn, a sensible-looking woman in her late forties, a slim, harassed-looking woman about the same age as him, a man in his late forties with a serious expression, and an older man with dark hair and thick glasses, waved towards his team.

"And of course, Georgia, who will be the finds manager," finished up Stacy.

Georgie stopped scowling and nodded curtly towards the team from the university. She still hadn't made eye contact with him.

He smiled at Stacy. "Thank you." He wanted to wipe his palms on his thighs. The room was roasting with the sun streaming in. "Let me introduce Sam, Patrick, and Sophie. All three will be on the dig team, but there will also be several volunteers helping with the dig over the summer. They'll mostly be undergraduate students, though we always have a few older regulars who come to help."

Sam, a tall red-head, and Patrick, dark-haired and serious-looking, both waved. Sophie simpered, batting her eyelashes. In the corner of his eye, he saw Becky's scathing expression at Sophie, before she dipped her head and studied her lap. He smiled to himself. Becky never had been one to keep her feelings to herself.

"Okay." He turned to the group, his nerves still fizzing. The fact they'd taken up opposing sides of the room didn't make it easy to address them as a whole. "I put together all the documentation on the site." He shrugged towards Georgie. "Which, of course, you guys will know inside out as you wrote it."

The Dig For It team smiled and nodded. Except Georgie.

"But, in essence." He shifted his gaze towards the uni staff. "Developers applied for planning permission for the site, and Dig For It did the initial field assessment. Much to the developers' dismay, the assessment suggested there might be an Anglo-Saxon, or, given the location, probably an Anglo-Scandinavian settlement under there. The local planning authority wants the whole site excavated and preserved, so that the developers can build on it without wrecking any heritage there."

He held his arms out to the side, then let them drop. Housing over history. Again. He couldn't deny there was a housing shortage, but it always seemed that new houses would be built over sites of interest, rather than the so-called brown-field sites.

"Anyway," he went on. "I'm delighted that we'll all be working together, and hopefully we can find out more about what was happening there in the ninth and tenth centuries. We'll be starting a week on Monday, with field-walking and geophysics, initially. Any questions?"

He didn't expect any. A couple of people looked at one another, but there was a general shaking of heads. Georgie had slumped even further down in her chair and stared at her notes.

"Okay, well, if any of you think of anything, just drop me an email. Thank you."

Stacy sprang up, beaming at him.

"Thank you, Dr Mortensen. I'm sure this will be a *fascinating* project, and we all look forward to working with you."

Everyone shuffled in their seats, and Anders swallowed. He should have made it a more informal session. Organised cakes or something. Something where the two groups might have actually *talked*, rather than glared across the room at one another.

He realised Stacy was speaking to him.

"Let me introduce our finds expert and our geophysics lead to you before you go. Um, Steve? Georgia?"

She beckoned to the scowling, middle-aged man with straggly hair, and Georgie, a few seats down. Steve reached the front first. Georgie was *definitely* dragging her feet. Behind them, everyone else drifted out of the room, half of them flapping at themselves to cool down.

Stacy made the introductions. Unnecessarily, since they'd already done that in the meeting. Anders smiled at Steve, hoping to thaw some of the frost coming from him.

"Hi, Steve. Nice to meet you. I wonder if you would be happy to talk me through all the geophysics that's already been done? I know you're extending the survey when we start, but I would really appreciate it if you'd go over the initial results with me. Reading surveys has never been one of my fortes, and I would appreciate your expertise."

Steve shrugged. "Sure. No problem. You've got my email address. Or at least your secretary does."

Anders laughed. "Yeah. I have it. Thanks. I'll try to fix something up in the next few days."

Steve nodded, and loped away.

He swallowed, trying to settle his nerves. Georgie stood in front of him, holding her jacket edges together over her chest and juggling a mug and a notebook. She must have been boiling, given the temperature of the room. She was certainly flushed, and Anders caught his breath, old memories filling his brain, unbidden. Her always wild, bright blonde hair had been snared in a hairband, but almost half of it was making a bid for freedom, corkscrewing around her face. It must have been annoying her, as she put her notebook and mug down, loosed her hair, fluffed it all out, and fastened it all back again. As she did so, her jacket fell open, and Anders smiled to himself as he saw that her top had only been ironed in places. No wonder she'd kept her jacket on. She'd be furious that her shirt wasn't pristine. He wondered why it wasn't.

Had she spent the night away from home and these were yesterday's clothes?

The thought slammed into him, almost knocking his breath from his chest, before he shook himself. So what if she had? It would be none of his business.

Georgie raised a defiant chin to him, her hazel eyes flinty. His armpits were sticky, and not just because the room was so hot.

"Hello, Georgie."

Electricity fizzed in his stomach, and he cursed himself. Why on earth was he *excited* to see her? She'd cut him out of her life like he'd been *nothing* to her.

She nodded at him, her lips thin. "Anders."

She pronounced his name more like 'On-desh', bringing back memories of the evening he'd spent sitting on a beach in Orkney with her, drinking beers, coaching her on the Norwegian pronunciation and teaching her a smattering of Norwegian. His heart pounded for a few beats.

"Ennesh? Oh, goodness, have I been pronouncing your name all wrong? I'm so sorry," said Stacy, flustered.

You're still *pronouncing it wrong,* he thought, but he smiled at her. "It's fine. Everyone calls me Anders."

In the corner of his eye, he saw Georgie shake her head. She'd always been more annoyed than he ever was at people pronouncing it 'Ann-ders'.

Stacy clapped her hands together. "Excellent. Well, I just wanted to introduce you as you'll be working so closely together, but you clearly know each other, so if you'll excuse me, I need to get on."

She busied away. Anders looked at Georgie. "How are you?"

"I'm fine, thanks. I didn't realise you were working at the university now. I thought you were still in Norway." She paused. "I almost didn't recognise you. You look, um, very *corporate*."

He laughed, trying to break the tension grinding his shoulders. "Okay… I started at the university about a month ago. Maternity cover for the head of department."

"Norway not work out?" Her clipped voice made him wince.

"Norway was fine." He shrugged. "But it was only a two-year post. And then this job came up, and it's a step up, albeit temporary, so…"

A brittle smile emerged, and she nodded. "Well. I'm delighted that your desire to climb the greasy pole is working out so well for you. I'm sure we'll be seeing each other on the dig. If you'll excuse me, I need to get back to my office."

He didn't want her to go. Not like this.

"Um. We should probably meet up. Before the dig starts. Just for a general chat about things."

She levelled her gaze at him, her eyes hard. "Sure. Though I do know how to manage finds, and I know you know how to run a dig, so I'm not sure why we need to meet. And it's *Georgia*. Only close friends call me Georgie."

He flinched. "Okay."

Before he could say anything else, she clasped her notebook to her chest and turned on her heel. He let his breath go in a long exhalation.

Well, that answers one question you had. Yes, she still hates you.

5

Back in her office, Georgia hurled her notebook on to her desk. Becky looked across at her, one brow raised. "I take it you're not happy to be working with him again?"

Georgia curled her lip. "Understatement."

She took her jacket off and draped it around the back of her chair. At least he hadn't seen how badly ironed her shirt was. It was bad enough that her hair was being such a pain today.

"He thinks we need to meet ahead of the dig starting," she ground out.

Becky pressed her lips together. "Not a massive surprise for the finds expert and dig manager to meet up ahead of a dig."

"He kept calling me Georgie."

"Well, he *did* call you that, in Orkney."

Georgia stared over the joint desk at her. "Well, he doesn't get to be that familiar with me *now*."

Becky scratched her ear, her expression patient. "How come he's here in York? I thought he'd taken a post in Oslo? Wasn't that why you split up?"

"Oh, clearly the Oslo job was just another stepping stone on his way to greatness." She peered at her empty mug. "Did you want another coffee?"

"Yes, please. Are you going to stomp around the place all summer about this?"

"I'm hoping that I can stay in the finds tent all summer and that he stays out of it."

She held her hand out for Becky's mug, then headed to the small kitchen down the corridor from their office.

While the kettle boiled, she spooned instant coffee granules into their mugs, adding two sugars to Becky's, her emotions churning. She'd been one of the team involved in the initial site survey and had been looking forward to this dig since its announcement. The *last* person she'd expected to be heading it up was Anders bloody Mortensen. She crossed her arms, scowling at her toes.

The kettle clicked off, and she poured boiling water into the mugs, splashed some milk in, and gave them a good stir.

Back in the office, she slid Becky's mug across their shared desk towards her, then sat down. She unsnapped the band from around her notebook and opened it, taking out the notes from the meeting and slamming them down on her desk.

"Georgie, do you still have feelings for him?"

Becky's question startled her, and her head shot up.

"For *Anders*? No!"

Becky smirked, her eyes dancing. "Really? Because you seem awfully wound up over someone you claim not to care tuppence for."

Georgia slurped her coffee. "No. That boat sailed a long time ago. To Oslo."

Though if that were true, why had she felt such a thrill at seeing him again?

"I almost didn't recognise him," went on Becky. "He's gone all…" She tailed off, flapping a hand at her head and body, the right word obviously escaping her.

"Tidy? I don't imagine you get to be the head of a department if you always look as if you've had a fight with a hedge and lost."

Becky poked her tongue into her cheek. "Time was, you *loved* him looking like that."

"Yeah. Well, not now… Can we change the subject?"

"Okay. Will you have time to work on that new brooch before the dig starts?"

A local metal-detecting club had found the new brooch in the field next to the one in which the dig would take place. The brooch was over in the finds store, a short distance from the Dig For It premises. The conservators had cleaned it up, but needed Georgia to determine what period of history it dated from. She was fairly sure it would be Anglo-Saxon and have originated from the dig site, even though it had been found just outside the boundary.

"I'm having a look at it this afternoon."

At least the brooch might be a distraction from the fact that Anders was back in her life, albeit tangentially, and hopefully only temporarily.

* * *

Anders reached the sanctuary of his office back at the university and sank down at his desk. How on *earth* was Georgie in Yorkshire, *on this dig*? The last time they'd spoken was in Orkney two years ago, when she'd put the key to his flat on the kitchen table and walked out of his life. Since then, she hadn't answered a single call, text, message… *nothing*. He grimaced, remembering all the calls to Becky, trying to find out where Georgie was, and getting nowhere. She had just *gone*, like the year they'd had together had meant nothing to her. Eventually, Becky had said that if he called her again, she'd block his number, and he'd given up.

His heart still raced, partly from the stress of having to stand up and talk to people he didn't know, but mostly because of seeing Georgie again. He rubbed a hand through his hair, swallowing. She obviously still loathed him.

He leaned back in his seat, closing his eyes. Georg*ia*. She'd made it quite clear that he couldn't use her nickname any longer.

"Do *not* get excited about seeing her. She's clearly not excited about seeing you. That's all history now. Move on."

But the idea of working with her all summer made his blood pound. And his heart sink. It was going to be hellish, seeing her every day when she patently had zero desire to see him.

Oh, God. What if she's seeing someone else?

"Of course she'll be seeing someone else," he muttered to himself. "She was never going to wait for you. She made *that* clear. For all you know, she's married with a kid now."

The thought made him screw his face up in pain.

A light tap sounded on the door, and he opened his eyes sharply.

"Yes?" he called, aware that his hair would be a mess from dragging his hands through it.

His secretary, Carol, popped her head around the door, looking more bird-like than ever, with her petite build and bright eyes. "Oh, you're back already. Did it go okay?"

He combed his fingers through his hair, trying to straighten it. "Oh, yes, fine thanks, Carol."

"Did you want a coffee?"

He smiled, his tension easing a fraction. "That would be wonderful. Thank you."

"No problem. Your eleven o'clock meeting has been moved to seminar room A4. And I've scheduled in a couple of quick meetings this afternoon for you: Dr Longstaff at three, and Dr Moore at half-past three. I hope that's okay. Your diary indicated you were free."

He breathed in deeply. "No, that's fine. What do they want to see me about?"

"Er, Dr Longstaff wants you to give three lectures to his Junior Honours students next semester. Dr Moore was wittering about a grant proposal he needs you to sign off on. I've put all the documents in that folder." She pointed to a buff cardboard folder on the side of his desk.

He nodded. "Thanks, Carol."

She smiled brightly and withdrew.

He studied his hands. They still trembled, and he curled his fingers to make fists, then stretched them out again. They looked too clean. He should have broken nails, dirt ground into his skin so deeply that even a scrubbing brush made no difference… working hands that had spent the day digging. Not these soft things that wielded nothing harder than a pen.

He peered out of the window, his heart yearning for wide-open spaces and a breeze in his hair. Instead, he had another meeting in another cramped seminar room looming.

With a heavy heart, he pulled up the notes for his eleven o'clock meeting on his computer and started to read.

6

Georgia exhaled steadily as she walked towards the finds store, the muscles of her shoulders knotting. Anders sodding Mortensen. She thought she was done with him. She *had* been done with him. What had promised to be an amazing summer, excavating the settlement, had now had every last trace of shine taken off it. She was going to be working with him every single day over the summer. A constant reminder that she'd not been enough for him.

She reached the stores and yanked open the door. Inside was a small foyer, with a turnstile to one side and a low desk. Behind the desk sat Mick, the guy in charge of access to the finds. She liked Mick. He was a big bear of a man, with salt-and-pepper hair, and eyes so dark it was impossible to distinguish the pupils from the irises.

"Afternoon," he said.

"Hi, there. Anyone else in?"

He shook his head. "Nope. Just you. Mrs Keeny Beany."

She laughed. "I'm in to look at that new brooch again. I need to finish my report on it before we start on the new dig."

He nodded, pressing a button on the desk to allow her through the turnstile, then turning his attention back to his computer screen.

The building contained a long, narrow room where finds could be examined and processed, next to a space filled with mobile shelving. Georgia logged in to a computer on a desk and looked up the location of the brooch. She scribbled the reference in her notebook, then rolled the shelving to access where the brooch was kept. The correct small box located, she took it over to a large table furnished with a magnifying lamp and various other pieces of equipment. She sat down, eased the brooch out of its container, and placed it carefully on a padded base under the magnifying lamp.

The disc brooch measured almost two inches across. Radiating lines decorated the central area, taking up about a third of the diameter. Outside that, interlaced lines covered the metal, forming a complicated knotwork pattern, though time had softened the once crisp edges.

The front of the brooch wouldn't really tell her where it was from. Not definitively. Metal-detectorists had found several brooches from the period, and they fell broadly into two camps: those made in Scandinavia, and those made in essentially the same style, but manufactured in England. Was this brooch brought over with The Great Viking Army? Or had a Viking settler had it made for a wife or daughter?

Georgia turned the brooch over and peered at the catch-plate, trying to ascertain its shape, and therefore its likely provenance. She was fairly certain that the brooch was Anglo-Scandinavian. In other words, Scandinavian in design, but made in England. As she studied the brooch, the room swam. She caught her breath and closed her eyes, waiting for the dizziness to go.

It didn't go. Her mind filled with strange images, and her eyes shot open again. The images didn't change.

Instead of being in the bright, white, harshly lit space in the finds store, her surroundings were dark and gloomy. The smell of a wood fire prickled her nose, and she looked around, alarmed.

Please don't let there be a fire in the storeroom!

She wasn't in the storeroom any longer. Her eyes widened and her breathing deepened as she tried to make sense of it all. She stood in a large space, hazy with smoke from a central hearth. The walls were too far away for her to see properly, but they had no windows piercing them. Under her feet, the floor was strewn with plants that gave off a herby scent, though it didn't completely mask the smell of dung, sweat, and urine that hung in the air. She looked down at herself. Her smart trousers and white shirt had gone, replaced with a long dress made of wool. A slim, tablet-woven braid belt hung around her waist, with a small pouch suspended from it. The sleeves of the dress covered half of her hands and over the top of it, she wore a long open coat, edged with braid. A pair of brooches, almost identical to the one she'd just been studying, held the neck of the long dress closed.

Fury flooded her body, though she had no idea what had suddenly made her so cross.

"Father, why?"

Her father scowled at her. "Because we lost, *child. Our leaders have made peace with Halfdan."*

"Made peace?" she spat. "Made peace? We have rolled over like puppy-dogs, and said, 'Here, take our land!' Some peace!"

Georgia's breath jammed in her chest, and she put the brooch down. Instantly, the room cleared, and the stark white study room replaced the dingy, smoky hall she'd been in. She still sat at the desk.

Her hands shook, and she folded them in her lap, staring at the brooch.

"What the…?"

She steadied her breathing, wondering what on earth she'd just dreamed. It had felt so real. Gingerly, she picked the brooch up again. A sensation of falling suffused her, and then she was back in the smoky hall.

"Aelfgyth, enough!" her father shouted. "I have already lost men – good *men – in this fight. I will* not *lose any more. We have made peace. We have sworn allegiance. It is not our land any longer. We* lost*! If we are lucky, this Einar will allow us to stay."*

Anger rampaged through her and she clenched her fists. "Allow us? Allow us? It's our land!"

"Not any longer, child."

"What else will they take from us?" she sobbed. "What else will we lose? Was it not enough that I lost my husband?"

Her father enfolded her in a comforting embrace. "Edmund fought bravely. We all did. But we were unprepared. Einar arrives tomorrow. He is injured, so I hear. You will tend to him. Be nice to him. We just have to pray that he is kind enough to allow us to stay. You will not *show him your temper and risk us being thrown out with nowhere to go. Do you understand?"*

He stood back, holding her at arm's length, his face serious.

"Yes, father. I will tend to him."

To his grave, she thought.

The vision faded, leaving Georgia staring at the reverse of the brooch, sweat prickling her skin. Who on earth was Aelfgyth? Had she owned this brooch? And Einar? It sounded very much like he was one of The Great Viking Army who had settled in the area after The Battle of York at the end of the ninth century.

Bracing herself, she picked up the brooch again, but whatever she'd seen – or thought she'd seen – had gone. Her hands shaking, she slid the pen out of her notebook, uncapped it, and made notes on the style of the reverse of the brooch, forcing herself to focus on the facts before her.

The brooch had almost certainly been made in England, though to a Scandinavian design. Made for a new wife or daughter of one of the invaders? Probably, though whether that wife had been born in England or in Scandinavia, she'd never know. There *had* been integration over the time the Vikings had run the north of England.

She carefully tucked the brooch back into its protective box. Maybe this feisty Aelfgyth had stopped swimming against the tide and settled down with one of the enemy.

The hairs on the back of her neck suddenly stood up, and she shook herself.

"Georgie, you're too old to be playing make-believe. Facts. What are the *facts*?"

She returned the brooch to its location, then bolted for the exit, suddenly desperate to see the spring sunshine again.

The finds store lay only a short walk from the building where her office was, so she loitered, breathing in deep lungfuls of air while she thought about what had just happened. The visions had felt so *real*, but how could they be? She clicked her tongue. It had just been her imagination. Goodness knows, she'd spent enough time as a child picturing the very time that the brooch dated to. In fact, she'd spent many a daydream imagining what it would be like to suddenly live with people who had taken everything from you. Nonetheless, she was glad not to be needing to handle the brooch again.

Having dilly-dallied on her way across the short path for as long as she thought she could get away with, she made her way back to her office. There, she logged into her computer, frowning, her mind still on part of the vision she'd had.

Becky eyed her across their desks. "All good?"

"Mmm. Just wanting to check something," she said, her focus back on the screen.

"Not conclusive whether the brooch was made in Scandinavia or made in England?"

"Hmm? Oh. No, I'm pretty sure it's Anglo-Scandinavian, probably from the very end of the ninth century; maybe the start of the tenth. Certainly no later."

She opened up a search engine and typed in 'Halfdan'. She scrolled through the results, looking for academic references, rather than characters from films or books, then found what she was looking for.

"Halfdan was one of the leaders of the Great Viking Army, which invaded the Anglo-Saxon kingdom of East Anglia in 865."

She skimmed down, looking for references relating to the local area, finding them further down the page.

"In 875, he settled his followers in Northumbria, founding the Danish kingdom of York."

She accessed an electronic version of The Anglo-Saxon Chronicles and found the entry for 875. She found what she was looking for in the entry for the following year: "*Halfdan divided up the land… and they were ploughing and providing for themselves.*"

"What are you checking?" asked Becky, peering over at her. "Something odd about the brooch?"

Georgia bit the inside of her lip. That would be one way of putting it. Not that Becky would believe that a brooch could cause visions of the past.

She checked herself. Did *she* honestly believe that? Not really. Her overactive imagination had surely just been… well, overactive.

"I was just thinking about the dig, and the period it might relate to. This entire area was probably parcelled up and given to the Viking men who had come over. The Anglo-Saxon Chronicles have such a throwaway line about it." She mimed air-quotes. "*Halfdan divided up the land.* In other words, *stole* the land from the Anglo-Saxons and handed it over to his men."

Becky stuck her bottom lip out. "Winner takes it all."

Georgia acknowledged the point with a flick of her brows and closed down the windows on her laptop.

Had her vision been real? *Had* one of Halfdan's men been called Einar, and been given Aelfgyth's father's lands? She sighed. She'd never know.

7

The following morning, Georgia tapped away at her computer, finishing up her report on the brooch. She kept it strictly factual, but her mind kept running back over the strange vision she'd had. *Had* it just been her imagination? It had genuinely felt as if she had been living it, just for a few minutes. She scolded herself mentally. Of *course* it had just been her imagination. What else could it have been?

Just as she finished proofreading the document, a 'new meeting proposal' flashed up in the corner of her computer screen and then died away, accompanied by a beep. A second later, her email pinged. She clicked on the email, irritation blooming in her chest when she saw it was from Anders. Begrudgingly, she accepted she was being unreasonable. She *had* agreed to meet with him ahead of the start of the dig, and her email address was linked to her diary, so he would have seen when they were both available.

Across the desk, Becky arched her brows. "From the fact your face looks like thunder, I assume that's something from Anders that's just arrived."

"Yep."

She clicked on the email. Along with the time and place for the meeting was a short agenda.

"God, Anders really *has* gone full academic," she muttered. "There's an agenda and everything. I thought it was just going to be an informal chat about the dig."

The saving grace was that Steve, the guy in charge of the physical surveys, had also been invited. At least it wouldn't just be her and Anders in the room.

"When is it?" asked Becky, jutting her chin up.

"Tomorrow morning. Ten. His office. Steve will be there, too."

Becky pulled a face. "You and Steve have to schlepp over to the university, rather than Anders coming here?"

She shrugged. "Well, he's a Big Cheese, now, isn't he? And we're just his minions."

Becky studied her, saying nothing. Georgia's computer beeped again, indicating that Steve had not only accepted the meeting into his diary, but added some paperwork to it. She opened it, to find the summary data from the preliminary survey that had been done.

"Are you going to accept the meeting, or what?" said Becky.

"Oh, he can stew for a bit. I'll accept it before I go home tonight."

Her office-mate rolled her eyes. "You *have* remembered the programme marks that you've opened all of it? Anders will know that you've seen the invite, *and* opened the agenda."

Georgia swore, then clicked on the 'accept meeting' button, gritting her teeth.

"Have you Googled him?"

Georgia tried to look innocent. "Who?" She'd spent at least an hour researching him before getting down to work that morning.

Becky gave her a sarcastic look. "Anders. The man you were totally in love with two years ago. What's he been doing since then? Why is he back in Britain?"

"He's been doing exactly what I expected he would. Publishing papers. Climbing the ladder. Following in his father's footsteps."

"Is that why he's back?"

"Seems so. The post at the university is another step up after Oslo, even if it is only maternity leave cover."

"Do you think he'll settle here?"

Georgia snorted. "Not if another shiny new role comes along. He's Haakon's son, isn't he?"

Professor Haakon Mortensen, world expert on twelfth century Scandinavian history. So focused on getting to the top, he'd forgotten he had a wife, son, and daughter to consider, or so

Anders had said one night, after a few too many whiskies. His mother had left Haakon when Anders was in his last year at primary school and returned to her homeland of England. Consequently, Anders had spent his teenage years split between Oslo and Oxford, and had told Georgia he struggled to describe either country as 'home'.

Georgia and Becky had met Haakon once. He'd come to the dig in Orkney, striding around as if it was him leading the dig, not Anders, openly criticising Anders in front of everyone, then whirling back to Norway, leaving a cloud of bitterness and animosity behind him.

Becky pressed her lips together. "I feel sorry for Anders being Haakon's son. How do you live up to his reputation?"

The hurt from Orkney flooded her afresh. "Well, he seems to be trying hard. The apple hasn't fallen far from the tree, has it? I bet he's spitting tacks he had to involve Dig For It in the new project. We might want to share the glory."

Becky put her head on one side. "I don't think you're being fair to him. He's not like that at all. Just see how your meeting goes tomorrow."

Georgia glowered across the desk, then checked herself. The Anders she'd lost her heart to was generous to a fault, and would have insisted that any glory was shared equitably.

She focused on her computer screen, her emotions in turmoil. It was easy to hate him when there was no contact with him. What if he was still just like the man she fell in love with two years ago? Where would that leave her?

Still heartbroken.

8

Anders looked at the clock for the umpteenth time, his armpits sticky with stress-induced sweat. On his desk lay a large-scale map with an area marked off with red – the area they would be digging. Steve, the man in charge of the physical surveys, had sent over the scans from the original dig, and Anders had printed them off to the same scale as the map. The new dig would extend the area to the west, but he wanted to get his head around what had already been scanned, before they started on anything further. He'd never found interpreting the various scans easy, and he needed to be absolutely sure about everything.

He'd also marked off the locations of the finds from the previous dig, with reference numbers next to them. It was these finds that had led to the new excavation, and he wanted to ask Georgie about them.

"Georg*ia*. Georg*ia*. Get it right, man!"

He closed his eyes, breathing out hard. A brisk knock on the door made him suck in a sharp breath and open his eyes.

"Yes. Come in."

The door opened, revealing Steve, looking as dishevelled as he had when they'd met the other day, and Georgie, clutching a tablet and a notebook to her chest like her life depended on it. Her light blonde curly hair was tamed by a band, though as ever, some strands were escaping, and she wore a neat dress that flattered her petite figure. Her hazel eyes regarded him coolly, making the stickiness in his armpits worse. He felt hot, and itched to take off his tie, but it was too late now. It would look weird if he suddenly did.

He waved a hand at the seats on the other side of his desk. "Steve. Georgie… *Georgia*. Sorry. Please. Take a seat."

He could have torn his tongue out. Georgie's eyes narrowed as she sat. She crossed her ankles and smoothed a hand over the skirt of her dress, then opened her notebook and clicked the end of her pen.

What was the phrase? Anders thought. 'You could cut the atmosphere with a knife.'

If Steve detected any atmosphere, he didn't let on. He plonked himself down in the other seat and leaned over to look at the papers on the desk, his gaze flitting between the scan results and the map.

"Did either of you want a tea or a coffee or anything?" Anders offered.

Georgie shook her head, but Steve opted for a coffee. Anders got up and stuck his head around the door to ask Carol to make a cafetiere of coffee and bring it through. He sat back at his desk just in time to see Georgie roll her eyes. Had she thought he should make it himself? Probably. But then, he would have offended Carol. He couldn't win.

"Thank you for coming over," he said. "I'm really sorry that we're holding this over at the university buildings. I would have come to you, but I am wall-to-wall with meetings today, and this was the only window when all three of us were free."

Steve shrugged a shoulder. "Nice to get out of the building."

Georgie said nothing. Instead, she pointedly tapped on the tablet in her hand, opening the agenda he'd sent. "You wanted to start by discussing the finds from the first dig. There was a full report written up after the dig, so I'm not sure what else you want to know."

He regretted sending the agenda. He hadn't intended to, but his predecessor had been finicky like that and as soon as he'd created a new meeting, his computer had prompted him to attach an agenda and the minutes of the previous meeting. He'd rolled his eyes, sketched out the briefest of agendas and stuck it on, just to shut the system up. One day, he'd remember to ask Carol how to stop it from doing that.

He met Georgie's eye, his stomach full of butterflies. "I know. But these things can be a bit dry. They're always just the facts. I wanted to hear what your gut instincts about the site were. Both of you," he added hurriedly. "You'll both have much more of a feel for the place than a report ever reveals. Georgie? You know the finds inside out. What are your thoughts?"

She raised her chin, blinking. Her pupils were dilated, narrowing the band of hazel. Was she angry with him? Stressed? He swallowed. Was she as anxious about meeting with him as he was to see her? He shoved the thought from his head and tried to focus.

"It would be easier if Steve talked you through the surveys first, then I can explain why we put the trenches in where we did, and perhaps then you'll understand the relevance of the finds."

He breathed carefully. She was angry, not stressed.

"Though it *is* all in the report. The survey. The rationale…" She threw her free hand up, then turned pointedly towards Steve.

Steve's eyes widened, then he collected himself and shuffled forwards to sit on the edge of his chair and lean over the desk.

"Okay, this set of results is the best to look at, because it indicates potential buildings." He moved one of the sheets closer to Anders, then traced areas that had darker shading. "We thought there were buildings here, here, here, and *maybe* here, though it's not all that clear. At this point, there was still no huge reason to expect anything significant, so we put in trenches here, here and here, to do sampling. They confirmed the buildings, but there were some important finds, which is why we're doing the whole site, right?" He cocked a brow at Anders.

"Yep." Anders glanced towards Georgie. "Talk me through the finds?"

She threw him a baleful stare. "As I've already said, it's all in the report."

"Humour me," he said softly.

She let a long breath trickle out of her nose, her face still stony. "Sure. Well, we wondered if this was a main hall, though it turned out to be more likely to be a smaller dwelling."

She talked him through what they'd found. A lot of pottery; some smaller items such as beads and individual coins; a buckle.

"But what really led to the excavation being extended was the hoard we found."

He scanned the pages in his hands. "Tell me about it?"

The report cited a pottery container that had been full of Anglo-Saxon coins. Both an unusual and a highly significant find.

"Hidden under a floor, we think, given the depth it was found at and the shading in the soil layers above it. The floor hadn't survived. Wood doesn't in this soil."

He knew that, but he said nothing.

"The coins all dated from the mid- to late eleventh century. My guess is that someone stashed it before the Harrying of the North, but wasn't able to come back for it."

"No coins later than 1069?"

The year the Harrying started, when William the Conqueror stamped out a revolt in northern England, reported to be one of the most brutal episodes in history, where whole villages were razed to the ground, livestock slaughtered, and tens of thousands were killed, or starved to death.

Georgie shook her head. Anders re-read some of the report, a frown settling. "Charcoal?"

"No, not really. We thought abandoned, rather than torched."

Many places had been burnt to the ground. Even by 1086 – the year that the Domesday Book was compiled – more than a third of viable land in Yorkshire was described as wasteland. Those settlements that weren't burned had been deserted.

"There's also a brooch, only found recently," added Georgie. "I finished the report on it the other day. Metal-detectorists found it at the edge of the next field, but I'm sure it's really part of this complex."

He arched a brow. "Anglo-Saxon?"

She twisted her mouth to one side. "Anglo-Scandinavian. I'll forward you the report."

She walked him through her reasoning, her posture softening, and her scowls turning to smiles as she talked. His spirits lifted a fraction. This was the Georgie he'd known. The bubbly, enthusiastic, smart woman he'd fallen in love with in Orkney.

Georgie finished and smiled at him, her eyes lively. His heart lurched a little.

Carol tapped on the door and carried a tray in, furnished with three china mugs, a cafetiere, some sugar, and a small jug of milk. Georgie's lips twitched with amusement.

"Did you want biscuits?" chirruped Carol.

Georgie's light smile widened before she lowered her head and stared at her notebook.

They all shook their heads, and Carol retreated. The rich scent of excellent coffee filled the room, and he breathed deeply.

"Sure you don't want one?" Anders asked Georgie softly.

"Oh, go on then. Since it's made."

He poured out three mugs of dark coffee and indicated for them to help themselves to milk and sugar. Steve loaded three spoonfuls of sugar into his mug and as much milk as he could fit in. Georgie still took hers white with no sugar, he noted.

"Can you show me on the map where they found that brooch?" he said, once everyone settled with their drinks.

Georgie leaned over, pointing to an area close to the field boundary. "Just there. I put both the GPS and OS coordinates in the report, so you'll be able to mark it exactly."

"Thanks. Appreciated. So, what's your gut feeling about what we'll find? Full settlement?"

She wrinkled her nose. "I think so. Steve?" She glanced at her colleague.

Steve nodded, making his lanky locks wave.

"Yeah. Another interesting bit might be over here." He reached over and pointed to a spot on the map showing a small wooded area, a little way away from the dig site, but still within the boundary of the permission. "It's maybe not part of the main settlement, but the ground is raised. It *might* be worth having a poke about in there. Or at least add it to the surveys we're doing."

Anders shook his head. "That's outside the main area and in the wrong direction. The finds were more concentrated towards this side of the field." He touched the map and ran his eye over the scan results again, planning the dig. "Okay. I'd like to have the finds tent set up over here, unless you can think of a good reason not to? It's close by, but not actually where we'll be digging. We have permission from the landowner to use this field for parking, Portaloos, finds processing etc. Which brings me to parking. There isn't a lot of space, so can you get the Dig For It team to organise lift shares? I'll sort out the uni guys. If you have any difficulties, let me know?"

"Yep. No problem," said Steve, even though Anders had been directing most of it towards Georgie.

She finished her coffee and replaced the mug on the tray, just as Anders did the same. His hand accidentally brushed hers, and an electric shock shot up his arm, making him catch his breath. Georgie jumped, also snatching at her breathing, then locked wide eyes with him.

"Static," she said, though she looked discomfited. "Nylon carpets."

"Probably." He cleared his throat, trying to ignore the fizzing running through his body. "Okay. Steve, can I get you to organise the surveys to start first thing on Monday? Georgie, if you can look after the finds tent, I'll get everyone else field-walking the new bit. See what shows up. There could be something really interesting under this field."

Georgie snapped her notebook closed and held it across her front like a shield again. The softness and animation in her face from a few minutes earlier had gone, replaced with a flinty look.

"Unless either of you have anything else you think we need to discuss, I'll let you both get back," he said, wondering what had caused the change.

Both of them shook their heads, and Georgie stood up.

"Barely worth an agenda, really," she said, smoothing her dress out. "See you at the site. And, *again*, it's Georgia."

He groaned internally. *That* was why her lightness had evaporated.

Steve also got to his feet and stood back to let her leave first. Anders hoped she would look back at him as she went. She didn't.

He swallowed, his spirits sinking. This could be a *long* summer.

9

Steve and Georgia strolled back to the Dig For It buildings together, Georgia's brain churning.

He's exactly the same as he was in Orkney.

Her fingers gripped her notebook as she tried to force her brain to think about the end of their time in Orkney, and not the middle. However hard she tried, all her mind would focus on were his forget-me-not-blue eyes, his easy smile, how much he'd made her laugh. How when he'd looked at her, he'd made her feel as if there was no one else in the world.

She gritted her teeth. *Yeah, and then he chose Oslo, remember?*

"I take it you know Dr Mortensen, then?"

Georgia jumped. Steve cocked his head at her, one brow raised.

"Sorry, I was miles away." She took a breath, then glanced away, trying to figure out how to answer him. "Mm. We were both on a dig in Orkney, a couple of years ago. He led it; I was involved in the finds tent."

"Not a fan of his? You seemed really pissed off with him in there. Is he a total arse to work with?"

Georgia weighed her words. "No, he's great to work with. He looked after the team in Orkney, and was fun to be around. He can just be very driven. Has more of an eye on what's coming next, rather than enjoying the moment, you know? He'll be hoping this dig *does* show up something brilliant, so he can write a book about it, or publish lots of papers, or get another promotion."

"Ambition isn't a *bad* thing."

"Hm." *That depends on whether chasing the next promotion is more important than settling down.*

They turned down a side road leading to their buildings.

"Is he related to *Professor* Mortensen? The Norwegian guy?" asked Steve as they waited to cross a busy road.

"Yeah. Professor Mortensen is his father."

Steve let out a low whistle. "I met him once at a conference. Not sure I'd want him as *my* dad. I guess that's why Dr Mortensen is so driven. Big shoes to fill."

Georgia sighed. "He could choose not to fill them and live his own life. There is that as an option."

Steve turned to her, scrutinising her closely. His eyes widened, and he grinned. "Have you two got history?"

She focused on the lights of the crossing, waiting for the green man to show, deliberately not answering. Steve chuckled.

"Oh, okay. That explains things."

"That explains what?" she snapped.

"Nothing."

The lights changed, and the crossing bleeped at them. Georgia hurried across, trying to ignore the amusement from Steve.

"So, it didn't end well, then?" Steve persisted. "It can't have done, given that you clearly hate him."

She huffed out her breath. "Steve, it was two years ago. It's not relevant. And frankly, it's none of your business."

He held his hands up. "Fair enough."

Georgia groaned internally. Steve could be the biggest gossip, so the fact that she had 'history' with Anders would be all over Dig For It by this afternoon, something she could definitely do without.

They reached the Dig For It buildings without further comment, and she escaped to her office. As she flung herself into her chair, Becky looked up.

"Oh. It went *that* well, then?"

"The meeting was fine. Anders was… Anders. Organised. Focused… *Anders*. Steve's twigged that there was something between us, though."

Becky stuck her bottom lip out. "So?"

She sighed. "*So…* everyone here will know that by this afternoon."

"I say again… so? What does it matter? Pretty much everyone

will tell Steve it's none of his business." She canted her head. "And it will be pretty obvious to everyone on the dig that there's nothing between you *now*. If you were any colder to him, he'd get frostbite."

Her comment provoked a smile in Georgia.

"Coffee?" offered Becky.

"No, thanks. I had one at Anders's office. Posh coffee. In a cafetiere and everything. His secretary made it." She pulled a face.

Becky huffed at her. "As head of department, he is allowed to have a secretary. It comes with the job."

"Yeah, I know."

In truth, she wasn't annoyed that his secretary had made the coffee. She'd just been reminded that he was promoted enough to *have* a secretary. Her mind drifted back over the electric shock she'd had when their hands had touched. Static from the carpets. That was all.

Except his office had wooden floors.

She pushed the thought out of her head. She was *not* going to fall in love with Anders again. He'd broken her heart once. She was damned if she'd let him do it again.

10

The first day of the dig rolled around. Steve, Becky, and Georgia had travelled in together in Steve's van, and he nosed it into a space on the grassed field set aside for parking next to the dig site. Two cars were already there – an ancient Land Rover Discovery, and a smaller hatchback – and Georgia wondered who they belonged to.

"Here we are, ladies," said Steve, climbing out. "Blimey. It looks like Dr Mortensen's got it all sorted."

Georgia scanned the field. Steve wasn't kidding. Two old army tents stood side by side, and there were a couple of Portaloos at the other end of the field. The smell of coffee wafted towards them, emanating from the army tent on the right. Between the two tents hummed a small generator. Becky came to stand next to her.

"Well, you have to give it to Anders. He knows how to look after his team," she murmured to Georgia.

Georgia couldn't argue.

The tents were almost certainly military surplus, and Georgia wrinkled her nose. Although they were often excellent shelters, they usually had a very distinctive odour of damp about them. A drab olive-green colour, they stood about nine feet high in the middle and could hold about fifteen people standing up. The openings were fastened back in each tent, and voices came from the tent on the right. Inside, Anders chatted to Sophie at one end, and Sam and Patrick stood at the other. Anders and Sophie looked deep in conversation, then Anders laughed loudly, and Georgia's heart raced for a couple of beats. He looked a lot more like the Anders she knew from Orkney this morning, clad in boots, walking trousers, and a rugby shirt. His hair was already getting away from him, even cut as short as it was. She smiled to herself. Her hair could have a mind of its own most days, but his hadn't been much better.

Becky jabbed her in the ribs. "I think there might be coffee. Shall we go and see?"

They made their way over to join the others. A folding table stood to one side, with a nearly full water-cooler bottle on it, alongside an urn of boiling water. Next to that were two boxes of Danish pastries, a large box of teabags, a jar of instant coffee, a bottle of milk, a bag of sugar, and a collection of teaspoons. A small pile of paper plates nestled next to the pastries. A second, smaller table held an array of bottles of sunscreen. Sophie had moved to the back of the tent to chat with Patrick and Sam, leaving Anders on his own. He stared into space, the fingers of his left hand tapping out a pattern against his thigh. Georgia hung back, but Becky marched straight over to him.

"Morning! Are we calling you Anders or Dr Mortensen?"

He laughed, then pulled a face. "Anders. Either pronunciation. I don't care. There's tea and coffee on the side table, along with some pastries. There'll be some volunteers joining us today so, once everyone's here, I'll introduce you all, and we can plan the day." He leaned around Becky to wave at Georgia. "Morning."

Her stomach flipped. Why did his eyes have to crinkle like that?

She gave a small wave in return, then joined Becky and Steve at the side table. While they all grabbed a coffee and a pastry, the tent filled until about a dozen people stood around. Georgia smiled to herself. All of the tall people had had to cluster in the middle of the tent, because that was the only place with enough head-clearance for them. Anders stood in a space towards the side, needing to bend his neck slightly to fit his six-foot frame in. He was empty-handed, but Sophie went over and gave him a mug of coffee and a pastry, earning herself a wide smile from him. He took small bites of the pastry, his gaze flicking over everyone, his posture tight.

"Jeez, he looks nervous," murmured Becky in her ear.

"I don't know why. It's not like this is his first dig," she muttered back.

But she *did* know why. She knew how much he hated speaking to a group, however friendly they all were. She'd seen exactly how stressed he got before a conference, to the point of vomiting once. She'd thought that he'd be cured of it by now, but he seemed as bad as ever.

He took another small bite of his pastry, then struggled to swallow it, his Adam's apple bobbing. His hand holding the mug of coffee shook and Georgia stared at him, torn. Other than her, she didn't think anyone would know just how anxious he would be at having to speak to the group. He glanced at his hands, then over to the table, then back to the pastry and mug, his colour fading.

Georgia took pity on him and scooted over to him.

"Want me to look after those for you while you talk?" she offered softly, nodding towards his coffee and cake.

He turned his sky-blue eyes with their darker blue edge to her, and his expression switched from panic to relief in an instant.

"Thank you," he whispered, handing her both items.

"It's okay." Her heart ached to see him so agitated. "Anders, relax. You're fine. You've got this."

His face fell. "That obvious?"

She shrugged. "To me… Come on. Deep breath. You're good at this."

She moved away to give him the floor. He took a deep breath in, moved closer to the middle of the tent, and squared his shoulders. He shot her another panicked look, and she gave him a tiny nod of encouragement. However much he'd hurt her, she hated seeing him flounder like this.

"Morning everyone!" he said, calling the room to attention. "Okay, introductions first. I think all of you either know me or have met me at least once, but for the avoidance of doubt, I'm Anders."

Georgia melted back to Becky's side while Anders introduced everyone, ran through the set-up of the site, pointed out the sunscreen and reminded everyone to wear some, covered a variety of safety notices, and then outlined the plan for the day. The first day would be taken up with field-walking and the geophysical surveys, and Georgia knew she'd be ensconced in the finds tent all day, looking at what was picked up. As well as the field-walking, some of the team were sweeping the field with metal-detectors. She could be busy. Or they could find nothing, and she would have a really dull day.

The meeting over, everyone else drifted out of the tent. Anders walked over to her, and she handed him his mug and the paper plate with the remains of his pastry.

"Thank you," he said quietly. "And thank you for the encouragement."

"It's okay. At least you weren't sick."

A wan smile crossed his lips. "It was touch and go with that pastry."

She studied him. "I thought you might be better about all that by now."

He shook his head, miserable. "No. And I've done I don't know how many courses on it. But my guts just knot up completely. I know. It's stupid."

He was so close to her, she could feel the heat from his body and smell his soap and shampoo. The familiarity made her stomach flip, and she looked up. If she wasn't mistaken, he hadn't bothered shaving. She preferred him with a beard. Was he going to grow it back in?

He held her gaze, his eyes soft, and she stepped back.

"Okay. Well, I'll be in the finds tent," she said, needing to be away from him.

He straightened. "Of course."

She hurried away, her heart racing.

Do not *fall for him again!*

11

Anders stared after her, confused. Did she still hate him for taking the job in Oslo, or not? She'd recognised just how anxious he was and been so kind to him just now. But if she still cared for him, even as just a friend, why had she ghosted him for two years?

He swallowed, trying to put it out of his mind and focus on the dig. As dig manager, his role involved more coordination than actual digging, although he was going to join the field-walk as soon as he could, if only to ensure that he knew the locations of any finds.

He sipped his coffee, but it had a slightly sweet, oily taste to it and he abandoned it. The pastry still made him feel nauseous too, so he tossed it in the bin. Outside, he took a moment to scan the field. The volunteers had been paired up with either the university team, or the people from Dig For It, and were walking in a slow, steady line across the ploughed field. Thankfully, it had been a fairly dry spring, so the ground underfoot wasn't thick mud. Steve and Becky stood close to the refreshments tent, fiddling with the equipment they'd retrieved from Steve's van.

Anders wandered towards them. "Got everything you need?"

Steve nodded. "Yep. We'll try not to get in the way."

"Oh, you guys have priority."

Becky grinned at him. "Can we quote you on that?"

Anders laughed. "You can."

Again, confusion tickled his brain. When he'd been desperate to fix things with Georgie, he was *sure* she was staying with Becky, but Becky had denied it, and eventually told him she would block his number if he rang her again. Yet, here she was, joking with him as if none of that had happened.

Steve moved away, and Becky picked up her equipment as if

to follow him.

"Becky?" said Anders.

She paused and turned back to him, brows raised. He waited until Steve was out of earshot, then took a breath.

"Um. Everything is okay with us?" he said, floundering a little. "After Orkney."

She nodded, still smiling. "Yeah, Anders. Everything is fine. Two years is a long time." Her gaze flicked towards the finds tent. "She didn't want to talk to you, that was all."

"Okay. Thanks."

She gave him a measured look before following Steve on to the field. Anders stood for a moment, gathering his thoughts, then grabbed a handful of small flags.

It wasn't long before a shout went up and someone stuck a small flag in the soil at their feet. Anders put his flags down to mark where he'd got to and hurried over to the find. Sam, the tall, red-headed man from the university team, held out something on the palm of his hand.

"Pin?" he said, offering his open hand towards Anders.

Anders peered at the mud-encrusted object. Even this close to it, it was hard to see *any* object in the lump of soil.

"Well spotted. You must have good eyes."

He took it from Sam and carefully brushed a little of the dirt away. The clump of mud encased a long, slim object, with a flattened disc at one end.

"Good find," he said, turning it over in his hand. "Yeah, I think it's a dress pin."

"Shall I take it over to Georgia?" said Sam.

"No. I'll take it. It's marked, yes?" Anders glanced down to check the flag number, then clapped Sam on the shoulder.

Sam grinned at him, then continued his slow walk across the field, his head down.

Anders drew a notebook out of his trouser pocket and wrote down the details of the find. Taking a steadying breath, he strolled over to the finds tent, ducking his head as he negotiated the opening. Georgie sat at a trestle table close to the opening where there was more light, unpacking a box of brushes and placing them next to a magnifying light in front of her.

"First find," he said, as she glanced up.

"Wow, that was quick."

He held out his hand with the pin in his palm. She picked it up, and the contact from her fingers sent a shot of electricity up his arm. At the same moment, she inhaled sharply, her eyes wide. So, she'd felt it too?

"Dress pin?" he asked.

He moved back a little while she looked at it. She carefully brushed more of the soil away, revealing more of the pin, then put it under the magnifying light.

"Yep, looks like it," she confirmed. "I would put it as Anglo-Scandinavian with this flat end. Nice find. Have a look."

She moved back so that he could take a better look, and he leaned in and peered at the pin. The smell of her washing powder and shower gel made his heart lurch, and he held his breath for a few seconds.

"Good start! Well spotted," she said, folding her arms tightly.

"Sam found it, not me." He tipped his head towards the table in the far corner of the tent. "I want to log it before anything else comes in."

He'd set up his laptop in the finds tent partly because he needed to be able to plug into the generator, but mostly because a masochistic kernel of him wanted to be in the same place as Georgie. He wandered over and booted the computer up, then unfurled the map of the site, pinning it down with mugs in the corners. His back prickled, and he glanced over his shoulder to see Georgie staring at him, her expression hostile. She turned back to her desk, her head down. Maybe setting up in here had been a mistake.

He finished recording all the details he needed to and closed the lid of the laptop, before hurrying back out into the sunshine.

Becky might think that two years was a long time, and that things were okay between them, but Georgie clearly didn't.

12

Georgia watched Anders duck back out of the finds tent, her emotions whirling. She'd seen his laptop. She'd *known* he would be working in there with her. So why had his presence unsettled her so much?

"Of *course* he's going to be working in this tent," Georgia muttered to herself. "Where else would he be? Did you think he'd just hunker down in the field next to the Portaloos? Or have his maps and laptop out with all the coffee?"

It would all be so much easier if there wasn't this *frisson* between them. That was twice now that their hands had touched, and twice that a pulse of electricity had shot up her arm.

She gritted her teeth and tried to focus on the dress pin, but it was no good. She might have walked away from him two years ago and cut all ties, but what had drawn her to him in the first place hadn't changed. His infectious excitement and enthusiasm, his kindness, those soft blue eyes with a navy edge to the iris, his wide, easy smile…

"He chose the *job*, not you. Get a grip!"

She was right. He *hadn't* shaved. Dark blond stubble covered his jawline. And the wayward lock of hair he had at the front was literally spiralling out of control. It always seemed determined to grow into a coil and, even with the major haircut, it refused to be tamed.

She closed her eyes, breathing out hard.

"Anglo-Scandinavian dress pin," she said firmly. "Flattened end, decorated with four ringed dots. Probably copper-alloy."

She wasn't seeing it, though. She was seeing the tuft of chest hair in the open neck of his rugby shirt.

And then she saw something completely different. She was

back in the low-roofed, dark, smoky building she'd had visions of in the finds store. She opened her eyes again, but the image didn't clear.

The room seemed smaller. She frowned. No, this wasn't the same building. She concentrated hard, slowly picking out features. There was a narrow bed. She could just make out the contours in the gloom. She looked down at her hands to find she was carrying a bowl of water with a cloth in it. Peering at the bed, she could see the outline of a man in it, though his face was turned away from her.

"I'm to tend to you," she said, her voice sounding strange. *"Though I don't know why I should."*

The man stirred, groaning, and turned over in bed.

She perched next to him and roughly drew the linen cloth covering the wounds on his shoulder to one side, making him flinch.

"Oh. Did that hurt? Sorry," she said, though there wasn't a trace of sorrow in her. "I thought you were a tough warrior. My error."

She was being rude; she knew. But he wouldn't understand her words. How could he? He was from another land. He should have stayed there.

"Who are you?"

She straightened, startled. The words were close enough to her own language that she could make out his meaning. How? How could that be?

"I am Aelfgyth. Daughter of Cenred. Cenred, whose estate this is. Was." She paused. "Did you learn our language before coming to steal our land?"

He struggled to sit up a little better. "No. But your people and my people share history. And enough language that we can make some sense of one another. Though I would like to learn your language better."

She studied him. Thick, wavy, dark blond hair tumbled around his face. One lock at the front grew almost in a spiral. Even in the dim light, she could see that his eyes were the colour of a spring sky, with a darker ring around the edge.

Georgia caught her breath, and the vision faded. The man on the bed had looked just like Anders, except with even longer hair and more beard than he'd had in Orkney.

Her hands trembling, she put the pin down. What on earth was happening to her? Why did she keep getting these visions? She folded her hands together on the edge of the table, taking long, steady breaths. She'd always had an active imagination. This wouldn't be the first time she'd sat in front of an object, imagining the person who might have owned it, or how they would have lived. These objects weren't just things from the ground. They *had* belonged to real people, who had pinned them in their clothes, been irritated that they'd lost them. Who had lost their land to invaders from Scandinavia.

This had felt different, though. She felt as if she'd *experienced* this. She shook her head. That was ridiculous. She'd been thinking about who might have owned the pin, and her mind had built on the same fantasy she'd conjured before, then stuffed Anders in as the Viking, just because he was half Norwegian.

She picked up the pin again to prove to herself that there was nothing supernatural about it.

"See. Perfectly normal. It's just a pin."

The room shifted, and she was drawn back into the vision before she could react.

"I'm to tend to you." She thrust the bowl forwards.

The man in the bed nodded. "Thank you. I am Einar."

"Oh, I know who you are."

Her eyes travelled over his broad chest and the light brown hairs covering it. He was certainly a powerful man. She wrung out the cloth and dabbed it none too gently on the raw wound on his shoulder. His breath hissed through his teeth, but he didn't yell out. She tossed the cloth back in the bowl, squeezed it out, then bathed the wound again, this time a little more gently. From her pocket, she drew a pottery jar, small enough to fit snugly in her hand. An incised pattern decorated the sides, and a wooden stopper covered the opening. She removed the stopper and slipped it back into her pocket for safekeeping. Inside the jar was a thick unguent, made from pounded herbs and animal fat.

"This might hurt," she muttered, applying a thick layer to his wound.

Again, his breath whistled, and he lowered his head. Even in the gloom, she could see how his colour had faded. She covered the area with a clean cloth.

"That should help it to heal. Was it from a sword?"

He nodded, his breathing still uneven.

"I will bring you food."

He raised his head, a smile tickling his lips. "Thank you. You are a fine healer. Blessed with gentle hands and a kind heart."

Her eyes narrowed. She could recognise sarcasm, despite the different language. She closed the jar, and stood, a sharp retort on her lips that died when she remembered her father's words. This Einar could throw them out; make them homeless. She was supposed to be being nice to him.

"I will bring you food," she repeated more softly, then gathered the cloth and bowl and retreated.

The vision faded, and the table of the finds tent came back into focus. Georgia put the pin down and pinched the bridge of her nose.

"Okay. This can just stop."

Was this going to happen with *every* artefact they found in this field? Her gaze spun out towards the dig, tightness settling in her shoulders. There could be *hundreds* of items found over the summer. How on earth would she get anything done?

13

Anders stood in a patch of late afternoon sun at the edge of the field, stretching his back, thinking over the day. It had been a pretty good start to the dig. The groups had gelled well; the geophysical surveys were rattling on; Steve said he'd have preliminary data for him to look at by the close of play; A steady stream of finds had kept Georgie busy, though only about a third of them had had any archaeological significance.

He scanned the site. The field-walk had finished a while ago, though the metal-detectorists were still going, criss-crossing the field, their heads down, and Steve and Becky were walking the final strip next to the hedge. Everyone else had decamped to the refreshments tent for a last coffee before packing up. He stretched again, hauling in a deep lungful of fresh air, and closing his eyes against the sun.

"Coffee?" asked a voice at his side.

He jumped, his eyes snapping open. Sophie held out a steaming mug to him, a wide smile making her cheek dimple.

"Oh. Thank you."

"I put oat milk in it for you again. And you don't look like a guy who takes sugar, so there isn't any in it."

Am I a guy who looks like he takes oat milk? And is that why it tasted weird this morning?

"Without sugar is perfect. Thank you. Where did you get the oat milk?" He'd only brought regular milk in.

She grinned. "Oh, I brought a small bottle with me."

He took the mug from her and sipped. The coffee had the same slightly oily, sweet taste to it that it'd had that morning. He didn't like it, but he smiled.

"Good first day, huh?" said Sophie, shielding her eyes from

the sun.

"Very good first day."

A mass of bright blonde hair caught his attention. Georgie had emerged from the finds tent and taken the band out of her hair, so it now tumbled around her face in mad corkscrews. He chuckled to himself, wondering how long it would be before she got irritated by it and tied it all back again.

"That's the woman who took your cake off you this morning and told you to get on with things, isn't it?"

He glanced down, surprised to see Sophie still next to him. "Um. That's not really what she did." His gaze spun back out in time to see a breeze send Georgie's hair into a maelstrom around her face.

"Did you know her before this dig?"

Anders tore his eyes away from Georgie. "Er, yes. I worked with a couple of people from Dig For It up in Orkney two years ago. Georgia and Becky. Er… Becky is the woman with the buzz cut, doing the geophysics with Steve."

Becky was just finishing up on the far side of the field, and Sophie's dark brown eyes appraised her as coolly as they had Georgie.

"It's a shame we had to include a commercial group. I always think it's better to keep things within the uni."

"That's a little churlish," said Anders, feeling defensive on their behalf. "It was their work that paved the way for this dig. And they're all professionals."

Sophie drained her mug. "Mm. But they're not academics, are they? They just do this for the money. They get asked to do an archaeological survey so that houses can be built, or supermarkets extended, or whatever. It's just a job. It's not actually *important* to them."

He thought of how animated Georgie had been on the Orkney dig; how excited she'd been when the finds had come in over the day. Sophie was quite wrong. It was *hugely* important to her.

Georgie turned in his direction, and he waved. She gave a small, hesitant wave in return. Sophie moved closer to him. So close that her arm brushed his and he could smell her perfume.

He shifted his weight, moving away from her, but not before Georgie had looked away.

He turned to Sophie. "If you'll excuse me, I really need to talk to Georgia."

Her lips thinned, but she said nothing.

Georgie sat on the grass at the edge of the field, her legs stretched out in front of her, her stripy top now untucked from her cargo pants.

He strolled over and sat next to her. "There's coffee on the go."

She tipped her head up towards him, her hair tumbling around madly. "Oh, I'm all coffee-ed out! But thanks." She eyed his mug. "I see Sophie has been looking after you again."

He snorted. "Mm. She brought me a coffee. She seems to think I take it with oat milk."

"Why?" Georgie's face crumpled. "Have you gone vegan since Orkney? No, you can't have. The pastries weren't vegan, and you had at least a nibble of one."

"No. I think she's vegan and is trying to convert me."

"Oh. Does she *ever* pronounce your name properly?"

He laughed, shaking his head. "No. I corrected her once, but she reverted to Ann-ders almost immediately. Life's too short to fret about it."

"Still. It's only good manners to make the effort."

Her attention shifted, and he followed her gaze. The last few people on the field were packing up their metal-detectors and heading towards the refreshments tent. Anders checked his watch, surprised to see that it was after five. He got to his feet, his stomach already twisting into knots.

"Quick team meeting?" he called across the field.

Those still out on the field nodded, or gave him a thumbs-up. Anders turned to Georgie, holding his hand out to help her up. She hesitated, then caught hold of it. He pulled her up, trying to ignore the fluttering in his belly, not sure if it was nerves at the idea of talking to the group, or the fact that Georgie was holding his hand. She faced him fully, still holding his hand, her hazel eyes bright.

"Thank you."

"Always a pleasure," he replied softly.

She pinked and let go of his hand. "Come on then. Address your minions. Try not to vomit on the way."

He laughed lightly. "One of these days I'll be as comfortable as you are at standing up and talking to people."

She snorted. "You know, I don't think you ever will."

She walked with him to the larger tent. With every step, his guts coiled tighter until, by the time he stood at the front, he felt queasy. Everyone turned expectantly towards him, and he hauled in a deep breath.

"Thank you everyone. Fantastic day today. If you can all remember to sign out, that would be helpful. It would also be really helpful if someone could wash all the mugs up. And guys, don't be sexist. It's *not* the women's responsibility. Thank you! Back here tomorrow at eight, please. Er, Steve, Georgia, can I keep both of you for a few minutes to go over today's finds and the survey results?"

The group dispersed, leaving Steve, Georgie, and Becky still in the tent with him. He glanced quizzically at Becky, then remembered that the three of them had all arrived together.

"Oh, Becky, sorry. I'd forgotten you would all be in the same car."

She grinned at him. "It's alright. I'm nosy enough to want to hear the full picture of the day."

They moved to the finds tent and stood around the table with Anders's notes on it. All of the day's relevant finds had been marked on the map.

"Were you kept busy?" Steve asked Georgie.

"Yeah, fairly busy. Only about a third of the finds were relevant, though. There were a *lot* of ring pulls and beer caps. And random bits from farm machinery."

"Give me the overview?" asked Anders. He didn't really need it, but he needed a reason for asking her to stay.

"You saw everything as it came in. Most of the finds were bits of broken pottery. A couple were so small I wouldn't like to date them with certainty without getting them to the lab, but the general picture is Anglo-Saxon. I don't think anything was later than eleventh century, apart from the ring pulls, bottle caps and random farm machinery things. The picture I got from today's finds was just Anglo-Saxon or Anglo-Scandinavian."

Anders nodded. "Steve, I know you won't have processed all the results yet, but any preliminary data you can share?"

Steve put a couple of print-outs on the table, showing black and white stippling of various densities.

"I wouldn't like to bet my mortgage on it, but there might… *might* be a structure here." His finger traced the merest differences in the shading on the print-out. "Which would be here on this map." He pointed again. "I should have a clearer picture for you tomorrow. I'll do a bit more processing of the raw data tonight. But there's a strong signal here, which might be a fire, and then this looks rectilinear just here." He rummaged through a sheaf of papers. "It's actually just about visible in the crop marks from this photo from a few years ago."

Anders studied the images, chewing a thumbnail. His hair fell forwards into his eyes, and he pushed it back, irritated by it. The shape Steve indicated lay close to where most of the finds had been.

"So, we have fragments of pottery, part of a comb, the dress pin, and a coin, all close to where you think the structure is?"

"And a spindle whorl," added Georgie. "Though the date of that's a bit vague. I'll put it as no more than 'not inconsistent with' the rest of the finds."

"Okay. Test trench in here?" He traced an area on the map. "And another here?"

Everyone around the table nodded enthusiastically.

"Perfect. Thanks for staying back. See you all in the morning."

Georgie's hair must have finally annoyed her enough, because she took the hairband off her wrist and tied it all back. She caught his eye as she did so, and he grinned at her.

Her smile widened. Then snapped off. She blinked a couple of times, then hurried after the other two without looking back.

Anders closed his eyes and fingered his brow, fresh pain searing his heart.

Don't go there. Don't hope that there might be a second chance. She didn't love you enough the first time, remember?

14

Back at their flat, Becky tossed her keys in the dish on the slim table by the door and kicked her shoes off, blowing her cheeks out.

"Jeez… Steve's driving gets worse," she muttered, shrugging off her coat.

Becky had ended up in the middle seat in the front of the van on the way back, with little to brace against on the corners. Georgia would swap places with her tomorrow.

"I need a beer," huffed Becky. "Want one?"

"Yes, please."

They headed to the small kitchen at the back of the flat. Georgia unfastened her hair and fluffed it out, wrapping the hairband around her wrist.

"So…" said Becky, flipping the top off a bottle of beer from the fridge and passing it over. "How are you feeling about working with Anders for the whole summer? You think you two will patch things up? You clearly don't hate him as much as I thought you would, though you blew a bit hot and cold with him today."

The bottle paused on the way to her lips. "What?"

Becky gave her a frank look. "You were kind to him when he was panicking about the group meeting. Then you moaned about him to me over lunch. You seemed chilled out around him just before we left, then suddenly froze him out. Make your bloody mind up."

Georgia put the bottle down on the worktop, about to argue, then sighed. Becky had a valid point. "It's difficult. He's the same man I fell for in Orkney. He hasn't changed. Apart from the haircut."

Becky twisted her mouth, studying her. "Would you go out with him again?"

Georgia shook her head. "No. Because as well as still being kind and funny and smart and *yes*... sexy as hell, he's still set on climbing the academic ladder, which means he would *still* drop me like a hot potato if a better job came up." Her shoulders slumped. "I was *so* excited about this dig, and then in he comes, all blue eyes and infectious enthusiasm, and it just punches another great hole in my chest and I'm hurt all over again."

Becky took a long pull from her beer, her eyes still on Georgia, then put the bottle down. "He asked me today if we – me and him – were okay. After Orkney."

Georgia chewed the inside of her lip. Becky had been an absolute rock when it had all ended with Anders, letting her crash at her place, fielding the non-stop calls from Anders... She knew Becky had found it difficult, because Anders had been her friend, too, but her loyalty to Georgia had won out.

"What did you say?" She picked at the label on the bottle.

Becky shrugged. "I said we were cool. That two years was a long time."

"I'm sorry our break-up meant you lost his friendship, too."

She said nothing, making Georgia feel worse.

Becky rubbed the back of her neck. "He also asked me today if you were seeing anyone."

Her stomach fluttered for a moment before she squashed her excitement down. "Did he? What did you say?"

"That you weren't. Do you think he's interested in getting back together with you?"

Her nail worried at the label on the bottle again. "I don't know. Moot point."

She was *not* going to let him break her heart again.

"I asked him if *he* was seeing anyone, and he blushed and said he wasn't."

"He probably abandoned someone in Oslo, the way he abandoned me in Orkney," she muttered, though the idea of him being with anyone made jealousy flash through her, leaving her cold. She dragged a hand through her hair. "Oh, Becks, it's so much more difficult than I thought it would be. When I saw him in his office, he was all corporate and academic, and I thought, 'Oh, maybe I didn't really know him. Maybe he really *is* a high-flying academic and the Anders I knew in Orkney wasn't the real him.' And then, I see him today, in his cargo pants and a rugby shirt, with mud in his hair, and he's in his element out there."

She ground to a halt. She *had* blown hot and cold with him over the day, but she just didn't know how to be around him.

"How do I survive this summer, Becks? I don't want to get back with him, even if that was on offer, which I doubt. But we're not *friends*. I don't even know if I could deal with being friends with him."

Becky sipped her beer, her gaze settling on her. "You're both grown-ups. Allegedly. And you're both professionals. Have a friendly, professional relationship. Like you do with Steve. And if Anders makes a pass at you, tell him, *politely,* that you're not interested. But from what I've seen, he's been nothing but nice to you, and acted the way an old friend might."

"I know." She rotated the bottle on the spot on the counter. "I just wish things could have been different."

She'd loved him so much, and then he'd chosen to move to Norway. Without her. That hadn't been the direction she'd thought the relationship was heading in. She'd thought they might get a place together, not him move to a different country. It had broken her heart to do it, but she'd cut him out of her life completely. It had been the only way she thought she could deal with everything.

And now he was back, and he was just the same. And *all* the reasons she'd fallen head over heels for him the first time around were still there in spades. Only this time, she couldn't just walk away and ghost him. She had an entire summer of seeing him every day.

* * *

Steve must have pulled an all-nighter, because when they arrived on site the following day, he had a set of processed scans to share with Anders. Georgia, Becky, Steve, and Anders all gathered around the table in the finds tent, and Steve laid out print-outs, his eyes shining with excitement.

"Wow. I wasn't expecting these to be ready this morning," said Anders. "Thank you!"

He beamed at Steve, deepening the smile-lines around his eyes. Georgia's stomach flipped, and she glanced away. Across the table from her, Becky raised a brow at her.

"Definitely a trench in here," Anders said, pointing to an area on the scans, and pulling her attention back to the dig. "And another here. But this anomaly might be interesting, too."

The four of them chatted about the results for a few minutes, and Georgia's excitement bubbled up, despite her stress. The field-walk hadn't shown up anything hugely interesting, but that was to be expected. This field had been ploughed goodness only knew how many times in the ten centuries since the Anglo-Scandinavian era. But the extended scan results suggested another building, which, coupled with the results of the previous dig, could mean they'd found a settlement. Or at least a significantly sized farm or estate. Would they find anything in this field that dated later than the eleventh century? And if not, what did that mean? Maybe any settlement really *had* only lasted until the Harrying of the North by William the Conqueror, and there would be some eleventh century stuff, but nothing later.

"Earth to Georgia."

She blinked.

Anders smirked at her across the table. "Oh. You're back with us."

"Sorry. What were you saying?" Cold shot through her at having been so unprofessional as to be day-dreaming during a team meeting, quickly followed by her face feeling burning hot.

His smile broadened, and his eyes sparkled, making her heart race for a few beats.

"That we'll start with a trench here and another here, and hold off on the anomaly until we see what they reveal."

"Okay. I'm so sorry."

He chuckled, shaking his head at her fondly.

Noise levels in the refreshments tent had risen, and he glanced over, his smiles fading.

"Okay. Quick meeting with everyone, and then we can get cracking."

Steve and Becky drifted towards the other tent, but Georgia held back. Anders raised his brows at her.

"I just wanted to apologise for not paying attention." She shuffled her feet. "I'm really sorry. That was unprofessional of me."

He tilted his head, his eyes crinkling. "You were wondering what we'd find; thinking about when the settlement might have ended. Right?"

Her clothes felt too tight, and she wriggled her shoulders. "Mm. But I should have been paying attention. I didn't mean to appear rude."

He chuckled. "Georgia, I've always *loved* your enthusiasm and the way you can disappear into your head, thinking about a dig. Don't ever change. And you certainly don't need to apologise to me about it."

"Thank you."

He looked over to the other tent, his shoulders tightening, all of his ease gone. "Okay. Time to gird my loins."

She wished she could take some of his anxiety from him.

"You've got this, Anders," she said softly. "Just don't try to eat a cake before speaking. Come on. Soonest started, soonest over."

"Thank you." He smiled wanly, his gaze intense. "You're the only person here who understands how much this bit stresses me."

She didn't know what to say, so just bunched her lips and nodded at him. He stared towards the refreshments tent, then pushed his hair back. The lock at the front coiled up like a spring, defying him, and she almost laughed.

"Come on," she said, canting her head. "No one is going to eat you."

* * *

After the team meeting, Georgia settled herself at her table in the finds tent. She pulled a tray towards her, half her attention on Anders's voice filtering in from outside. He and Sam were talking about what to do with the new volunteers who were due later in the week, but it wasn't the discussion of the dig that distracted her. She rubbed her forehead. It would all be so much easier if Anders could just be cold towards her, but he was sweet and friendly, and she missed being able to talk to him.

Don't go there.

Becky was right. They *should* be able to have a professional relationship. The problem was, they never had. From day one in Orkney, they had been completely comfortable around each other, laughing together and teasing each other as if they'd been friends for years. It had taken less than a week for this to have progressed to them going out, and then, when they'd split up, there had been nothing. Zero. Zilch. Nada. Because that's what she'd needed.

She drew in a long breath. She couldn't exactly have zero contact with him now. He was leading the dig. But if she relaxed around him, there was every danger she'd fall for him again. Her fingertips worried at her brow. Maybe her best option was just to be completely aloof.

She picked up one of the finds, her mind made up.

Cool and aloof.

15

Late that afternoon, Anders stood just inside the refreshments tent, sipping a coffee, his gaze on the dig, but his mind elsewhere. After apologising to him that morning for not paying attention, Georgie had barely said two words to him. Had he said something wrong? If he had, he couldn't think what.

He hated needing to tread on eggshells around her. It had *never* been like that between them. But now, whenever he took a find to her, or he did some work at his desk, the frost coming off her would make the Arctic seem positively balmy. She hadn't been rude or unpleasant. She'd been perfectly civil in fact, but he couldn't get out of the finds tent fast enough, and on the rare occasions when he'd managed to dig, he'd preferred to send Sam in with any finds.

Should he move his laptop into here? His nose wrinkled. Apart from the long trestle table where all the drinks paraphernalia was, there was nowhere he could put his laptop, and certainly nowhere he could spread out the maps and the scans. He'd just have to accept that she still hated him.

He took another sip of his drink, regretting that it was instant coffee. Tomorrow, he'd bring in a flask of some proper stuff. He stretched his back and neck, checking the time. Time to wrap up the day. Instantly, a lead weight settled in his stomach. Would he *ever* get past that? It was a small, friendly team, not a huge conference he needed to address. Nothing to break sweat over. He drained his mug and glanced towards the neighbouring tent. Despite the frost, he should talk to Georgie about the day's finds before the wrap-up talk.

He sighed. Maybe it *was* better that she was cool and professional towards him. How much harder would it be if she were laughing and joking with him all the time? She'd moved on. He should too. As Becky had said, two years was a long time. Swallowing hard, he ducked out of the refreshments tent.

* * *

Georgia filled in the last bit of paperwork and packed the finds into one of the stackable plastic crates that sat towards the back of the tent. Anders had popped in and out over the morning, and she'd forced herself to be polite but reserved, trying to imagine him as his father. Not long after lunch, she realised Sam was coming in and out more often, not just to bring finds, but also to log stuff on Anders's laptop. She wasn't sure what to make of that. Was Anders annoyed with her? Did he want to avoid her as much as she did him? Maybe that was for the best.

She turned back towards the opening to the tent just as he walked in. He gave her an uncertain smile and pushed his hair back. "Hi. I was hoping you could give me a quick overview of the finds before I do the wrap-up."

She nodded, concentrating on keeping her face neutral. "Sure."

He loitered next to her chair, and she flicked her head towards his desk. "Shall we sit at your table? Then we can spread the map out."

She picked up her seat and carried it across. He joined her, still looking wary. As she walked him through all the finds, pointing to their marked locations on the map, his shoulders softened, and he grew more animated, asking detailed questions about some of the objects. Despite her best efforts, his enthusiasm drew her in, and her insides fizzed as she looked at him.

She blinked hard. *Think of him as Haakon.*

The trick worked. Imagining Anders to be his father allowed her to keep a cool, diffident demeanour as she wrapped up her debrief.

When she finished, Anders sat back. "Thanks. I might pick your brains tomorrow morning if Steve has got all the geophysics reports to me. See where you think we should prioritise."

She straightened in her seat. "Okay. But you're the leading authority on Anglo-Scandinavian settlements."

He laughed, softening his features. "Kind of you to say, but I'm not sure it's true. And you know the full site better than me. I value your opinion."

That shattered the Haakon trick. His father would never in a month of Sundays say he valued anyone else's opinion.

A thought struck her. "Is that Steve and Becky finished now?"

"I think so."

"Oh. Then I'm going to need to find a new car-share. Is there anyone in the uni team with a space? The Dig For It car is already full."

He met her eye, pausing for a moment. "I could give you a lift. I don't have anyone else in the car."

She swallowed, trying to find a reason to turn him down and failing. He was a colleague. This was what colleagues did.

"Um, sure. Thanks."

A hurt expression flickered across his face. "You'll need to give me your address. The only contact details I have for you are your work ones."

She hesitated, then held out her hand. If he was going to be giving her a lift in, he *had* to have her number. "Give me your phone?"

He slid it out of a pocket, unlocked it, and passed it across. She called her number with it, hung up, then handed it back. "There you go. You have my number, and I have yours. I'll text you the address. Let me know when you need me ready by?"

"Okay."

She indicated the other tent. "You'd better hold your debrief before the natives get restless."

His gaze shifted to the opening in the tent, all of his earlier animation gone. "Yeah."

He tidied away the maps and scans while she finished up at her desk, then the two of them headed toward the refreshments tent. There, Anders stood in the middle, where he had some headroom, and cleared his throat.

"Thanks everyone. Another great day, and some amazing finds. Prizes to Sam, *again*, who always seems to be the one finding them. Tomorrow, I'd like to extend trench two to the north a little, and finish up recording trench one… Yes, Steve?"

"Er, unless you want us to survey anywhere else, I think we're done. I'll email you the final processed files."

"No, that's great. Thank you for the work you did. It's been excellent."

"Can someone give Georgia a lift, then?" Steve glanced around, brows raised.

Sophie lifted her chin. "I could come in with you, Anders, and that would leave a space in Sam's car."

Behind her, Becky snorted, and Georgia fought to keep a straight face.

Anders looked wrong-footed for a moment, then shook his head. "No, that's not necessary. I'm giving her a lift in."

Georgia looked across at Sophie in time to see her scowl, confirming her suspicions over how Sophie felt about Anders. Her guts squirmed with jealousy. Sophie was tall, slim, and attractive, with shiny, *sensible*, brown hair tied back neatly in a ponytail that she'd threaded through her baseball cap. And she was an academic. Great match for Anders.

She chastised herself internally. What was it to her if they got together? She didn't want him.

Anders tugged at the hem of his top, dislodging a bit of dirt. "Unless there's anything else, I'll see most of you back here tomorrow. Thank you, everyone."

Everyone milled about, collecting belongings and preparing to leave. Sophie made a beeline for Anders, but Georgia was too far away to hear what she said to him. He had his 'politely patient face' on, though, which gave her a shred of comfort.

Becky appeared at her elbow. "If you can peel your eyes off the man you're not supposed to care two hoots for, we're ready to go."

Georgia gave her a withering look. "Ha, ha. Yes. I'm ready."

"Come on, before Steve pips at us to tell us to get a move on."

Georgia cast another glance in Anders's direction. He suddenly tipped his head back and roared with laughter at something Sophie said, making the green-eyed monster emerge in her again. She grabbed her things and hurried out to Steve's car.

Cool and aloof, remember. Cool and aloof.

* * *

Anders checked his phone for the umpteenth time, but there was still no text from her. He put his phone back down on the low table in front of him and closed his eyes.

She was just the same as she'd been in Orkney. Smart, capable, enthusiastic, knowledgeable, beautiful. He'd been head over heels in love with her, whereas she'd clearly seen him as nothing more than a stop-gap. He thought of that awful morning, when they'd been packing up after the Orkney dig.

"I can't do this any more, Anders. I'm sorry."

And then she'd just left the key to his flat on the kitchen table, walked out, and never replied to a single text, message, email from him… nothing. The dig finished, and she vanished from his life overnight.

He fingered his brow, pain bubbling up in his chest.

He knew why she'd left him. It was the job application to the post in Oslo. She'd had a job in Cumbria to go to, but he'd had nothing lined up for after he'd written up the Orkney project. He'd wanted to be able to offer her a settled life with him, but he needed to climb the ladder before he could land a permanent job in academia. The only suitable university post available had been in Oslo, not England, and it had been a perfect job for him in so many ways. He'd never intended to make a permanent move to Norway. It was only ever a stepping stone. But she'd seen the application, asked him if he'd take the job if he was offered it, then left him, barely giving him the chance to talk about it with her.

If she'd loved you, she'd have made it work for the time you were in Oslo. She didn't. Move on!

He leaned back, folding his arms across his brow, his eyes still closed.

He couldn't read how she felt about him now. Sometimes she seemed relaxed and happy, giving him glimpses of the summer two years ago. Mostly she had her barriers up. He wanted to ask her why she'd ghosted him. Why it had been so easy for her to walk out of his life and never look back?

He swallowed. No. If he was being brutally honest, he wanted to ask her that, and for her to say she'd made a huge mistake, and there was zero chance that would happen.

His phone beeping made his heart race for a few beats. He sat up and peered at the screen. Text from Georgie. His hands shook slightly as he opened the message up, then his heart fell at its baldness.

I'm at 14a Orchard Road. When do you need me to be ready?

He pulled up Google maps to see where her flat was. It was in the exact opposite direction to the dig. They would literally drive past his place again on their way from hers to the site.

He composed a text back, suggesting about half-past seven to pick her up, then hesitated over signing off. Should he put Anders? A.x? Just an A? In the end, he didn't put anything. She'd know who it was from. He clicked on send, then tossed his phone down on the sofa next to him.

It was going to be a *long* dig.

16

Georgia stood outside her flat, her collar turned up against the chilly wind that had picked up overnight. The day ahead promised to be sunny, though not especially warm, but at least there was no rain scheduled.

Anders turned on to her road in an ancient navy blue Land Rover Discovery that looked as if it had done so many miles, the milometer had probably ticked past zero more than once. He drove past her to turn in the space at the end of the road, then pulled up next to her. She got in, almost kicking over a Thermos flask that was wedged in the foot-well in front of the passenger seat as she did so.

"Morning. Nice car," she said, fastening her seat belt and tucking her bag into a space next to the flask.

He scrunched his face up. "Really?"

She rolled her eyes. "No, Anders. It's a museum piece."

He laughed, put the car in gear, and pulled away. He gestured loosely towards her feet with his left hand, in between changing gears.

"I realised it's stupidly early, and that if you'd had a lift with anyone else, you'd have been picked up later, so there's a coffee for you in the foot-well."

"With oat milk?" she quipped, leaning forward to retrieve the flask.

"No. Regular milk. No sugar. Don't pour any yet. The next road has a load of speed bumps."

"Okay. Actually, I'll leave it until we get there."

"Is that a comment on my driving?"

"No. Don't be such a sensitive soul."

She shook her head at him, laughing. He flashed an affable

grin back at her, and her stomach fizzed.

Cool and aloof, remember.

"So, whereabouts do you live?" She peered out of the side window, trying to calm her emotions.

"Er. We're about to pass it, near enough. Next street on the left."

She turned back to him, her mouth dropping open. "Oh, I'm sorry! I'm in totally the wrong direction for you to be giving me a lift."

He shrugged. "I don't mind. I'm driving you, not carrying you."

They left the outskirts of the town and turned on to the country road leading to the dig site in silence. Georgia smiled to herself. Anders never talked much when he was driving. Becky had asked her if the two of them had had a huge row after a long and utterly silent drive once. The question had taken her by surprise. She was used to not talking when he drove. He didn't mean to seem standoffish or unfriendly; he just didn't chat when he was behind the wheel. Anders didn't really chat, period, most of the time.

Anders flicked his indicator on and turned the car on to the field being used for parking, pulling up tight next to the hedge line, close to the refreshments tent. He climbed out of the car and went around to the boot, Georgia following, clutching the flask of coffee. Anders reached in and retrieved a backpack. The air between them was charged with an awkwardness they'd never had, even when they first met.

Anders jutted his chin towards the flask. "Coffee? Now I've stopped driving."

A smile tugged at the corners of her mouth, but she tucked her chin down, refusing to meet his eyes.

"Yes, thanks."

She tailed him to the refreshments tent, where he held his hand out for the flask. She handed it over, still struggling to know how to be around him. He grabbed two clean mugs, then poured out the coffee. A glorious fragrance filled the tent.

"That isn't instant coffee," she said, taking a mug from him and inhaling deeply.

"No. I mean, I'll suck it up over the day with the stuff here, but if you're going to drink coffee, drink the proper stuff, right?"

He grinned at her, and she felt a familiar lurch in her chest.

"You said you might pick my brains over the dig." Work would be a safe topic. She could stay cool and dispassionate while discussing the best locations for trenches.

He stared at her for a moment, as if about to say something, then blinked, pushing his bottom lip out. "Er, sure. Shall we take these through to my desk?"

He picked up the flask and led the way to his desk. There, he spread out the scans and the map.

"I'm waiting for Steve to send me his final report, but I was thinking of extending this trench out to here—" he pointed to the map "—and maybe putting in one over here."

She took a moment to study the documents. The scent of his soap drifted towards her, shredding her concentration. She dragged her focus back to the site and outlined her thoughts, trying to concentrate on how the current extension to the original dig clarified or disproved their original ideas. To her relief, Anders slotted into work-mode, weighing everything up, seeking more details, challenging her when he didn't agree on a point… keeping her brain just about too busy to think about how close he was sitting to her or that the light was highlighting his cheekbones beautifully.

As their discussion wound to a close, cars arrived in the field, and the sounds of doors closing and chatter drowned out the birdsong from the hedge. Anders raised his gaze to the tent opening, breathing in slowly. Georgia frowned.

"It sounds like more people than were here yesterday."

"Mm. There's an extra load of volunteers arriving today. I'll introduce them, but talk to them separately. None of you lot will want to hear the safety announcements a third time." He flashed her a weak smile.

"Why don't you get Sam to do it?" she offered softly. "He's a million times better at it than you."

A hurt expression slipped over his face. "Thanks."

"Oh, you know what I mean!" She flapped her hand at him. "Sam could talk the hind legs off a donkey. And he knows all the safety stuff as well as you do. You lay out the day to us, then get Sam to show the volunteers the ropes."

Anders's shoulders softened, and he finished his coffee. "Okay. You talked me into it." He shot a nervous gaze towards the refreshments tent, and she shook her head at him.

"Come on. You'll live."

* * *

By the end of the day, Anders was wondering whether offering Georgie a lift in had been a stupid idea. Again, she had barely spoken to him over the day, and he'd tried to spend as much time away from her as possible. Not a simple task, given that his laptop sat on a desk about six feet away from her.

Sam had done an excellent introductory talk with the volunteers. Afterwards, Anders had caught him and suggested he do all of them. Sam had given him a cheeky grin and said, "Of course, boss. I know how much you hate them."

He liked Sam. As well as the fact the man appeared to have detectors in his fingers for finding artefacts, and eyesight that would put a golden eagle to shame, he was smart, with a dry sense of humour. Certainly smart enough to have realised all was not rosy between Anders and Georgie, though he hadn't said anything directly. He *had* volunteered to do some of the paperwork for Anders, allowing Anders to stay in a trench for longer than he would have managed otherwise.

The day's wrap-up chat finished, he stood just outside the refreshments tent, waiting for Georgie. He studied his hands, the cool breeze ruffling his hair. There was dirt under his nails, and his skin felt as if it had been lightly sanded. He picked at the grime, a smile tweaking his lips.

Bright blonde hair in his peripheral vision drew his attention, and he straightened.

"Sorry, have you been waiting long?" said Georgie, looking flustered.

"No. Relax."

He flashed her a smile, and she returned it. Almost immediately, her face fell, and she turned towards the car. Anders pulled his car keys out of his pocket and grabbed his bag, his heart sinking. Would they ever be able to find a new equilibrium? One where they could smile at each other and things not be tense?

In the car, she stared resolutely ahead. He knew the look. She was working herself up to say something she would find difficult. He clicked his seat belt on, put the car in gear, and reversed out of the parking space, waiting. She took a breath, then said nothing and gazed out of the window.

They drove in complete silence back to her place. He'd never been one for talking while he was driving, and he could recall plenty of times when they'd barely spoken during a journey, but today, the silence was oppressive. She turned to him as he pulled up outside her flat, and he braced himself, wondering what she was going to say.

"Shall I make the coffee tomorrow?"

He wasn't sure what he'd expected, but it hadn't been that. He blinked. "Sure. Strong. No sugar."

She snorted. "I remember how you take your coffee, Anders."

He wanted to ask her what he'd asked Becky – were they okay? – but the words died on his lips. It was patently obvious they weren't.

"Thanks for the lift. I'll see you tomorrow."

She snatched up her bag from the foot-well and hurried out of the car before he even had a chance to say goodbye.

He caught a breath, staring out of the windscreen.

"Move on," he muttered. "She didn't love you. It'll be better in the long run if she's barely even friendly to you, because you will *never* be The One for her."

17

By late morning the following day, a backlog of finds had built up. Anders had popped in and out with some of them, but hadn't stayed long on any occasion. Georgia wondered if they would ever get the chance to clear the air; say that things were okay between them. She'd almost tackled it in the car the evening before, then bottled it. Maybe she'd get the chance today.

She scanned the excavated objects. So far, they fell into two distinct time periods: the one they were interested in, or modern. From the number of fizzy drink bottle caps, it would seem that whoever farmed the area about forty years earlier, had taken a bottle out on the tractor, and tossed the caps in the field when he was done.

Of the historical artefacts, more broken pottery had turned up, plus another dress pin, and part of a buckle. Still nothing from later than the late eleventh century, as far as she could tell on first inspection.

She was delicately brushing some soil from the dress pin when Anders joined her, his face flushed with excitement.

"Look at this!"

He held out a grimy hand with a dirt-encrusted object on the flat of his palm. She picked it up, curious, and eased some of the soil off it, to reveal a pot about the size of a tangerine. Its sides had the same incised decorations as on the pot she'd imagined holding in her vision, and her eyes widened.

"Oh my god, it's the pot! I can't believe it's survived and you found it."

She was absolutely certain that she held the same pot that had contained the ointment Aelfgyth had applied to Einar's wound.

"*The* pot?" queried Anders, cocking a brow at her.

Georgia caught herself. "Um. I just meant I can't believe the entire pot has survived intact."

Anders held her gaze for a moment, but didn't challenge her.

"Nice find," she added, putting it down carefully on the table. "Much better than another bottle top."

He opened his mouth as if to say something more, then closed it again abruptly, his eyes still full of enthusiasm and curiosity, but his body tense.

"What?" she asked.

He smiled awkwardly. "I was going to ask if I could watch you clean the pot up, but you won't want me in your way."

She paused. In Orkney, he'd often watched her clean up a find, and the two of them would spend ages chatting over its importance or construction. Did she want to do that again? Not really. Things were hard enough as it was.

Becky's words rang in her head. They *were* both grown-ups. It *had* to be possible to have a professional relationship with him. And anyway, he was in charge and could follow whatever he wanted.

"Stay. It's your dig."

Surprise flashed across his face. "Thank you. If there's a shout from the field, I'll have to go."

She nodded.

He retrieved his chair from the other desk and plonked it down at her side. "Sure you don't mind?"

She took a deep breath, her guts knotting, then looked him in the eye. "Anders, shall we tackle the elephant in the room? We went out together; we broke up. That was all two years ago. *Lots* of water under the bridge. I'm sorry if I've been frosty. I honestly hadn't known you were back or would be involved in this. It came as a surprise, that's all. We're colleagues. Let's just be cool about it all."

He blinked, and his Adam's apple bobbed as he swallowed. "Sure."

It didn't really cover what she'd wanted to say, and it had come out crisper than she'd meant. She tried to pin a bright smile on.

"Okay. Let's have a look at this pot."

She picked it up, along with a soft brush, and brushed gently at the soil clinging to the outside of the pot. The room blurred, and she focused hard.

Come on. Don't get pulled into your imagination again. Just clean the pot up.

But however hard she tried to keep her attention on the task in hand, the vision of the dimly lit room with an injured man in a bed insisted on coming to the fore.

His wound was healing well. When she went in to tend to him, he was sitting up in the bed, though still stripped to the waist. She couldn't help but stare at his broad chest with its fuzz of dark blond hair. When she finally looked into his eyes, he smirked at her.

"Good morning, Aelfgyth."

His language sounded strange and yet similar enough to be familiar.

"Good morning, Einar. How are you feeling?"

"Well. And tired of lying in bed."

"Hm. Let me inspect your wound. I don't want you opening it up again after I've been so careful."

Did he detect her sarcasm? But then, after the first day, she had *been careful when she'd been tending to him.*

She peeled the cloth back, pleased to see the edges of his wound knitting together.

"Perhaps tomorrow this will be healed enough for you to get up," she said, raising her head.

The heat from his skin warmed her, and she could smell the herbs in the ointment. She bent her head to smell the wound, to check that it didn't fester. His body tensed. When she moved back, his eyes were dark, and he swallowed.

"You are the lady of the house?" he asked. "You have no mother?"

She shook her head, wringing out the cloth in the basin of water. "No. She died. A few years ago."

"And your father has not arranged a marriage for you with another family?"

She straightened, her eyes narrowing. "He did. I was married. To a fine man called Edmund. He was killed in battle."

She bathed the wound, her hands hard.

"I'm sorry," said Einar, softly.

"Not sorry enough to stay in your own land." She dropped the cloth in the water, then drew the pot of healing ointment from her pocket. "Greed is

a sin."

"And famine is a curse."

She raised her head. "Oh, is that why you came? I was not aware that man could eat gold."

"He can't. But he can buy food with it. When food is scarce, the cost is high. And I am not here to plunder, but to farm."

She took the wooden stopper from the pot and scooped up some of the thick ointment.

"And I pray you will be kind to my people. We did not choose to be invaded. We did not choose to go hungry. We did not choose to lose our land."

"I know. I understand."

She smeared the ointment over his wound and covered it with fresh linen. "You should rest."

He caught her hand as she replaced the wooden stopper in the pot. "I will try to be kind. As you have been kind to me. You could have nursed me to death, but you did not."

Heat rose in her cheeks. "I was tempted," she said, the words out before she could stop them. "But it is a sin to take another man's life."

He laughed hard, then kissed her knuckles, his lips soft against her skin. "I see honesty is a virtue to you."

Her heart raced, and she pulled her hand away. "You should rest."

The image of the dark room faded, and Georgia blinked, her heart thumping hard. The small pot came into focus and she put it down on the table, her hands shaking.

"Where did you just go?" asked a soft voice at her side.

She turned to the man sitting next to her, confused, half of her head still in the vision. "Einar?"

The man frowned, smiling at the same time and making his face lopsided. "*Einar*? I've had some weird and wonderful pronunciations of my name in my time, but never so wrong as to sound like *Einar*."

She breathed deeply, recognising him properly. "Sorry. Anders." She rubbed her brow, her hands still trembling.

"Who's Einar?" Mirth rippled through his voice. "And where on earth did your head just go? You gave the pot one brief brush, then just sat there and stared at it."

She peered into his blue eyes, her skin hot and prickly. "Nowhere. I… I was just imagining the pot being made and used." She tried to laugh, but it came out tight and awkward. "You know me. Too much imagination."

"And there was an Einar in this imagination?" His lips twitched with amusement.

"Yes. Um… I'm going to get a coffee. Did you want one?"

"I'll make them. I don't trust you not to wander off into fantasy-land and pour boiling water over yourself."

He slid off the chair, still giving her an amused look, then wandered over towards the other tent. She watched his broad back, berating herself, then turned back to the pot.

Curiosity burned her, and she picked it up again.

Almost instantly, the finds tent morphed into the low-roofed, dark room. Georgia wanted to put the pot down, but something inside her made her keep hold of it.

"This looks healed," said Aelfgyth, removing the linen cloth from the site of the wound.

The skin had joined together well, leaving a pink area where the blade had bitten deep.

"Good. Let me dress, then you can show me around the farm and tell me about it."

Her back stiffened at Einar's words. He had been kind enough to let all of her father's men remain on the farm, but it still rankled that the land was no longer her father's. Some of Cenred's men had been killed in the fighting, and their huts and places reallocated to Einar's men. Some of the invaders had brought their women with them, but not all, and tensions had been running high for a day or two. Perhaps if Einar was up and about, he would stop his men from harassing the girls.

Einar threw back the covers and swung his legs out of the bed.

"I will let you dress. I will wait outside," she squeaked, and fled the room, Einar's chuckles echoing behind her.

She stood outside the hut, her fingers worrying at her dress. Why did she *have to show him around? Oh. Perhaps he thought it would be humiliating for her father to do it. Perhaps he was saving her father that embarrassment.*

One of Einar's men approached, leering at her.

"What do we have here? Do you think you can catch the eye of Einar? Or do you just fancy a bit of real man instead of your local weaklings?"

He caught hold of her roughly, and she pushed him away.

"Get off me!"

He was much taller than her, and far stronger. His hands grabbed at her skirts, pulling at them and exposing her legs. She wriggled and squirmed, but this only encouraged him, and his hand moved higher. She shrieked. The man backhanded her, and she fell to the ground, tasting blood in her mouth.

"Georgie? Oh, god, Georgie!"

She opened her eyes to find herself pressed tightly against Anders's torso, his one arm around her back, his other at her hips. She peered into his face, her skin clammy with sweat. He stared back, his breathing rate high.

"What… What happened?" she mumbled.

Nausea bubbled in her throat, and her face hurt as if someone had just punched her. She poked her tongue around her teeth and the insides of her lips, expecting to find at least a loose tooth, but the pain had faded, and everything was intact.

"You tell me," he said. "I was bringing the coffees back, and you were standing next to your chair, eyes totally glazed. Just as I put the mugs down, you jerked backwards and swooned in my arms."

She met his eye and arched a brow. "I swooned in your arms?"

He shrugged, demonstrating neatly that she was, indeed, still in his arms. She pulled away and sat on her chair, then bowed her head, closing her eyes. He had felt so familiar, and it had felt so *right* to be held by him, that she wanted to cry.

He sat next to her. "Are you okay?"

"Mm. Just give me a minute."

She opened her eyes and scanned the table. The pot lay safely on a small bed of cotton wool. The two mugs of coffee sat to one side. She focused on her breathing.

No one hit you, you idiot. It was your imagination going mad. Anders is going to think you've totally lost it.

"Um… Were you having a fit or something?" Anders asked.

She shook her head. "No."

He rested his shoulder against hers, the gesture both comforting and too familiar. "I'm worried about you, Georgie. I mean, your eyes hadn't *quite* rolled up to the top of your head, but you looked like you were totally out of it."

He shifted position slightly, releasing a puff of air from his rugby shirt that smelled of his soap and deodorant. She drank it in, still too close to tears for her liking.

"I'm fine. I don't know what came over me. Maybe I'm just too hot, or something," she said lamely.

"Did you want some cold water instead of a coffee?"

She moved away from him before her heart cracked any further. "Yeah, that would be nice, actually. Thanks."

He scraped his chair back and stood up. "Don't faint while I'm not here to catch you."

She smiled wanly.

Once he was gone, she leaned her elbows on the table and buried her head in her hands. What was happening to her? Why was she getting these visions? And why did the man in them look like the spitting image of Anders?

She massaged her scalp, her gaze settling on the jar. Gingerly, she touched the very tip of her index finger to it. Immediately, her vision filled with sky-blue eyes peering concernedly at her.

"Aelfgyth? What did he do to you?"

She struggled to sit up, her face sore. Einar held her closely, a worried expression on his face.

"What did he do to you?" he demanded, his voice thrumming with anger.

"He tried to push my skirts up, then he hit me when I cried out."

"He will be whipped for that. I will not have any *of my men mistreating anyone. Let me help you up. You can show me the farm another day."*

He drew her to her feet, then held her hands. Rough calluses covered his skin, but she suddenly felt safe with him.

He gazed into her eyes, making her heart skip a couple of beats.

Georgia snatched her hand back, blinking away the vision of Einar-Anders. Aelfgyth had felt so comforted by Einar, just as she had by Anders. She scrunched her face up, pressing the knuckle of her thumb into her brow.

"Aagh! Anders! Get out of my head!"

18

Anders grabbed a mug of cold water in the refreshments tent, his mind whirring. Georgie had looked completely out of it. If he hadn't caught her, she would have hit the deck. It was almost as if she was sleep-walking, but it was the middle of the day and she hadn't been asleep.

Did she suffer from epilepsy? She'd never said so when they were together. Surely she would have told him if she did?

He hurried back to the finds tent. Just as he was about to enter, he heard Georgie say, "Aagh! Anders! Get out of my head!" and his feet stumbled to a halt.

He peered around the edge of the opening of the tent. Georgie sat at the table, her head in her hands, her mass of hair shielding her face. He joined her and put the mug on the table next to her.

"You okay?" he asked.

She raised her head. Her skin was pale, and she looked pinched.

"Yeah, I'm fine," she said unconvincingly. "Thanks for getting me a water."

She sipped at the water, her hands shaking badly.

"Georgie, do you have epilepsy?" he said, keeping his voice soft.

Her eyes widened. "No."

"Are you sure? You looked so… vacant… out of it… and then you jerked backwards, like someone had punched you in the face."

Her colour faded even further, and she had to put the mug down.

"I don't have epilepsy. I'm fine."

He folded his arms, leaning back in his seat. "You didn't look fine."

She scowled at him. "Anders, don't fuss."

He tilted his head, studying her, debating whether to ask the question that was burning inside him. Curiosity won out. "What am I *doing* in your head for you to want me out of there?"

Despite being alabaster-white the moment before, her cheeks flushed pink at his words.

"Nothing," she mumbled.

He gave up. He knew her too well. She'd only talk when she wanted to, and she clearly didn't want to. The more he pushed, the more she would back away and put the shutters up. And anyway, not half an hour ago, she'd said they were just colleagues, nothing more. He squashed down his feelings and hunted for a safe topic.

"Tell me about this pot?" He jutted his chin towards it.

Her eyes widened, and she gave him a wary look. "What about it?"

His breath huffed out. "It's rare to find an intact pot. I thought you'd be more excited. When does it date from? What would it be used for?"

Her posture softened, and her face relaxed. "Oh. Yes. Late ninth, maybe early tenth century?"

"Based on?" Getting her talking about artefacts was usually the best way to distract her or cheer her up.

She scrunched one side of her mouth up. "Gut feeling, mostly. Anglo-Saxon pots can be notoriously hard to date. Normally, they get dated by what they're found with, rather than the pot itself being diagnostic. But nothing else in this dig – so far – dates from later. The clay the pot is made from is consistent with other pots that *have* had a more reliable date. And this series of lines as decoration is in the same style as other pots that have been dated better."

She used the end of the soft brush to point at the jar, as if reluctant to actually handle it.

"What would it have been used for?"

"It had ointment in it. Like an antiseptic."

"Really? Oh, god, is there still some in it?" He leaned forward to peer into the jar, excited beyond belief. *That* would be an incredible find.

She shook her head vigorously. "Oh. No. I just meant that's what might have been in it. It's too small for food stuffs, so…" She trailed off.

He wanted to keep her talking. "How would the jar be sealed? We didn't find anything else with it. No lid or anything."

"No, it had a wooden stopper. You see how the sides slope? It had a wooden top with the same slope, and you just pushed it down to close it. Like a cork in an oil dressing bottle. Same kind of idea."

Her words made him chuckle. "Oh, I *love* your imagination. You can *see* it being used, can't you? Things found on a dig are never just dry objects for you. Even a tiny bit of broken pot. You'll look at it and imagine what it looked like when it was new, what it was used for, how it was treated. Was it a treasured object, or commonplace…?"

Her face fell, and her eyes narrowed, so he shut up. She gathered her hair up and fastened it back, giving off strong vibes that she wanted to be left alone. He sighed internally. Probably for the best. She'd made it abundantly clear that she saw him as a colleague and nothing more.

"Okay. I'll leave you to it," he said, standing up and carrying his chair back to his desk. He gave her a long look. "If you don't feel well, give me a shout and I'll run you home."

She nodded briskly, a tight smile on her lips. "Thanks, Anders."

He ducked back out of the tent, trying to forget how *right* it had felt when he'd held her.

"We're colleagues. *Colleagues*," he muttered.

It didn't help.

19

Almost a week passed, and the site kept Anders busy. Sam proved adept at managing all the volunteers, giving Anders enough space to dig occasionally. He still had to balance his departmental responsibilities with leading the dig, meaning that however much he wanted to spend all day outside with a trowel in his hand, he had to work at his desk in the finds tent for much of the time.

He and Georgie had settled into a relationship that straddled a 'professionally friendly' line. Every now and then, there were glimpses of what they'd had when they were together, but invariably, Georgie would immediately switch to being more distant. Anders caught himself doing the same. His first thought whenever anything was found was to share it with her; anticipating how her face would light up and her eyes sparkle. And then he'd remember how strained things were between them, and his enthusiasm would fade. He'd watched her clean up a couple of finds, but there had been no repeat of her looking completely spaced out, or of fainting, thankfully.

He was in the middle of sketching one of the trenches, when a shout came up from the other side of the field.

"Boss!"

"Yeah?" He looked over, brows raised.

Patrick waved a trowel wildly, beckoning him over. "*Big* post-hole!"

Anders straightened. "Really?"

Would they actually be able to find evidence of the main hall? So far, all the traces had been of more minor dwellings.

He jogged over to stand next to the trench. Patrick circled an area of earth that was a slightly different colour from its surroundings.

"What do you reckon?" Patrick asked, squinting up at him.

Anders crouched down, touching his fingertips to the earth for balance. "I think you could be right. If so, that *is* a significantly sized post. For a roof beam?"

He scanned the trench, mentally positioning other posts in the building, based on the scans of the site and the layouts of other structures dating to the same era. In the corner of his eye, he saw Georgie emerge from the finds tent.

"Something good?" she called across.

He straightened, grinning at her. "Post-hole. A big one."

She reached his side, picking her way carefully around the margin of the trench. "Ooh. Does that mean…?"

"Definitely a building, and probably a large one, yes," he said.

She beamed up at him, her eyes shining. The rest of the group looked a little less enthusiastic, especially the volunteers. He sighed. No, perhaps post-holes were not as exciting a find as a pot full of coins, or a buried hoard, but they could be significant. Georgie got it, even if the others were less impressed.

She jammed her knuckles against her hips, her eyes flicking over the site, making him smile. He knew *exactly* what was running through her head. She'd have pulled up a mental image of the survey results that she could overlay over the field, and her brain would be mapping everything out. He'd never known anyone to be able to do that quite as well as she always had.

She turned and caught sight of him, then looked sheepish.

"Got it all mapped out?" he said, unable to keep the grin off his face.

"Mm." She smiled, melting his heart. A stiff wind licked across the site and she shivered, rubbing her arms briskly. "Well, happy digging, guys. I only came out to see what all the shouting was about."

She wrapped her arms tightly around her torso, dipped her head, and made her way back to the finds tent. Anders watched her go, his heart sore, wishing things could have been different between them, then dragged his focus back to the trench.

* * *

Georgia returned to the tent and settled back at her desk. In front of her was the pot that had been found the previous week, and she eyed it warily. She'd cleaned up and catalogued everything else that had come in, but the pot remained snuggled up in its protective wrapping, still half caked in mud. She sighed. There was only so long she could avoid dealing with it.

What on earth *were* the visions she'd had? She hadn't just been lost in her imagination. It had all felt more real than that. Her mouth had *hurt* after the man had struck her. Struck Aelfgyth, she corrected herself. And actually, it hadn't hurt. Not when she'd poked her tongue around it.

She sighed. She *must* be imagining it all. What other rational explanation was there?

Her hands trembling a little, she peeled the wrappings back, easing the fragile pot out. So far, so normal. She selected a small, soft-bristled brush and a toothpick to remove the mud from the pot.

As she began picking at it, she realised she was holding her breath, her muscles braced.

"Stop being ludicrous," she muttered, making a conscious effort to relax.

She brushed the loosened soil away and turned the pot in her hands. Her vision blurred, and she gritted her teeth.

"No… not happening. Get a grip."

But it was no use.

"Good morning, Aelfgyth."

Einar strode towards her, a wide smile on his face. She was relieved to see him fully dressed, in rough woollen trousers with a blue, woad-dyed, thigh-length tunic over the top, belted around his middle. He wore simple leather boots, but had woollen strips bound around his lower legs. A woollen cloak wrapped his shoulders, fastened at the neck with a clasp. A knife in a leather sheath hung from his belt.

"Good morning, Einar. I see you've healed well enough to be up and about."

"You ministered to me well. Perhaps you can show me the farm this morning, since you were not able to the other day."

She was about to comment that she should know it well enough, as it had been her father's and she had grown up here, but she held her tongue. He chuckled at her.

"I would rather that you showed me than ask your father. I would not shame him that way. And you are a far more beautiful guide."

She clicked her tongue at him, pretending to be offended at his words. Inside, she was grateful for his respect for her father. "Come, then."

They walked from his hut towards the hall in the middle of the settlement. Timber-built, with a thatched roof, the hall was the largest building by far. It was where her father and his men ate, and where some of them slept. No doubt Einar would oust her father from his section at the end of the hall, and Cenred would have to build a new hut to live in. Smoke trickled through the roof from the fire in the centre of the hall, and there was the lively noise of everyone going about their work.

Behind the hall lay a scattering of buildings: the weaving hut to the north of the hall; the blacksmith's hut to the south; along with various huts for the families who worked in the settlement. On the far side of the settlement, an enclosure held pigs, and next to them were some sheep, all penned in by willow hurdles.

Einar questioned her closely about everything, from the crops that grew in the fields to the south of the animal pens, to the state of repairs of the huts, to the cloth that was woven.

"Both of these huts need the roofs repairing," he said, as they passed some of the outer dwellings. "And some planks of the wall are rotten. Why did Cenred not see to this?"

"He might have been too busy defending his land," she said, unable to curb her tongue. "But as you now own it, perhaps you can assist these families. Both of them are elderly, and both of them lost their sons in the fighting."

He turned soft blue eyes to her, smiling. "You are quite right. They are my responsibility now. I will see that their huts are mended."

The vision faded, and Georgia blinked, breathing hard. Everything had been so *real.* This couldn't all just be her imagination running riot. There was no way she would have been able to fill in so many details.

Her brain matched up the layout of the buildings from her vision with the post-hole that had just been found. The main hall would be exactly where the post-hole was, and would have had many posts holding up a substantial roof. More, if one end was partitioned off, as her vision had implied. Other huts in the settlement would have been smaller and simpler in construction and may only have had a couple of posts holding up the roof.

Anders drifted through her thoughts. However much he admired her ability to map out a site, he would need solid evidence, based on the survey results and any post-holes found. She couldn't tell him she knew the location of the main hall because she'd had a *vision*.

She pulled up her mental images of the geophysical surveys again, summoning both the current dig, and the preliminary dig that held led to this project. Her brow creased as she struggled to remember all of the details. Reluctantly, she slid off her seat and made her way back out to the dig. As she approached, she could see Anders in a trench, his mad lock of hair caught by the breeze. Patrick and Shona worked at the other end of the trench, and Georgia's guts tightened as Sophie's sleek head leaned in close to Anders.

"More post-holes?" Georgia asked Shona, sitting on her haunches next to the trench.

"One. Anders and Sophie have just found it."

She glanced down the trench towards them. Sophie was talking to him, but his head was turned towards Shona's end of the trench, his gaze on Georgia.

"Anything wrong?" he asked, cutting across what Sophie was saying, patently not listening to her. "Or did you just want to come and dig for a bit?"

Sophie closed her mouth and gave her a death-stare.

"I was just wondering if you had the geophysics results to hand, but it's not urgent if you're busy."

He straightened up, easing out his back with a click. "Sure. Have you plotted it all out in your head and now want to check the surveys?"

She laughed. "Something like that. Have you got both sets of surveys?"

"Yep."

He clambered out of the trench and dropped the trowel so that it landed point first in the loose soil on the ground next to the trench. Shaking his head to flick his hair back, he brushed the soil off his hands, and then dusted his trousers down. Sophie's jaw bunched, and she bent her head back to the excavation. Patrick looked from Sophie to Anders, his brows raised, but said nothing. Georgia wondered what Sophie had been talking to Anders about before she'd arrived. Sophie really didn't know him well if she was expecting him to be chatty. Georgia had worked in a trench with him for three hours in Orkney once, and he hadn't spoken to her at all, other than to offer her a coffee. And that was when they were together.

"Sorry to pull you away from the trench. I know you like to get your hands dirty every once in a while."

He smiled. "Mm. Come on then, let's find these results for you."

A thought struck her. What would it mean if the surveys lined up exactly with her visions? That she'd subconsciously integrated the information into her imaginings?

Or because the visions *weren't* just her overactive imagination?

20

They reached the finds tent, and Anders stood back to let Georgie go in first.

"What are you thinking about?" he asked.

"There was a paper in one of the archaeology journals a while back, about the layout of Anglo-Saxon settlements."

"The one by Blair? Yeah, I remember it."

"He talked about settlements being on a grid. I can't quite recall the dimensions he was talking about." She scratched her head, scrunching her face up. "Do you have print-offs of both the preliminary dig results and the current ones? Thanks."

He rummaged through a sheaf of papers in a folder on his desk, selecting several sheets and passing them across. Georgie laid them out on the table, arranging them to mimic the landscape, then hooked her foot around his chair to pull it towards her.

"Got a pencil?" she asked, her eyes fixed on the papers.

He passed one across, then leaned on the table opposite her. "What are you thinking?"

She sat on his chair, leaving him standing. "Just give me a minute? Where are the post-holes you just found?"

"Er… here, and here." He pointed at the scans. "I think you can just about see them."

"Can I draw on these?" She glanced up at him, pencil poised.

"Sure. I can print more off if I need to."

She shaded the marks corresponding to the post-holes, making them stand out, then squinted at the pages.

"They're faint, and I'd ideally like to ask Becky or Steve about it all, but do you think there are more, here, here, here…" She indicated a line of slight smudges.

Anders peered at the page. “Maybe. The traces aren’t strong.”

She shuffled through the papers. “Okay, humour me? If there *are* post-holes there, this would be a significant building.”

“Main hall?” He could buy into that.

“Mm. With a partition across here? Which would make sense, because the lord of the manor won’t want to be kipping down with everyone else in there. He’d want a private area. That would leave this space for the main hall, so where would you put a fire pit?”

He studied the grainy images, then touched his finger over a darker mark in the scan. “I would say that anomaly there would be a prime candidate.”

“Exactly. So, if this is the hall, let’s think where other things might be.” She peered up at him, smiling, her enthusiasm infectious.

He walked over to her side of the tent to fetch her chair, then sat down opposite her. She studied the sheets, then closed her eyes, frowning a little.

“North of the hall. South of the hall.” She looked at the papers, re-orientating them so that north was towards him. “That would put the weaving hut about there, and the blacksmith’s hut about there.” She pressed her fingertip into the paper. “Mm. Okay, well, that would fit.”

He frowned, trying to figure out what had led her to say that. Yes, there were darker smudges in the traces which might suggest buildings, but what had made her so certain that they related to a blacksmith’s hut or a weaving hut?

“Georgie? Let me in? What are you talking about?”

Her head shot up, her hazel eyes wide. “Oh, jeez. I forgot you were there! Sorry!” She pinked. “Um. I was kind of thinking about the settlements we know about and thinking of the layout.” She sat back in her seat a little. “A settlement this size would have had a blacksmith, a weaving hut, maybe a pottery.”

He held up a hand, laughing. “Whoa! Slow down. We don’t *know* what size it is. That’s the whole point of the dig! We have two post-holes, and a handful of artefacts. Stop letting your imagination overtake the data.”

She seemed to have forgotten he was there again and was

studying the scans, muttering to herself. "If that's the weaving hut, why is it showing up so dark on this? It was on the shady side of the hall. North. And that definitely looks like the long axis running east to west. Blacksmith to the south… Which would be there, and that *is* dark, but then, it would be." She slumped back, gnawing at the end of the pencil he'd given to her. "I don't get it. Why is it dark?"

He tried to follow the thread of her musings, but failed.

"Hey. Georgie." He waited until she was looking at him, then arched his brows, resting his cheek on his hand. "What aren't you telling me? Because you're looking at these results and talking about there being a weaving hut here and a blacksmith's hut there, and I'm looking at them and just seeing a couple of dark marks that *might* be something, but might also be nothing."

She huffed out a breath. "But the weaving hut *shouldn't* be dark. That's the problem. There should be post-holes and maybe, *maybe* a trace because of a pit or a fire."

Anders rubbed his brow, still not following her. "Or… it's not a weaving hut at all?"

"Well, it's *something*."

She pulled the sheets towards her again and lightly outlined several rectangles. With an eye of faith, he might concede that she'd outlined structures, but the traces were faint.

He leaned back in his seat and grabbed his laptop, pulling up saved documents. He eventually found what he was looking for and checked the scale of the map. She was right. The rectangles she'd just sketched over faint marks in the scans lay on a grid structure, with the same spacing as outlined in the journal article she'd talked about.

When he raised his head, she looked at him across the table, her eyes shining.

"We've found the full settlement. These are so rare! Anders, this could be the find of a lifetime!"

Her enthusiasm brightened his spirits, but the sensible, hard academic side of him – the side that sounded suspiciously like his father – urged caution.

"Let's just wait and see what we find, yeah? You're *way* ahead of the data."

And, just like that, all of her excitement disappeared, and her expression turned flinty. "I'd have thought the lure of a find of a lifetime would have had you sprinting to put a trench in. Onwards and upwards to a shiny new job and all that."

His mood prickled, and he folded his arms in a barricade across his chest. "Not fair, Georgie. If you hadn't ghosted me for two years, you'd *know* why I went for the job in Oslo." He pushed his chair back. "Let's see what we find. Excuse me, but I want to get back to the trench."

He stalked out of the tent, his good mood gone.

* * *

Georgia watched him go, instantly regretting her words. The crack about him chasing a new job had been unfair. She'd said it because she'd been so excited about them finding a settlement, but then he'd been all 'academic' and distant, reminding her why they'd broken up, and the words had been out before she could stop them. She should go and apologise. They were supposed to be professionals. Colleagues. Technically, he was her boss on this dig. She massaged her temples, wishing she could strike the right balance with him. Her gaze drifted towards the entrance to the tent, her brain itching to put things right with him.

He needed to cool down first, though. If she went out to him now, he'd still be too pissed off with her to accept any apology. Nonetheless, she pulled her phone out to text him.

Sorry. That was unfair of me.

She clicked on send. He'd probably read it and ignore it, but at least she'd apologised.

She tidied all the scans away, then dragged her chair back to her side of the tent. The pot still sat in the middle of her desk, caked in mud, and she eyed it.

"What is it you're trying to tell me?" she murmured.

She picked it up, readying herself for more visions.

None came.

"Because Einar is healed now?" she wondered. "So he has no connection with a pot of gunk?" She clicked her tongue at herself. "Healed *now*? It's been more than a millennium since he was alive. If he ever existed. And even if he *existed*, he almost certainly didn't look like Anders."

She scraped gently at the mud inside the pot, focusing on the cleaning.

By lunchtime, she'd finished with the pot, and a steady stream of other finds that had come in from the trench demanded her attention. Now that the team was down past modern layers, all of the finds dated from the late Anglo-Saxon or Anglo-Scandinavian eras. She noted Anders hadn't brought any of them in to her, but had dispatched Patrick or Sam. Sam had stopped to chat for a while; Patrick hadn't.

She took her pack of sandwiches out of the tent and sat on a foam kneeler at the side of the field. Anders glanced over at her from his trench, then turned away. Sophie still clung to his side, chattering. He still didn't appear to be listening to her.

Shona joined her, sitting on a picnic blanket and unwrapping her lunch. One of the older members of Dig For It, Shona was a woman Georgia liked well, with her no-nonsense Yorkshire bluffness and kind heart.

"You pissed the boss off?" Shona asked, raising her eyebrows at Georgia.

She pulled her gaze away from him. "Mm. I'd hoped he would have cooled off enough for me to apologise to him, but I'm not sure he has."

Shona's short, dark brown hair fluffed in the breeze, and she rubbed a grubby finger under her nose, sniffing. "Sophie is driving him up the wall, chattering away to him."

Georgia laughed. "Has he replied? I worked with Anders in Orkney, and he was never one to chat."

"Not really. She's upsetting Patrick as well, but I think that's because Patrick fancies her, and she clearly fancies Anders."

Georgia's guts knotted.

"Mind you," Shona carried on. "I don't think Anders is interested." She turned her sharp brown eyes to the man in question. "His head seems elsewhere. What did you piss him off about?"

Georgia didn't answer for a moment. "Oh, we were disagreeing about how extensive the dig might end up."

Shona chewed her sandwich, then swallowed. "We're getting

excellent finds now we're down to the Anglo-Saxon layer. Nothing later, though. There's been absolutely zilch from the last thousand years."

"I suspect if we have found a settlement, it was abandoned."

"You think we have?"

"My gut feeling is yes. The finds don't support that yet."

Shona snorted. "You quoting Anders there?"

Georgia grinned. "Yep. Pretty much." She finished her lunch and looked across the site.

Anders clambered out of the trench he was in and tidied his trowel and small brush away. Patrick joined him, and he, Sophie, and Anders laughed about something for a few moments. Eventually, Sophie and Patrick drifted towards the refreshments tent.

"If you want to talk to him without Sophie, there's your chance," said Shona, crumpling up her sandwich wrapper and stuffing it into the pocket of her fleece.

"Yeah."

She stood up. Shona took the kneeler from her to stop it from blowing away, and Georgia strolled towards Anders, not entirely sure how to phrase things. He stared at her, unsmiling, as she approached, making her heart sink further.

"Hey," she said when she reached him.

"Hey."

His gaze was cool, and she jammed her hands in the back pockets of her trousers. "I'm sorry. I was out of line. On several counts. It's your dig. And it's your career. Of course you're going to want a decent job. I'm sorry."

She ground to a halt. He still hadn't smiled, and his posture was tight. He glanced over her head, then half closed his eyes, sighing, and she turned to see what he was looking at. Sophie and Patrick headed towards them, Sophie clutching two mugs, her gaze flicking from Anders to Georgia and back again. She handed Anders a mug of coffee, and he mustered a feeble smile.

"I'll catch you later," Georgia said, walking backwards away from the group. Both Patrick and Sophie looked glad she was going. Anders had reverted to a stony expression. None of them said anything.

She raised her brows at Anders, wondering if he would acknowledge her *at all.* He stared at her for a moment, then buried his nose in his mug.

Oh, stuff you! she thought. *I've apologised!*

She turned and stomped back to the finds tent.

21

It turned out to be a productive day. They had found enough post-holes to convince Anders that there *was* a hall there, and there had been plenty of finds coming out of the floor level of the building. More than he'd expected, if he was being honest.

He'd held the briefest of debriefs, and now everyone had left apart from Georgie, who was still in the finds tent, packing things away. He looked in that direction, drawing in a long breath. Her comment about the job had irked him, but he should have accepted her apology. They still had to work together.

Time to make peace with her.

He squared his shoulders and made his way to the finds tent. Georgie had her head bent, carefully wrapping finds and filling in paperwork.

"Hey," he said, pausing in the tent's opening.

She raised her gaze to him, her eyes wary. "Hey."

He jutted his chin towards the table, floundering a little. "We've kept you busy today. *Lots* of finds."

She nodded, and went back to dealing with them. He scrunched his face up.

"Georgie, I'm sorry. I was narked about your jibe about the job."

"I apologised," she murmured, still not looking at him.

"I know." He breathed deeply. So much of him still wanted to have the row they should have had when they split up, but never did. What would be the point, though? She'd said it herself: there was a lot of water under that bridge. Dredging everything up wouldn't change anything.

"Can I chat to you about the dig? Or are you still too pissed off with me?" he said, not wanting to head home with her still so cold to him.

"Sure. Let me just finish what I'm doing."

"Can I help?"

"No."

He sighed. "Georgie, I'm trying to make peace here. I'm sorry. I was just hurt by the jibe."

She finally looked up. "I know. I'm sorry I had a pop at you." She hesitated. "Sometimes it's just hard."

His heart rate quickened. "Hard?"

She lifted one shoulder and let it drop. "To find the right balance."

He swallowed, unable to take his eyes off her. "Yeah. It is."

Pain flickered through her eyes, and she turned back to her desk. "I need to finish this."

He wanted to talk to her about what she'd said, but from her expression, the topic was over. Once she'd finished processing the last piece, he canted his head at her, brows raised.

"Okay, I'm done," she said, still looking troubled. "Let's talk about the dig."

He rubbed the back of his neck. "Sure. Bring your chair over to my desk? I want to spread the survey results out again."

She carried her chair across while he laid out sheets of paper, then sat opposite him, avoiding looking at him.

"Well, you'll be pleased to hear that I'm coming around to your idea that this *is* the main hall," he said, smiling at her, trying to find the ease they usually had when talking about the site, rather than the awkwardness that had surrounded them all day. He marked up the papers with the locations of the post-holes and the day's finds. "I would tentatively say an east-west orientation, unless the building is a lot bigger than I'm expecting, and this is the width and not the length. What's the latest date in the finds so far?"

"Late Anglo-Saxon. Nothing after that."

He pursed his lips. "Thoughts?"

She wriggled her nose. "I'm still thinking any settlement ended with the Harrying of the North, but that's mostly gut feeling. We may turn up something with a later date tomorrow that would blow that idea out of the water."

He scratched his cheek, his finger rasping his stubble. "There's no sign of the hall burning down, so abandoned, rather than torched." He met her eye. "Extend this trench out to here? See if there are more post-holes?"

"Yeah, I think so."

"Okay. Talk me through today's finds?"

She did, finally becoming more animated as she spoke. Anders let her chatter, delighted to see her relax around him at last. When she finally finished and leaned back in her seat, he smiled at her.

"I promise to excavate where you think there's a weaving hut."

"Thank you."

He gathered together the papers and put them back in the file on his desk. Georgie moved her chair back to her desk and tidied everything away, then grabbed her bag, waiting for him.

On the drive back, his brain chewed over things. Why was she finding it hard to strike the right balance? Did that mean that she *did* have feelings for him? Or did she mean she was struggling to be friendly to him because she still hated him? He hoped that wasn't the case, but maybe he'd been misunderstanding things. Maybe when he'd been thinking things had been relaxed and easy between them, she'd been forcing herself to be nice to him. An icy feeling slithered through his body. Was her default feeling towards him one of animosity?

"Anders, is there something between you and Sophie?"

The question took him by surprise, and he glanced across, eyes wide. "Me and Sophie? No. Why?"

Georgie stared straight ahead through the windscreen. "I think she might hope that there was. And she is your type."

"My 'type'? What's 'my type'?"

And where the hell was this coming from? Had he somehow given off the impression that he liked Sophie?

"Tall, leggy, pretty. Academic."

He spluttered a laugh and looked across at her. "You think that's my type?"

She couldn't be much further from the truth. If he had a type at all, it would be someone small and curvy; someone who could make him laugh. Someone kind and funny and smart.

Georgie, basically.

"So, why not?" she persisted. "She's definitely interested in you."

"Er... because I'm not interested in her." He paused, changing gear, worried. "Am I giving off signals that I am?"

"No. You mostly seem to either barely notice she's there, or have zoned out because she's talking non-stop."

Her words didn't comfort him. "Shit. Am I being really rude to her?"

Georgie snorted. "Um... you're being very you, sometimes."

What did *that* mean? Was he rude to people? He never meant to be. God, was he more like his father than he feared?

They'd reached her road, and he pulled up next to her door, then turned towards her, troubled.

"What do you mean, I'm being very me? Am I being like Pappa?"

She smiled softly. "Not at all! You're just not chatty. Sophie doesn't seem to have twigged that yet."

"Okay." His teeth worried at the inside of his lip, as his brain ran back over the day. Georgie's light laugh drew his attention back to her.

"Don't look so worried, Anders!"

"But I am. Am I rude to people?" His words came out in a rush.

She reached across and rested her hand over his, her expression kind. "No. You're not." She paused, tilting her head to one side. "At times you can be very intense, but in a good way."

She squeezed his hand, surprising him. He stared at her, wriggles of electricity coursing through his skin from her touch.

He cleared his throat. "Are we good? I'm sorry I was an ass with you today."

She nodded. "Mm. We're good. I shouldn't have had a dig at you. I'm sorry. See you tomorrow. I'll make the coffee."

She released his hand, grabbed her bag, and headed into her flat, leaving him staring after her, his brain whirring. *Did* she still have feelings for him?

Did he want her to?

Yes.

***

Later that evening, Georgia and Becky finished streaming the last of their latest box-set binge. Georgia would probably have to watch them again, because her brain had been on the strange visions and not on the show. However much she tried to convince herself that they had just been her imagination running wild, she couldn't shake the feeling that they'd been actual glimpses into the past, however mad and unlikely that seemed.

She clicked the TV off and looked over to Becky, who sprawled in a chair on the other side of the room, her long legs draped over the arm.

"Can I talk to you about something?"

Becky rolled her head towards her. "Is it about Anders and the fact you've finally accepted you're still totally in love with him?"

Georgia shook her head. "No. It's about the dig and the geophysics results."

Becky swung her legs off the arm of the chair and sat up properly. "Go on."

"I think there's a significant settlement under the field."

"I know. You said so over dinner. And I agree with Anders that it's too early to know for sure. Yeah, there are marks on the surveys that *could* imply buildings, but he was right; they could also imply several other things."

"It's more than that." She trailed off, wondering how to phrase things. "I've had a couple of really odd experiences."

Becky frowned with one eyebrow while the other arched, making her face lopsided. "Right…"

"Hear me out? I *know* this is going to sound utterly bonkers, but I have to tell someone."

She sat forward, clasping her hands together, rubbing her thumb over her knuckles, then her words tumbled out. She told Becky everything she'd seen, and how clear it all was, and that the survey results married up with the vision where Aelfgyth had shown Einar around. With every passing minute, Becky looked more incredulous. By the time Georgia ground to a halt, Becky's brows were almost in her hairline.

"Are you being serious about all this?" she said.

"Yeah. I've *tried* to write it off as me just being me and my imagination going into overdrive, but I can't." She closed her eyes, shaking her head. "The visions were all so clear. It was as if *I* was Aelfgyth."

Becky stared at her, her mouth slightly open. "Oh, god, you really *are* serious about all this. Georgie, you *can't* be seeing the past, just because you have an Anglo-Saxon pot or brooch in your hands. Be sensible. You've looked at the geophysics results, some kernel of your brain has remembered that paper about the grid layout, and your imagination has run wild and filled in a load of blanks."

Georgia had known, deep down, that Becky wouldn't believe any of it, but part of her had hoped she might.

"It was all so real," she said, sounding lame even to her own ears.

"But you managed to clean up the pot in the end. You had a couple of 'visions' when you were looking at it, but then you didn't. You're not even being consistent."

Georgia gave up. "Okay. Forget I said anything."

"Shall we talk about you still being in love with Anders instead?" said Becky, settling back.

"And that's where *your* brain is having flights of fancy. I'm not still in love with him."

Becky laughed. "You are a *terrible* liar."

Georgia scowled at her, about to argue, and found she couldn't. "Oh, okay, *yes*, he's still as attractive as he was. But it didn't work out between us. He left me for a job in another country, remember, so while I was wondering if he might be The One, *he* was thinking about moving to Norway so that he could further his career."

"How do you think he feels about working with you again?"

She shrugged. "I dunno. Sometimes I think he's struggling with it all as much as I am. Other times I think he's moved on. He keeps calling me Georgie."

"And have you told him not to?"

"Not recently." She pulled a face. "I quite like it, actually."

She'd deliberately not questioned herself over that fact too closely.

"Hm. Don't tell me you don't still love him. I can count on the fingers of one hand the number of people you allow to call you Georgie."

"Fair." She settled back, troubled. "We had a bit of a spat today." She stopped and corrected herself. "No. I had a go at him, and then he cut me dead all day, even though I apologised to him. And then he was trying to mend things, and I blurted out that it was hard to find the right balance with him, which kind of let the cat out of the bag that part of me still fancies him, even if I still think it might be a bad idea to get back together."

Becky's brows rose. "And how did he react to that?"

She scrunched her face up. "He agreed it was difficult."

Her brain had gone over that nugget since he'd said it. Did that mean he still had feelings for her? Or was she reading too much into it?

Becky eyed her. "You should talk to him. Maybe two years away from you has made him realise you *are* The One, but he thinks you hate him, so is keeping his distance."

Her heart thrilled at the idea, but she squashed her emotions down. "What if he says I never was, and never will be The One?"

Becky gave her a firm look. "Talk to him. Worst-case scenario: you aren't The One for him, in which case, fine. Move on. At least you'd know. *Best-case* scenario…" She waggled her eyebrows.

Georgia held up her hands. "Okay! Fine! I'll try to talk to him."

22

The following afternoon, Anders settled down to dig in the main trench, his brain busy. During the drive in, Georgie had seemed quieter than usual. Was she still upset with him over the day before? He didn't think so. He sighed. Were they destined to spend the entire summer treading on eggshells around each other? They seemed locked in a dance of advance and retreat. The evening before, she'd squeezed his hand and made him wonder if they might have a future together after all. This morning, she'd been aloof again, as if she'd crossed the line and needed to retrench.

He considered for a moment as he dug. Was she really being aloof? Or just professional? Shona wouldn't have squeezed his hand. Was that what she'd meant about struggling to find the right balance? That, because of their history, it wasn't easy to be strictly professional with him?

Did he *want* things to be strictly professional? He didn't know. Every time she backed off, it reminded him of how she'd cut him out of her life like he'd meant nothing to her, and it not only opened up the wound but poured lemon juice in it, too. He wouldn't let himself get hurt like that again. But what if things could be different this time?

Sophie moved down the trench to work next to him. Her perfume irritated his nose. Was Georgie right about her having a thing for him? He hoped not. He was fairly sure he hadn't given her any indication that he was interested in her. Almost immediately, she started talking, making tension creep into his back and neck. He raised his head, glancing down the trench. Sam caught his eye.

"Sophie? There's more space down this end. Want to come

and work by me?" he called over.

Anders smiled gratefully.

Sophie sat up, looking at Sam as if he had just suggested that she fly to the moon. "No, I'm grand here, thanks."

As she turned back to her work, Sam gave Anders an 'I tried!' look, and Anders had to stifle a laugh.

By lunchtime, they'd found enough post-holes to convince Anders that the structure in the main trench was a large hall, and he decided he would put a test-pit in where Georgie seemed sure there would be a weaving hut, partly to check out her theory; mostly to get to dig on his own for a bit.

He grabbed his lunch, praying to be left alone while he ate it. Instead, the day's volunteers clustered around him to grill him about the site and all the finds. Partway through, Georgie shot him a sympathetic glance. Had she understood how much he didn't enjoy being the centre of attention? Probably. Did that mean she really cared about him? Maybe not.

Lunch over, he left the main team and grabbed some sticks and twine to mark out the test-pit, desperate for some solitude. The weather was still being kind, with long bouts of sunshine interspersed with slightly chillier cloudy spells, but although the clouds threatened rain, none had been forthcoming so far, making the light earth easy to work.

The square marked out, he knelt down and scraped at the soil, taking his time, enjoying the feel of the sun on his back and the breeze on his neck. He made slow, steady progress, occasionally looking up to see others in the team scurrying back and forth to Georgie's tent. Mid-afternoon, she came out of the refreshments tent and made her way over to him, two mugs in her hands, and his heart lifted at the sight of her.

"Anything good yet?" she asked as she crouched next to him and passed a mug across.

He stood up, stretching cramped legs and flexing his back. "Still early days. Have you run out of finds?"

She laughed. "No. I just needed a break and some fresh air, so I thought I'd bring you a coffee."

He smiled. "Always appreciated. Thank you. Want to dig for a bit? There's a spare trowel here. Or are there too many finds for you to deal with?"

"Oh, I'd love to dig for a while. Thanks. The finds can wait for an hour. They're not going anywhere."

"It'd be nice to have your company."

She gave him a sneaky look. "I'm sure Sophie would keep you company. You'd only have to bat those baby blues at her, and she'd be here in a second."

He snorted, not gracing her remark with a reply.

A cotton scarf kept her hair back from her face today instead of her containing the madness with a band. It was a simple square, folded to make a triangle and knotted at the nape of her neck, in a pretty Liberty pattern in greens and browns that emphasised her hazel eyes.

He'd clearly been staring at it for too long, because she arched her brows at him. "What?"

"Sorry. I was just admiring your scarf."

She rolled her eyes. "Oh. My hair's driving me *insane* today. I'm half tempted to do a Becky and shave it off."

"Please don't do that. I love your hair. Even in its maddest state."

"Yeah. You don't have to live with it." She twisted her mouth to one side. "After I left Orkney, I got it cut short. *Big* mistake! I thought it would look good in a bob. Clearly, gravity doesn't act on my hair, because it just grew out horizontally. I haven't had it cut since, except to tidy up the ends."

He chuckled, trying to imagine it. "Why on earth did you get it cut?"

She glanced away. "Oh. Just living out a cliche."

He frowned, but she bent her head back to the trench. Tension settled around them, chasing away the lightness that had just been there. Should he say something to break it? What? *"Why are you being weird around me?" "Do you still hate me?" "Did you ever really love me?"* He blinked hard and focused on the soil in front of him.

"You've forgotten your coffee," she said a few minutes later.

He looked up. She pointed with her trowel towards his mug. A clod of mud dropped straight into her coffee as she did so, and he burst out laughing.

"Nice! Here, have mine."

He passed across his mostly untouched drink, but she shook her head.

"You're okay. I'll make another one."

"You'll get trapped in the finds tent again if you go. Want me to make you a fresh one?"

"You'll get trapped by everyone wanting your attention," she countered. "And I know you. You're doing a test-pit over here to get away from everyone."

He grinned wryly. "Rumbled. Share then?"

"Yeah. Go on."

She sat back on her heels and accepted the mug, and they took it in turns sipping from it.

"So, you think we'll find a weaving hut here?" he said.

She shifted uncomfortably. "I don't know. Maybe."

She handed him back the drink, and he peered into it. "Not sure I can spin this out to two more mouthfuls. Can I finish it?"

"Sure. It was yours to start with."

He drained the mug, and they drifted into a comfortable silence, only broken by the sounds of their trowels on the soil. As he cleared a patch, the soil colour changed to black.

"I'm getting to a pretty solid bit of charcoal here," he said.

She worked so close to him that their heads almost touched. "Mm. Me too. I think it's a burnt plank. Wall? Floor?"

"If a hut burned down, I'd expect the walls to fall in, so my money would be on that, rather than floor."

He picked away until he could lift the piece. Underneath it, half hidden in a burned layer, he could see the edge of a loom weight.

"Hey, Georgie." He waited until she looked over. "Guess your hunch about it being a weaving hut was right." He pointed to the loom weight, still half buried in the trench.

Her eyes widened, and she swallowed hard, her face blanching until she looked like a ghost.

23

At least half of her hadn't wanted to find anything remotely like a weaving hut. Then she would have been able to dismiss all the visions as being nothing more than her imagination running riot. But exactly where Aelfgyth had pointed out a weaving hut to Einar, there was a weaving hut.

"Georgie? You okay?" asked Anders.

She looked up, straight into his eyes, and her heart beat harder for a few seconds. He dipped his head, brows raised.

She flapped a hand at him. "I'm fine."

"You're white as a sheet. What's up?"

What on earth could she say? Certainly not the truth.

She plastered a bright smile to her face. "Nothing's up. I'm always pale. I don't tan like you do!"

Anders kept his focus on her, making her hot with embarrassment at her reaction. Maybe it was a coincidence. All settlements would have had a weaving hut, and the survey results *had* indicated a building here. But she couldn't shake the feeling that she'd *seen* the hut. That she'd known it would be there.

She met his gaze, sweat prickling her skin. "I might just head back to the finds tent, if you don't mind."

His face fell. "Okay. It was nice to have your company, albeit briefly."

She hurried away. In the finds tent, she sat at her desk, thinking, trying to be as rational as Anders always was. Subconsciously, she'd thought about the layout of Anglo-Saxon settlements and their spacing, and that was why she'd imagined it would be a weaving hut. In fact, now she thought about it, wasn't the layout exactly the same as another Anglo-Saxon settlement found in the south, a couple of years earlier?

Having talked herself around to it being no more than chance, she scanned the trays of finds waiting to be processed. An amber bead caught her eye. With it was a sheet of paper covered in Patrick's neat writing, along with a sketch made with the bead still *in situ* in the trench.

"Nice find," she mused. "And not Sam finding it for once!"

She drew the tray towards her, ready to clean the bead up and complete the paperwork. As soon as her fingertip touched it, her vision swam, and she snatched her hand back.

"No. Just no," she muttered.

She forced herself to breathe deeply and relax, then reached a shaky hand towards the bead again. Around her, the room looked fuzzy, with two images overlapping. She swallowed, closing her eyes and giving in. Whether it was just her imagination, or something else entirely, it was going to happen, so she should just roll with it.

Sunlight streamed in through the open door of the weaving hut, picking out dust motes dancing in the air. Aelfgyth sat on a stool in the corner, carding fleece ready for spinning. It was her least favourite job in the weaving hut. She far preferred actually weaving, but Hilla had got to the loom before her.

The fleece to be carded lay in a basket at her side. It was thick and dark, from the small, sturdy sheep that lived on the estate. Aelfgyth picked out straw and sticks from a clump, then pulled it through the two carding combs, working it back and forth until the dense, matted lump had become separated and fluffy, ready to be spun. It was hard work, and she wished more fresh air would blow in through the open door, but the wind was in the wrong direction for that today.

She piled the carded wool into another basket, watching Hilla weaving. The stones weighting the warp threads clanked together near Hilla's feet, and the periodic rhythmic beating of the weft threads upwards punctuated the stillness. Hilla wasn't one to chatter much, unlike Eanswith, the young woman spinning next to her.

"I thought he'd be a brute, but he's been kind so far," chirruped Eanswith. "Einar, I mean."

Hilla gave her a sharp look, but Eanswith wasn't looking.

"I mean, he could have been awful. There are other farms where everyone was thrown out," she carried on, heedless.

"Concentrate on your spinning, Eanswith. Your threads are always

lumpy," said Hilla. "You need to draw the thread more evenly, otherwise the cloth is a mess."

Eanswith pulled a face, though Hilla wouldn't have seen. Aelfgyth smiled to herself.

A shadow filled the doorway, making all three women look up. Einar stood, blocking the light, his eyes resting on her in a way that made her insides tingle.

"Aelfgyth? May I speak to you outside?" he said.

Eanswith giggled at her, earning another sharp look from Hilla. Aelfgyth put her carding to one side, smoothed a hand over her skirts, and joined Einar outside the hut.

"I have a gift for you," he said, his sky-blue eyes twinkly. Over the month since he'd arrived, he'd been working hard at learning her language and had become far more proficient.

She averted her gaze. Less from modesty and more to make her heart beat more slowly. His eyes were far too enticing. "A gift? Why?"

"Do I need to have a reason?"

"Yes."

He chuckled. "Then my reason is because you are beautiful, and I wished to give you something." He showed her a necklace made of amber beads. "You are fiery. These make me think of you."

Her insides fluttered at his words, and she pinched herself, reminding herself that he had stolen her father's land, however kind he seemed.

He drew a circle in the air with his finger, indicating for her to turn. She did, and he put the beads around her neck, caressing her skin as he did so.

She stepped away briskly, her heart pounding, and faced him.

"Do not think that you can help yourself to everything that is not yours! Is it not enough that you have my father's land? I am not for sale. Or do you intend to take me by force like you did the land?"

His face fell, and his hands dropped to his sides. "I would never do that. To anyone. I swear to you. The beads are a gift. I meant nothing more by them. Forgive me."

He bowed his head, then turned away, his broad shoulders tight. Aelfgyth stared after him, her fingers brushing the beads, then she returned to the weaving hut.

Hilla eyed her carefully. "Those are a fine gift. I think you have caught the eye of our new lord. You could do worse."

She said nothing, taking her seat, and picking up her work again.

"Ooh," said Eanswith. "If you had his children, they would inherit the land and it would return to your family."

Hilla arched a brow. "You could do worse," she repeated.

Her face felt hot, and she bent her head to her work, trying to erase the sinful thoughts that had just poured into her mind.

The surface of the desk came back into focus, leaving Georgia caught between the two worlds for a moment. Surely, this was something more than just her imagination? The interior of the weaving hut had been so detailed to her. The loom weights, the frame, the smell of the wool, the feel of it in her fingers as she'd worked…as *Aelfgyth* had worked, she corrected herself. As for the 'sinful thoughts'… they had been all too clear and, she had to confess, largely based on her and Anders. She fanned herself with her hand, her skin suddenly hot.

"Did you want a coffee… without added mud?"

She whirled around in her seat to find Anders sitting at his desk on the other side of the space, a smile lifting one side of his mouth.

"Shit, you made me jump! I didn't know you were there. When did you come in?"

"About ten minutes ago, while you were staring at whatever it is you're working on. The bead?"

"Yeah." She turned back to it, dipping her head, trying to get her heart rate back under control.

"And what have you been imagining about it?" he asked.

"What?" Her head whipped back to him. How the hell did he know?

He snorted. "You're *always* imagining how things were used, or what their story is. What have you come up with for the bead?"

"Oh. That it was part of a necklace given by a Viking, called Einar, to an Anglo-Saxon woman, called Aelfgyth, if you must know."

He quirked a brow at her. "Einar? Good Viking name. And who was Aelfgyth?"

"The daughter of the man whose land this was before Halfdan gave it to Einar."

He chuckled, his attention back on his laptop screen. "Oh, Georgie, I *love* your imagination. Don't ever change." He peered at her over the top of the screen again. "Does Einar look like me, by any chance? Is that why you got my name wrong the other day?"

She folded her arms. "He may have a passing resemblance, yes. I thought you were digging the test-pit."

"I was. And then I came to log a couple of things and found you staring into space. I stayed in case you needed me to catch you if you fainted again."

Humour danced over his lips.

"Well, as you can see, I'm not fainting, so you won't need to catch me. You needn't worry about me."

"That's a habit I am neither able nor willing to break," he said, his voice low and full of intensity.

Her stomach flipped, and they stared at each other for a moment.

"Tell me about the bead before I go back out to the test-pit?" he said, closing down his laptop.

She forced her head back to work and what she could say about the bead that was factual, rather than fanciful.

"Scandinavian style. I suspect Scandinavian in origin, rather than made in England. Which would imply being brought here. Still consistent with late ninth century. I can tell you more when I've finished cleaning it up."

He nodded, his eyes still locked on hers. "Are you sure you're okay? That's twice now that I've found you staring into space, pretty out of it. And not just like you were day-dreaming, but totally spaced." He cleared his throat, his face troubled. "Georgie… I know things ended badly between us, but I will always care about you. And I'm always here if you need to talk, or if things are difficult. If something's going on, don't think you have to face it on your own."

"Anders, nothing's going on. I'm fine. But thank you. That's very sweet of you."

He gave her a long look. "Okay. I'm heading back out to the test-pit, but just text me if you need me and I'll come back."

"Please stop worrying about me. I was just day-dreaming."

She didn't sound convincing even to her own ears, and Anders pushed his hair off his brow, still looking at her.

"Have it your way," he said eventually. "You know where I am."

He eased himself out from behind his desk and made his way out of the tent. Georgia stared after him. Did he really still care about her? One of these days, the two of them would *have* to actually talk.

24

The following Thursday, Georgie flew out of her door, her hair still wet. She *hated* being late. Anders's car already sat at the kerb, and she scrambled in, knocking a flask of coffee over with her foot as she did.

"I'm sorry! I'm sorry! Have you been waiting long?" She pulled the flask upright.

He smiled at her. "Chill. I literally just put the handbrake on."

She clicked her seat belt fastened, breathing out hard. "My phone died in the night, so I had no alarm, and Becks is away."

"Did you want to go back in and dry your hair?"

She did, but she'd already kept him waiting. "No, it'll take far too long. I'll just shove it under a hat if I get cold."

"Sure? We've plenty of time."

She nodded, and he pulled away.

At the site, he parked up and walked around to the back of the car.

"Georgie? Do you have a spare hand free? Can you grab these bags for me?" he called over his shoulder. "Oh!" He clicked his tongue. "Sorry! Georg*ia*. Sorry."

She reached him. "Relax. It's okay. Georgie's fine. You've called me that for days now. If you start bugging me, I'll just pronounce your name wrong in retaliation."

"What, and call me Einar again?"

The cheeky look he gave her made her insides go a little wobbly.

He opened the boot of his car and lifted out two water-cooler bottles.

"Do you need a hand with them?" she said, looking dubiously at them.

He grinned. "No offence, but I don't think you can lift these. They weigh about twenty kilos each!" He nodded towards a carrier bag and a backpack still in the boot. "If you can bring those and the coffee, that would be a help."

She slung the backpack over one shoulder and picked up the carrier bag, tucking the flask of coffee from the foot-well into it. Anders closed the boot and grasped the handle of one of the water bottles. He headed towards the refreshments tent, carrying the bottle with ease, then ducked back out to retrieve the second bottle, which he put in the washing-up area of the tent.

He started up the generator and rummaged in the carrier bag. A box of teabags, a new jar of instant coffee, and a carton of milk joined the mugs on the side table, then he filled the hot water urn from the half-empty cooler bottle left next to it, and hefted the new one up.

"I'd almost forgotten you had muscles under that fleece," said Georgia.

He turned to her, a wide smile on his face. "Is that a compliment?"

She laughed. "I guess."

Everything ready, he waved the flask of coffee at her, and she nodded. He poured her a fragrant mug and passed it over, then rested against the table, stretching out long, lean legs. She perched on a chair opposite him. His eyes settled on her over the rim of the mug, and her heart fluttered.

"Can I ask you something?" he said.

She shrugged, wondering what was coming.

"How come you're in Yorkshire? The last I heard, you were working in Cumbria. When did you move here?"

She shook her hair back from her face. "Just after Christmas. It's the same job. The company has relocated."

"Oh. That must have been a pain. What if you were settled in Cumbria?"

She savoured another slurp of coffee before answering. "A few people were, and they weren't all that chuffed. It wasn't much of an issue for me and Becky. Steve was pretty annoyed. His kids have had to change school, and his wife is still struggling to get a job here."

He looked as if he had follow-up questions he wanted to ask, but said nothing.

"What about you? How was the job in Oslo?"

He blinked, and stuck his bottom lip out. "The job was great. I was lonely. It's a long time since I lived there. Most of my old friends had moved away. Or got married and had kids."

She cocked her head at him. "What, is my big, gentle Norwegian still shy?"

He held her gaze for a moment, making her insides tingle. "I'm only *half*-Norwegian. And I only seem big because you're tiny. And I'm not shy. I'm just quiet."

And you're not mine any more, either, she thought, with more of a pang than she'd expected.

"You're just quiet?" she said sarcastically. "Okay. If you say so. But you *are* quite big. Tall."

"Not by Norwegian standards. And you are quite tiny. With *massive* hair."

She laughed. "Fair enough. Can we agree on my half-big, half-Norwegian man, still being half-shy?"

"Yeah. We can agree on that."

They drifted into silence, each sipping their coffee, watching each other over the rims of their mugs. The air crackled, as if an electrical storm was about to strike.

Georgia finished her mug of coffee, then cleared her throat, needing to break the tension. "You got some excellent papers out while you were there."

He twisted his mouth to one side, his eyes full of humour. "Have you been Googling me?"

Her cheeks burned, but he just chuckled at her. "Yeah. I got some good papers out. They helped me to get this job."

"Your dad might have some competition over who's the more prestigious Mortensen soon."

He choked on his coffee. "Oh, that'll never happen. I can't imagine Pappa ever retiring for a start, so he'll always have a thirty-year head start over me! Mind you, it would be wonderful to be introduced in meetings and people *not* look disappointed that the 'wrong' Mortensen has come."

She stuck a lip out sympathetically. "That must be tough."

He shrugged one shoulder, twitching one brow. "I'm used to it."

"He still giving you a hard time over everything?"

Anders drained his mug. "Yeah. Though he was happy when I finally got my hair cut."

Georgia chuckled, remembering the one time she'd met his father. Haakon Mortensen had visited the dig in Orkney, and found fault with *everything* Anders did, but his most excoriating comments had been about his longish hair and scruffy beard.

"He might be less happy that your face doesn't look like it's seen a razor in well over a fortnight."

He rubbed his palm over his jaw, making a rasping sound. "Well. He's not here to see it."

"You growing your beard back in?"

"Maybe. It's pretty much past the itchy stage, at least." He shook the flask from side to side, eliciting a slight sloshing sound. "More coffee?"

"Go on then."

He straightened up and poured her out another mugful, then drained the flask into his mug. Georgia took a moment to study him. He might not describe himself as tall, but he stood at just over six feet, with a strong frame and broad shoulders. Today, he had on dark grey-brown walking trousers, with a pair of grubby boots peeking out beneath the hems, and on his top half he wore a half-zip fleece, in the neck of which sat a buff. His lock of hair with a mind of its own had fallen forward and was trying to curl into a tube. Her fingers itched to push it back from his brow.

She realised he was watching her, and heat flashed into her cheeks again.

"What?" he asked. "You're looking at me weirdly."

"Does that bit of your hair at the front *ever* behave? I thought it was always a bit mad because your hair was long, but it's still mad, even with the corporate look."

He barked a laugh. "That's rich, coming from you! Have you seen what your hair looks like today?"

Since she hadn't had time to dry it, she assumed it would appear to be growing out of her head at right-angles in a mass of tightly coiled corkscrews, giving her a bit of a Medusa look.

"Okay, that's fair," she said, grinning. "You look more natural in all that—" she waved her hand at him "—than you do in a shirt and jacket."

He crossed his arms, resting his mug on his forearm by his elbow. "By 'natural', do you mean scruffy?"

"I meant it was more 'you' but now you come to mention it, yeah, scruffy fits."

His arms still folded, he made a rude gesture with his middle finger against his biceps, making her laugh.

From the field outside came the sound of a car pulling up, and they both turned to the entrance of the tent. Sophie bounced in, along with Sam and Patrick. Sophie zeroed in on Georgia, her expression steely, then flashed a brilliant smile at Anders—who was still looking at Georgia's hair.

"Morning," he said without turning. "The urn should be hot, so help yourself to tea or coffee."

The three of them made themselves drinks, then joined Anders in leaning on the table. Sophie managed to get the spot right next to him, her hip jammed against his. Anders looked as if he was about to shift down a bit, but Sam rested on the table on his other side, and Anders settled again, though his posture stiffened, and his knuckles tightened around his mug.

Another car drew up outside, and the four members of the Dig For It team arrived. They too bundled into the tent and grabbed drinks, but took up position on Georgia's side of the tent, looking expectantly at Anders.

He flashed a wide-eyed look at her, then levered himself away from the table and moved to stand in a space where everyone could see him.

"Morning all. It's a bit chilly today, so try to keep warm, and come and warm up in here if you need to. The urn will be on all day. Please remember to keep it topped up, so it doesn't boil dry. No rain is scheduled, which is always a bonus. Everyone knows what they're doing today, right? We don't actually need a team talk, do we?"

The group grinned, shaking their heads, and Anders drifted back over to Georgia.

"Okay, titch. I'm going to go and be scruffy outside."

She tilted her face up to him, surprised. "Did you just call me titch?"

He didn't answer, just wrinkled his nose at her affectionately, then headed out to the main dig site.

She breathed deeply, her insides fizzy from the look he'd given her.

25

Georgia settled at her desk once everyone had headed out to the dig. Her head was cold from her wet hair, and she rummaged in her bag to find the woolly hat she'd grabbed at the last moment. She jammed it on, wishing she'd picked something more stylish than the hand-knitted beanie she'd made from leftover bits and bobs of wool. Damp corkscrews of hair still sat against her neck, making her shiver. She should have taken Anders up on his offer of going back in to dry it. Or at least gone back in and grabbed her hair dryer.

The finds had been coming in at such a rate of knots, she was doing little except logging the barest of details. She certainly hadn't kept up with getting them all cleaned up. Much of that would have to wait until she was back at the Dig For It premises. Some finds were too fragile to deal with on site, anyway. She expected that most of her day would involve packaging things up, ready to be taken to storage. Tugging her coat tighter around her, she started to sort the finds into those that would definitely need to be dealt with elsewhere, and those she could deal with here if she got a moment.

Halfway through the morning, Anders poked his head in. "Hey. I've brought you a coffee. How are you getting on?"

She smiled up at him. "I'm getting swamped. But I can't be upset, because the wealth of finds is just amazing."

He passed her a drink, then perched on the edge of his desk, blowing on his coffee. She wrapped her hands around her mug, trying to warm them, still cold from her damp hair.

"You okay?" He peered at her. "No, you're frozen, aren't you? You could have gone back in and dried your hair this morning. I'd have waited."

"Well. Too late now."

He eyed her. "Want me to braid it so you can fit it in your hat?"

"Can you remember how to?"

Anders had a sister with hair almost as thick as hers. Fairly early on in Orkney, when her hair had been blowing around her face and annoying her, he'd offered to plait it for her. She'd been impressed with how neatly he'd done it, and he'd confessed to being made to play hairdressers with his sister as a child. Georgia had always struggled to French-braid her own hair, feeling as if she needed another three or four fingers on each hand to manage, and had asked him to do it for her on many an occasion.

"Just about," he said. "Hang on, let me get some more of the grot off my hands first."

He disappeared, returning with some damp paper towels. He sponged his hands, taking off the worst of the grime.

"Right. Come and stand here. You don't have a comb on you, do you?"

She shook her head, moving to stand in front of him. She unsnapped the hairband from around her wrist and passed it to him. He put it around his own wrist, then grabbed a pencil off her desk.

"I can't promise how neat this will be. It's been a while since I did this."

He was so close behind her, his body heat warmed her. Steadily, he pulled up sections of her hair with the pencil and plaited them together. The feel of his hands in her hair brought back so many memories, she had to bite the inside of her cheek.

He tied the band around the bottom of the braid. "There. Done. Turn around?"

She did, and he laughed. "Sorry. It's not all that straight. Want me to try again?"

She shook her head. "No, you're fine. Thank you for plaiting it for me."

She held out her hand for her hat, but he hung on to it.

"Your neck will be cold once you tuck your hair up. Here."

He pulled off the merino wool buff that he wore and passed it to her. She put it on, drawing her braid free so that it hung outside the neck-warmer. The wool was warm against her skin, and the buff smelled of him. She breathed in a deep lungful of memories that made her insides tingle.

He turned her hat around in his hands, studying it. "Did you knit this?"

"Is it that obvious?"

"No, it's lovely. I like the colours." He handed it back to her. "Very you."

She stuffed her hair under the hat. "I was about to ask if you'd be cold without your neck-warmer, but you're always like a blast furnace."

He laughed. "True." He swallowed, tilting his head. "I'd offer to give you a hug to warm you up, but I'm not sure you'd accept."

The idea of being snuggled up in his arms, toasty-warm, was *very* appealing.

"Hm. If you did, Sophie would arrive in 3… 2… 1." She arched her brows expectantly, looking towards the entrance to the finds tent.

Only a few seconds late, Sophie bounced in. "Anders? Can I steal you? I need a hand with something in the trench."

He burst out laughing, winking at Georgia as she gave him an 'I told you so' look.

Sophie's gaze shifted from Anders to Georgia and back, and her brows furrowed. Anders straightened his face. "Sure."

Sophie gave Georgia a triumphant smile and shepherded him out of the tent, jabbering away about what she'd found in the trench.

Georgia finished her coffee, relishing the warmth from the buff, her mind full of thoughts of her and Anders. It would be so easy to get back together with him. But his post was only temporary, and he was too proud and too ambitious for his next job to be at anything other than at least the same level that this one was. Would a high enough ranking job come up in the UK?

She shook her head, determined to focus on the finds. One of the many treasures that had been unearthed was a bone comb, and her fingers itched to clean it up and examine it, but it was too fragile to deal with in the tent. The little she could see of it that wasn't covered in dirt was exquisitely made, with beautiful decorations along the plate holding the teeth. She gathered together what she needed to pack it carefully for transport, then picked it up, ready to protect it and store it.

The double-image of the finds tent superimposed over something much, *much* older, made her feel woozy, and she closed her eyes before letting go of the comb.

"Jeez, Anders is *not* going to find me looking spaced *again*. Just pack it away, and deal with it off-site."

But it was no use. As soon as she picked the comb up again, she was back in the ninth century, at least in spirit, if not actually physically.

"Good morning, Aelfgyth."

She looked up, smiling at Einar. His pronunciation of her language was getting closer, but it still wasn't right.

"Good morning, Einar," she said slowly, emphasising where he had been wrong.

His blue eyes danced. "Good morning," he repeated.

She grinned at him. "Much better."

"What are you doing today?"

"Spinning."

"Can you spin and teach at the same time?"

She straightened, puzzled. "You want me to teach you to spin? It is women's work."

He threw his head back and laughed. "No, Aelfgyth. I wish for you to teach me your language while you spin."

She twisted her mouth to one side. "I do not think that the other women will like you spending all day in the weaving hut with them."

"Then sit outside in the sunshine with me. You can bring your fleece and your spindle, yes?"

She hesitated. The thought of spending a couple of hours with Einar, sitting in the sun, made her insides thrill.

"Can none of the men teach you the language?"

"None of the men are as pretty as you." He tilted his head to the side, his eyes soft. "And I desire your company, not theirs."

Her heart skipped a few beats at his expression.

"You are my lord and master. If you order me to teach you, I cannot refuse," she said, arching a brow, meaning only to tease him.

His face fell. "Aelfgyth, I would never order you to do something you did not wish to do. I merely wanted your company."

She smiled, and his shoulders relaxed. "I will fetch my fleece and spindle, Einar. The sun is warm, and your company will be welcome."

"Thank you."

The images faded, and Georgia chuckled to herself. "Was this your comb, then, Aelfgyth?"

She packed it carefully, then worked her way through the rest of the tray of artefacts, getting all of them safely stored with no further trips to the ninth century.

By lunchtime, she felt as if she was no further forwards than she'd been at the start of the day. As soon as she had finished processing one tray of finds, Sam had arrived with more. She slithered off her seat and went to find Anders. He stood next to the main trench, chatting with Patrick, but he turned to her, full of smiles.

"Hey."

"Hey. Sorry to bother you, Anders. Could you guys either find less stuff, or could I steal someone to help me at least pack things up to take back to the stores? I'm getting swamped in there."

He grinned at her, making her heart skip. "Of course."

Shona poked her head up from the other end of the trench. "I'll help. Give my knees a break. All this kneeling in the mud is a young person's game."

"Thanks, Shona. I'm going to grab my lunch now, but if you could give me a hand this afternoon, that would be perfect."

"Sure. It'll be nice to see everything together, actually."

Was she imagining it, or had Anders just looked disappointed? Had he hoped to be the one helping her? He glanced back at her and caught her eye, smiling again immediately, but there was a yearning expression in his eyes that made her heart flip.

26

That afternoon, Anders walked around the site, his brain running back over him and Georgie teasing each other. He'd wanted to hug her, and not just because she was frozen. He missed her. He clicked his tongue, correcting himself. He missed *being* with her. As friends. As lovers. From the first day they'd met, he'd been completely comfortable in his own skin when he was around her, something he almost never was. He could be Anders. He wasn't 'Professor Mortensen's son.' Or 'the other Mortensen' as he'd been referred to far too often. That summer with her had been the happiest he could remember.

And then she'd ghosted him for two years.

He'd thought them working together and her being cold to him would be unbearable, but somehow, this was even worse. Why had she been teasing him this morning? Why had he been teasing her? His heart had been pounding so hard when he braided her hair, he was surprised it was still in his chest. She'd always used a coconut product to stop her curls from becoming frizz, and the scent of it had made him yearn for her, deep down in his core.

He closed his eyes and tipped his head back, letting the cool wind ruffle his hair. Had she changed her mind about him? About them? *Could* they get back to what they'd had, or was there far too much water under that bridge now? He didn't want to only be colleagues with her. He wanted what they'd had.

He stared across the field, hoping to catch a glimpse of her, but the opening to the finds tent was empty. She'd be busy with Shona, cleaning up and cataloguing the finds. She almost certainly wasn't thinking about him.

He made his way to the trench excavating the weaving hut.

The number of loom weights he'd found buried under the burned planks suggested that the hut had burnt down while still in use. He'd extended the trench twice, and had now almost finished uncovering the whole hut, but he wanted to draw it and finish the photography off before any further excavation.

He was in the middle of sketching when Patrick came over.

"Er, Anders? You're needed. Sam's found bones."

"Animal or human?" he said, scrambling up.

"Dunno."

He glanced towards the tents. "Get Georgia. She's pretty good at identification."

Patrick nodded and turned towards the tents. Anders hurried over to Sam, his brain running through options. Human bones would be exciting but a pain in the neck, because the dig would have to stop until they'd been dealt with, and there was a ton of paperwork involved. Animal bones would be less exciting, and much more likely, given that they already thought the trench went through a midden.

He reached the trench and squatted down just as Georgie arrived. Sam pointed the tip of his trowel at the end of a bone sticking out of the soil.

"I think it's pig rib, but I'm not a hundred per cent sure."

Anders turned to Georgie. "What do you reckon?"

"Can I get in the trench? I can't see it well enough from here."

Sam offered her a hand, helping her down. She crouched, peering at the exposed bone, then borrowed Sam's trowel to clear a little more of the soil away.

"Yep. I would say that's a pig rib. Flatter cross-section than human. Which is a relief, because there are also clear cut-marks." She raised her face to Anders, smiling. "Sorry to disappoint you. There would have been a published paper on the horizon if it *had* been human, because these ribs were eaten!"

He laughed, though the idea was pretty gruesome. "Odds were it would be animal. Thanks."

He held out a hand to her, and she grasped it. A familiar bolt of electricity coursed up his arm, making his breathing catch. He hauled her out of the trench, but didn't want to let go of her hand. He couldn't keep holding it, though. He settled for squeezing it lightly, then releasing it. She gave him a quizzical look, but said nothing.

"Did you want to stay out here instead of being banished to the finds tent?" Sam said. "Otherwise, you might be backwards and forwards if we find a load of bones. You can even have a trowel, if you fancy digging."

She glanced up at Anders, holding his gaze for several seconds longer than necessary, then shook her head. "No, I'd better get back to Shona."

Anders's insides fizzed at the look she'd just given him. Did she feel more than friendship towards him? Had she finally forgiven him for going to Oslo?

He watched her walk back to the tents, then cleared his throat, suddenly aware that Patrick was studying him. "Okay. Catch you all later. I'm going to finish up over there."

He scurried back to the trench over the weaving hut, his cheeks burning.

"Sort yourself out," he muttered to himself as he bent back over the soil. "You don't need the whole team knowing your feelings."

27

Anders found Georgie just as she'd finished packing up for the day. Other than for brief moments, their paths hadn't crossed much over the day, and he was no closer to knowing what her earlier look had meant.

"Ready to leave?" he asked. "Or do you need a bit longer?"

She smiled warmly, making his heart sing. "Nope. Ready. Thanks for sorting my hair out this morning and for lending me your neck-warmer. Let me give you it back before I steal it. It's really cosy!"

She made to take his buff off, but he signalled to her to keep it on.

"Keep it. I can always get another." He twisted his key ring around his finger. "Can we do a detour to my office on the way? Sorry. I've had the last of my stuff sent over from Oslo, and it was easier to get it sent to work than to arrange a time when I'd be in."

Georgie shrugged. "Fine. Need a hand with any of it?"

He smiled apologetically. "Probably. Do you mind?"

"Depends how much there is."

She gathered her things together and followed him out to the car.

"I think there are three boxes," he said as they set off. "Mostly books, I'm afraid."

"If they're too heavy for me, you're on your own."

He grinned. "Fair enough."

At the university, he parked up, then rummaged in his wallet for his pass to get into the building. His office was on the third floor, and they walked up the main stairs together, their footsteps echoing in the empty building.

"I've always thought office buildings feel weird out of hours," said Georgie. "I can remember doing a summer project when I was a student, and the university buildings without the students in them made me think of that hotel in The Shining. I wouldn't have been at all surprised to turn a corner and find a small child on a tricycle pedalling down the corridors."

He laughed hard. "I know exactly what you mean. The buildings are designed with the idea of several hundred more people occupying them. In the summer, it can be like a ghost town. A lot of the staff are away then, too. Fieldwork, or holidays, or working from home. I never really like academic buildings in the summer. Even the air smells wrong."

They reached his office, and he unlocked the door. Piled on the floor in front of his desk were three boxes, neatly parcelled up with a variety of labels on them. They had originally been used for packaging reams of paper, which meant that they all had handle-spaces in the sides, making them easier to carry.

"If you can manage one, I can take the other two, but if it's too heavy, say, and I'll do two trips."

"Pass one up. Let me see."

He lifted the top box, trying to judge its weight. Georgie held her hands out, and he passed it to her. She sagged a little, but nodded.

"Yeah, I think I can manage this. Watch your back, picking the other two up."

He gave her a withering look. "Yes, Mum."

He picked up the other two, doing as he was told and protecting his back. Out in the corridor, he bent his leg and balanced the boxes on his thigh while he re-locked the door, then hefted them back up into his arms.

Georgie headed down the corridor and stopped in front of the lift doors. Anders carried on towards the door to the stairs.

"Oh, no," she said, shaking her head. "It's three floors. I'd be happy to take the stairs *if I wasn't carrying a massive box of your stuff.* We're taking the lift."

He stopped and turned back to her, adjusting the two boxes in his arms. The box he'd handed over to her *was* heavy, and it was his stuff. She raised her brows at him, jamming her foot in the lift door to keep it open, and he relented. Georgie balanced the box awkwardly to get a hand free, pressed the button for the ground floor, and the doors slid closed behind him.

The interior of the lift was smaller than he remembered, and the boxes made it feel even more cramped. At least Georgie barely took up much room. He pressed his back against the wall to keep his balance as the lift lurched into life.

Two moments later, the lift jerked to a standstill with a horrible screech of metal, and a red light glowed on the lift's control panel. He caught her eye over the top of the boxes, his heart rate picking up.

"Georgie? Don't tell me the lift is stuck."

She manoeuvred around him to put her box on the floor in the corner, then took his from him one by one and stacked them on top.

"Er, yes, it seems very likely that the lift is jammed. Hang on. Let me see if I can get through to someone on the intercom."

He kept his back hard against the wall as she pressed the button to speak to someone, trying to give her more room. A crackle emerged from the intercom, then a chipper male voice.

"Hello?"

"Oh, hi," said Georgie. "We're in the lift in the archaeology building. We were going from the third floor down to the ground, and from the lights, I think we've left the third floor, but haven't quite reached the second. The lift isn't moving."

"Yeah, I can see that. Um… there's two of you in there?"

Anders scanned the interior of the lift, locating the small camera in the top corner.

"Yep. Plus a pile of boxes. Is there a problem?"

"Um… well, duh, *yeah*, since you're not moving. I've alerted the engineer."

Georgie's jaw bunched, and she closed her eyes, her lips making a thin line. Anders stifled a smirk.

"Thank you," she said through gritted teeth. "Any idea how long it'll be before we get moving?"

"No idea. Sorry."

"Thanks. *Du var veldig hjelpsom. Ikke.*" You were very helpful. Not.

Anders spluttered a laugh.

"What was that?" asked the now less than chipper man on the intercom.

"Nothing. Thank you."

"I'll keep you posted about the engineers."

With that, the intercom crackled again, then went silent.

"You still remember your Norwegian?"

She threw an amused look at him. "Only the phrases where I can be snarky." She turned and rested her shoulders against the wall behind her. "You okay?"

"Been better, but I'm fine."

He hated confined spaces, and sweat was already beginning to trickle between his shoulder blades.

"We should have taken the stairs, after all," mused Georgie.

"Mm."

"Did you want to sit down?"

He looked at her, scrunching his brows. How was there space for them to sit down?

She folded herself into the empty area of floor next to the boxes, sitting cross-legged, leaving him enough room to sit down next to her. He tucked his backside into the corner of the lift and stretched his legs out until his feet hit the door, his knees still bent.

She splayed out her hands. "See, there *are* some advantages to being this small."

"Yeah. Except if I hadn't braided your hair, it would be taking up at least half the available space."

She laughed. "Very true. Thank you for sorting it for me this morning."

He shrugged.

The lift was stuffy and hot, with a faint tang, as if someone had mopped it out with disinfectant. He undid all of the buttons of his rugby shirt, then rolled his sleeves to the elbow. Next to him, Georgie rested her head back against the metal wall, her shoulder in contact with his. Silence stretched between them, and he wondered how long it would take for the lift to get fixed. He plucked at the front of his top, trying to get some air against his skin to cool it down, nudging her shoulder as he did so. "Sorry,

I'm boiling in here."

She turned her face to him, her expression open. "Take your rugby off if you're too hot. I can see you have a t-shirt on underneath."

He shook his head, acutely aware that his t-shirt would have damp sweat patches.

Half of him wanted to clear the air between them; ask her how she felt about him. A good chunk of him was scared about what the answer might be. What if he was misreading any lightness between them? Maybe he'd just been *hoping* to see that she was as conflicted as him, when, in reality, she couldn't care less about him.

What if, like before, she did like him, but not enough?

After a few minutes, Georgie turned her head towards him. "Can I ask you something?"

"Mm," he said, wary.

"Why did you go for the corporate look?" She waved a hand at him. "The hair, the suit, the beard gone. Though the beard seems to be trying to make a comeback."

He smiled ruefully. "It went with the desk job."

She arched a brow. "Mm. That doesn't suit you, either."

"What do you mean?"

She sighed softly. "You love being outside. You love the breeze on your face and the sun on your back. You relish being in the trench, picking away at the soil to uncover things. I *never* understood why you went for a desk job."

He tensed. *Were* they finally going to talk about what happened at the end of the Orkney dig? Now the moment was come, he wasn't at all sure he still wanted to.

She looked at him, clearly waiting for a response.

"I needed to work, Georgie. You had your position in Dig For It. I had nothing." He steadied his breathing. "I needed a job."

"In Oslo."

"No. It didn't *have* to be in Oslo, but that's all there was."

"There was another post in Dig For It. You could have applied for that."

He lowered his head, tension making his skin prickle. "I wanted to stay in academia."

"More than you wanted to stay with me."

It was a flat statement, not a question.

"I thought I could do both," he said quietly.

She glared at him. "I don't have dual nationality, Anders. It would have been difficult for me to see you in Oslo."

His breathing juddered. "It wouldn't have been impossible. And it wasn't long-term. We could have made it work."

She turned to stare at the lift doors opposite them, her lips pressed together, her shoulders taut. They lapsed back into a silence that was almost worse than them finally talking.

A few minutes later, the intercom crackled. "Hello?"

Georgie scrambled up and pressed the button. "Hello?"

"Hi. There's an engineer on their way."

"Okay, great. Thanks. Any idea how long they'll be?"

"No."

The line went dead.

"I hope he got a refund from Charm School," muttered Georgie as she sat down again.

Anders sniggered, despite the tension. "God, I've missed you making comments like that."

"Then you shouldn't have left me," she said sharply.

He blinked. "Excuse me? You're the one who left. You took your key to my place off your key ring, put it on the table, and just walked out of the door!"

"You were hoping to move to *Oslo*. I thought I meant more than that to you. Clearly not."

He stared at her, his mouth turning dry. "I've already told you. I needed a job. That was all there was going. And it was perfect for me then. We could have made it work, but you just *left* me."

She studied her shoes. "Anyway, that's all two years ago. Water under the bridge."

He breathed steadily for a few minutes, mustering the courage to ask the question that wouldn't stop eating at him. "Why did you ghost me?"

His voice came out smaller than he'd meant, and as fragile as glass. She didn't answer, and he tilted his head to see her face better.

She still didn't look at him. "What do you mean?"

"You froze me out completely… and I don't understand how we went from what we had, to *nothing,* in a day. You never answered any of my calls or messages; none of my texts. You didn't tell me where you were. I tried to ask Becky, and she wouldn't tell me and threatened to block my number if I kept asking. How could you walk away like that?"

She picked at a bit of skin at the side of her nail, not replying for several breaths. His pulse quickened. She was going to say he wasn't enough. He was *never* good enough, so why would she feel any different?

"It was the only way I could cope," she said eventually. "I was too hurt to talk to you. I thought I meant a lot to you, and then when the crunch came, you chose work instead of me. We'd been *so close,* and instead of us settling down and spending more time together, you were going to move to another country. So… I didn't answer when you called because I was too hurt. And then I didn't think I could cope with you being just a friend. Not after what we'd had. It hurt less to cut you out than to compete with work and lose."

He flinched at her words, and his breathing stalled. "Is that really how you felt?"

She chewed at her lip, nodding.

"Wow… Okay…"

"You'd made your decision, Anders, and it didn't involve me."

"It would have done if you'd *talked* to me." He scraped a hand through his hair. "I loved you so much, and you walked out of my life like I was *nothing* to you."

Her eyes widened.

"You were *never* nothing to me," she whispered. "You were *everything.*" Her breathing became broken. "But I thought, 'It doesn't matter how much you love him. It doesn't matter that you feel as if you've known him for eternity. You can't stay with him. You can't put your life on hold while he figures out if you have a future together. You have to walk away.' And it was the hardest thing I have ever done."

His brows rose. "It didn't look like it from where I was. It looked like it was really easy."

She shook her head. "No."

"Where *did* you go? Becky's?"

"Mm."

"She swore blind you weren't there."

"I know. I made her promise not to tell you."

A tear slid down her cheek, and she swatted it away, turning her head. He stared at her, his heart aching to see her cry, then, almost on reflex, he slipped his arm around her shoulders and drew her against him.

"Hey, come here."

She wiped her palms over her face, sniffing. But she didn't pull away.

It felt so right to hold her. He studied the nails of his free hand, trying to pluck up some courage, still scared of what she might say.

"So… if I was gutted that you left me, and you were gutted that I went to Oslo, what about now?"

She turned her face up to him. Tears still brightened her hazel eyes. "What about now?"

A drop of sweat trickled down his back. "Can we try again?"

She said nothing for several seconds, making his pulse quicken, then she blinked, unsmiling.

"What, until the next great job turns up?" Bitterness laced her words. "Anders, I want kids. I want stability."

"I know. And that's what I've always wanted. Academia hasn't always offered me that."

He swallowed, trying unsuccessfully to wet his mouth. His current post was only temporary.

"Is this job permanent?" she asked, arching her brows. From her tone, she knew it wasn't.

"No," he managed.

"And when it ends, will you piss off back to Oslo again?"

He gazed at her. "Not my first choice, but if I *had* to go, maybe you could come with me."

Her face fell a mile.

"No," she whispered. "Not after what happened to Amelia."

His blood turned cold, and he could have torn his tongue out. Amelia. Georgie's sister. Who had followed her boyfriend to Germany, then died in his flat from a drug overdose, less than six months later. Memories of Georgie sobbing on him on the anniversary of Amelia's death swept through his brain, and he took a long breath, appalled at himself for having forgotten.

"Anders, I'm even less sociable than Amelia." Georgie's voice came out tiny and full of pain. "If *she* couldn't cope with moving to a new country, how do you think *I* would?"

He reached across to hold her hand. "You would be fine," he said firmly. "For a start, I know for a fact that you wouldn't even smoke a joint, never mind take anything stronger. And second, I like to think I would spot if you were lonely."

From what Georgie had said, Amelia's boyfriend, Karl, certainly hadn't noticed how isolated Amelia had felt.

Tears rolled down Georgie's cheeks. He released her hand so that he could brush them away, then drew her closer to him, cradling her against his body.

"I couldn't move to Norway," she mumbled against his skin.

"Sh. Shh. I know."

He couldn't find the right words to say, so he squeezed her closer, hoping that would compensate.

They were still sitting in silence when the intercom burst into life a few minutes later. "Engineer's here. You should be moving soon."

It went dead again before either of them could respond.

Georgie eased herself away from him and scraped her hands over her face. He kept his arm around her shoulders, rubbing his thumb against the seam of her top. Banging started up above their heads, then the lift juddered to life before almost immediately stopping again. Twice the lift jolted with a scraping sound that went right to his bones. Finally, it slid gently to a halt, and the doors opened to reveal the ground floor foyer. A disembodied voice floated down the lift shaft, muffled by the lift itself.

"All okay?"

He tipped his head towards the ceiling. "Yeah. All okay. Thanks."

Georgie pulled out from under his arm and stood up, then held her hand out to him to help him up. He grabbed the top two boxes and waited for her in the foyer while she retrieved the last box. She still hadn't said anything, and he ducked into her field of view.

"Georgie? Are we okay?"

Her face was still blotchy from crying, and she sniffed. "Yeah. We're okay."

"Can we try again? Please?"

She squared her shoulders, adjusting the box. A long breath trickled out of her nose. "I don't know, Anders."

"Will you at least think about it?"

She stared at him for so long that he thought his heart would beat its way out of his chest.

"Yes. Okay. I'll think about it."

His spirit soared. "Thank you."

28

Georgia followed Anders back to his car, the box of books heavy in her arms. Neither of them had spoken since she'd said she'd think about them trying again, but Anders's expression shone.

She waited while he juggled his two boxes and opened the boot of his car, then slid her box in next to his.

"Thanks." He cocked a brow at her. "Fancy a drink before I take you back?"

"No, I'm fine, thanks," she said automatically.

His face fell, and she felt her defences rising.

"I said I would think about it. Don't push."

He blinked, then nodded. "It was just a drink."

She walked around to the passenger side of the car, her brain churning. Anders slid into the driver's seat, not looking at her, and turned the engine over.

"I'm sorry," she said softly.

He glanced across, his hand on the gear stick. "As in, sorry you just snapped at me for suggesting we go for a drink? Or sorry, but no, you don't want to try again?"

"I'm sorry I snapped." She took a steadying breath. "I'm just scared of getting hurt again, Anders."

He held her gaze for a few seconds. "That makes two of us."

She didn't know what to say.

They drove back to her flat in silence. She could smell Anders's body spray, mingled with fresh perspiration, and the scent took her right back to long evenings in Orkney with him. Times when they'd been to ceilidh dances together, struggling to learn the steps, but having a blast anyway. Evenings where they had sat on beaches while the sun still rode high in the sky, even though it was really late. Nights lying entangled in his arms.

She blinked. Hard on their heels, came other memories of crying herself to sleep. Of burying herself in work, trying to forget him. Of feeling worthless. She opened her eyes wide, trying to chase away the tears that prickled.

They reached her street, and Anders turned the car and parked at the kerb outside her flat. He shifted in his seat to look at her, and she met his eye, praying that she didn't look as close to tears as she felt. The beaming enthusiasm that had filled his face when she'd said she would think about things had been replaced with a wariness that pulled at her heart.

He peered earnestly at her. "I won't go back to Norway again. Not if it meant I couldn't be with you."

If she could be sure he was being absolutely honest with her, she would rush back into his arms. She turned away and stared through the windscreen, trying to sort her feelings into words.

"Anders, I loved you so much. And then it all fell apart, and it broke my heart. I can't go through that again."

"I know. Nor can I." His voice was low and gravelly.

She nodded. She needed to think, away from him.

"I'll see you tomorrow."

"Yep. See you tomorrow. Thanks for helping with the boxes."

She hurried out of the car, waving as he drove off, then headed into her flat.

"You're home late," said Becky, looking up from her phone as Georgia stood in the doorway to the lounge.

She shrugged out of her jacket and tossed it over the arm of the sofa, relieved that Becky was in so that she could talk to her about everything. "I got stuck in a lift with Anders."

Becky put her phone down in her lap, grinning. "You got what?"

Georgia flung herself into the chair opposite Becky. "Anders asked me to give him a hand with some of his stuff that he'd had delivered to his office. We got stuck in the lift at his department."

Becky straightened up in her seat. "Okay. And how was it, trapped in a confined space with him, for however long?"

She scratched her cheek. "Er… Hm. We ended up talking about what happened when we split up."

"In a good way?

"I don't know. Maybe…" She tailed off. "I need a glass of wine. Want one?"

"No, I'm fine, thanks."

She fetched a drink and returned to the lounge, taking up her seat again.

"Come on. Spill the beans," Becky chivvied.

She tucked her feet up under her, then told her best friend everything that had been said, but not that he'd asked if they could get back together.

"He thought he'd meant nothing to me." She fiddled with her wineglass, still upset that she'd hurt him so much.

"You cut him out of your life completely. If he hadn't rocked up to a job here, you'd *still* not be in contact. I can see why he would think that."

In fact, Becky had told her so at the time, but Georgia had ignored her.

"I didn't think he'd care."

He'd clearly cared a lot, and she gripped the stem of her wineglass tighter.

"He asked me if we could try again," she blurted out.

Becky's brows rose. "And? How do you feel about that? In your heart of hearts."

She sighed heavily. "That's the problem. My heart still loves him and is yelling, 'YES!' at me. My head sees he's still exactly the same about work: driven, ambitious, career-focused… I'm scared that we'll get back together, have an amazing time, then his current post will end, and he'll follow the work and leave me. Again."

"Or… you have an amazing time, then his current post ends, and he gets another job in Britain," Becky countered.

"There's no guarantee of that." She hesitated. "Anders blithely said I could go to Norway. Said I would be fine."

Becky gave her a reassuring smile. "You would be. Amelia had problems long before she went to Germany."

Georgia peered into her wine, swirling it until it almost breached the rim, trying not to think of her sister dying alone with a needle in her arm.

"It's alright for Anders. He's half Norwegian. He grew up in both countries; he speaks both languages. He can flit back and forth without batting an eyelid." She closed her eyes, her brain running over how she'd felt when he'd held her; how they had teased each other that morning; how her legs had barely been able to hold her up while he'd been braiding her hair. "Oh, Becks. It is *so easy* to be around him. Sometimes it's like things were, just before we got together, and everything's light and fun, and we're joking around together. And then, *bam*, I remember why we split up." She pulled out the band fastening her hair and ran her fingers through the braid, unravelling it all. "He *could* have stayed in Britain after Orkney. There was a great job going in Dig For It, and he would have been ideal. But he chose academia, even though he loves being outside, and absolutely *hates* standing up and talking in front of people. That's what really hurt. I see him with his short hair and corporate look, tying himself in knots over giving a team meeting to *eight* of us, and I just don't get it. I don't get why he chose that over leaving academia and staying with me."

"Then ask him about that," said Becky. "If that's the sticking point, talk to the man."

Georgia sipped her wine, her emotions churning. Did she believe in her heart of hearts, that when his current post finished, he wouldn't still chase after promotion and kudos in academia? He'd broken her heart once. Could she ever trust him with it again?

29

In the morning, Anders pulled up outside Georgia's door, his mind churning. His mind had churned all night, in fact, going over and over everything. Would she have thought about them trying again and decided against it? She'd been so upset in the lift. He'd never meant to hurt her, but she never gave him an opportunity to talk; to explain why he'd applied for the job. Would she give him a second chance? How on earth was he going to get through the rest of the dig if she said no?

She emerged from her door clutching a flask. She smiled as she got in the car, but he couldn't quite read the meaning behind it.

"Morning," she said brightly. "Don't take this the wrong way, but you look knackered. Maybe I should have made two flasks of coffee."

He scratched his head. "Yeah. I didn't sleep well."

Her smile dimmed, and she averted her gaze. He put the car in gear and pulled away, his heart sinking.

Throughout the drive, she stared straight out of the windscreen, her fingers twisting around one another. He itched to ask her about what was happening between them, but had enough sense not to. If she'd decided she *would* give him a second chance, she'd tell him. In fairness to her, if she'd decided she wouldn't, she'd also talk to him.

"Will you finish up that trench over the weaving hut today?" she said eventually.

"I don't think so. It definitely looks like it burned down while it was still in use, by the way. All of the loom weights I've found were sandwiched between two layers of burned planking."

"Wall and floor," she murmured. "I wonder why that was

burned, but the main hall wasn't."

"I'm not sure we'll ever know. Accident, probably. They had thatched roofs. It would have been a common hazard for them to catch fire."

They fell back into silence until they arrived at the dig site. There, she helped him to set up, ready for the day ahead. Once everything was done, she waved the Thermos at him. He nodded, standing in the middle of the refreshments tent so that his head didn't skim the canvas roof, his guts knotting. She poured out two steaming mugs of coffee and handed one across, then stood next to him, sipping at her drink. He waited.

"I'm sorry I hurt you so much," she said at last. "I should have answered your calls and messages."

She still hadn't looked at him. He wasn't sure what to say. 'It's okay'? Except, it really hadn't been okay. *He* hadn't been okay. He peered into his coffee, but no inspiration sprang forth.

Finally, she raised her head to him. "Can you forgive me?"

He blinked slowly. "Yes. But don't *ever* do that to me again."

"I won't." Her face crumpled a little.

She drank some more of her coffee, staring at her toes, her body taut. He knew better than to press her. Just as she opened her mouth, there was the sound of a car pulling up in the field outside.

"Never mind," she said, almost too quietly for him to hear.

The four members of the Dig For It team poured in, chatting noisily, and the moment was shattered. She flashed him a weak smile, then studied her shoes again.

The Dig For It team clattered about making coffees. Hard on their heels came the university group and the volunteers, and the tent filled with people and noise. Anders stole another look at Georgie, but she was staring into her mug, her posture tight.

His heart sank. That wasn't the body language of someone excited to try again. That was the body language of someone rehearsing how to say no.

* * *

By late afternoon, Anders was more than ready to leave the site. Shona had been helping Georgie all day in the finds tent again, packing up objects ready for them to be transferred to storage, giving him zero chance to talk to Georgie on her own. He'd spent most of the day in the trench over the weaving hut, leaving him plenty of time to think. Some days, spending an entire day with only his thoughts for company wasn't a bonus. Today was one of those days.

"You were never nothing to me." That's what she'd said. He'd been back and forth over that exchange for hours, but he was no closer to knowing what she wanted.

He went into the finds tent to pack away his desk. Georgie and Shona had just finished processing the final set of finds, and a small stack of boxes sat on the ground next to them.

Georgie stretched her back, smiling at him. "Done! Oh, thank goodness it's Friday!"

"Time for the team talk?" asked Shona, straightening up and catching his eye.

His heart sank, but he nodded. Georgie rolled her eyes at him, giving him a soft look.

"Come on. The sooner you start, the sooner it's over," she murmured to him.

The team had assembled in the refreshments tent, and all heads turned expectantly towards him when he went in, making his stomach clench even further. He braced himself and stood in the middle of the group.

"Well, guys. I think we might have found a settlement," he said, forcing himself to smile through his nerves.

Whoops and cheers went up, and Georgie caught his eye, winking at him. His heart fluttered, and not from the stress of having to talk to the group.

"So, because we might have found a settlement…" He paused, while a couple of them cheered again. "If anyone wants to come to the pub, the first round is on me." He raised his brows at the group. "Blacksmith's Arms? Seven?"

Most of them nodded, but Denise, a woman from the Dig For It team, shook her head. "Thanks for the offer, but I've two small kids I need to get back to. Maybe another time?"

Anders's face crumpled. "Oh, Denise, I'm sorry. I forgot you had a young family."

She flapped a hand. "Don't be sorry. No offence to anyone, but I've spent all day with you. I don't need to see you tonight."

They all laughed. The Dig For It team drifted towards Bob's car, the three from the uni made their way towards Sam's, and the volunteers packed up and headed off, leaving Anders and Georgie as the only ones on the site. They strolled over to the finds tent to retrieve the boxes, and he faced her, yearning to ask her if she'd made a decision over them yet.

She twitched her shoulders, her eyes steady on him. "Stop looking at me like that, Anders. I'm still thinking.

He held his hands up. "I didn't say a word!"

She picked up the nearest box. "You didn't have to. I know you too well. Come on. Let's get all this in your car."

He grabbed the other crates and tailed her out of the tent.

As he drove them to the Dig For It storage unit, his brain kept chipping at him, like there were two people in there, arguing it out.

She hasn't said no yet… True, but surely if it was a yes, she'd have said so by now. It must be a no and she's just figuring out how to couch it… No, she's never shied away from tough decisions, so maybe it's a yes. I mean, she's pretty relaxed around you now. It's not like the permafrost there was when you first saw each other again…

"Anders, will you stop already?" she said, snapping him out of it.

"What?" He glanced across, eyes wide.

"I can *hear* your brain whirring. Do you still never have a quiet head?"

He snorted a laugh. "No."

One night in Orkney, they'd lain in bed together, and he'd asked her if she had an internal monologue. It turned out she didn't. Thoughts were just thoughts. They weren't vocalised. She didn't have an almost incessant chatter going on in her head. She'd been amazed, and a little aghast, when he'd told her it was never quiet in his head. That there was a non-stop voice chirruping away. The only time it really stopped was if he had a song in his head, though if he was particularly stressed, the chatter would play out over the top of the song.

"So, what are you churning about? Because you're looking like it's even noisier in there than normal."

He grinned. "Oh… A million things at the moment. Is it really a settlement? How much should we dig? Should we be conservative and come back another season? Should I extend the team? What if we found graves? You. How does your hair grow like that? If you ever shaved your head like Becky did, how would it grow back? Have we got enough crates for the finds? Where can I get more if we need them?" He looked across at her. "That's actually just the tip of the iceberg. That only covers some of what my brain is thinking about." The rest of the iceberg was all about them, but he kept that to himself.

She blinked at him, her mouth slightly open. "How do you sleep?"

He laughed. "Badly, often."

They'd arrived at the stores, and he parked up. She got out and swiped her access card while he unloaded boxes, then Mick lumbered around from behind his desk to hold the door open until they had everything inside.

"Hi, Mick. How are things?" she said.

"Oh, all grand, thanks. This all from the Mortensen dig?"

Georgie chuckled. "Yep. Mick, meet Anders. He's the Mortensen of The Mortensen Dig."

"Oh, sorry! I thought it was someone else entirely who was running the dig. An old guy."

Anders shook his head. "No. I think you're thinking of my father."

"Ah, maybe. Sorry. Right, Georgia, shall I get all these logged in and processed for you? It might not be tonight. I'm about ready to go home."

"Just put them somewhere safe and get to them when you can. There's paperwork in each crate."

"Always is with you. Is it looking good? The site?"

"So far, so good. We might be keeping you busy."

She finished signing in all the finds, then bade good evening to Mick, who mock-saluted her.

As they walked back to his car, she bumped Anders with her shoulder. "Sorry."

He looked down. "What for?"

"Mick, thinking the Mortensen must be your father."

"Oh. Don't worry. I'm used to that."

"Still."

He shrugged. If he got too upset about it every time it happened, he'd be permanently miserable.

He drove her back to her place and parked up, still hoping that she would talk to him; say that she wanted to try again.

She swivelled in her seat to face him, and he held his breath.

"I don't know how many of the volunteers will come tonight," she said.

He blinked, blindsided, his brain having been rehearsing reactions to her saying no to him. "Um, no. Probably not. Not sure The Blacksmith's Arms is their kind of pub."

Most of the volunteers that week were undergraduates getting a bit of dig experience, who would think The Blacksmith's Arms was a pub more suitable for their parents, even though it could be lively at times. The couple of retirees who came and helped were about as likely to come to the pub as they were to go water-skiing.

"Well, at least buying a first round won't bankrupt you."

"True. Did you want me to come and pick you up?"

She scrunched her face. "You're not driving, are you?"

He laughed. "I meant I would walk there with you."

"Oh. No, I'll be fine, thanks. I'll see you there."

She held his gaze for a moment, smiling, and making hope bloom in his chest. Was she going to say yes, after all? His heart rate climbed. "Yeah, see you at the pub."

30

Georgia's feet slowed as she approached the pub. She'd spent all day thinking about her and Anders, and she knew he'd be hoping for *some* kind of sign from her tonight, one way or another. The problem was, she was still torn. So much of her wanted to say 'yes' and them get back together, but a little voice in her head kept sounding a warning alarm she couldn't ignore. She found she'd reached the pub entrance without even getting close to deciding what to do, and squared her shoulders.

Let's just see how the evening goes.

She poked her head around the door, trying to spot where everyone was. Just as she located the group clustered in a corner next to the window, Anders waved at her, smiling.

"Over here. Come and grab a seat. The first round is on me, so what are you having?" He stood up as she joined the group, his long legs stepping out into a space next to the chairs.

She put out a hand to steady him. "I'll have a long vodka, if you're paying. Thanks."

He grinned at her and headed towards the bar. She tried not to admire his backside in the jeans he wore and focused on finding a space to sit. The group had assembled around a long table with a bench along the window side and a handful of seats on the other. Patrick shuffled along the bench to give her space to sit at the end next to him. Shona sat on the other side of Patrick, with Sam next to her. Georgia smiled to herself that Sophie had nabbed the seat next to Anders. Scott, from Dig For It, had the last chair. Bob, also from Dig For It, had said he'd be there, but wasn't yet. Entirely as expected, none of the student volunteers had come, and nor had the older couple.

Most of the group had gone home and changed into clean

jeans and t-shirts, like Georgia had. Only Sophie had pushed the boat out, now sporting a full face of make-up and a low-cut top over a straight, knee-length skirt that was riding up a little. It had caught Patrick's eye, at least.

Anders returned with her drink and sat again, smiling across at her. Almost immediately, he was back on his feet to get Bob a drink. Bob crammed himself in on the end of the bench next to Sam. A similar age to Shona, he wasn't known for being sociable. Georgia was a little surprised he'd come to the pub, if she was being honest.

Anders raised his glass to everyone. "Cheers!"

"*Skål*," she said, catching his eye. His grin widened. Her gaze drifted over the soft blue, long-sleeved t-shirt he wore that hugged him in the right places and emphasised his eyes. After three weeks of not shaving, his stubble was making a concerted effort to be a beard, and his hair was undoubtedly too long for his father's approval. Georgia thought Anders looked much more himself now that the neatness had blurred somewhat.

She dragged her attention away from him and focused on the surrounding conversation. The group chatted excitedly about the finds and the possibility that they had found a complete Anglo-Scandinavian settlement.

"It would be an amazing discovery, Anders," said Sophie, leaning in towards him, and showing more cleavage than necessary. "That would *really* get your name out there."

Anders's gaze rested on her chest for a fraction of a second, then he looked across at Georgia, a blush pinking his cheeks. "It's not just *me* who's finding it. It's the whole team. And we wouldn't have been digging there at all if it wasn't for Dig For It."

"Yeah, but you're *leading* the dig, Anders."

Georgia's patience thinned to nothing. "Oh, for goodness' sake, Sophie, could you at least *try* to pronounce his name right?"

Sophie blinked, her face falling. Anders gave Georgia an admonishing look, and she shrugged at him, brows arched.

"How should I be saying it?" Sophie asked quietly.

"More like Ond-esh, but it's fine. I answer to most versions." He gave Georgia a pointed look. "Including Einar once."

Georgia let her gaze drop. If she was being honest with

herself, she was less bothered by the fact that Sophie never pronounced his name correctly, and more by her lack of appreciation for the Dig For It team. And that Sophie was so interested in Anders. *And* that Anders had clearly just checked out her cleavage.

Something pressed on her foot, and she looked up. Anders flicked his brows up at her.

"*Beklager,*" she mouthed. Sorry.

He smiled.

"Anders, can I get you another drink?" asked Sophie.

Georgia's lips twitched. Her pronunciation was better, but still not quite right.

"Er, I'm in a round with Georgia," he said, surprising her. When had they agreed that?

She pointed at his empty pint glass. "My shout then, since you got the first. What are you drinking?"

"I'll come up to the bar with you."

Sophie's lips thinned even further.

"Come in a round with me and Sam," offered Patrick, before looking over to the Dig For It team. "Is that okay? That would leave you three in a round together."

They all nodded, and that was that.

Georgia stood up, and Anders joined her. He stood close behind her at the bar, then leaned down to murmur in her ear, his breath tickling her skin.

"Give Sophie a break. She's trying."

She turned slightly so she could see his face. "Oh, she's *very* trying, believe me! Considering she's wanting to get into your bed, the least she could do is get your name right."

"She's not getting into my bed. Chill."

The heat of his body warmed her, making her heart race. "She could be nicer about the Dig For It team, too. We found the site."

He canted his head. "Okay, I agree with you on that."

She tried to concentrate on why they'd come up to the bar. "What are you drinking?"

"Double whisky, if you're buying." Her eyes widened, making him laugh. "Just a beer is fine!"

"I'll get you a double whisky, if that's what you want."

"Nah. It's too early, and I'm not stressed enough for whisky. What have they got on tap?"

He leaned around her to scan the pumps, his chest brushing her shoulder. As he did so, a crowd of rowdy young men poured into the pub, jostling him. He caught Georgia around the waist, pinning her firmly against his body while he put a hand out to brace them against the bar. The barrage of people bumped him again, and he gripped her tighter. A chorus of "Sorry, mate," flew up around them, then the crowd thinned.

Anders suddenly made a smacking sound with his mouth, along with, "Ugh!"

"What?" She turned her face up to him, looking over her shoulder.

"I just got a mouthful of your hair."

She laughed. "Sorry! Maybe I should get you to braid it again."

He squeezed her closer, his gaze intense, and she automatically leaned back into him. For a moment, she thought he was going to kiss her, but he just blew on the end of her nose.

"So, are you buying me a pint, or what?" he said, his eyes still locked on hers, making her heart go into triple-time.

"What do you want?" Her voice came out more throatily than she'd meant.

He tore his eyes away to look at the pumps. "Er, the Black Sheep they have on tap. Thanks."

He still had his arm around her waist, holding her spine tight against his torso, even though the rowdy group had dispersed. His thumb rubbed the bottom of her ribs, the way he often had when they were together. Did he even realise he was doing it? She didn't mind.

The barman took her order, and Anders eased away from her to pick up the pint. She missed the contact immediately. She paid, then followed Anders back to the table.

"Patrick? Swap seats?" said Anders, standing next to his chair. "I want to talk to Georgia about something. Thanks!"

Patrick looked all too happy to trade places, given that it meant he was then sitting next to Sophie. Sophie looked less enamoured with the move. Anders indicated to Georgia to move down the bench so that he sat on the end. She tucked in next to

Shona and leaned forward to give him more space.

"Okay?" he said, frowning.

"Yeah. Your shoulders are too big."

He smirked. "You've never complained about them before." He leaned around the back of her. "Shona, are you okay if I stretch my arm along the back here?"

Shona shrugged. He turned slightly and rested his arm along the back of the seating, then nodded at Georgia to lean back.

"Better? Because if not and you make me move down to fit my shoulders in, I'll only have one butt cheek on the bench."

She smirked. "Yeah. You're fine."

The evening passed in a buzz of conversation and laughter. At some point, Georgia realised Anders had his arm resting on her shoulder, rather than along the back of the seat, but she couldn't remember when the change had occurred. His arm wasn't exactly *around* her. More that it had slipped down to lie along her shoulders. She wasn't entirely sure that Anders had even noticed he'd done it.

The group settled into a couple of conversations. Sophie had abandoned trying to chat up Anders and seemed engrossed in what Patrick was saying to her. The rest were discussing previous projects. As ever, Anders listened intently and said little, though it would be a close call whether he or Bob was the quieter.

After several drinks in, she was feeling a little fuzzy around the edges. When Shona checked her watch and announced she ought to go, Georgia tilted her head to Anders.

"I'm probably going to head off, too."

"Walk you home?" he offered.

"Yeah. Thanks."

He glanced past her. "Shona, how are you getting back?"

She grinned. "Scott and Bob are walking with me. I'm in the same direction as them."

"Great. Patrick? Sam? I'm going to walk Georgie home. Can one of you make sure Sophie gets home safely, please?"

"Sure."

The Dig For It group and Anders all got to their feet. As she stood, Georgia caught her foot against the table leg, lost her balance, and pitched towards Anders, needing to plant her palms flat against his chest to brace herself. He sniggered.

"Are you a little unsteady on your feet there, Georgie?"

She poked him in the belly, not deigning to answer, and he laughed, his eyes crinkling.

They drifted out of the pub, saying their goodbyes to Sam, Patrick, and Sophie. The Dig For It team waved and set off, leaving Georgia standing next to Anders. He offered her the crook of his arm and she slipped her hand into it.

"I've just remembered that my place is in the opposite direction to yours. You should have left one of the others to walk me back," she said.

"It's fine. We're not exactly miles apart, and I enjoy your company."

They walked slowly, not really talking. Georgia wished she'd had a couple of drinks fewer than she had, as she'd shifted beyond pleasantly merry and was needing Anders's arm to keep herself steady.

About halfway to her flat, Anders glanced down at her. "One of the many things I've always loved about you is the fact you don't have the urge to fill silences."

She laughed, squeezing his arm. "Ditto."

They reached her house, and she eased her hand away from his arm and turned to face him. "This is me."

He chuckled. "Yeah. I know."

He pulled her into a deep hug, tugging her close to him. He was so familiar, and she fitted against his body as if she was meant to be there. She cuddled in, breathing in the smell of his soap and warm skin, her face buried against his broad chest. His palm caressed her back, his other hand fussed with her hair at the nape of her neck. He drew away slightly, dropping his hands down to lock together at the small of her back, then he leaned in and planted a kiss on her lips, surprising her. He brushed the end of his nose against hers, then kissed her again more tenderly, his lips soft against hers, his beard a little tickly against her skin. Slowly, he straightened, his arms still around her, his breath light on her skin. She stared at him, her breathing quickening.

"Goodnight, Georgie."

Her heart fluttered. "Mm. Goodnight."

She wondered if he was going to kiss her again. She would have kissed him, except he was too tall, and she couldn't reach. She *wanted* him to kiss her again, but he didn't.

He held on to her for another moment, his gaze intense. "*Jeg elsker deg,*" he said, his voice little more than a breath. Then he tipped his face upwards, closing his eyes. He squeezed her lightly and pulled away, swallowing.

She gazed hungrily at him, yearning to feel his arms around her and his lips on hers again. She didn't want him to leave, but before she could do anything, he turned on his heel and hurried away.

"Anders?"

He turned, his feet hesitating, then he walked backwards, blowing a kiss to her. He reached the end of her road, blew her another kiss, then turned again, striding off and out of sight.

She touched her fingers to her lips, wishing she wasn't so tipsy and could think a little straighter, but alcohol swirled in her brain. She gave up trying to analyse what on earth was happening between them and headed into the flat. She could think about it all the following day.

31

Sun filtering in through the curtains woke Anders. He squinted at the light, then groaned and closed his eyes. His mind produced memories of the previous night with a flourish, and he groaned harder.

He shouldn't have kissed her.

He folded his arms across his face, covering his eyes. He'd done it because he was a little drunk, and because he loved her, and because it had felt *right,* but had he overstepped the mark?

She hadn't *seemed* like she'd minded.

He sucked in a long breath. What if she'd just been as tipsy as him and in the cold light of day would regret it?

"Jeg elsker deg."

He sighed hard. He *did* love her, but should he have said that?

He threw the covers back and pulled on his running kit. Downstairs, he grabbed a piece of toast and a glass of orange juice, then headed out the door, needing to run hard enough that he couldn't think too much.

Ten fierce kilometres later, his fitness watch beeped at him, reminding him not to spend the entire morning running. He hauled air, his legs aching, and turned on to his road. The run hadn't helped to clear his head. If anything, he was in more turmoil than when he set off.

As he ran down his road, a shock of bright blonde hair caught his eye. Georgie was walking towards him. His feet stumbled to a halt, and he stopped his watch, panting hard.

"Hi."

She smiled. "Hi. Good run?"

"Um. Hard."

Her gaze travelled over him, making him acutely aware of the dark sweat patches all over his top.

"I came out for a walk, then wondered if you might want to join me," she said, still eyeing his t-shirt. "Sorry. I maybe should have texted, but I was literally passing the end of your road, so took a punt."

"Um. Sure. I need a shower first!"

"Er, yeah! Want me to go away and come back?"

"No, come in and wait for me in the house."

She fell into step next to him, and they walked down to his house.

"Would you like to have lunch?" he blurted out as they reached his door.

Her smile dazzled him. "That would be lovely. Thanks."

He opened the door and kicked off his trainers, his brain whirling. Georgie balanced precariously, a hand braced against the wall, while she took her boots off.

"Did you want to grab a coffee or something while I get a shower?" he said, picking up his shoes and tossing them into a plastic box in the hall.

He showed her through to the kitchen at the back of his house, and pointed out where coffee and mugs and spoons were. She shooed him away.

"Don't take this the wrong way, Anders, but you need a shower more than you need to tell me how to make coffee."

He laughed hard. "Okay, okay! I'm going."

He dashed upstairs to have a swift shower.

As he stood under the water, his brain worried over why she was there; why she wanted to go for a walk. Was she about to tell him that there was no chance of them getting back together? Had she only been relaxed around him at the pub because she was tipsy?

But then, she'd looked happy at the idea of lunch, so…

He didn't want to get his hopes up.

He turned the water off, towelled himself down, and found some clean jeans and a light top. Dressed, he hurried downstairs to the kitchen, half expecting Georgie to be in there, but the room was empty. He grabbed a glass of water and found Georgie walking around his lounge, looking at the books on his shelves, a mug of coffee in her hands.

"That was quick," she said, smiling up at him. "Are these what we got from your office the other day?" She tilted her head towards the books.

"Some of them. There are more upstairs. Did you want to sit down; finish your coffee?"

She perched on the sofa, jiggling one foot. He sat on the chair opposite her and fiddled with his glass of water, his skin prickly.

"Nice place," she said, breaking into his thoughts. "You must be on better money than me."

"I don't have an answer for that," he said, half laughing. "I mean, what can I say that isn't crass?"

"You do the very British thing of saying, 'Oh, this dump? It *looks* nice, but really, it's completely rat-infested and falling apart' or something similar."

He rubbed his nose, smiling. "I think I'm too Norwegian for that."

"Yeah, you are." She grinned at him. "Okay. I've finished my coffee. Thank you."

He downed the remains of his water, then held his hand out for her mug, and took things through to the kitchen. She waited for him in the hall while he grabbed a jacket and some boots.

Outside, he debated with himself over offering her an arm, deciding against it in the end. They strolled to the pub mostly in silence, and he sneaked a peek at her as they walked. She definitely looked like she had something on her mind that she needed to say, and his stomach knotted again.

At the pub, she finally looked up at him. "Is it too cold to sit outside? The sun's nice, and it looks pretty packed inside."

He scanned the wooden picnic benches on the grass outside the pub. "I think that one's pretty sheltered. Want to have a drink first and see? If it's too cold, we can go in."

Georgie sat at the bench, tugging the cuffs of her jacket down over her hands.

"What do you want to drink?" he asked, still standing.

"Lime and soda? My head's still a bit muzzy after last night."

He left her in the sunshine and fetched their drinks and a couple of menus, then slid on to the bench opposite her. He clinked his glass against hers. "*Skål.*"

"*Skål.*"

She took a gulp of her drink, then pulled the menu towards her and studied it. She chose her food, and he took the menus back in and put the order in. When he returned to the table, she smiled brightly, knotting her fingers. He swung his legs over the end of the bench and faced her, itching to hold her hands.

"Anders, can I talk to you about something?"

"You can always talk to me. You don't need to ask permission." He smiled across at her, but his stomach had a thousand butterflies beating their wings inside it. From her face, it looked as if it was going to be a 'letting him down gently' talk.

"I'm half waiting for Sophie to pop up," she said, picking at the corner of a scruffy beer mat.

"If Sophie comes bouncing over today, I will personally throttle her."

She laughed, easing the tension a fraction. "I think after you sat with your arm around me last night, she might have got the message that you're not interested."

He breathed carefully. "Are you mad at me for that?"

"No." A smile tweaked one side of her mouth. "I don't think you'd even realised you'd done it, had you?"

He shook his head. "I was a little drunk. Sorry."

She shrugged, then hauled in a deep breath and set her shoulders. He braced himself.

"Anders, I'm sorry. I should have returned your calls. I should have talked to you after I left… It wouldn't have changed the outcome… we would still have split up… but it would have been fairer to you. I never meant for you to feel that you hadn't been important to me; that our relationship wasn't amazing. It was. You were. I loved you more than I have ever loved anyone else."

She paused again to take a breath. His heart pounded at her words, but he was sure she was winding herself up to saying no to a second chance.

"I sense there's a 'but' coming," he said softly. "You loved me, but… You don't want to try again, do you?"

She raised her head to look at him, and tension gripped his shoulders and back.

"Oh, this is so difficult," she whispered. "Anders, I still have so many feelings for you. I *really* want it to work between us, but I don't understand why you left me for a job in academia. You *hate* speaking to a group, even a small group you know. I mean, look at you on this dig! Every morning, and every evening, I watch you sweat and tense up, and look as if you'd rather die than have to stand up and say even a few sentences. And I see you digging in a trench, and you are absolutely in your element. You *love* being outdoors. You *love* excavating. So why did you choose a desk job in Oslo? I just don't get it."

The green in her eyes was vivid with emotion.

"I told you. It was all there was."

"That's just not true, Anders! There was a job at Dig For It. Stacy's job. You didn't *have* to go to Oslo." She closed her eyes, her face screwed up as if in pain. "I understood you choosing post-doc positions after your PhD, because they were still mostly fieldwork. And I know that you're always living in this massive shadow of your father. But Anders, he will *never* be happy with you. You could win a Nobel prize for archaeology, and he would still sniff and turn his mouth down and say it wasn't as prestigious as his paper in whatever journal. He would say that someone with a Nobel prize should know how to use a razor and get a haircut. *Why* do you care so much about what he says?"

Her words landed like physical blows, and his breathing grew jagged.

"Not to diminish your point, but there isn't a Nobel prize for archaeology."

"Don't," she snapped. "Just don't. Stop running away from answering me."

His gaze spun out over the top of her head. "I don't know." His voice came out strangled. "I don't know why I care so much about what he thinks of me. Or why I spend so much of my time and energy trying to live up to his impossible standards." He rested his cheek on his fist, looking at her. "I didn't apply for the job at Dig For It entirely because of how he would react. It would have been yet another example of me not being good enough. 'Only good enough for a commercial job.' That's what he would have said."

"Is that what you think? That a commercial job is vastly inferior to academia? Do you think that *I'm* only good enough for a commercial job?" Her words were full of sharp edges and pain.

"No. Not at all. You're the smartest person I know. Smarter than my father! Most certainly *far* smarter than me." He sipped his drink, needing to wet his throat. "The job in Oslo seemed perfect in so many ways. It was only ever for two years, and I thought I could juggle it with still seeing you. I saw it as a stepping stone to a permanent position in academia, and that once I had that, I could settle down, have kids. Stop running on the treadmill. I've spent so much of my life going back and forth to Norway, it doesn't feel like a big thing. I only realised it would be a huge thing for you after you left me. I was going to turn the job down; stay in the UK. But then, you never picked up, and you never replied, and I left because being in the same country as you and not being with you would have killed me. I thought I'd meant nothing to you."

Tears nipped at his eyes. This was the sticking point. His chest tightened, and his breathing shuddered.

She mimicked his pose, leaning her cheek on her knuckles, but her focus was on the side of the pub building.

"Talk to me," he murmured. "Please?"

Her gaze sidled back to him. "I'm scared of getting hurt again. I'm worried that we'll get back together and then some amazing project will come along, and you'll put me second again. Time is ticking, and I want kids, and if it's *never* going to work out properly between us, then I'd be better off cutting my losses and starting somewhere else."

His guts churned at the idea of her having kids with someone else.

"I won't put you second again. I promise. I lost you once. I *never* want to lose you again." He focused on her eyes, studying the flecks of green in them. She was so beautiful. "Georgie, I love you. *Please,* can we try again?"

She turned her head away, and he held his breath. It felt like an eternity before she looked at him again.

"I love you too. But I swear, Anders, you hurt me again, and I will hate you. There's no third chance."

The iron bands around his chest disappeared, and he grinned at her, his heart bursting. He reached across the slats of the table to hold her hand. "I promise."

32

Georgia squeezed his hand back across the picnic table, praying that she'd made the right decision. It felt so *right* to be around him. When he'd pulled her against him at the pub the night before, she could have stayed with him like that all evening. And when he'd hugged her outside her house, she'd felt completely at home in his arms.

Their food arrived, and he slid his hand free from hers. "God, I'm ravenous! This looks great." He glanced up. "Are you still warm enough?"

She smiled. "Mm."

He held her gaze, radiating happiness, settling her nerves a little.

She picked up her cutlery. "*Bon appétit.*"

"*Håper det smaker godt,*" he countered, making her laugh.

Over the meal, she studied him. The tension that had stalked him since that first meeting in the seminar room seemed to have lifted off his shoulders. Each time he caught her eye across the table, his face lit up, and the smile-lines around his eyes deepened. She'd always loved his smile. It was wide and open, and always made her think he was filled with sunshine that was bursting to get out of him.

He had on a grey-blue top that made his eyes look less blue than usual. She preferred the long-sleeved t-shirt he'd worn the night before, that had made his eyes look like a summer sky.

They chatted lightly as they ate, Anders slowly loosening up enough to talk about being lonely in Oslo.

"The job was fine." He paused, clearly planning his words. "My friends had all moved on with their lives, which was hard. They were married, or had kids, or both. And I was single. Our lives didn't have much in common, and so I threw myself into work. And funnily enough, that's not great for meeting people you don't already know."

"Was there no one?"

Half of her didn't want to know, but her curiosity had won.

He shook his head softly. "No. Not really. A friend tried to fix me up a few times, but it was hopeless. *I* was hopeless. None of them ever wanted to see me again." He laughed, self-consciously. "It turns out that dates expect you to have witty repartee. Or at least *some* ability to make small talk for five minutes. Apparently, sitting there saying almost nothing isn't the way to a woman's heart." He rubbed his eye, then rested his chin against his knuckles. "What about you? When I first saw you in that meeting, I wondered if you'd be married with kids by now."

"No. You were a hard act to follow." She shrugged lightly. "There was one guy for a little while, but… it wasn't right. Becky kept sending me off on blind dates, and they were all terrible."

He chuffed a laugh.

She finished as much of her meal as she wanted and put her cutlery together.

"Are you done with that?" he said, eyeing her plate.

"Anders! You are still the biggest Labrador! Yes, I'm done. Feel free to finish up what I've left."

He grinned at her and swapped their plates over. She shook her head at him. He'd always wolfed down food like he was about to starve, but always burned it all off. He probably ate twice as many calories a day as she did, but never gained an ounce.

"Mm. This is good," he said, his mouth full.

"You know, if your metabolism was like any normal person's, and you weren't a human blast furnace, you'd be the size of a house."

He chuckled, shovelling up another forkful.

She waited until he'd cleared her plate, then caught his eye. "Do you still want to go for a walk?"

He smiled. "Sure."

She remembered the state he'd been in when he'd finished his run. "Oh. How far did you run this morning?"

"Ten K. But I'm fine."

He stood next to the table, waiting for her to climb out from the picnic bench, then slipped his arm around her shoulders. She automatically tucked her hand into the back pocket of his jeans. It was what she'd always done when they were together before. His waist was a fraction too high for comfort, and anyway, she'd always quite enjoyed having her hand where it was.

She almost took her hand straight back out again. They were starting again, not picking up where they'd left off. Anders squeezed her shoulders and dropped a soft kiss on to the top of her head.

"I'd almost forgotten you used to do that."

"Do you mind?"

He snorted. "Do I mind your hand on my arse? No." He pulled her closer. "Where did you want to go?"

"There's a beautiful walk along the old railway line," she said, tilting her head up to him.

"Sounds good."

She leaned against him to get him walking in the right direction, and they headed up the path to the disused viaduct. There, Georgia propped her arms on the parapet, drinking in the view. Anders rested his weight against her, his chest against her back, his arms wrapping around her shoulders. She reached up and held his forearms, relishing the solid feel of him against her. As ever, he radiated heat, his body warm against her. He smelled of washing powder and the woody body spray he wore. She closed her eyes, deep contentment bursting from her core and seeping out to fill every part of her. His lips brushed the side of her head, and she turned in his arms, settling her back against the stone, her face tipped up towards his, her palms resting lightly against his broad chest.

He dipped his head and kissed her, taking his time. A tingle went from her lips right through her entire body, leaving her insides fizzy, and she reached up a hand to tangle her fingers in his hair.

He drew back slowly, his gaze boring into her. "Oh, Georgie, I have missed you *so much*."

She drew his face closer so that she could kiss him, and he rested his hips against her, pressing her gently against the parapet.

"Is my beard scratchy? I can shave if you want."

She smiled. "No. It's gone beyond the scratchy stage now, and anyway, I prefer the slightly wild look to the polished one."

"Wild? Okay."

She fluffed her fingers through his hair at the back of his head. "Yeah. Wild. If this gets much longer, it'll go curly."

"My hair's wavy, not curly. *Your* hair is curly!"

"Mm. You keep telling yourself that, Anders." She coiled her finger around the wayward lock at the front. "*This* is beyond wavy."

"Hmm."

His lips touched hers again, making her groan softly and pull him closer.

A cyclist rattled past them on the path, muttering, "Oh, get a room!" and both of them burst out laughing. Anders pressed his lips to hers again, then pulled back, breathing deeply.

"I could kiss you all afternoon," he murmured.

A thrill ran through her at the idea. "That sounds like a plan. Shall we walk back to yours?"

* * *

They didn't manage to spend the entire afternoon kissing, after all. Georgie offered to make dinner for them both, but Anders had almost zero food in the house, so after the walk along the viaduct, they'd ended up strolling around a supermarket, pushing a trolley together like an old married couple. To Anders, it had felt both perfectly normal and utterly weird. Normal, because he was so comfortable around her, and they'd done grocery shopping together umpteen times before; weird because this wasn't how he'd imagined any 'first date' with her would have gone when he'd been hoping they would get back together again.

She'd made an amazing pasta dish, but if he was being totally honest, she'd made the same amount that she'd have made for her and Becky, and he could have done with at least half a plate more. He wouldn't say anything, though.

The meal over, he stacked the dishwasher, then nodded to Georgia to go through to the sitting room. He folded himself into the corner of the sofa, and she leaned back into him.

"Thank you for making dinner," he murmured. "I'd almost forgotten what a great cook you are."

"Did you want me to tie my hair back?" she said, sweeping some of it over her shoulder and out of his way.

Her hair still tickled his face, but he didn't really mind. He smoothed a stray lock down and tucked his arms around her. "No, you're okay." His thumb caressed the border of her ribs. "I missed you so much when I went to Oslo."

Tightness crept into her shoulders, and he swallowed, suddenly feeling awkward. He shouldn't have mentioned Oslo.

"Can we take things slowly? Please?" she blurted out in a rush.

He nodded, though she probably couldn't see.

"I feel *so* comfortable around you, Anders, and it would be too easy to go straight back to where we were, but that was two years ago."

"It's okay. I know what you mean. From the very first day I met you, I've felt like I've known you forever. Now that's a hundred times more. We can take things as slowly as you want."

She wriggled around so that she could see his face, and pressed her lips to his. "Thank you. What was it you always used to call me?"

"A Norwegian word?"

"Mm."

He smiled. "*Elskling*… Darling. Sweetheart."

She screwed her nose up. "See, *elskling* sounds lovely. Darling and sweetheart sound rubbish and a bit patronising."

He laughed, adjusting her in his arms so that her shoulder didn't dig in to him, then smoothing her hair down again.

"It's in your face, isn't it?" she said, unsuccessfully trying to move her mass of curls out of the way.

"It's just a bit tickly. Stretch out with me?"

They both shuffled about until Anders lay on his back along the length of the sofa, with Georgie stretched out on top of him. He rested one hand lightly on her bottom, his other arm around her shoulders.

"Am I heavy?" she asked.

He snorted. "No."

She pulled his top free from the waistband of his trousers and slipped her hand underneath.

"Mm. I've missed the fur," she murmured, teasing her fingers through the hair on his chest.

"Fur? I'm not *that* hairy!"

She wriggled her nose. "No, I guess you're not really. Perfect amount."

His fingers traced patterns over her shoulder, while his brain filled with memories. The feel of her fingertips on his skin sent ripples of electricity through him, and his body didn't seem to have got the memo about them taking things slowly. He tried not to think about how much he wanted her, with the exact opposite result.

She raised her head to peer at him. "Why are you so tense suddenly? Oh… I recognise that look in your eyes."

He groaned lightly. "Mm. My head is saying take it slowly. My body is saying take you to bed."

She smiled, then leaned in to kiss him.

"Wonderful… but not helping," he murmured when she finally moved back.

She pressed her hip into him, her eyes mischievous.

"Oh, that's *definitely* not helping," he said.

He shifted her to the side, returning her smirk, then kissed her languidly. She tangled her fingers in his hair, making soft, happy noises that made his pulse quicken.

"Well, if I'm *not* taking you to bed, I suppose I'd better take you home," he said, drawing back slowly.

She glanced over his head towards the clock on the wall. "Mm. I suppose you better had."

They took their time walking to Georgie's place, his arm draped around her shoulders, her hand dug into the back pocket of his jeans. At her door, he pulled her back into his arms to kiss her.

"Did you want to come in?" she said, when he drew back.

He did, but he shook his head. "No… if I come in, I won't want to go. Am I seeing you tomorrow?"

She screwed her face up. "No. I have chores to do tomorrow. Becky will kill me if I don't help with housework and laundry. I'll see you Monday. Who's making the coffee? Me, or you?"

"Me."

He kissed her, lingering over her lips, then finally pulled away, letting his hands trail over her arms, then holding on to her fingers until he had to let go.

"Thank you for a lovely day. I'll see you on Monday. I'll talk to you tomorrow," he said, walking backwards.

She waved and blew a kiss at him, then turned and went in.

He let a long breath trickle out of his nose. *Please let it work this time.*

33

Georgia sipped at the rich dark coffee Anders had brought, her gaze settling on him. It was Monday morning, and they were in the finds tent, sharing the last of the flask of coffee after setting up ahead of everyone arriving. Anders sat on the edge of his desk, facing her, his long, lean legs stretched out and crossed at the ankle. His eyes met hers over the rim of his mug, and from the crinkles that developed, she knew he was smiling, even though she couldn't see his mouth properly. A thought struck her.

"Anders? There's no issue with us being together, but you technically being my boss on this dig, is there?"

The crinkles faded, and he lowered his mug, screwing his mouth up. "Um. I don't think so. If you were in the same department, there might be a problem, though as I'm only temporarily head of department, maybe not. Given that you work somewhere else, and there's no conceivable way I could have influence over your promotion or prospects, then I don't think there could be an issue." He scratched his cheek. "You're not about to accuse me of being inappropriate in the workplace, are you?"

She grinned. "No. I don't think you *have* actually been inappropriate in the workplace with me, have you?"

He gave her a more serious look. "Let's keep work as work? I don't want anyone else saying I was inappropriate with you."

"Sure."

From the field outside came the sound of cars pulling up, heralding the arrival of the team. Anders peeled himself off the table, and they sauntered through to the other tent.

As ever, Sophie bounced in first. She gave Georgia an even filthier look than she usually did, but flashed a big smile at Anders.

Georgia rolled her eyes, and Anders buried his laugh in his mug of coffee.

Everyone else bundled in and grabbed drinks, and Anders gave the morning team talk and plan for the day, finishing up with, "Please can you all try not to need me too much today. I have a lecture to prepare, and a paper to write this week. It would be lovely to get them done during the day and not have to take them home with me."

The team filtered out to the dig site, and Anders and Georgia headed to the finds tent together.

"Can I help with either the lecture or the paper?" Georgia offered.

He shook his head, pulling a face. "Thanks. That's nice of you to offer, but I don't think you can."

He settled at his desk and started up his laptop. She watched him for a few moments, but he was deeply engrossed in the screen, making her smile.

She got to work herself, filling in paperwork on various finds from the previous week. It didn't take long before Patrick came in with something for her to look at and date. He laid it down carefully in front of her. To an untrained eye, it looked like a series of rusted nails in a clod of earth.

"Oh, nice wool comb!" Georgia exclaimed. "Where was this found? The weaving hut?"

"Yep. Under some charred boards. I think it must have been trapped, or burnt beyond bothering salvaging it."

Georgia examined the lump of soil, then looked up. "It looks like most of the binding plate has gone, which is a shame, but not uncommon."

"How does it work?" asked Patrick, his brow wrinkling. "I mean, I've seen them, but I don't really know how you'd use one."

Georgia pulled some scrap paper towards her and sketched out what the combs would have looked like before rust and decay took their toll, starting with a T-shape.

"They work in pairs, so there would be two of them. The nails would have been driven through the top of this shape, and this bit—" she pointed to the down-stroke of the T "—would have been the handle, so you'd be holding it and the nails would come out at right-angles to the handle. You have a lump of fleece on one comb and drag the nails of the other through it to untangle it. Hang on…" She took her phone out of her pocket and pulled up a video showing their use. Patrick peered at it, his face clearing.

"Oh! I thought at first they were just a pile of nails."

Georgia laughed. "Yeah. Common mistake. That's a really nice find."

Even Anders was intrigued enough to wander over from his desk. Georgia passed him her phone, and he watched the short video, then peered at the clod of earth in front of her.

"Double row or single row of teeth?" he asked.

"Single, I think, just lying in a way that makes it look less clear."

He nodded, then returned to his desk. Patrick drifted back out to the dig, leaving Georgia looking at the remains of the wool comb. It really was a cracking find.

She drew it towards her, ready to photograph it and sketch it before preparing it for a 3D scan. Once the soil was removed, the teeth of the comb would fall apart, and she wanted to capture the details. The edge of her finger brushed lightly against one of the metal teeth, and her vision blurred. She snatched her hand away, then glanced over towards Anders. His focus was locked on his laptop screen, and she recognised his expression. It would take something like an earthquake or another natural disaster to make him look up.

She moved the lump of soil with the wool comb a little closer to her, then, after a last check on Anders, rested the back of her index finger against one of the teeth.

"Aelfgyth? I need to talk to you about something."

Her father stood in the doorway to the weaving hut, and she laid down the two wool combs, smoothed out her skirts, and followed him back to their hut.

There, he indicated for her to sit, a serious expression on his face that jangled her nerves.

"I need to discuss something with you. I know that this is not what you might have imagined for your life. You had Edmund, God rest his soul. But I must think of the future."

She twined her fingers around themselves, her stomach knotting. Clearly, her father had plans for her. And clearly, he didn't think she would like them. Had he seen that she had caught Einar's eye? That she didn't discourage him? Was he angry with her? Another thought caught her. Maybe he had arranged for her to marry someone else.

"Einar has come to speak to me," her father went on. He held his hands up. "I know. I know. He is a heathen who has taken our land."

Her mind raced. Why had Einar been to see her father? Had she misunderstood how he felt about her? Had he told her father to marry her off to someone else? Her mouth dried, and her belly fluttered.

"I understand that what I am about to ask of you will make you angry. And if you are truly against it, I will not make you. But I am thinking about the future."

He criss-crossed back and forth in the small space, making her dizzy.

"Aelfgyth, Einar wishes to marry you." Again, he held up his hands. "Please. Hear me out before immediately saying no."

Her heart pounded, and her head spun. Einar wanted to marry her? She opened her mouth, then closed it again.

"Aelfgyth, I know you will not want him. But I have watched him these last few months, and I believe him to be a kind man. He has been honourable and fair to the families here. He has ensured that no one goes without. I wonder if you might learn to love him. Or at least learn not to hate him."

She went to speak, excitement and joy bubbling up in her, but he held up his palms. "No. Hear me out. Your children would inherit this land. I have no son. Edmund would have had everything when I died. But you and Edmund were not blessed with children before he was killed. This farm; this land… will all go to Einar's children. If you married him, they would be your children, and the land would return to my family."

Her insides fizzed. Einar had asked for her!

Her father turned and paced back across the small space. "Einar said that he did not think you would have him, because he is a heathen. He has promised to convert, if you will agree willingly to the marriage. He was insistent that you not be forced." He stopped and faced her. "Aelfgyth. I know that this will have been an unwelcome surprise, but consider his offer. You would save his soul, as well as my heirs inheriting their rightful lands."

She tried to hide her glee and look suitably demure and chaste. "Father, let me consider it? I can see that there would be significant benefits to the marriage."

He crouched before her and grasped her hands. "If you are truly against it; if the idea is abhorrent… I will not force you. I will make another match for you elsewhere."

She lowered her eyes, not trusting that they didn't sparkle with delight. "Father, I will pray about his offer and seek guidance from God. I think I might learn to tolerate Einar."

"Thank you, child." He straightened. "You may return to your weaving."

She stood, and it was everything in her power not to grin like an imbecile.

"Father, thank you for allowing me to choose."

She hurried back towards the weaving hut. As she crossed the path leading to the animal pens, Einar caught up with her.

"Did I just see your father speaking to you?" he said as he fell into step with her.

"You did. He told me that you had asked for me in marriage, but that you would not force me to have you."

"And what did you say?"

They had almost reached the weaving hut, and she turned to face him. "That I would pray to God for guidance. But I am sure that God will tell me to accept the proposal. Especially as it will save your soul when you convert. I could hardly be so selfish as to damn your soul."

He laughed hard, the crinkles around his blue eyes deepening. "And saving my soul is the only reason you would agree?"

She smiled. "Perhaps it is not such a sacrifice I would be making."

With that, she tweaked his beard playfully, and ducked back into the weaving tent.

The vision faded, and Georgia drew her finger back.

Oh, Aelfgyth, I hope you were happy with him.

She glanced over her shoulder. Anders face was fixed in a half scowl, his attention on his screen, his chin on his knuckles.

"Anders? Did you want a coffee? Take a break from your screen?"

Nothing.

"Anders!"

Still nothing.

Georgia screwed up a bit of scrap paper and threw it at him, hitting him squarely in the face. He looked up, blinking.

"Sorry, were you talking to me?"

"Mm. Do you want a coffee? And some fresh air. You weren't built to sit at a desk for hours."

"I need to finish this." He turned back to his screen, distracted.

She watched him for a moment. His frown didn't lift, and his shoulders bunched. If he sat like that all day, his neck would be sore by the evening, and if he didn't get out into the fresh air, his mood would plummet. However much he might aspire to the upper reaches of academia, it would suck every drop of life out of him, and she wished he could see that.

She slithered off her seat and made them both a coffee. As she slid his mug on to his desk next to him, she brushed the back of his hand.

"Go take a walk around the site. You've been staring at your screen for too long."

He shook his head. "No. I'll get distracted by something in one of the trenches, and I need to get this done."

"Then take a break now, with me."

He smiled weakly. "Lovely as that would be, *elskling*, I really need to focus on this."

She gave up and returned to her own desk.

At lunchtime, Anders finally peeled himself away from his computer and took a saunter around the site. Georgia grabbed her packed lunch and sat on a kneeler at the edge of the field, admiring him. He always looked more natural in walking trousers and a fleece than the crisp shirt, jacket, and tie he'd had in his office. His hair was growing out from the short-back-and-sides, and the wind ruffled his curls.

Shona plonked herself down next to her. "Have you and the boss *finally* figured out that you were made for each other and got back together?"

Georgia rapidly swallowed her bite of sandwich. "Um… yes."

Shona sniffed, unwrapping her lunch. "Thought so. I mean, you seemed pretty cosy at the pub on Friday, but looking at how relaxed Anders is today, I assumed you two had sorted out whatever was stopping you from getting together again." She snorted suddenly. "I guess Sophie's not quite so observant."

She nodded across the field towards Anders. Sophie had

wandered over to him to bend his ear about something, and Anders listened patiently. Partway through whatever it was Sophie was talking to him about, he glanced over the top of her head to look at Georgia, and immediately broke into a warm smile. Even from the other side of the field, Georgia saw the wink, and she grinned back. Anders turned his 'politely patient' face back to Sophie, who spoke for a little longer before flouncing off. Anders picked his way over to Georgia and Shona, took his fleece off, folded it, and sat down, stretching out his legs in front of him.

"Did you want a kneeler? Your fleece will get muddy," said Georgia.

He shook his head, leaning back on his elbows and tipping his face up towards the sky, his eyes closed. "I'm only perching. My lunch is through there." He bent his head towards the finds tent.

"Would you two be interested in going to see a Viking re-enactment day?" asked Shona.

Anders opened one eye. "When? Where?"

"This Saturday, over at Tildale."

Georgia smiled to herself, knowing *exactly* what would be going through his head. "I think that would depend on how accurate it all is."

"Oh, pretty accurate. It's the Viking Society running it, and they have a load of historians and experimental archaeologists involved. My nephew's in it. He's involved in the battle re-enactment bit, but there's a ton of other stuff going on. They try to recreate the tented villages that the Viking Great Army would have been in as they moved around the country."

Georgia looked at Anders hopefully. "Shall we go? It sounds good."

He nodded, smiling benevolently at her. "Sure. But one glimpse of a horned-helmet, and we're out of there." He sat up. "I need food. Can I get either of you a drink while I'm up?"

They both shook their heads, and Anders scrambled up, shaking out his fleece. It *was* muddy, but Georgia didn't think he'd care.

"I think even Anders will be happy at the re-enactment," said Shona, once he was out of earshot. "And if either of you spot something historically inaccurate, just let them know. They're dead keen on getting it right."

Anders returned with his lunch and a kneeler and sat next to Georgia again, close enough that his shoulder brushed hers, sending a light thrill through her body. She leaned against him, and he smiled, his gaze on the dig site, his eyes bright with happiness.

A light shiver ran down her spine as she thought about the end of the summer. Would things work out with Anders this time? What if no jobs came up for him when his current post finished?

What if the only jobs that came up were in Norway?

34

That weekend, Anders drove them to Tildale for the re-enactment day. The event was taking place at a large open-air showground, and a marshal directed him to park his battered old Land Rover in a field to one side. The entrance lay a little way away, across the field, and they strolled over. Anders draped his arm around Georgie's shoulders, smiling to himself as he felt her hand slip into the back pocket of his jeans. He squeezed her and kissed the top of her head. He still thought that the whole thing was likely to be an inauthentic pastiche of Viking life that would grind his gears. But Georgie had wanted to come and have a look, so he'd kept his thoughts to himself as much as possible.

She tilted her face up to him. "Thank you for coming to this. I know you think it's going to be awful."

He laughed. "I'm hoping it won't be as bad as I fear."

The showground had been transformed into a tented village, set up to mimic how the Viking Great Army had travelled over Britain in the late ninth century, and there was a variety of things to see, from demonstrations of weaving and wood-turning, to weaponry. Later in the afternoon, there would be a battle re-enactment.

They sauntered amongst the first line of tents. To his relief, everyone wore authentic outfits. The men wore woollen trousers with a woollen tunic belted over the top. The belts were made of leather, and woven braiding decorated the edges of the tunics. Over their lower legs, some of them had what looked like leg-warmers on, made of strips of dense wool wrapped around their legs. The women wore long apron-dresses over the top of an under-shift or serk, and the children wore miniature versions of their parents' outfits. The colours were delightful, ranging from blues and yellows through oranges to reds and the occasional green, and the patterns in the braids were brightly coloured and intricate.

At one of the first tents they passed, a middle-aged woman appeared to be sewing something, and Anders peered at it. Although she was clearly only using one large needle, the finished product resembled knitting rather than cloth, and he assumed she was nålbinding, a Viking practice for making woollen garments. He slowed to a stop, and she smiled up brightly at him.

"Hello."

"Hi. Is that nålbinding?"

"It is! I'm surprised you've heard of it."

"I know a little about it," he said. "And I've seen it done before, but not for a long time. Could you show me, please? Slowly!"

"Of course."

Georgie moved so that she could see more clearly, and the woman demonstrated what she was doing. At the dig, they'd found a handful of large, flat, bone needles, similar to the one the woman used, and Anders watched closely to see how she transformed the lengths of yarn she had in a basket at her side, into a thick material. The woman passed across a finished mitten for them to look at. He turned it around in his hands, studying the rows of stitches.

"Because it's essentially knotted, it doesn't fray if it gets a hole in it," said the woman, picking up a sock to show them. It had a hole worn in the sole, but the fabric hadn't deteriorated any further, and it looked as if it would be a fairly simple procedure to repair it.

Anders watched her for a little longer, working out how what she did with the needle produced the thick material in his hands. Once he'd finally got his head around it, he passed the mitten back to her, then caught Georgie's grin.

"You figured it out, then?" she said, her eyes full of mirth.

He pulled a face at her. "Yes."

She laughed, then nudged him to move away. "Did you want to find someone doing tablet weaving? That will *definitely* give your brain a workout! I've watched umpteen videos about it and still can't quite figure it out."

"I know how tablet weaving works," he said smugly.

She looked up, surprised. "Yeah?"

"Mm. On one of the first digs I remember, we found some tablets, and I couldn't understand how they worked, so I got one of Pappa's colleagues who was into experimental archaeology to show me. I must have been, ooh, about seven?" He scrunched his face up, trying to remember. "It was before Mum and Pappa split up, so it would have been in Norway. I used to join Pappa on the digs, and he would show me what had been found."

"I sort of understand it, but I don't think I have the same kind of brain as yours. If there's a demonstration, can we have a look? I can just about get my head around it when I can see it, but I still struggle to imagine it from a diagram or a pattern."

She slipped back under his arm, and they walked down the line of tents. Anders glanced around. There was one tent set up as a weaving tent, across the other side of the camp, and he leaned into Georgie to steer her over towards it.

"I think they have someone over there doing it."

There was indeed someone weaving a long braid, similar to those decorating the edges of the tunics worn. Anders smiled to himself at Georgie's furrowed brow as she studied the young woman weaving. The pattern she wove looked complicated, with perhaps twenty square tablets manipulating the warp threads. They'd found a couple of bone tablets on the dig, but the woman's were made of small squares of leather, about eight centimetres across, with a hole in each corner. The original inhabitants of their dig site probably also used leather, though they wouldn't find any as they wouldn't have survived being in the ground for over a thousand years.

Anders and Georgie stood quietly, watching as the woman rotated the leather squares, then took the weft thread across and changed the tablets again. Some of the tablets rotated in one direction, some in the other. The resulting braid had a highly intricate pattern on it, with the coloured warp threads crossing and criss-crossing the piece.

"That pattern is based on a piece found in a dig in Norway," murmured Anders, following the threads with his eyes as they twisted and turned.

The woman making the braid glanced up, smiling. "It is indeed. How did you know?"

"Oh, I'm an archaeologist," he said, a little flustered. "This era is my area of interest."

"Yeah? You should talk to my husband. He's an experimental archaeologist. He'll be over doing weapons demonstrations. We both do these re-enactment days as a hobby."

Anders's interest was piqued. "What's his name? If you don't mind me asking."

"Josh Holmes. I'm Libby."

The man's name didn't ring a bell, but if he was a similar age to his wife, he would be in his early twenties, Anders thought, and their paths probably hadn't crossed.

"I'll find him. What does he look like?"

Libby studied him. "About your height. Chunkier. Black hair and dark eyes."

Anders nodded. He always enjoyed talking to experimental archaeologists. Part of him half wished he'd gone down that branch instead of the more academic side.

He checked on Georgie, who still studied the braid intently. "Got your head around it yet?"

She laughed. "Sort of. Maybe."

Libby smiled. "I think you only really understand it if you actually do it. Want to have a go?"

Georgie took a step back, making Anders chuckle.

"No, I don't want to mess it up. It looks so complicated."

"Well, if you change your mind, just come back. I'm more than happy to let you have a go. There are also some kits for sale at the shop tent."

"I'll buy you a kit and show you how it works," said Anders. "Once you've got your brain around it, it makes sense."

They made their way over the grass towards a group of people clustered around a display of swords and shields. Anders thought he could spot which of the men was Libby's husband, and the two of them made a beeline towards him.

"Josh Holmes?" asked Anders, raising his brows, hoping that the burly, dark-haired man in front of him was the right man.

"I am indeed. How can I help?"

Like the other re-enactment men, Josh wore dun-coloured woollen trousers with a coloured tunic over the top. The neckline, cuffs, and hem of the blue tunic were decorated with braids that Anders was sure Libby had made. Around his middle was slung a leather belt with a pouch hanging from it on one side, and a knife on the other. Josh stood next to a collection of round wooden shields, painted with a variety of designs, and held a long sword in one hand.

"Hi," said Anders. "We met your wife, Libby, and she suggested we come over and say hello. She said you're an experimental archaeologist?"

Josh nodded. "I am. I did an archaeology degree, but to be honest, the practical side of it all always interested me more, and I did a Masters in it, and now I'm doing that full-time, really."

Anders held his hand out. "Anders Mortensen. This is Georgia Cooke. We're both archaeologists."

Georgie leaned around him to shake Josh's hand. "Hi."

"Mortensen?" Josh's brow knitted.

Anders's stomach clenched, and he braced himself for the inevitable disappointment that he was *Anders* Mortensen, not Haakon.

"As in the Mortensen who wrote the papers on Anglo-Saxon settlements and the influence of the Vikings?"

His tension dissipated, and he laughed. "Er. Yes. The very same."

Josh's dark eyes studied him, amusement flickering over his lips. "You look surprised that I've heard of you."

Anders shrugged. "Yeah… Normally I get, 'Mortensen? As in the guy who wrote the books on late Viking burials in Norway?'"

"Is he a relation?"

"He's my father."

Josh shook his head. "No. Not heard of him. Is he important?"

Anders wanted to laugh, imagining his father overhearing their conversation. "Er… He's a big name in Norway. And an expert on late Scandinavian Viking burials. Writes a lot of books."

"Ah. I focus more on the British Viking stuff, rather than the

Scandinavian. Their integration into Anglo-Saxon life is fascinating. Sorry not to have heard of him. I clearly wasn't forced to write an essay on his work when I was at uni!"

Anders screwed his face up. "Oh… Does that mean you were forced to write an essay on *my* work and hated it?"

Josh shook his head, his eyes crinkling. "No. I found your papers really interesting."

A warm feeling settled in his belly, and the tightness in his shoulders eased.

"Actually, I'm really glad to meet you," said Josh. "I would *love* to pick your brains about something." His face fell. "Oh. Shit. Sorry. You're off duty and trying to have a fun day out."

Anders chuckled. "No, you're fine. What did you want to ask?"

"It was about the layout of settlements, and whether there were regional variations between those where the Vikings had influence, and those in the south."

Anders blinked. "Ooh. That's a shortish question with a *very* long answer."

Josh nodded, looking a little crestfallen.

A couple with an excited child approached, clearly itching to ask Josh about the sword he was holding, and Anders grabbed his wallet and rummaged in it to find a business card.

"Do you break for lunch any time?" he asked, handing it over. "If so, I'm happy to chat about it with you over lunch, when *you're* off duty. If not, or you get pulled away, drop me an email or give me a ring. It's a discussion that would work well with a beer. Do you live locally?"

Josh wrinkled his nose. "Not all that locally. I'll probably grab lunch with Libby at about one."

"Okay. I'll try to find you." Anders grinned. "Nice to meet you."

"Yeah, you too."

He slipped his arm back around Georgie, and the two of them wandered away.

"He seemed nice," said Georgie, squeezing closer.

"You didn't mind me saying we'd find him over lunch?"

"Of course not." She tucked her hand back into his back

pocket. "You know, I've sometimes thought that you would make a great experimental archaeologist. You have the right kind of mind for figuring things out, and you're good with your hands."

Anders snorted, and she punched him lightly in the midriff.

"No, I'll take that," he said, still laughing. "If you think I'm good with my hands, I'm happy! Come on. Let's buy a tablet weaving kit for you, and check out that less than delicious-looking stew thing they're selling in the food tent."

They headed towards the tent selling gifts, and he ran back over the first part of what Georgie had said. Should he think about a shift from academia? Widen his horizons when this job came to an end?

Instantly, his father's voice rang in his head, disparaging and dismissive. *"Anders, you were blessed with a brain that can analyse data; make sense of things. Why on earth would you waste it on play-acting? I despair of you sometimes."*

He breathed unevenly. His father would be right. He'd be wasting all of the hard work he'd put in, building up his reputation.

Georgie nudged him. "You okay?"

"Yeah, yeah. I'm fine."

She scrutinised him for a moment, a slight frown marring her brow. He fixed a smile on his face, trying to reassure her, but he couldn't quite shake the cloud that had descended on him.

* * *

As the afternoon wound to a close, Georgie bunted Anders with her shoulder as they walked. "Are you ready to head off?"

"Mm." He nibbled his lower lip as he looked at her. "Did you want to stay over at mine tonight?"

She hadn't spent the night with him yet. Not since they'd got back together. She held his gaze for a moment, a soft smile creeping over her face. "Yeah, actually."

"Shall I cook you dinner? What would you like?"

"Anything except a stew with barley and dried meat in it."

He laughed, tightening his arm around her shoulders. "It wasn't actually that bad. I've certainly eaten worse things in my time. And I don't think you can pass judgement on it when you wouldn't try it."

They strolled back towards the exit, passing the tents of craftsmen and women. As well as the nålbinding and tablet weaving, there had been displays of wood-turning using a pole lathe, carving, leather-work, blacksmithing, and jewellery-making. Anders had, as promised, bought her a tablet weaving kit, but he'd also bought himself a Viking-style tunic, and she'd bought herself a small carved box. They'd caught up with Josh and Libby over lunch, where Anders had braved some authentic stew and Georgie hadn't, and the four of them had spent over an hour chatting and laughing together. Libby was an art teacher, but she'd contributed as much to the discussions about life in late Anglo-Scandinavian times as the three archaeologists had, and clearly relished the re-enactment stuff that she and Josh did together. While the two men had bickered good-naturedly over the construction methods of Anglo-Scandinavian houses, Libby had spent a little time showing Georgie how to set up her new weaving kit. At the end of the lunch, they had all swapped numbers, and Anders hoped they would catch up again some time.

The traffic out of the event was heavy, and the late sun streaming in made the car stifling. Anders rolled his window down and rested his arm on the sill, his face boiling, and his hair damp at the nape of his neck.

"Are you too hot?" Georgie asked.

He laughed. "I'm always too hot. I blame it on my formative years being in Norway."

She fanned him with the brochure about the day, making him laugh harder. The traffic thinned a little, and he pulled away, nosing out on to the main road. Once the car was moving, more air circulated, and Georgie abandoned fanning him.

A few minutes later, he pulled up outside his house and turned the engine off.

"Drink in the garden?" he asked. "I still need to cool down."

In the kitchen, he busied himself making cold drinks. Georgie tucked her arms around him from behind and pressed her cheek against his shoulder blade.

"Thank you for going to that with me. I know it wasn't really your thing."

He turned in her arms and rested his elbows on her shoulders, his fingers ruffling her hair. "It was a lot better than I thought it was going to be."

"Not a single horned-helmet to be seen. Josh and Libby were nice."

"Yeah, I liked them." A puff of air emerged from his top, and he laughed, embarrassed. "Oh. Sorry! I have clearly been too hot all day. I'll grab a shower in a minute."

She pushed her lip out, holding his gaze intensely. "I kind of like you a bit sweaty."

"Oh, really?" He blinked and frowned.

"Mm. Well, maybe it was more how you ended up getting a bit sweaty with me…" Her eyes danced. "Maybe not *that* sweaty, though," she added, wrinkling her nose but still smiling.

He shifted uncomfortably. "I'll go and shower."

He pulled away, but she held on to him, her eyes locked on his. "Can I share it?"

"Oh, I know *that* look," he said, his pulse quickening. "Yeah. You can definitely share it."

35

The weather over the following week held bright and sunny, with a light breeze, lifting everyone's spirits. The finds still poured in, keeping Georgia busy. Anders was splitting his time between the finds tent, where he worked on various papers and admin, and the trenches, where he was in his element.

Mid-morning, he sauntered in, the knees of his trousers grubby, his hands caked in mud, clutching a tray with something in it.

"Look!" he said, his eyes alight.

He slid the tray gingerly on to the table in front of Georgia and she peered at its contents. Nestled in amongst the mud and earth was a beautiful belt buckle, intricately decorated with entwined animals. Just visible at the head of one of the animals was a red eye, and Georgia looked up.

"Gemstone? Or glass?"

Anders sucked his teeth. "Won't know for sure until it's cleaned up and examined properly, but given the quality of the decorations, I wouldn't be surprised if it was a gemstone. Ruby maybe? Garnet?"

"It's a fantastic find." She smirked. "Sam?"

"No. Sophie."

"Let me guess, she was *delighted* to bounce over to you to show you."

He nodded, rolling his eyes. "I think she must be the only one on site who hasn't figured out that I'm seeing you."

Georgia gave him a look. "Oh, no, I'm sure she knows. She's just wishing it was otherwise."

He shrugged, looking uncomfortable. "I'd better get back out there. Cracking find, though?"

"Fabulous! Okay. Back to the trenches with you. See you at lunch."

He winked, grinning, and strolled back out of the tent.

Georgia drew the tray a little closer to her and selected a soft brush. Almost the moment she picked up the clod of earth and her fingertips touched the buckle, she was back in the ninth century.

The early summer sunshine made the lush grass glow with vitality. Aelfgyth sat outside the weaving hut, her hands busy spinning, her eyes watching her son, Magnus, as he tottered around on the ground before her. He'd arrived barely nine months after she and Einar had married. No real surprise there, given the passion of their relationship. Magnus had inherited his father's blond hair and blue eyes, and, given how sturdy he already seemed as a child, was likely to be as big as Einar, too. Maybe even bigger.

Einar sauntered over with something in his hands, making a sound like a horse's hooves galloping. "Tick-a-tick, tick-a-tick, tick-a-tick."

Magnus beamed at his father, holding outstretched arms to him, demanding to be picked up.

Einar swung him up, settling him on one solid arm, then held a small carved horse out, miming it galloping through the air while he made the sound again. Magnus's eyes widened, and he gurgled with joy, making Aelfgyth's heart sing. Magnus took the wooden horse in his fist, waving it around in a clumsy impression of a gallop.

"That's it. Tick-a-tick, tick-a-tick, tick-a-tick." Einar sat down next to her, smiling, their son still in his arms. "And how is my second son? Still kicking?"

He nodded towards her swollen belly, and she rested one hand on it.

"Still kicking. But maybe it's your daughter kicking me, not another son."

"Maybe. Perhaps I will have a daughter as feisty as her mother!"

She continued spinning, watching the two men she loved playing together. As well as the little horse, Einar had carved a sheep for the boy, its sides covered in spirals to mimic its fleece, but of the two toys, Magnus had always preferred the horse. She wasn't entirely sure where the sheep was. Maybe it had been dropped in their room somewhere. She would try to find it later.

She caught her breath as the baby inside her womb gave her another mighty kick. Einar's gaze shot to her, his voice tailing off mid-gallop. Magnus turned, his mouth making a small circle, and she smiled to reassure him.

"Oh, it's nothing, Magnus. Just your little brother or sister wanting to play, too."

She leaned back, letting the sun warm her. Einar had proved to be a good lord: the farm thrived; all of the people were happy and well fed. It also seemed as if there would be a new stability in the country. Halfdan had brokered peace with Wessex; Yorvik city had been rebuilt. She knew other farmsteads had been less lucky. Other men who had been given land hadn't been so kind as Einar. Some people whose land had been given away had ended up as slaves, working their own land for little more than enough food to prevent them from starving, and a hovel to keep most of the rain off them. She shivered. She'd been so lucky. She almost laughed to herself when she remembered she had half planned to nurse him to his death-bed.

"Cold, wife?"

She shook her head, smiling softly. "No. Just happy."

The room swam a little, bringing Georgia back to the modern day. She brushed her fingertip over the belt buckle, wondering if it would show her anything more, but it didn't.

"I wonder if we'll ever find the little sheep you lost? Or that horse?" she mused.

It wasn't likely. Most wooden objects didn't survive long in the ground. It was a shame. The toy horse had looked adorable.

A piece of patterned paper caught her eye, tucked underneath a tray towards the back of her desk. She pulled it free, then a broad smile settled on her lips. It was an origami 'puzzle purse' – a carefully folded square of paper, which would reveal a hidden message if you opened it in the right order. Anders had made dozens of them for her in the past, hiding little notes, or saying he loved her in them. Judging from the pristine creases in the paper, he'd made this one off-site, when his hands weren't covered in grime from digging.

She prised it open. Inside, in minuscule writing, Anders had written out one of her favourite love poems: Elizabeth Barrett Browning's Sonnet 43. She read it, a smile tickling her lips, then re-folded the paper and slipped it into her pocket.

Her gaze spun out over the site. She could just see the top of Anders's head, the sunlight catching his hair and making it look much more blond than reality. Would she and Anders ever have kids? When she tried to imagine her life in the future, she definitely wanted Anders in it, and she definitely wanted children. She'd seen Anders with his nephew and niece once when they'd come over to visit him in Orkney, and he'd been amazing with them. Katya's little boy, Oliver, had been three, and the little girl, Emma, was just a year old. He'd had endless patience with Oliver, carrying him on his shoulders and galloping around the field, while the boy yelled "Giddy-up!" over and over. Anders had looked in his element. He'd also had a great knack for getting Emma to stop crying. So much so, Katya had wanted to take him back home with her so that she could get some sleep.

She smiled at the memories, happiness bubbling out from the centre of her core to fill every part of her.

"You will make *such* a great dad, one of these days, Anders," she murmured, her eyes following him as he moved around the site.

Reality slapped her. For Anders to feel settled enough to start a family, he would want to have a permanent job in academia, and these could be as rare as hens' teeth. She knew he already had half an eye on the website listing academic posts and that there was nothing coming up.

She forced herself not to stress about it.

"There's still plenty of time before his current job is up," she said through gritted teeth.

If she said it enough times, maybe she would believe it.

36

Later that week, Anders scooped up the post from the doormat as he entered, then kicked his shoes off, sifting through the mail as he did so. One letter caught his attention: his father's handwriting; Norwegian stamps; a thick, brown, A5 envelope.

He strolled through to the kitchen and flicked the kettle on, discarding the flyers for pizza places and taxi services straight into the recycling bin. He opened the envelope from his father while the kettle boiled.

Inside was a job application form and a covering letter in his father's tight handwriting. He skim-read the job summary paper-clipped to the form. The post was an academic job in Norway. It was another step up from his current post, and as he read the description of the 'ideal candidate', he wasn't sure if he ticked a number of the boxes. He turned to the letter from his father.

Dear Anders,

I hope you are well and that your dig is as important as you thought it might be. Katya tells me you have got back together with Georgia. I hope she is worth it this time around.

I thought you might be interested in this post. It's a step up from your current role, and you perhaps don't have enough publications of sufficient impact, but I know the director and will put in a good word for you. My name carries weight. And perhaps your dig will prove to be of significance, and you can get some articles out that would help. I know that your current employment will end when the woman comes back from maternity leave, so you would do well to consider your options. This would be a great opportunity for you to cement your status in your area. You would need to work on your aversion to public speaking, but I have never believed this to be insurmountable.

The second page of the letter shifted topic to describe

Haakon's recent publications and work, and Anders laid it down on the kitchen counter, trying not to grind his teeth.

He skimmed through the application form again, his brain automatically thinking about how to fill in some of the boxes, then he clicked his tongue, and stuffed both the form and the letter from his father back into the envelope.

"You can't," he muttered. "You'd lose her. Again. There would be no third chance."

The ever-present voice in his head asked him what he *was* going to do when his current job ended, and he closed his eyes, trying to silence it. To no avail.

He shook his head and made a cafetiere of coffee. While it brewed, he booted up his laptop and pulled up a website listing academic jobs. He'd already looked at it enough times to have a variety of filters in place, limiting the results to suitable jobs in the UK. He poured his coffee, refreshed the search, and settled down to scroll through the results.

Almost immediately, his eyes drifted back to the envelope from his father. There had been nothing on the website. Not just nothing suitable. *Nothing*. Not a single post in his field. Nausea spiked in his belly at the thought of not having any job at all in a few months.

Should he broach it with Georgie?

He dismissed the idea instantly.

"Something will come up," he muttered. "It has to. You have time yet."

He finished his mug of coffee and poured another. He removed a couple of the filters, widening out the search. Two jobs appeared, but even a cursory glance told him they weren't suitable. He reinstated the filters and re-saved the search parameters.

What if nothing came up?

Out of curiosity, he pulled the job application back out of the envelope to check the closing date. Still a few weeks away.

A voice chittered in his head. *If she really loves you, she'd find a way to make it work, even if you went to Norway. If she* really *loved you, she'd go to Norway with you.*

He wished he could shut the voice up. He stuffed the form

and the letter together again and tucked them behind the edge of the bread bin.

Something would come up. It had to.

37

The weather continued to hold, allowing the dig to progress at pace. Georgia had escaped the finds tent for an hour, desperate for some fresh air and a bit of sun. She headed towards the main trench over the great hall, hoping to dig for a bit. Shona scraped gently at the soil where the post-holes suggested a separate room, and she waved Georgia over. Georgia picked up a trowel and started working at the other end of the trench, where they believed the edge of the hall would have been.

A few minutes later, Shona's head shot up. "Georgia? Come and have a look at this?"

Georgia picked her way down to where Shona sat on her haunches. The older woman pointed to something in the soil with the end of her trowel. "Another belt buckle?"

Georgia crouched down and used the tip of her own trowel to expose a little more of the object.

"I think so. Not as fancy as the one Sophie found, but a belt buckle, all the same." She raised her head and scanned the site, looking for Anders. He stood talking to Sam on the far side of the site, and she made a circle with her middle finger and thumb, stuck them in her mouth, and whistled to him.

Shona chuckled. "Whistle and he'll come to you."

Anders sauntered over, his hair a tangle, and mud caking his boots. A dark V of sweat darkened his t-shirt over his chest. "What have you got?"

"Another belt buckle." She scraped a little more, enough to extract the buckle from the surrounding soil.

As soon as her fingers touched the metal, the world shifted. She could smell smoke from a fire. The wall dividing the end room from the great hall appeared before her, made of wattle and daub. She pulled her hand back from the buckle, and the world shifted back to the 21st century.

"You okay?" asked Shona, peering at her.

"Just a little hot," she lied. "And maybe my blood sugar's a bit low." She emphasised her hands shaking. "Could one of you take it to the finds tent for me? I'm scared I'm going to drop it."

"Sure," said Anders. "Let me get you a drink, too."

He finished exposing the buckle and recorded it, while Georgia sat on the side. The visions she'd had of the past had been fun and interesting, but now their unpredictability and intensity were making it a challenge to get her work done. Why did she get them, and no one else did? Or *were* others also getting them but, like her, saying nothing?

Anders moved the buckle to a tray and straightened up. He held his free hand out to her to help her up, releasing it again as soon as she was standing.

In the finds tent, he put the tray on her desk, then hurried off to the other tent, returning with a cold drink and a couple of biscuits for her, which he put on the desk in front of her.

"Thanks," she said, picking up the cold drink and pressing it to her face. "Sorry. I'm too hot and a bit tired."

Should she tell him what was really going on? Much as he might love her, he was never in a month of Sundays going to buy into her having visions of the past that could be considered anything other than her overactive imagination.

"Cool off in here for a bit," said Anders. "It's getting warm out there, even under the awnings."

She nodded, though the canvas of the tents trapped the heat as much as the awnings did.

"Want me to stay for a bit?" he asked.

"No, I'm fine. But thank you." She wanted to see what the vision would tell her.

"Sure?"

"Sure."

He glanced towards the site, then back to her, before leaning across to kiss her quickly. "Okay. See you later."

Once he'd gone, she drew the tray with the buckle towards her and touched the metal, her hands trembling a little. Her surroundings shifted in and out of focus until eventually, the tent around her disappeared, replaced by an image of the interior of a small building. Einar lay on a bed, his face deeply lined and his hair and beard grey, his eyes closed.

She drew the covers up to his chin, trying not to wake him. His breathing was definitely worse. His chest rattled with every breath now. At least he'd abandoned insisting on walking around the settlement every morning. Magnus had everything in hand. Magnus was now older than Einar had been when Halfdan had given him the land. Oh, that was so long ago now.

She sat next to the bed, wishing she had something to occupy her hands. Should she get a basket of wool and do some spinning? Her fingers were getting too stiff for that these days. She studied the backs of her hands, covered in lines, the joints swollen and disfigured.

"Oh, Einar. When did we get so old?" she murmured.

He coughed wetly. "Years ago, my love. We just didn't realise it."

She smiled at him. "I thought you were asleep."

"I was, but now I'm not. Help me up?"

"You should rest." She brushed his wild grey hair back from his deeply lined face.

He caught her hand, kissing her fingertips. "Don't fuss. I am fine."

She planted the knuckles of her free hand on her hip. "You are not fine, Einar. You are a foolish old man."

He chuckled, his breath crackling in his chest as he did so. "Ah. I am that. But I will not lie in my bed all day. Help me up."

His breathing rasped, making her heart ache. Time waited for no one, and Einar was unlikely to see spring.

She stood, her bones creaking, and leaned over. Einar might be a shadow of his former self, but he was still a big man, and she puffed and wheezed as she helped him to sit up.

He took her hands in his large ones as she sat again. "Aelfgyth? I need to talk to you about something. When I die—"

"I don't want to talk about that," she cut in.

"Aelfgyth. Please. I am not afraid, and you should not be, either. Magnus will look after you when I am gone."

Tears filled her eyes. The idea of life without Einar was unbearable.

"Hush now," he said, his voice low and soothing. He lifted her hand to his lips and kissed it. "When I die, I want to be buried with my sword."

She blinked. "You are a Christian. Why do you need your sword?"

He sighed. "I converted so that I could marry you. But my bones… ah, my bones they are a warrior's. Please. Bury me with my sword and weapons."

"I am not burning you in a boat! You will be buried as a Christian."

He kissed her hands again. "Bury me as a Christian if you must… but also with my weapons." His eyes glistened. "Oh, Aelfgyth, I do not fear death itself. I fear what comes after. What if my gods are angry that I abandoned them?"

"What if God is angry that you have not embraced him?"

"I tried. But I do not think your god is for warriors."

She swiped at a tear, tipping her head to look up at the roof-beams of their hut.

The vision faded, leaving Georgia with tears stinging her eyes. Aelfgyth's love for Einar was so deep, and her turmoil over his request so profound. How difficult it must have been for her, to love him so much but to fear that she might damn his soul if she followed his wishes. Or the doubts that she might damn him if she *didn't.*

Excitement flickered in her chest. What if Aelfgyth *had* followed his wishes? Could there be a Viking-style burial on the site? Where? That would be the find of a lifetime!

She closed her eyes, pulling up mental images of the site surveys. As far as she could remember, there was nothing either in the current field, or in the one Dig For It had excavated previously that would suggest anything even remotely resembling a Viking burial site, but there were still the adjacent fields to consider. Maybe the burial was in there?

She still itched to tell Anders, but sense prevailed, throwing ice-cold water over her. She could hardly say to him, "Hey, Anders, I reckon there's a Viking burial on the site somewhere, because when I was cleaning this buckle, I saw it all in a vision."

She chewed the end of a pencil, taking a breath. *You're getting ahead of yourself. There's no evidence of a burial.*

There had been no evidence of the weaving hut until they found it, exactly where she'd been shown they would, either. In fact, every vision had led to her understanding the site and discovering something important, and it didn't get much more important than a full burial. It would be the find of a lifetime, and Anders might finally step out from behind his father's shadow.

She chewed her thumbnail. Maybe the dig would find something tangible that would point them in the right direction. In the meantime, she would try to figure out a way to tell Anders about it, without him thinking she'd lost her marbles.

38

"You head in. I'll grab the shopping," said Anders the following evening, closing his car door and tossing his house keys over to Georgia.

She caught them deftly. "Sure you don't want me to carry something?"

He shook his head and opened the boot.

Georgia unlocked his front door and kicked her shoes off, Anders close behind her. He carried the grocery bags into the kitchen and dumped them on the counter, then turned to her. "Can I leave you to unpack while I nab a quick shower?"

"Sure. Though I don't actually mind you being hot and sweaty."

She shot him a mischievous look, and he rolled his eyes and scooted upstairs to shower. Georgia unpacked the shopping and tidied it away, then filled the kettle and switched it on. As she put the last of the groceries in a cupboard, her attention snagged on an envelope with Norwegian stamps on it, tucked behind the bread bin. Curious, she pulled the bundle of papers towards her and leafed through them. Her Norwegian wasn't good enough to understand much of either the handwritten letter that must be from Haakon, or the printed sheets, but she could recognise a job application form when she saw one, and felt sick.

She re-scanned the job summary again, picking out a few words she could understand. She couldn't translate most of it, but if Anders had kept this, did it mean that he was interested in the job? Cold flashed through her. Was he thinking of going back to Norway, after all the promises he'd made?

Just as she finished studying the form, Anders pattered back in to the kitchen, his hair damp and uncombed.

"Glass of wine?" he said, before stumbling to a halt, his focus on what was in her hands. The colour drained from his face.

She held the pages up, her brow raised, not trusting herself to speak.

He bit his lips together, his eyes wide. "My father sent it all to me. I did *not* ask him to, I promise you. I knew *nothing* about the job. I swear, Georgie."

Her hands shook. "And yet, here they are, *not* in the bin. Are you going to apply for it?"

He walked over and took the papers from her to toss them into the box of recycling, then held her hands. "No. I'm not applying for it. Georgie, I promise you, I knew nothing about it. He just sent it all over."

He released her hands so that he could put his arms around her, drawing her closer. She rested her palms against his chest, her body tight, pushing him away.

"Don't hurt me again, Anders," she whispered.

"I won't. I promise you. I love you."

"You said that last time, and still left me for a job in Norway."

"I didn't have any other work then."

"You have nothing else now. Not when this post finishes."

He closed his eyes briefly. "I know. And to be honest, that scares me. And still being honest, the job is a great step up, and there is *nothing* coming up in the UK. But I don't want to lose you again. You mean so much more to me than any job."

She swallowed. "I saw my name in Haakon's letter. What did he have to say about me?"

He shrugged. "Just that Katya had told him we were back together."

She didn't think that was all of it, but didn't press him. Haakon's opinion of her was about as high as her opinion of Haakon.

Anders hugged her. "I'm not applying for it." He kissed her lightly. "Did you want a glass of wine?"

She nodded. "Thank you." She gave him a squeeze. "I'm sure something good will come up in the UK."

An expression flickered across his face, almost too quickly for her to see, then he smiled. But she had seen it. He was terrified.

He kissed her again, then eased out of her arms. "Let me get you a drink."

Two glasses of wine poured, they sat together on the sofa. Georgia cuddled in against him.

"Something will come up. And if not, you'll just have to be a kept man for a bit."

She'd meant it light-heartedly, but he tensed up next to her and his breathing tightened. She wriggled around to face him and rested her palm against his cheek.

"Seriously, Anders. Something will come up. Let's not worry about it tonight. The end of your post is ages away."

None of his tension dissipated, and she rubbed her thumb along his cheekbone. "My Norwegian isn't good enough to have read all the details, but it was perfect, wasn't it?"

He shook his head sadly. "No. It had two *big* problems. The major one is it's in Norway. And you're here."

"And the other one?"

"I'd probably have to do a lot of presentations and lectures."

"But otherwise, it'd be great, yeah?"

He said nothing. She kissed him tenderly. "We'll figure something out."

* * *

Anders could shoot himself. Why on earth had he left the stuff from his dad out? Why hadn't he thrown it all in the bin? He knew *exactly* why Georgie had gone cold on him tonight, and she had a point. If he was never going to apply for the job, he should have tossed the papers in the bin.

But he hadn't.

He rubbed his brow, his other arm loosely slung around Georgie, who leaned against him on the sofa. They'd had a relaxed enough dinner and now were supposed to be watching a film together, but his mind had been elsewhere, and from the tension in her shoulders, hers was too.

Should he say something? Talk to her? He traced his fingertip along his eyebrow. What could he say that wouldn't stir things up?

He knew why his father had sent the details over. The job was great. Apart from being in Norway. Okay, there would also be presentations to give, but he muddled through those well enough. He'd never entirely got on top of his nerves, but he'd found a way to at least *appear* confident when giving talks.

I hope she really does love you. If you don't apply for this and then she dumps you again…

He closed his eyes, willing that nagging voice to be quiet. It wouldn't be.

Don't throw everything away for the woman who cut you out of her life without hesitation. You've always loved her more than she loves you. Idiot.

He ran back over what she'd said earlier. *Could* he cope with being a 'kept man'? He didn't think so. What if he waited and waited for a job to come up in the UK and it never did? The gap in his career would look awful. He wanted to make a life with Georgie; offer her stability; be earning enough that they could think about kids even. Buy a house with a garden… Ending up living with her and Becky because he didn't have anything and couldn't afford his own place was *not* in the career plan. He breathed in, filling his lungs, then let the air trickle out of his nose.

Georgie squirmed around until she faced him. "What's up?"

He opened his eyes, smiling weakly. "My brain won't shut up. Sorry."

She cocked a brow. "The dig?" Her face fell. "That job?"

He brushed her hair back over her shoulder. "I'm churning about upsetting you. I should have thrown the papers away when they arrived. I'm sorry."

Her face softened, and a strange expression filled her eyes. "Maybe you'll find something in this dig that's so amazing, you'll get headhunted for a fabulous job in the UK."

He smiled wanly. "It would have to be beyond amazing for *that* to happen."

She smiled back, still giving him an odd look. "Well. You never know."

He studied the flecks of green in her eyes. "I'm sorry I upset you. I never meant to."

"I know." She drew in a deep breath. "I wish I found it easy to think about hopping from one country to another the way you can, but after what happened to Amelia…" She blinked, averting her gaze.

"Hey. It's okay. I understand."

He knew they'd been close. He knew that Amelia dying after taking a drug overdose had shattered Georgie. But from what he could tell, Amelia had been a very different person to her sister. She'd followed her boyfriend to Germany, but barely spoke the language and had felt isolated. Georgie had said that she knew Amelia had taken drugs before she went to Germany; she just hadn't realised how addicted she'd been. The inquest had decided that the overdose was accidental, but Georgie hadn't found any comfort in that.

He drew her closer to him, kissing her gently.

"We'll figure it out," he murmured. "I'm sorry I've been so wound up."

She snuggled in against him. "I think we both need distracting."

He laughed lightly. "Uh, huh? And have you got any suggestions for what the distraction might be?"

She tipped her head up to him, smirking. "Oh, yes."

The mischievous expression in her eyes made him catch his breath. "I know that look."

She clicked the TV off, twined her fingers in his, and led him upstairs.

39

A week passed, and the dig revealed more of its secrets. So far, the finds had exceeded Anders's expectations, and he knew he would get some decent publications from it all. The little voice in his head that rarely shut up had also pointed out that they would land him the job in Norway if he just pulled his finger out and applied for it.

He and Georgie had settled into spending most nights together, either at her place or, more usually, at his, but tonight she'd said she should spend a bit of time with Becky before she complained of being abandoned. In his head, he knew that was why she wasn't with him that evening, but it hadn't stopped his fears from inveigling their way into his brain and making themselves at home. Had she changed her mind about him? Was she about to ditch him again?

He poured himself a drink and opened up his laptop, automatically clicking on the jobs website and running his saved search.

Still nothing. Well, nothing in the UK.

Panic fluttered in his chest, and he forced himself to breathe slowly. There was probably one more month of digging, but then the weather would change, the academic term would start, and the dig would close. As far as he knew, his predecessor would be returning from her maternity leave, leaving him out of a job by Christmas. However much Georgie said that this was still months away, when he factored in the time it would take from a job advert appearing to the closing date for applications, then the selection process, interviews, second interviews and so on… those months were almost all taken up. He needed something amazing to come out of the dig if he was going to get a decent post after this one.

And he needed a suitable job to come up soon.

He closed the laptop lid, rubbing his brow. What if nothing came up? Georgie had said he could just move in with her and Becky, and lovely as it would be to live with Georgie, he'd assumed that would happen because she'd moved out of her shared flat and in with him, not that he was unemployed and sponging off her.

In the kitchen, he stared into the fridge, wondering what to make for dinner. He pulled out a few ingredients, his heart not really in it. He hated cooking just for himself.

His phone buzzed, and he peered at the screen, hoping it was Georgie. His heart sank. "Hi, Pappa. How are you?"

"Are we speaking English tonight? No. Norwegian, please."

He sighed, switching language. "Okay. How are you?"

"I'm very well, thank you. I was talking to Professor Gundersen today, and I asked him if he'd seen your application. He said that he hadn't."

Anders put the food back in the fridge and wandered through to the sitting room. "Er, no. I'm not applying for the job."

"What? Why on earth not? Has something better come up? No. This would be the perfect position for you."

He tucked himself into the corner of the sofa. "Well, not really. It's in Norway, and my life is here."

Haakon sniffed. "By that, I suppose you mean your girlfriend?"

Anders didn't grace him with an answer.

"What have you got lined up after your current post, then?"

Anders closed his eyes, a sick feeling bubbling in his stomach. "Nothing at the moment, but there's plenty of time."

"Anders, this is the opportunity of a lifetime for you. I would understand if you had a better offer in your hands, but you don't. A gap in your career will look terrible. You'd struggle to get another good post."

"Pappa, there's plenty of time. And I'm not going back to Norway. I want to build a life with Georgie, and I can't do that if I go to Norway."

There was a pause on the line, then, "I assume you mean marriage and children?"

"Mm."

"And *how* do you think you can support a wife and children without a good job, Anders? You need to get your prospects sorted out *first* and then worry about settling down."

Anders rubbed the back of his neck, biting his tongue. His father focusing on his job prospects had led directly to his mother leaving him and returning to England when Anders and Katya were still young.

"And Georgia wants this, does she? She wants you to make this sacrifice for her?" Haakon clicked his tongue. "If she was as keen as you are on settling down, she would be prepared to make some sacrifices and move to Norway to be with you. Her job is in the commercial sector. She could easily move."

"Georgie doesn't speak Norwegian," he said, trying to quell his rising annoyance with his father.

"You could teach her. And she could speak English here. Are you *sure* she wants to settle down with you? She's already left you once. Make sure you're not squandering the opportunity of a lifetime over someone who is only lukewarm about you."

"Pappa, I'm not moving back to Norway. Can we talk about something else?"

"Fine. I'm coming over to England. Yorkshire. To see you."

Anders's heart sank. "When?"

"Two weeks."

Anders breathed slowly. He should offer to put his father up, but he couldn't face the thought of it.

"Are you coming to visit the dig?"

"Yes, it would be nice to see it. Thank you. Will you be able to provide a room for me?"

"Um… not really. I've converted the spare room to a study. And Georgie often stays over."

And Georgie would *not* appreciate sharing the house with Haakon.

His father harrumphed on the other end of the line. "Well. I'm sure you will find a suitable hotel for me."

Anders wondered meanly which hotel might be the most run-down and horrible in the area.

"Pappa, lovely as it is to talk to you," he lied. "I'm afraid I have to run. Let me know the dates you're coming over, and I'll book somewhere for you."

Another harrumph. "Think about that job. If she does actually love you, she would support you over it. The closing date is coming up. Don't miss it."

Anders ended the call before he said something he'd regret, and tossed his phone down on the seat next to him.

His father's words nibbled away at his brain. It *was* an amazing opportunity. The *only* reason he wasn't going for it was because it was in Norway, and Georgie was in the UK. Even if she couldn't contemplate moving to Norway, surely they could manage for a couple of years with each of them going to see the other?

What if he was wrong, and she didn't love him as much as he loved her? What if he ended up not applying, and then she broke up with him?

The chatter in his head wouldn't stop. He picked his phone up and called her.

"*Hei, elskling.*"

"Hi. Something up?" She sounded grumpy.

"No. I just wanted to hear your voice."

She sighed heavily. "Anders, you spent all day with me."

"I know. Sorry."

"Becky and I are in the middle of making dinner. Were you just wanting to chat, or was there something important?"

He rubbed his brow. "Just wanted to chat. No worries. I'll see you tomorrow. I love you."

"Yeah. Love you too."

She ended the call, leaving him staring at his phone. The commentary in his head instantly started up again, and his gaze drifted out towards the kitchen. Maybe if he read the job details again, he'd realise it wasn't a great post, after all.

He headed for the kitchen and rummaged through the paper recycling box. He read over the pages again, then laid the application form and sheet outlining the details on the side, closing his eyes.

The job would be fantastic.

* * *

The following morning, Georgia waited on the doorstep for Anders to pick her up. Bright morning sun threatened to provoke a headache in her, and she shoved a pair of sunglasses on as Anders pulled up next to her.

"Morning, *elskling*," he said as she got in.

She leaned across to kiss him. "Morning."

He kissed her back, then took a deep breath as he eased the car away from the kerb. She looked over, wondering what was coming.

"Pappa called. He's coming over to see me."

Her heart sank. "Oh. He's not staying with you, is he?"

He chuckled. "No. I have to find him a hotel." He kept his focus on the road. "He wasn't happy that I didn't apply for the job."

"Well, I'm sure he'll live." She turned in her seat to look at him. "Did he give you a hard time about it?"

"Yep."

"You're *not* applying for it, are you?"

"Nope."

She moved back to face the front. She could imagine the conversation Anders had had.

"You going to get your hair cut and have a shave before he arrives?" she asked.

He glanced over. "No." He tilted his head. "Maybe. I'll have to before the new academic year starts."

"Why?"

He gave her a withering look and didn't answer.

"I like your beard. And your curls."

"My hair's not curly. It's wavy."

She laughed. The wayward lock at the front was currently doing a loop-the-loop.

"Any jobs in the UK come up yet?"

He shook his head, staring out at the road. She sucked her teeth.

"You want to apply for that one in Norway, don't you?"

He didn't reply, making her heart go into triple-time.

"I'm not applying for it," he said eventually. "But I have to confess that my stress levels are sky-rocketing at the fact there's nothing else coming up."

She reached across to squeeze his thigh. "I know. We'll figure something out."

He pulled into the field next to the dig and parked. They both clambered out and went to the back of the car, ready to unload things. She stopped him before he opened the boot.

"Hey, come here."

She held her arms out wide, and he stepped in. She hugged him close, stroking his broad back.

"I know how stressed you are, both about the job, and about your dad coming over. We'll work something out, I promise."

His back muscles bunched under her hands. "I know. Come on. Help me get set up for the day."

He pulled free, opened the boot, and grabbed the heaviest things, his face turned away. She rubbed his shoulder, wishing she could ease his stress.

Everything set up, she poured him a coffee from the Thermos he'd brought and passed it across.

"Talk to me?" she said.

He peered into his coffee. "I'm just stressed. I'm getting anxious about what I'll do if nothing comes up work-wise, and Pappa's just going to bang on about how I'm wasting my life." He shrugged. "But you know all that."

"Yeah, I know. I wish I could ease some of it, though."

Would finding a Viking burial help him?

Yes. But it might also mean she lost him. It would be exactly what Anders needed to nail the job in Norway. Would he really blow a hole in his career just to stay with her?

40

Aelfgyth finished bathing the body, then wiped her eyes, sniffing hard. Einar, her beloved Einar, had gone to sleep but never woken. Where was he? With God? Or with his gods?

She was old, and he was still heavy, despite age stealing some of his strength, so Magnus's wife, Synne, had helped her to dress him in his finest tunic. Aelfgyth fastened his belt, letting his pouch settle on one side of his waist, and his knife nestle into the folds of his tunic on the other. Synne raised her brows, but kept silent. Aelfgyth drew a small object from her own leather pouch and fastened it around Einar's neck. A simple silver cross hung on a leather cord, and she tucked the cross into the neck of his tunic. Synne smiled.

Aelfgyth and Einar had discussed his burial over and over. He'd been insistent on having his weapons with him. Resting on the bed next to him at the moment was his sword, ready to be taken with his body to the burial site. He'd been too stiff and too old to wield it properly for some years, and Aelfgyth knew Magnus had expected it to be given to him on his father's death, but it would be buried alongside its owner. She'd held her ground, too, which was why a cross now lay on his chest.

His body would be taken to the nearby knoll to be buried. She'd argued with him over this. She yearned for him to be buried at the church, but he was adamant he didn't want that.

"Your god finds those who die in battle and who drown at sea, doesn't he? Then he will find me, even if I am not next to the church."

She straightened her back, fresh tears slipping over her cheeks at the memories. She would pray for his soul, and hope that God could accept that he had been a good man. Maybe that would be enough.

Four men arrived at the door to the hut, carrying a willow hurdle. She and Synne moved back, making space for them to lay it on the floor, ready to lift Einar on to it. They were the sons of Einar's men; friends of Magnus. They would be Magnus's men now.

They lifted Einar's body down on to the hurdle, and Aelfgyth adjusted his clothes, making him look neater in death than he had in most of his life. Once she was ready, she signalled to them that they could take him. The four men each took a corner of the hurdle and lifted Einar up. Despite his age, he was still a big enough man that two of the hurdle-bearers grunted with the effort, making a small smile creep over Aelfgyth's lips.

They carried him out of the hut and towards the clearing around the great hall. Magnus and Synne lived in the room at the end of that now. The whole settlement had gathered in the clearing, ready for the procession to the knoll. Aelfgyth walked immediately behind the hurdle, her eyes on her beloved husband, Magnus and Synne flanking her. Behind them, men carried the goods that would be buried with him: his sword, his axe, his shield. Einar had asked for his comb, his whetstone, and his flint to be buried with him, too. Aelfgyth didn't know what use he would have for them if he was with God, but she'd agreed. It had been important to him. She had them in the leather pouch hanging from her belt.

The procession wove its way between the scattered huts and on towards the small hillock, singing. Each of the men carried a wooden shield and rhythmically beat the hilts of their knives against them. The sound made the hairs on the back of her neck stand up.

They reached the mound. A space had already been dug for Einar's body, and the four men lowered him into the hole, using ropes tied to the handles of the hurdle. Einar might be being buried with his weapons, but Aelfgyth had insisted on the grave being cut in an East-West line. Einar's gods didn't care, but her God might. Aelfgyth knelt at the side of the grave, opened the leather pouch, and leaned down to tuck his comb close to his cheek, his whetstone close to his right hand, and his flint close to his left. For the final time, she tweaked his tunic and cloak, neatening them both.

Synne helped her back to her feet, then the two women stepped back, and the men carrying his weapons moved towards the grave. One laid Einar's magnificent sword along his body, the hilt at the top of his breastbone. Another placed his axe between his ankles, and a third rested his shield over his chest, the hilt of the sword just visible beneath it.

The villagers processed past the grave, still singing; still beating their shields. Once everyone had paid their respects and circled the grave, they made their way back down to the great hall, where the drinking and feasting would take place.

Aelfgyth lingered at the knoll, staring at the man she had first hated but soon loved. The father of her children. The leader of the settlement. The man she had thought would be a brute, but who had turned out to be the kindest, gentlest man she knew. The man who had adored her and loved his children and grandchildren. She brushed away her tears, offered up a silent prayer, and hoped that they would meet again in the afterlife.

Georgia woke suddenly, tears nipping her eyes. She stared into the darkness, her brain slowly leaving the tenth century, and recognising Anders's bedroom as her surroundings. The dream had been so real. She could still smell the smoke in the air, the meat for the feast roasting. Still hear the singing and the banging of shields.

Why had Aelfgyth come into her dreams? There were no finds from the dig here in Anders's house. Was it because all of the finds linked to the burial were *in* the burial, and therefore couldn't be found unless they looked for the grave?

Or maybe none of the visions are real and it's all coming from your imagination.

She checked the clock. Just gone five. Light crept in through the blinds, and she peered across at Anders sleeping next to her. He lay curled on his side, facing her, his hair tumbling over his eyes. One hand rested on her waist, and one leg was hooked over hers. She gazed at him, tears still wetting her lashes, her brain half seeing him as Einar. Reality cleared the last vestiges of her dream away, and she blinked.

"No. You're not Einar. And you're not dead. And I haven't just buried you," she murmured.

Anders's eyes fluttered, and he made a soft sound, not quite awake and not quite asleep. She smiled at him, waiting for him to fall back to sleep. He wriggled a little, tucking her closer, then settled.

As ever, he radiated heat. Georgia stuck her free leg out from under the duvet, trying to cool down. Now she was awake, and the sun was up, she wouldn't go back to sleep. Should she make herself a coffee downstairs? Sit at the table in the garden and listen to the birds? The songbirds were already in full voice, audible through the open window.

Sticking one leg out hadn't cooled her enough, so she eased away from Anders and slipped out of bed. She pulled on a few clothes, then padded down to the kitchen and filled the kettle. While it boiled, she rested her hips against the counter, thinking. Had Aelfgyth and Einar actually existed?

She sighed. She'd never know. Her brain ran back over the dream, linking the burial procession to the site. Einar's grave would be in the small wooded area next to the site. There *was* a mound there. The ground in the middle of the thicket rose. Her heart raced. If they surveyed it, would they find a full Viking burial, with sword, axe, and shield? Those were so rare on this side of the Pennines. Oh, if Anders led a team that found that, it would make his name!

Would that make it more likely he would stay, or leave? Would he get headhunted by a university in Norway, and offered a job he couldn't turn down?

The kettle clicked off behind her, and she spooned ground coffee into a cafetiere, a nervous sickness in her belly. Was she enough to keep him here? Or would he be offered something so good that he couldn't say no, and would leave her again?

Her mind churned while she finished making the coffee. She poured out a mugful, added some milk, then took it out to the back garden. Cool, fresh air washed over her, and she sat, listening to the birds as they heralded the day. The early sun had a cloudless sky to itself, and although the temperature was perfect just then, the day was going to turn into another scorcher.

Her thoughts flip-flopped over whether to tell Anders about the burial. She wanted him to find it, but not if it meant he would leave. But maybe if he found it, a university in the UK would headhunt him.

She couldn't tell him it was there based on a dream, though. He would look at her with patient eyes and a kindly expression, and dismiss it entirely.

Before she could ponder any more on how to get him to believe her, the man himself emerged through the back door, carrying a mug of coffee and clad only in pyjama bottoms.

"Couldn't sleep?" he asked, sitting down.

"Vivid dream woke me, and then you were boiling and the room was too bright, so I just got up. Sorry. Did I wake you?"

He shook his head, stretching out his legs. "No. What was the dream about?"

"Vikings."

He chuckled, and blew on his coffee. Georgia's eyes travelled over him, her stomach flipping. After working outside for so long, he had a lot of blond in his hair, highlighting the curls, but his chest hair was still dark. And although he was no gym-bunny, he had a broad, lean build that always looked toned.

"You can have a very hungry gaze, sometimes," said Anders, smiling at her over the rim of his mug.

"Well, you have a very attractive body," she replied.

Pink tinged his cheeks. "I'd rather be admired for things I've actually *done* than things I've had no control over."

She leaned over and tweaked his nose. "It's fine. I love you for your mind as well as your body. But you *are* sitting there half naked and *utterly* gorgeous."

He shook his head and turned back to his coffee, his blush still colouring his cheeks. Georgia laughed to herself. He'd probably never realise just how attractive he was, especially looking this gloriously dishevelled and straight out of bed. Her body thrummed with desire.

"Breakfast?" she said. "Or back to bed?"

His lips twitched. "Back to bed, given how you're *still* looking at me."

She grinned. "Right answer."

41

Later that morning, Georgia chewed the end of a pencil, studying the map of the dig site spread out in front of her on Anders's desk. Anders had marked every find on it, along with the building outlines. There were also other scribbled notes in his tight, neat handwriting. She gathered the map to one side and spread out the survey results instead, hoping to find some solid evidence pointing to a burial that she could show to Anders.

It didn't matter. She still couldn't put her finger on anything that would suggest there was a burial in the trees. It would be in entirely the *wrong* location, based on findings from other settlements. In fact, Steve had suggested the wooded area might be of interest all those weeks ago in Anders's office, and Anders had dismissed his ideas instantly.

The mid-morning sun streamed in through the tent opening, and a trickle of sweat worked its way between her shoulder blades. Outside, Anders had erected some gazebo-like structures to give the team some shade from the sun, making it reasonably pleasant to work outside. Here inside the tent, the canvas trapped all the heat, making the space absolutely stifling, now that the breezes of the last few days had dropped.

She closed her eyes, re-living the dream she'd had about Einar's burial, focusing on the buildings and where the sun was. She half opened her eyes, peering through her eyelashes so that she could just about see the map and the surveys, but still also visualise the burial.

"Past the weaving hut, over the slight rise, veer right a little…" Her finger followed the path the procession had taken. It definitely finished in the small wooded area.

"He won't buy it," she muttered.

She wanted him to find it, though. The site was already turning into the dig of a lifetime, but if he found a Viking burial, replete with sword and weapons? Well *then,* he might finally escape from the shadow of his father. *Then* when people heard 'Mortensen', they might think of Anders first, rather than Haakon.

She pulled her phone out and texted him: Coffee? Cold drink?

A few moments later, a reply came back: cold drink ♥

She fetched a couple of drinks from the cooler box in the refreshments tent, meeting Anders as she came back out. His face was flushed, and the hair at the nape of his neck was damp with sweat.

"Perfect timing," he said, smiling. "I was just thinking I needed to re-hydrate."

"How's it all going?"

They'd reached his desk, and he ran his eye over the maps and surveys, distracted for a moment.

"Er… yeah… fine. What's all this?"

"Something I've been thinking about."

He hooked a foot around a leg of his chair, pulled it towards him, then sat, pressing the cold drink to his face. "Going to tell me?"

"I think you'll shoot me down in flames." She cracked open her drink and took a slurp. "You'll say there isn't enough evidence for what I'm thinking."

"Go on. Tell me anyway." He leaned back in his seat, flapping the neck of his top to get some cooler air in.

"I'm wondering if there's a burial," she said.

He arched a brow, but didn't comment. He didn't have to. His expression said everything.

"Given that the site is in the right area to have been reallocated by Halfdan to someone senior in his army, and given that we think the site was probably abandoned around the time of the Harrying of The North, it's not a huge stretch to think that the settlement was more Scandinavian than Anglo-Saxon over this period."

Anders opened his mouth, then closed it again, folding his lips in.

"We never really looked at the wooded area over here. It

wasn't surveyed, but it's possible that the person the land was transferred to by Halfdan didn't convert to Christianity. That they were buried as a Viking."

Anders pinched the bridge of his nose. "No. Walk me through your reasoning from the start. You've given me your conclusions, but not shown me your evidence."

Her eyes narrowed. "Don't treat me like a student. I'm not one of your undergraduates, Anders."

He leaned forward, his colour rising slightly. "No. If you were, you'd know better than to present me with half-baked ideas with no foundation. Georgie, you have a degree in this! Come on! Walk me through your evidence and reasoning."

His words stung. She glared at him across the desk. He threw a challenging look back at her, in full-blown academic mode, and she drew a breath, organising her argument.

"We think the settlement probably changed hands after the Battle of York," she started.

"Evidence?" he cut in.

She ground her teeth. She'd seen him like this before, going over things with one of the Honours students helping out on the dig in Orkney. At the time, she'd thought he was being a brilliant teacher. Right now, he was infuriating.

"There are some finds that are Scandinavian in origin – some of the combs, the amber bead, the knife, and so on – and scholars don't believe there was much trade between this region and Scandinavia at the time. Therefore, I would argue that there was evidence of the settlement being occupied by someone who originated in Scandinavia, not long after Halfdan parcelled out the land to his pals."

"Cut the attitude, Georgie," Anders said softly. "I just asked you to back up your argument."

She scowled at him. "Would you agree that there is some evidence that supports my assertion that the land changed hands at around the time of the Battle of York, Dr Mortensen?"

He turned his head away for a moment. "Why are you so mad at me? Why are we fighting?"

"Because you're treating me like one of your students."

He breathed deeply. "I thought I was treating you like an

academically qualified colleague. If you can't reason out your theories, why are you presenting them?" He pressed the drinks can against his other cheek. "Okay. The land changed hands. That still doesn't mean there's a burial here."

She backed down a little. "You agree that this area would be considered more Scandinavian than Anglo-Saxon over the period between The Battle of York and the Harrying of the North?"

"Yes. I agree the finds support that argument."

"Thank you."

He flashed her a conciliatory look. "I actually don't have a major issue with your claim that the area was abandoned. We've found nothing after the late eleventh century. How did you get from that to saying you think there's a full Viking burial in the woods?"

"We've found nothing overtly Christian. No sign that the people here converted."

"We've found nothing that says they didn't," he countered.

She took a long drink, her eyes on his over the rim of the can. "You can be *so* annoying when you're in this mode."

He raised his chin, his eyes flashing. "In what mode? Dig director mode? You're building towards asking me to do a geophysical survey of the wooded area, but not telling me any valid reasons why I should."

She squared her shoulders. "We haven't found any burials on site. Where were they buried?"

"In a long-lost churchyard, probably."

"I just think we should survey the woods and the next field over. I think there's more to find."

"If there *were* any burials, that would be the wrong direction. I would anticipate any burials being in the ground beneath us. And you've still not argued your case effectively over there being *any* burials."

How could she convince him to survey the woods? If he just *did*, he would find it all. Her gaze skimmed the papers on the desk, but he was infuriatingly right. She had no evidence that would sway him.

"I can see it, Anders," she blurted out. "Full burial. Sword. Shield. *Everything*. Where the trees are."

He blinked. "You want me to commit resources to surveying the woods? Based on what, Georgie? Your imagination? The visions you think you have? It's in the wrong direction. There's *nothing* over that side of the site that leads me to believe there would be anything worth finding in the woods."

She held her hands up. "Fine… I'm sure you're needed out on the dig."

His brows shot up. "Are you throwing me out? I'm sitting at *my* desk, in *my* dig."

Defeated, she tidied his map away, her jaw clenched.

He caught her hand. "Why are you so mad at me?"

She softened. "I'm not. I'm annoyed that I can't convince you. I want you to find something amazing, so that you can throw it in your father's face."

A smile tweaked his lips. "*Elskling*, I could have discovered Stonehenge and he still wouldn't be impressed." He squeezed her hand. "I can't survey the area just because you imagine there's something there. I have to write all of this up and justify all the costs. I have to explain why I thought there would be something there. So, if you can't explain it to me, I can't argue for it."

She knew that, which only deepened her frustration.

"I know. I'm sorry I got cross with you."

He pushed his chair back. "Back to the heat I go."

He dropped a kiss on to the top of her head and headed back out to the dig. She stared after him. How *could* she convince him to check the place out? She *did* only have her visions leading her to this conclusion, and although he humoured her when she told him about them, he didn't actually believe in them.

42

That evening, Becky slid into the seat opposite Georgia and passed a drink across. The Blacksmith's Arms heaved with people, and they'd been lucky to get the last couple of seats. Admittedly, this was the table next to the toilets, so it was always going to be the last one to be taken, but a table was a table. The heat of the day hadn't diminished one iota, and despite all of the doors and windows to the pub being wide-open, the temperature was uncomfortably high.

"Cheers," said Georgia, clinking her glass against Becky's.

"Cheers." Becky slurped the froth off the top of her pint of beer. "Okay. Tell me about the dig. What have you found?"

Georgia itched to tell her about the burial site. Or, more accurately, the potential burial site. Instead, she filled Becky in on the other finds of the week and the current theories over the site. Becky listened closely, asking about a few details, but mostly keeping quiet. As Georgia finished her update, Becky scrutinised her.

"I get the feeling that there's something you're not telling me. Oh, has Sam found a massive hoard of gold, and you're all sworn to secrecy?"

Georgia laughed. "No. Though if anyone on the dig was going to find a hoard, you're right, it would be Sam." She took a sip of her drink, wondering whether to tell Becky. She'd scoffed at her when she'd told her about her visions before.

"Come on… spit it out," Becky prompted. "There's clearly something you want to talk about from the dig."

Georgia sighed. "Okay. But hear me out? And don't shoot me down in flames. I had enough of that from Anders today."

Becky held her hands up, palms out, offering peace.

Georgia bit the inside of her lip, then told Becky everything. Every vision she'd had; how she'd been 'shown' the weaving hut before they'd found it; Aelfgyth and Einar growing old; Einar asking to be buried with his weapons; the burial procession. To her credit, Becky said nothing, though her expression screamed utter disbelief. Georgia eventually ground to a halt, her enthusiasm for telling Becky about it gone.

"And you told Anders all this?" Becky asked.

Georgia rubbed the end of her nose. "Yeah. He bought into it about as much as you look like you have."

Becky shrugged. "Are you surprised? He's an academic. I'm a scientist. Neither of us really deal with odd visions triggered by random objects dug up out of the ground, and dreams. Let's face it, Georgie, you do have an overactive imagination. These 'visions' are just you looking at objects, dreaming about what they might have been like when they were new, and weaving in information you've gleaned from reading research papers, or building on things from previous digs. The weaving hut is where you imagined it to be, because the weaving huts in most settlements were probably in pretty similar locations. The bead is Scandinavian and therefore probably brought over by someone in the Viking army. It's the kind of thing given to a woman. It's not unreasonable to imagine that a Viking man fell in love with an Anglo-Saxon woman and gave her amber beads as a gift. None of that means any of it was true." She paused. "What did Anders say about the possibility of there being a burial in the wooded area?"

Georgia wriggled her shoulders. "He said it's in the wrong direction."

"He's the expert, whatever his father says. If anyone knows about Anglo-Scandinavian settlements, it's Anders."

"But I saw it. I wasn't just imagining things. I know I can have wild flights of fancy sometimes, but I promise you, I saw all of this."

Becky didn't answer, but her brows remained close to her hairline.

"Do you think you or Steve could survey the area?" asked Georgia.

"Not without say so from Anders. It's his site. He'd have to sign off on the use of the equipment. I mean, Dig For It would have to bill for the use, and unless we have a bit of paper with his agreement on it, we wouldn't get paid."

Frustration turned to desperation in her. "Could you not just borrow the equipment? Do it on the sly?"

Becky's mouth fell open. "What, because you think you've seen something in a vision or dreamed there's something there? No!"

Georgia took a breath. "How can I convince you to do a survey of the area?"

"Bring me a bit of paper with Anders's signature on it."

Georgia swallowed. She had no chance of getting that.

"Why are you so bent out of shape over it?"

She fingered her brow, her skin clammy to the touch from the heat. "Because I am genuinely convinced there's a Viking burial there, and I want Anders to find it."

Becky sipped her pint, thoughtful. "If he did, it would make his name. I mean, even more than now. He'd be headhunted. You sure he'd be able to resist the lure of that job in Norway? Or do you think you can get past your anxiety about the idea of going to Norway with him?"

Her guts knotted. "Maybe he'd be offered an amazing job in the UK. He's the expert in *Anglo*-Scandinavian settlements."

That was what she was holding on for.

Becky's expression softened. "Look, I can talk to Steve about it. Maybe he'd be happy to do the survey for nothing, or charge it to you personally, rather than to the project."

Her spirits lifted. "If Steve is happy to invoice me for it, I'll pay for it."

"You'd still need to okay it with Anders. We can't just march on to the site and start surveying things if he isn't on board about it all, even if the project *isn't* paying for it. He's the dig director."

She nodded, but if she couldn't talk him around, maybe they could do the survey when he wasn't there.

"Thanks, Becky."

"Steve hasn't said yes yet. Don't get your hopes up."

Some of Georgia's pent-up tension evaporated. Steve already

thought she was a little eccentric and wouldn't be surprised that she'd had some madcap idea. And Anders? He'd probably humour her too if he didn't have to write it up.

Excitement fizzed in her blood. The burial was there. She knew it. And once she had the survey results, she could convince Anders to dig there, and he would find it.

43

The date of Haakon's arrival crawled around. His father had been with him for less than an hour, and already Anders had had enough of him. His opening words to Anders had been, "Dear God, what do you look like?" and things had largely gone downhill since then.

He'd picked him up from the station and taken him to the hotel he'd organised. Haakon had been disparaging about the car, the hotel, the weather… after a night of little sleep, stressing about the visit, Anders's reserves of patience had hit empty.

He parked up in the field next to the dig and glanced across. "Coffee?"

"Yes. And then you can talk me through the site. And we speak Norwegian."

Anders shoved his rising irritation back down and scanned his father. His steel-grey hair was cropped close to his head, and his pale blue eyes peered out from behind wire-rimmed glasses. He stood a little shorter than Anders, with a slim, almost gaunt frame. Like Anders, he wore walking trousers and boots, but somehow, he managed to look smart in them. Probably because there currently didn't seem to be a speck of mud on them, unlike the trousers and boots Anders had on.

Anders stuck his head around the finds tent and waved at Georgie. "Hey. I'm back. All good while I was gone?"

"Yep. Couple of nice finds, but I can talk you through them later."

"Okay. Coffee? I'm making one for Pappa."

"Please."

Coffees made, he found a spare chair and carried it through to the finds tent, plonking it down next to his desk. His father had already made himself comfortable in Anders's chair. Almost before Anders could sit, Haakon launched into a discussion about the site.

"Show me the map of the site? And the survey results?" he barked in Norwegian.

From the other side of the tent, Georgie shot him a sympathetic look over her shoulder. He unfurled the site map, anchoring it at the corners with mugs and books, then started to talk him through it all.

As ever, his father spoke over the top of him, snapping out questions that he'd have had the answers to if he'd just shut up and listened. As Anders finished describing the site, Haakon butted in.

"What papers will you get out of it? Have you submitted any yet? Let me see them."

"Er, nothing submitted yet. I have some drafted, and I have the site report to finish."

Haakon turned his steely gaze to him. "No papers submitted yet? How many papers do you think you'll get? Have you at least thought where you'll be sending them when they're written?"

Anders had, but he didn't especially want to discuss it with him.

"I have a few journals in mind," he said, trying to dodge the question.

"Which ones?"

Reluctantly, Anders told him.

"Pht. You think you'll get a paper in there?" Haakon's gaze travelled over Anders, his eyes narrow. "Show me the drafts."

Anders leaned over and pulled up the files on his laptop. His father changed his glasses, pulling out a slim pair from a case in his pocket, and peered at the screen. Anders waited while he read, feeling like he was fifteen years old again, and his father was checking his homework.

"Hmph," said Haakon when he finished reading. "I can see where you're going with them, but the structure could be better. They're early drafts, I assume? What have you been doing with your time?"

Anders swallowed, his throat dry. "Managing the site.

Digging."

Haakon sneered. "That, boy, is the problem. You're the project manager, not some junior like Georgia."

Anders's gaze flicked to her. She'd stiffened in her seat, but her head was still bent over her work. How much Norwegian did she understand?

Haakon leaned back in his seat, his arms crossed over his narrow chest. "Wake up! You are *wasting* your life and *wasting* opportunities. Professor Gunderson would be *delighted* to have you on his team, and you haven't even contacted him." He paused, his lips thinning. "So, you haven't applied for that job; you're not focusing enough on publications… what *are* your plans? What jobs *have* you applied for?"

His stomach clenched, and he said nothing.

"There are three other jobs going in Norway that would suit you. Nothing as prestigious as the one with Professor Gunderson, but still fairly reasonable. Please tell me you're considering them."

"Pappa, we've had this discussion," he ground out, acutely aware of Georgie's body language on the other side of the tent.

Sam poked his head into the tent. "Anders? Can you come and look at something? Oh! Sorry! I didn't realise you were in a meeting." He nodded at Haakon. "Professor Mortensen."

Georgie raised her head. "What is it, Sam? Anything I can help with?"

Sam brightened. "Yeah. Do you mind?"

She shook her head and scrambled off her chair to follow him out. Haakon's narrowed eyes followed her, his jaw bunching, then his gaze swung back to Anders, and his nose wrinkled.

"Look at you, Anders! You look a mess! In fact, you look *feral* with your hair so long and your nails full of dirt! You have no coherent plan of where you're going in life. You are throwing away your career. Over her?"

Anders switched to English, painfully aware that Georgie could return to the tent at any moment. "Pappa, Georgie can't move to Norway. I realise love is an alien concept to you, but I love her, and I would rather be unemployed and with her than go for a job in Norway and lose her."

Haakon stared at him, his pale blue eyes piercing. "You are a bloody fool, Anders. I am *ashamed* of you. Ashamed that a man with as much talent as you would throw away his career over a woman. Especially a woman like Georgia. She's not an academic! Her job is just commercial. She clearly has neither the ability nor the drive to have a proper career. She could work anywhere. And if she loved you even half as much as you claim to love her, she would go to Norway with you."

Right at that moment, Georgie stepped back into the tent, and Anders regretted to his core that he'd switched the argument to English. Her steps faltered, then she re-took her seat, her back to them, her shoulders bunched.

Anders glowered across the desk at his father. "There's more to life than a career. But you clearly never learned that, or Mum wouldn't have left you!"

Haakon sniffed, his lip curling. "If your mother had been less selfish, she would have seen that I was right to pursue my goals. If I had stayed in some *backwater*, focusing on what she'd wanted, I would have made nothing of my life. Are you really content to be a nobody, with nothing to your name except a woman who is so vastly inferior to you?"

Anders shook with anger. He tried to breathe steadily, but couldn't. His voice, when it came, was low, and thrummed with fury.

"Get out. Now. I will not have you speak about Georgia like that."

Haakon blinked at him. Anders held his nerve, glaring back, his heart pounding. His father harrumphed, then pushed his chair back and stalked out of the tent.

* * *

Anders let his breath go slowly, then raised his head to look over at Georgia. "I am so sorry he said all that. That is absolutely *not* how I feel!"

She swivelled in her seat, then slid off it and walked over to him. "I know. You okay?"

She slipped her arms around him, rubbing his back, and he dipped his head to rest his forehead on her shoulder.

"No. Not really."

She could feel his heart thumping against her chest, and cuddled him closer, wishing she could ease some of his stress.

"Just ignore him. Don't let him get under your skin."

He trembled. "But he's right, though, isn't he? I'm *not* focusing enough on papers or publications. I *don't* have a career plan."

She dusted the side of his head with a light kiss. "So? There's more to this life than work. Surely it's more important to be happy?"

"Is it not possible to have both?"

She kissed his temple again. "I'm sure it is. I am. I'm also sure it's possible to be more patient than you are."

He raised his head, leaning back in her arms, his face drawn. "Academia isn't very forgiving of career gaps."

She moved one hand up to fuss with his curls at the nape of his neck. "Anders… choose *your* dreams, not Haakon's dreams for you."

Fear filled his eyes. "They overlap, Georgie," he whispered. "My dreams are to be known in my field. To be introduced somewhere and people not be disappointed that 'the wrong Mortensen' is there."

She wondered where she figured in his future. Where exactly did she rank? He might *say* he would rather be unemployed and with her than in a great job without her, but when push really came to shove, would he stay in the UK with her and ignore all the jobs in Norway?

"Do you have any painkillers?" he asked, breaking her train of thought.

"Yeah. In my bag. Headache?"

He nodded miserably.

She eased away from him to rummage in her bag for the packet of painkillers she knew was in there. She handed him a strip, along with the bottle of water from her desk, and he smiled weakly.

"I wish I could take some of this off you," she murmured. "You're wound so tightly right now."

He took the tablets, throwing his head back as he swallowed them, then handed the plastic strip and the water back to her.

"He'll be gone the day after tomorrow."

"What are the three jobs like in Norway that he mentioned?"

He studied her. "I don't know. I haven't looked at them... How much of the Norwegian did you follow?"

"Enough." She shrugged. "Too much."

"I'm sorry."

"Never apologise for another person. That's not your responsibility. It's theirs."

He snorted. "You might wait a long time for that with Pappa. That would involve him realising he was out of line."

From outside the tent came the sounds of Haakon barking at someone on the team, demanding that they tell him about the trench and how it fitted into the wider site findings. Anders closed his eyes, pinching the bridge of his nose.

"I'd better go out before he pisses *everyone* off."

Georgia rubbed his arm, and he gave her a wan smile, then headed out to the dig.

She wandered back over to her desk and turned on the radio, trying to oust Haakon's words from her head, but they ricocheted around incessantly.

"If she loved you even half as much as you claim to love her, she would go to Norway with you... Her job is just commercial... She could work anywhere."

She gnawed at the end of a pencil. He was right. She didn't have a career the way Anders did, but she was perfectly happy doing what she did, and despite her job being commercial, she was well known in her field. That said, she *could* move to Norway with him, and get a similar job over there, technically.

She closed her eyes, a lump forming in her stomach. The idea of upping sticks and moving to a new country where she knew no one and didn't speak the language filled her with dread. It was easy for Anders to flit back and forth. He was bilingual and had spent half his life in Norway and half in Britain. What if she moved and then felt as isolated and lonely as Amelia had?

Icy fear made her shiver, despite the stifling heat in the tent. Did Anders think her reluctance to go to Norway was because she didn't love him? She did. More than anyone else she'd ever known.

She needed to decide what she would do if nothing came up for him in the UK. *Was* she so selfish that she wouldn't move? It wouldn't have to be forever.

She didn't want to lose him again.

44

Anders returned to the finds tent near to the end of the afternoon, taking Georgie and Haakon a coffee each. After annoying everyone on site with his snapped questions and disparaging looks, Haakon had taken up residence at Anders's desk there. He'd talked more about the site to Anders over the day, but in the end, Anders had needed to get away from him and had spent as much time in a trench as he could.

"No wonder you've not drafted anything out yet. You're spending all your time digging," Haakon said, looking up from the desk. "Here, I have put some ideas together for you, for potential papers. Clearly, you will have to write them, but perhaps it will give you some ideas on where to start."

Anders turned away and took a long breath. Georgie caught his eye and pulled a face, making him have to work hard to stifle a laugh.

"Anders!"

He sat at the desk, resigned to another blistering session. Haakon shuffled some papers around, and Anders's heart sank at the sheaf of densely annotated pages.

"Right. Well, I think you could get four papers out. Perhaps five. It depends on some of the finds. I assume you trust your finds manager's skills?" Haakon arched a bushy, grey eyebrow.

Anders bristled on Georgie's behalf. "Of course. She's the most knowledgeable person in the UK on Anglo-Scandinavian finds."

"Hmph. If you say so."

He moved on to lecture Anders on the site, as if Anders was his student, and this was Haakon's dig. Anders zoned out a little. None of what his father was saying was news to him. He knew the site inside out. He knew exactly what papers he could write on it. He didn't need his father giving him 'cheat-sheets' or a leg-up. History told him to suck it up, though. Let his father witter on and feel as if he had imparted dazzlingly unique insights to him. If Anders dared to say he knew all of this, Haakon would chastise him for not having drafted the papers yet.

He sipped his coffee, letting the words wash over him, waiting for his father to run out of steam.

He wondered what the three jobs in Norway were. Presumably they were all in academia. His father wouldn't countenance anything else. Curiosity prickled, even though he wasn't going to apply.

"Anders! Are you listening?"

"Yes," he said in a flat tone, even though he hadn't been.

Haakon narrowed his eyes, then carried on.

Anders leaned back in his seat far enough that he could look at Georgie without his father realising he wasn't fully focused on the pages on the desk. Her head was bent, and she was concentrating on the finds in front of her, but he just wanted to look at her.

Next to him, his father ground to a halt, and Anders sat forwards again, taking the proffered sheets.

"Thank you. Very helpful. Appreciated."

In the corner of his eye, he saw Georgie turn her head, her lips twitching, before she turned back again.

"Well. Time to go home," said Anders, getting to his feet and gathering the mugs ready to be washed. "Georgie, Pappa and I are going out for dinner. Are you joining us?"

She threw him a look that told him exactly what she thought of that idea.

"No. Thank you." She flashed him a sweet smile, full of sarcasm.

Anders left the two of them alone while he washed up. Everyone had gathered in the refreshments tent, and looked over expectantly at him. He wasn't in the humour to do a team talk.

"Thanks, everyone. Um… I'll be dropping Georgia off in the morning, but then I'm taking Professor Mortensen in to the university for some meetings he's arranged. Sam, can you act as me until I'm back? I shouldn't be long."

Was he imagining it, or had everyone instantly relaxed when he'd said his father wouldn't be there the next day?

He finished tidying up, then went to rescue Georgie.

When he joined her, her colour was high. Words had clearly been exchanged, and nothing good from the looks of things.

"All okay here?" he asked nervously.

"Fine. Just clearing the air a little," said Georgie, her voice brittle.

He swallowed, not liking the sound of that. His father glowered at Georgie, who tilted her chin up, defiance in her eyes.

"Shall we go?" Anders said, jamming his thumb through his key ring.

The ride to Georgie's was frosty and silent. Georgie sat in the back, behind him; his father sat stony-faced in the front. When he pulled up outside Georgie's flat, he got out of the car and walked with her to her door.

"What was said in the 'air-clearing' at the site?" he asked in a low voice.

She pressed her lips together. "Haakon told me what he thought of me. And I reciprocated."

His heart sank. "Okay. I'm sorry if he was rude to you."

She shrugged. "Don't apologise for him. And I'm not sorry I was rude to him." She caught his hand. "Come over after dinner if you want. You might sleep better in my bed."

He smiled. "Mm. I will. Oh! I just remembered. Josh messaged me."

"Re-enactment Josh?"

"Mm. Did we want to catch up with him and Libby one weekend?"

She grinned. "Yeah, that would be great."

He kissed her softly, then drew back, groaning. "I'd better go. See you later."

She stood on tiptoe to kiss his lips. "See you later. Try not to kill him."

He waited until she was inside, then returned to the car.

"*She* is the most ill-mannered, disrespectful woman I have ever come across," said his father as soon as Anders closed his door.

"Why? What happened?"

"She called me a nasty, bitter, unpleasant old man."

He wanted to laugh. "Uh, huh? And what had you said to her that provoked this?"

"Nothing."

He glanced across. Haakon stared out of the windshield, his face hard. He'd winkle it out of Georgie later, but he was pretty sure *something* had been said, and he had a good idea what.

He pulled away from the kerb, chuckling to himself. Well done, Georgie, for standing up to him.

* * *

Inside her flat, Georgia kicked off her shoes, still smarting from Haakon's last set of comments.

"I have never understood what my son sees in you. You are a silly and selfish woman. He has the opportunity of a lifetime, and you are sulking and whining and wanting him to stay in England with no job, rather than making even a small sacrifice and moving to Norway."

Was it a small sacrifice? Was she building the idea of moving to Norway up into something much bigger than reality because of Amelia?

The flat was empty, and Georgia pulled out her phone to message Becky.

Had a shit day. Can you pick up takeaway?

Almost immediately, Becky messaged back. *Sure. Usual? I take it H has been an arse?*

Georgia smiled. *Yes. And yes. See you soon.*

She headed to the kitchen and made herself a coffee, then sat down at the breakfast bar with a pad of paper and a pencil, trying to draw up a list of pros and cons over Norway while she waited for Becky to get home. Obviously, the major pro would be that she would be with Anders, and he would have a good job and be happy. Except she wasn't entirely convinced that he *would* be happy in a desk job. He might *say* that his dream job would be a permanent academic position, but was it?

The major issue over her going to Norway was the fact she was very far from being fluent in Norwegian. Without the language, would she find a job? Make friends? She chewed the end of the pencil. She could learn more. It wasn't as if she didn't have a native speaker on hand, 24/7. She could ask Anders to only speak Norwegian to her. Or at least spend more time speaking Norwegian so that she felt less at sea. Her heart sank as she thought about it all. She doubted she would learn enough to be confident in a job in Norway, and she didn't know if she could even get a work visa.

She opened up a browser on her phone, but before she could check what she needed for a work visa in Norway, the front door banged, and Becky joined her in the kitchen clutching a bag of takeaway. Georgia sniffed appreciatively.

"Crispy duck pancakes?" she said, one brow quirking upwards.

"Yep. And beef in black bean sauce, with extra peppers."

"You're a star. Thank you."

Becky fetched plates and served up, sliding Georgia's food over to her.

"Okay. How bad was it?" she asked, passing across some cutlery and sitting opposite.

"Haakon? About as bad as you might imagine. He harangued Anders all day, strode around the dig like he was running it, and generally pissed everyone off." She took a bite of her food, chewing and swallowing swiftly. "And then, just before we left, he told me I was a selfish bitch for not wanting to go to Norway with Anders."

"Did he actually use those words?"

Becky looked aghast, and Georgia relented. "Not exactly, but that was the gist. He thinks Anders should apply for the job, and that I should stop whining and go with him if he gets it."

"And what did Anders say?"

"He didn't hear that bit, although earlier, Haakon called me a nobody who was vastly inferior to him, and Anders didn't react well to that." She stabbed at her food. "I don't know why he keeps looking at jobs in academia," she said, though this wasn't really what was stressing her. "He loves being outside, and he hates all the bureaucracy and desk-stuff. And giving lectures."

"Have you asked him?"

She sighed. "He says it's because it's all he knows. But he knows what I do. He could work for a commercial company. I wish he would stop chasing what Haakon wants for him." She glanced over at Becky. "And yes, I have said that to him. He still claims it's what he wants, when it's patently obvious it isn't what would suit him."

"*Are* there any commercial jobs going?"

"No."

"Then it's a moot point." Becky manoeuvred some food on to her fork. "You have four options. One. A job comes up in the UK, and everything is hunky-dory. Two. He gets a job in Norway, and you go with him. Three. He doesn't have a job anywhere, and he moves in here until he does. Or four, you break up with him and let him get a job in Norway without you. But it's not me you need to discuss this with."

"I know." She focused on her food, wishing Becky wasn't always so clinical about everything.

Becky sighed. "Georgie, you two are going to have to have a proper discussion about all this at some point. I only see him on and off, and even I can see he is in full-on panic mode about the fact there are no jobs coming up here." She arched a brow. "And it's not like *we* haven't talked about it!"

"I know."

As she finished her meal, an image came back to her of the fear in Anders's eyes that morning. He was so terrified about not having a job; so worried that his career was slipping away from him. He wasn't applying for jobs he wanted, entirely because of her, and it was turning him inside out.

How could she do that to him if she loved him?

45

That weekend, Anders decided to take Georgie out for a day at the beach. Although everyone else's spirits had lifted the moment Haakon had left, Anders hadn't quite been able to shake off his tension. The closing date for the job in Norway crept ever closer, and each day, Anders checked the website for academic jobs, but there was still nothing suitable appearing. Maybe a day out at the beach would help unknot his shoulders and take his mind off things.

The sun danced in and out of scudding clouds chased along by a stiff breeze. As soon as Georgie got out of the car at the beach, her hair blew across her face, making both of them laugh.

"Want me to braid it for you?" he offered, opening the boot of the car to grab a rolled-up picnic blanket.

They ducked into the lee of a building, and she stood in front of him while he tamed her hair into a French plait, chuckling at her. Her hair sorted, he held out his arm, and she ducked underneath it, slipping her arm around his hips.

They strolled down to the beach and found a dry area of sand out of the wind to sit in. Anders spread the picnic blanket out and sat, gesturing to her to join him. She sat between his legs and leaned back against his chest. His arms snaked around her middle, and he rested his chin on her shoulder. In front of them, the North Sea sparkled in the sunshine, though the wind whipped the tops of the waves into white horses.

Anders twined her fingers in his, his brain running over all the things his father had said during his visit, however hard he tried to think of something else.

Georgie tweaked the end of his fingertip. "You okay?"

He blinked. "Yeah, fine. Just got a busy head. As ever."

He tried to chase the thoughts away, but they drifted back to him like an incoming tide.

"Talk to me?" said Georgie.

He took a long breath and squeezed her closer. "Oh, just stuff my father said when he was here."

"Him being so cross about you not applying for the job?"

"Mm." His stomach knotted. He really didn't want to talk about all of this. They were supposed to be having a relaxing day at the beach.

"Still nothing coming up?"

"Not in the UK, no."

"There's still plenty of time."

He closed his eyes, trying to squash down his stress. "Except, there isn't. At least a month between the job advert appearing and the closing date; a month or more to go through the applications; the notice needed to give to a shortlist to get them in to give presentations; the time taken to check references… there isn't still plenty of time."

His heart pounded, and he forced himself to take long, deep breaths.

"Can I do anything?" she asked softly.

"Consider moving to Norway?" he said, sounding flippant, but meaning the words. "There are several jobs there."

He rested his cheekbone against the top of her head, his eyes still closed, glad not to be able to see her expression. She probably looked horrified at the idea.

His father's voice rang in his head. *"If she loved you as much as you love her, she'd be prepared to make some sacrifices and go to Norway with you!"*

She tensed in his arms, and he wished he hadn't said anything. He cuddled her closer, breathing in the coconut scent of her hair. Overhead, gulls wheeled, squawking raucously against the background of the waves crashing on the shore.

"Are you being serious?" Georgie's voice came out as little more than a breath.

"No… Well…" His guts coiled tightly. "Georgie, I never, *ever* want to be without you. I love you so much. But I can't pretend I'm not terrified about not having anything lined up for when

Angela comes back from maternity leave." He paused. "I didn't want to talk about this today. I wanted to have a fun day out."

"We can do both. Anders, I hate seeing you so chewed up. I know you've been stressing about not having a job, and your father's only made that a hundred times worse. Stop listening to him."

He rubbed his cheek on the top of her shoulder, his brain so busy he thought it might finally explode.

"I know that what happened to Amelia makes you terrified about moving to Norway, but if it was the only way for us to be together, would you come?"

The words were out before he could stop them, and he cursed himself.

She shifted in his arms, raising her head. "But it's not the only way. You could live with me and Becky. You could get a non-academic job. Anders, you're determined to keep chasing jobs in academia, and I still don't understand why."

"Because it's all I know," he said softly. "And it's what I want." He squeezed her fingers. "I genuinely didn't mean to talk about this today. I'm sorry if I've upset you."

"It's okay. We have to talk about it at some point."

"I know, but can we talk about something else now? Please?"

"Such as?"

"I don't care. Just not jobs, or Norway, or my father."

She snorted. "He really hates me."

"No, he doesn't."

She barked a short laugh. "He thinks I'm selfish… And he's right, because I want you to stay in England, even though you have no job, rather than move to Norway with you where you could get an amazing position. That does make me selfish."

He didn't know what to say. Him wanting her to come to Norway with him was also selfish, especially as she was far from fluent in Norwegian. *One* of them had to give in if nothing materialised in Britain.

She cleared her throat. "Okay, the time to have said, 'No, no, Georgie, I don't think you're selfish' has passed."

The day was squirming away from him, and he screwed his face up. "I *don't* think you're selfish. Well, no more than I am for wanting you to think about Norway."

She nestled back against him, and they lapsed into silence again. His focus shifted to the white-topped waves of the sea, his brain churning. In his arms, Georgie's breathing tightened, and her posture stiffened. He dusted the side of her head with light kisses, racking his brain for something else to talk about.

"Can we compromise?" she said suddenly, startling him. "You keep looking in Britain, and if nothing suitable has come up by the time Angela actually returns, you move in with me, and start looking at jobs in Norway as well as here. In the meantime, teach me more Norwegian, so that if a job comes up in Norway for you, we can both move."

Anders swallowed. "You would really come to Norway with me?"

"Mm. I mean, I'd rather stay in the UK and you get a job here. But I know how stressed you are, and I know how important it is to you. I need to know more Norwegian, though. I don't want to move there and have no job and be isolated."

"Thank you," he whispered, his breathing suddenly easy. "I know how much you're scared about that."

She wriggled until she could see his face, and he kissed her tenderly.

"First lesson," he murmured. "*Jeg*… I… *elsker*… love… *deg*… you."

She smiled. "I already know that one."

He rubbed the end of her nose with his. "*Jeg vil kysse deg*… I want to kiss you… *hele ettermiddagen*… all afternoon." He touched his mouth to hers again.

A wide smile crept over her lips. "Mm. I like lessons like this. But I'm not sure they'll help me get a job." She gazed at him as he drew back. "I'm sorry I'm so scared about moving to Norway. It would just be a huge step for me."

"I know. I've spent so much of my life going back and forth between the two countries that I forget that it's a big thing for others. I tried to imagine how I would feel if you were fluent in French and suggested we both move there to follow your job."

"And?"

One side of his mouth twitched. "Yeah. I get why you don't

want to go to Norway. You have a job you love here; your friends are here. This is your home."

She studied him, serious all of a sudden. "What were the other jobs like? The ones your father talked about."

He bit his lips together. "They're all in Norway."

"Yeah, I figured that. What are they like?"

His breathing juddered as he exhaled. "They're in Norway." He swallowed, blinking. "But one of them looked great."

"You want to apply for it, don't you?"

Anders paused, then shook his head. "It's in Norway. We just agreed to compromise."

Georgie stared at him, her eyes troubled. "I'm sorry. I'm not ready to go to Norway yet."

He wished she was. It would make everything so much easier. Even if he got the job, he wouldn't be starting it for a few months. She could learn some more Norwegian in that time; look for a job herself.

She already has a job. You're being just like your father and expecting the world to bend to you!

He closed his eyes, feeling pulled apart. Georgie pressed a soft kiss to his lips, and he kissed her back, sliding his arms tighter around her.

"I'm sorry," he murmured. "I'd meant for us to have a lovely day out today."

"Keep kissing me like that and we will," she said.

He laughed.

A harsh gust of wind lifted the dry sand around them, and Anders flicked his head sharply.

"Agh!" He rubbed at his eye, then peered up at her, his left eye streaming with tears. "Much as the idea of sitting here kissing you all day appeals on many levels, I'm getting sand-blasted here, and you promised me an ice-cream. Shall we go?"

They stood, and he shook the blanket out, smiling at her. She caught his hand. "Are we okay, Anders?"

He coiled an arm around her waist and pulled her towards him, then kissed her softly. "Yeah. We're okay."

46

His nerve broke midweek. Not only had he scoured the jobs website incessantly, but he'd rung a few colleagues around the UK, asking if there was anything brewing. Was anyone up for retirement soon? Did they know if anyone was likely to be leaving? Nothing on any front.

He sat in his office at the department, the details for the job with Professor Gunderson in front of him, along with one of the three other jobs his father had flagged up during his visit. He twirled a pen through his fingers, nausea flickering in his stomach. What if he didn't apply for either of them, had *nothing* lined up, and then she didn't actually love him as much as he loved her? She said she would move to Norway to be with him in a few months, but what if there was nothing available then? What if this was his big opportunity, and he didn't even go for it?

He closed his eyes. How long would they last together if he was unemployed and sponging off her?

Drawing in a deep breath, he pulled up the online application form for the job with Professor Gunderson and read it for the umpteenth time. It would be a major step up if he could land this job. Anxiety made his skin prickle. The closing date was now only days away.

She said she understood how stressed he was, so maybe he was fretting over nothing, and she would say 'go for it'.

He twirled the pen again.

Was he being just like his father and putting his career first? Georgie's fear of moving was bone-deep. What if her anxiety overrode her feelings for him?

He tipped his head back and stared at the ceiling, torn.

There was no guarantee he would get the job. In fact, there

was no guarantee he would even get called for an interview. Was this a fight to have down the line? Worry about how Georgie would react if, or when, he got shortlisted? If he didn't apply, he *definitely* wouldn't get the job. And she'd said she would move to Norway with him. If he got the job, surely she would come with him?

He grabbed a pad of paper and started drafting out what he would put in the application form.

47

The following Sunday, after a lazy lunch out at a country pub together, Anders parked outside his house and glanced across to Georgia. "I won't be long. I just want to pick up a couple of things from the office. Make yourself at home."

He'd already spent all of Saturday in his office, writing papers and drafting the site report, and she caught his eye. "Don't get wrapped up in stuff."

He grinned. "I won't."

"Hmm. Remember that I know you! Just pick up the books you need and then come away. Don't get sucked into anything!"

He laughed. "I promise. I really will try not to be too long."

He leaned across the car to kiss her.

She scruffed his hair up as she moved back. "See you soon."

She watched him drive off, then let herself into his house, kicking her shoes off just inside the door. She headed to the kitchen on the hunt for coffee. Anders always had the best stuff.

A cafetiere of strong, expensive coffee made, she wandered around the ground floor of his house, inhaling the rich aroma of the coffee. Anders had clearly continued working at home the day before, because there was a pile of papers, and a notepad covered in his neat, tight writing, on the table in the lounge.

Intrigued, she scanned the pages, wondering what angle he was taking in the articles he was preparing, and how far on he was with the site report. The top few sheets were handwritten, planning out the structure of the papers. Like her, he 'thought best on paper' and would map out ideas by hand, rather than type straight into a laptop. She skim-read the notes, smiling to herself. He might be utterly at home outdoors, but he knew how to put an academic paper together alright.

Below the notes lay a mind-map of his site report and a print-out of what he'd written so far. She flicked through the pages, the bundle seeming too thick to be just the report, and her eyes widened and her blood froze. Beneath the draft of the report were the job descriptions of two posts: the one with Professor Gunderson, and another that she recognised as the job in Norway that Anders had described as 'great'. She shuffled through the rest of the sheets, her heart rate spiking, and her palms clammy. More handwritten pages, but these appeared to contain detailed notes for each of the sections of the application form for the job with Professor Gunderson.

Her stomach went into free-fall. He had sworn blind to her that he wouldn't apply for either of these posts. That he understood she didn't want to move to Norway. Not yet. They'd *agreed* that they would compromise and he would wait, in the hope that a suitable job would come up in Britain. Her hands shook as she flipped through the pages, willing them to be notes on the site. Maybe her Norwegian wasn't good enough, and she'd misunderstood. Right at the bottom was a print-out of a completed application form. Cold fury flashed through her.

She hauled in a deep breath, closing her eyes.

He loves you. He wouldn't apply without talking to you. You must be mistaken.

She sat on the chair next to the low table and sifted through the pages again, separating off the ones that were clearly in English and relating to either the site report or the articles, and keeping hold of the ones in Norwegian. She took another slurp of coffee, taking her time to look at the pages. Even with her limited Norwegian, she could see that he'd re-written the section headings from the application form, and then drafted and re-drafted his responses.

Maybe he's just practising what he would write, in case something similar came up in the UK.

She knew she was clutching at straws. He was perfectly fluent in English. He wouldn't need to draft in Norwegian and then translate.

Which only really left one reason for him having a completed application form in Norwegian.

Just as her temper reached boiling point, the front door banged.

"See!" Anders called to her. "I promised you I wouldn't be long! Ooh, have you made coffee? Any left for me?"

Anders strolled into the lounge carrying three books, beaming at her. His smiles vanished when he saw what was in her hands, and he stumbled to a halt.

She leapt to her feet and brandished the pages at him. "You lied to me!"

He put the books down on a chair and held his hands up, his eyes wide, his breathing uncertain. "It's not what it looks like."

"Really? Oh, do tell me what it *is*, because it looks exactly like you're filling out an application for the job with Professor Gunderson! The one you *promised* me you weren't going to go for."

He hurried over to her, his face stricken. She took a step back, maintaining the distance between them.

"I was only drafting it out," he said, his voice strained. "Just in case."

She paused, then her anger surged again. "Don't treat me like I'm an idiot, Anders. The closing date for this one is *tomorrow*. You've applied for it, and you haven't even *talked* to me about it!"

"Georgie, I swear. I have *not* applied. It's just a draft."

She stared at him, breathing hard. "On a scale of one to ten, how ideal would this be if it were in Britain?"

He didn't answer for a moment, and she raised her brows, prompting him.

He swallowed. "It's a moot point."

"Like hell, it's a moot point! You're drafting out your responses to the sections! Don't *lie* to me! Both this job and the other one you've printed off are exactly what you want, aren't they? Are you applying for that one, too?"

The colour had leached from his face, and he didn't speak.

"Anders?"

"Come with me," he whispered. "To Norway. You said you would if nothing had come up by the time Angela returned. Come sooner than that. There's *nothing* coming up in the UK. Georgie, I love you, and I don't want to be without you, but I need a job."

She blinked hard, trying not to cry. He *knew* how hard it was for her to think about moving. Her chest constricted at the idea of living in a country where she knew no one and didn't speak the language, and she struggled for breath. Both of the jobs were high level. If he got either of them, Anders would be working long hours just to get started in the role. She would be alone, jobless, friendless…

"When were you going to talk to me about all of this?" she said, her voice uneven.

He hesitated, and her breath stalled again.

"You weren't, were you? You were going to apply without us even talking."

He took a step forward, and she moved back.

"There's no guarantee I'd even get shortlisted," he said.

"That's not the point, Anders. I thought we were a partnership. That we made *joint* decisions. We literally only decided a *week* ago that we would compromise." She stared at him, anger colliding with her fear. "Career first. Me second. Again. You are *exactly* like your father."

She flung the papers down on the table and marched past him. He caught her arm, but she batted him away. "Don't!"

"Georgie? Georgie!"

She jammed her feet back into her shoes in his hallway. He tried to catch her hand again.

"Georgie, *please*? Can we talk?"

She whirled around. "Too late, Anders! The time to talk to me about this was *before* you decided you were applying." She breathed hard, fighting tears. "I can't do this any more, Anders. I keep hoping that you love me enough this time to stay, and then find out *by chance* you're planning on leaving. I guess we were never meant to be, after all."

She snatched her hand away and stalked out, slamming the door behind her, hardly able to see the street through her tears.

48

Anders stared at the door, his world collapsing. His breathing caught in his chest, and he brought his hand up to cover his heart, bending over as he did so.

"Georgie," he gasped. "I'm sorry."

He wanted to run after her, but he knew she wouldn't listen to him.

Dots appeared in his vision, and he closed his eyes and wrapped both arms around his middle, letting out a long wail.

"You stupid, *stupid* idiot!"

His legs buckled beneath him, leaving him crumpled in a heap on the floor. He still couldn't breathe properly, and he rested his forehead on his bent knees. He'd lost her. Again. She wouldn't come back. He *should* have talked to her. He deserved everything he got.

He clasped his fingers together at the back of his head, weeping, his heart split in half. When his tears finally dried, he scrubbed at his face with the heels of his hands, then stumbled through to the kitchen. There, he poured himself several fingers of whisky, then sank the lot in one go, coughing afterwards at the burn. Another two inches of scotch went into the glass and he meandered through to the lounge, the neck of the bottle in the fingers of one hand, the glass in the other.

His legs gave way again, and he slumped in a chair, his gaze resting on the papers. Why had he left them out?

Why had he even filled them in?

He gulped at his drink. He knew why. He'd filled them in because the fear of being unemployed and jeopardising his career plans had overwhelmed his fear of losing Georgie, and because his father's assertion that if Georgie loved him, she would consider moving to Norway had bounced around his head, giving him no peace. Although he'd filled in the form online, he hadn't submitted it yet. Some corner of his brain had recognised he should talk to Georgie about it first. He just hadn't found the right moment.

The first tumbler of whisky settled in his brain, fuzzing his thoughts. His sorrow shifted to hurt, and then to anger. Why didn't Georgie see how stressed he was over not having a job? Why did she expect him to throw everything away? She *could* move to Norway. Her job *was* less career-based. He knew she wasn't interested in climbing any higher in Dig For It because she was happy doing what she did.

He finished the second glass of scotch and poured a third, just as large.

She'd said she *would* go to Norway with him if nothing came up in Britain. This job was perfect, so why wouldn't she just move their plans sooner?

Because she didn't love him enough.

The third glass of scotch disappeared down his throat, and he poured a fourth, his hand unsteady.

"Why did you ever think she was The One?" he muttered. "If she was, she'd move heaven and earth to stay with you. You're throwing away *everything* and she doesn't care."

A small voice of reason tried to put her perspective forward. The thought of moving terrified her. They'd agreed to compromise and wait, and she would work on her Norwegian. Then, if she moved, she'd be less at sea; less isolated.

The more inebriated part of his brain argued that if she was prepared to go *then*, he might as well apply for a job *now*. What were a few months if the job was right? And even if he got the job, there would be time before he started for her to learn some more Norwegian and get used to the idea.

"If she actually loves you and you get the job, she would move to Norway. If you get the job and she won't move, then she doesn't love you enough, and so you might as well apply and be done with her."

He opened up his laptop, finding it hard to focus on the screen, then navigated to the online application and read it over.

His finger hovered over the track-pad, his brain swirling.

"If she doesn't love you, you'd be better off in Norway. New start."

He blinked twice, then clicked on 'send'.

* * *

Georgia stumbled blindly down the road back to her flat. How could he have done this to her a second time? She was a stupid, gullible fool. He didn't love her. Not the way she'd loved him. He was *always* going to be more concerned about his career than he was about her. She should never have believed he would wait.

A couple of passers-by shot her concerned looks, but she put her head down and kept on walking, wishing she could stem her tears.

"He's not worth it!" she muttered to herself.

As she dug in her pocket for her keys, she found one of the origami puzzle purses he'd left her weeks ago. She stared at it, her guts coiling. It was the one which, when opened, revealed a spiral of tiny writing, quoting one of her favourite love poems. She crushed the small square in her fist, ruining it, and opened the door to the flat.

"Hi! I wasn't expecting you back!" Becky called out from the lounge.

Georgia headed straight for her bedroom and flung herself down on the bed, her tears still pouring. Becky tapped on the door and poked her head around it, her eyes wide.

"What the hell's happened?"

"He's applied for the job with Professor Gunderson."

Becky sat on the end of the bed. "Oh. I take it he forgot to discuss it all with you first?"

Georgia sat up, smearing her tears down her face. "He didn't *forget*. He was going to see if he got it and *then* talk to me. We'd talked about all of this last weekend, and he *agreed* that if nothing had come up by the time Angela came back, that he would look in Norway as well as the UK, and I would go with him. But, oh no, he couldn't wait that long. He'd printed off the application form and drafted out what he would put. He *said* he hadn't submitted it yet; that he was just drafting it out, but the closing date is *tomorrow*. I'm not stupid."

"What else did he say?"

"He wanted me to go to Norway with him sooner than the agreement."

Becky canted her head. "Not entirely unreasonable if an amazing job has come up for him, given that you've said you would consider it if nothing came up here."

"He should have talked to me about it! But no. He's Anders. And his career comes first. I don't speak enough Norwegian to get a job at the moment. That was the whole *point* of waiting. I could learn more Norwegian and look at stuff for me, just in case. But what *he* wants comes first. I would be over there, with no work, no friends nearby, and Anders at work all the time. Just like Amelia was with Karl!"

Her sobs stopped her from speaking for a moment. Becky shuffled up the bed to put her arm around her.

"You're stronger than Amelia. And Anders isn't Karl. Anders would do his absolute damnedest to make sure you didn't feel isolated."

She swallowed a hiccupy sob. "Would he? He *knows* why it's such a big thing for me to up sticks and move to a new country, and he still wants me to do it. He's more scared of losing his career than he is of losing me."

Becky squeezed her shoulders. "Not sure that's fair to him."

Georgie scowled.

"How did you leave things?" asked Becky.

"We're done. I've had it with him. I'm tired of coming second."

She reached over to grab a tissue from the box next to her bed and blew her nose. Next to the box was a photo of the two of them, and she slammed it face-down on the table.

Becky gave her a long look. "Don't you think you should talk to him? Maybe you misunderstood things."

She sighed, then pulled her phone out and sent him a text: *Have you applied for the job? Honest answer!*

She waited, her heart rate climbing, praying that he would message her back to say that he hadn't and that he loved her.

Nothing.

What would she do if he said no? Maybe he *had* been drafting things out. Maybe he'd intended to talk to her tonight, and she'd jumped the gun. She breathed shakily, staring at her phone. If he said no, she'd go round and talk.

What if he said yes? Her stomach roiled, and she swallowed.

"He loves you," said Becky softly. "He's not always brilliant at talking about stuff, but deep down, he loves you."

She looked up at her friend. "Does he love me *enough*? That's the question. Or is he always going to put me second to his career, the way Haakon did his mum?"

Her phone pinged. Hands trembling, she opened his reply.

Yes. Come with me if I get it?

Fresh tears welled up, and she turned her phone around so that Becky could read the screen.

"I guess that says everything," she said through her tears. She wiped her nose and put her phone on the bedside table. "Do we have any empty cardboard boxes?"

"Er. There's one on top of my wardrobe," said Becky cautiously. "Why?"

Georgia didn't answer. She slithered off the bed and retrieved the box from Becky's room, then worked her way around the flat, lobbing everything belonging to Anders into it. As soon as she'd packed all of his stuff, she taped the box up and put it by the door.

A sudden wave of nausea washed through her, and she pressed her fingertips to her lips, waiting for it to subside. It didn't, and she dashed to the bathroom to be sick. As she sat back on her heels and flushed the toilet, she caught sight of Becky in the mirror.

"Sick?" Becky said, one brow arched.

She shrugged. "Just from crying. Though I don't know why I'm so upset. He's clearly not worth it."

Another wave hit her, and she waited until her stomach settled, then got up to rinse her mouth out at the sink.

Becky still leaned in the doorway. "You should talk to him. It could all be a huge misunderstanding."

"Not today. I'll say things I can't take back."

"Well, maybe in the car in, tomorrow?"

Georgia groaned. She hadn't even considered that he would be giving her a lift in. The *last* thing she wanted was to be stuck in a car with him. "Shit!"

Her brain rattled through options. Maybe Shona could give her a lift? She scrolled through her phone, hunting for her number. Nothing. She'd never had to call Shona outside of work.

"Becky, do you have Shona's number?" She knew she was clutching at straws. If she didn't have it, Becky was even less likely to, as they worked in different areas.

Becky shook her head. "You're going to have to hope Anders picks you up in the morning."

Georgia closed her eyes. She'd be perfectly happy never to see him again.

49

The following morning, Georgia waited outside her flat, torn, wondering if Anders would come and pick her up. She hadn't texted to ask, and he hadn't messaged to say he wouldn't, so she had to assume he would arrive. Half of her would be happy if she never saw him again. The other half of her wanted to get to work.

Bang on schedule, his battered car turned on to her road, drove past her to turn at the end, then pulled up next to the flat. She got in, her heart beating too fast.

"Hey," he said softly, as she fastened her seat belt.

She stared out of the windscreen, too upset to talk. He turned the engine off.

"At least have the decency to say good morning to me."

She kept her focus on the road in front of them. "Good morning, Anders."

He still didn't start the car. In the corner of her eye, she saw him turn in his seat so that he faced her. Reluctantly, she looked across at him. He looked hellish. Dark circles shadowed under bloodshot eyes, his face was drawn, and his hair looked even wilder than normal.

"Thank you," he said. "Can we talk? Please?"

"I don't think there's anything to talk about." She shrugged. "We'd agreed to wait. And then you applied for a job in Norway without even discussing it with me. So, no, Anders, we *could* have talked, but you chose not to. Don't ask to talk now. It's too late."

She shifted in her seat to peer out of the side window. Next to her, Anders sighed and started the car.

Neither of them spoke until they reached the site. There, she helped him to set up, then sat at her desk.

"Coffee?" he offered.

The aroma tempted her to say yes, but her stubbornness won out. "No. Thank you."

He poured out a mug for himself from his flask, then pulled a chair over to her desk. She glared at him.

"Okay. You won't talk. But you can listen," he said.

Tension ground her shoulders.

He held his hands up. "I'm sorry. I'm a complete idiot. I *should* have talked to you." He breathed out deeply. "I only applied last night, after we rowed. I got drunk, and I sent it in. It was a mistake. I should have talked to you instead. I swear to you, I hadn't applied before then."

She arched a brow. "So, you were drunk enough to send it in last night and it was a mistake, but you'd already typed it all in and finessed your application, and that wasn't a mistake?"

He shifted in his seat, glancing away.

"Go away, Anders. I'm trying to work."

He didn't. He stayed in the seat, rubbing his brow.

"I really thought you were The One," he whispered, his voice broken.

"Clearly not."

How could she be The One for him if he was prepared to leave her again? The One to just trail around after him? The One to put everything on hold for him, because he was more important?

A car pulled up in the field outside, shortly followed by the sound of voices in the refreshments tent. As the second car pulled up, Anders stood, scrubbing his hands over his face, then carried the chair back to his desk and stalked out.

"Morning all!" His voice rang with false bonhomie.

She stared after him, her heart broken.

"I thought you were The One, too. Guess we were both wrong."

* * *

Anders headed for a trench as soon as the team talk was over, hoping his body language made it clear that he wanted to be alone.

"Clearly not," she had said.

Meaning he was right. She didn't love him as much as he loved her, and he was a fool for ever thinking she was The One.

His head still pounded after the excess of whisky the night before, and the bright sunshine was only making him feel worse. He wished he had a pair of sunglasses with him. By the time he'd gone to bed, he'd finished all the whisky, and the bottle had started out at least three-quarters full. He couldn't remember how he actually got to bed, but given that he'd woken that morning still in the day before's clothes, he assumed he'd stumbled up the stairs, fallen on the bed and instantly gone to sleep. He probably shouldn't have driven in.

He closed his eyes. The pillows had smelled of coconut. She had a toothbrush and hairbands and toiletries in his bathroom, and a pile of clothes in his closet. The fridge was full of food she liked.

He tried to focus on digging, softly scraping at the soil, but tears blurred his eyes, and his brain churned constantly. In the end, he knew he was in danger of potentially ruining the trench, and he headed towards the finds tent, his feet heavy.

Georgie scowled up at him as he entered, then bent her head back to her work. His heart lurched. How could he make her love him? He couldn't imagine his life without her, but he didn't want to be with her if she didn't feel the same way.

He opened up the papers he'd been working on, but he couldn't concentrate.

"Coffee?" he called across to her, his voice unsteady.

She threw him a baleful stare, then nodded curtly. "Thank you."

He made the drinks, then slid one on to her desk, next to her. "Please, can we talk?"

"Is it about work?" she said, without looking up.

He sighed. "No."

"Then no. We're at work. Be professional."

He pushed his hair off his brow. "Will you talk to me when we're not at work?"

She didn't answer, her eyes fixed on the object in front of her.

"Georgie?"

She raised her head, her eyes stony. "Thank you for the coffee,

Anders. I'm working."

He held his hands up. "Fine. If I call you later, will you answer?"

"No."

"You won't talk to me here, you won't speak to me outside of work, and you won't reply to any of my calls or texts—"

"Maybe you should pick up on the very large hint in there," she cut in, before turning back to her task.

He closed his mouth, memories of Orkney flooding back to him. She had cut him out completely then, too. They had gone from everything, to nothing, overnight. He was an idiot for thinking it would be different this time. He hadn't meant enough to her then, and he clearly didn't now.

He picked his coffee up and retreated to his desk, suddenly glad to have sent in the job application. Maybe starting again in another country was exactly what he needed to do.

* * *

At lunchtime, Georgia sought out Shona, and they took their packed lunches over to a quiet area, away from everyone else, and especially away from Anders. Georgia had hoped that since the finds tent was boiling with the sun on it, that Anders might have gone off and dug in a trench somewhere far away from her, but he hadn't. Although he'd left fairly early on, he'd returned pretty quickly. Then, after she'd told him to leave her alone, he'd sat at his desk, working on his laptop, the two of them maintaining a stony silence.

"I guess you and Anders have split up, then?" said Shona as they sat.

"That obvious?"

Shona unwrapped her sandwiches, half laughing. "Er, *yes*. What happened?"

Georgia flapped a hand. "Doesn't matter. A repeat of why we split up two years ago, really. I never learn."

"Do you want a lift in with me?"

Georgia smiled gratefully. "That would be great. I know you're in a lift-share with all the other guys from Dig For It, but if you could give me a ride in, that would be brilliant. Thank you."

"No problem." She paused. "If it's any consolation, I think Anders is in bits."

Georgia chewed her sandwich, feeling queasy. "Well, it's his fault we've split up."

Shona tilted her head to one side. "He's still in bits. No chance you can sort things out?"

Georgia shook her head. "No." She put her sandwich back in her lunchbox, her appetite gone.

"Shame. You two always looked like the perfect couple."

Georgia shaded her eyes, her gaze drifting over the site. Anders sat on the opposite side of the dig, a little way from the tents. Sophie was making a beeline for him.

"She's not wasted much time," commented Shona, nodding towards Sophie.

"She can have him."

"I don't think he's interested."

"No. She talks too much."

Shona laughed. "I think it's more than that. Like the fact that he's totally in love with you."

Georgia lay back, folding her arms over her face. "Oh, Shona, I wish that were true. He just *thinks* he's in love with me."

Shona made a non-committal sound in the back of her throat, which Georgia chose to ignore.

Lunch over, the two women drifted back towards the refreshment tent. Anders was already there, making a coffee, Sophie fluttering around him.

"Anders?" Georgia said.

He raised forget-me-not-blue eyes full of hope to her, and her heart cracked.

"Shona's giving me a lift in from tomorrow, so you don't need to pick me up."

The hope in his eyes faded, replaced with pain. He nodded, swallowing. Behind him, Sophie raised her chin, her eyes glittering with triumph.

You're welcome to him. Hope your Norwegian is good, or that you're a quick learner.

She made herself a drink, then turned her back on both of them and retreated to her desk in the finds tent.

* * *

Anders worked silently at his desk on and off over the afternoon, but he didn't try to talk to her. She threw herself into her work, ignoring him, thankful that they were approaching the end of the dig. They would have to work together for a while, but they were grown-ups. They could maintain a professional relationship, surely?

After the end-of-day summary, he caught her eye, and her heart sank.

"You ready to go?" he asked, hovering by her side.

"Mm, hm. Let me just grab my bag."

Sophie's eyes narrowed as she looked across at them, but then she must have picked up on the atmosphere because the gleeful look returned.

Georgia couldn't help herself, and called across, "*Ha det!*" to her.

Sophie blinked, her glee turning to confusion and confirming Georgia's suspicion that she didn't even know 'bye' in Norwegian. Anders gave her a puzzled look, but she turned and picked up her bag, then followed him out to the car.

As she fastened her seat belt, he looked over to her. "Will you still not talk to me?"

"I don't think there would be any point."

He started the engine and pulled away. Neither of them spoke for the rest of the journey.

At the end of her road, Anders turned the car. "How do we fix this, Georgie?"

She glanced across, surprised. He *never* talked while he was still driving. His attention was currently on the road, but his jaw had tightened, and his breathing was all over the place. Half of her wished they could fix things, but she knew it was all beyond repair.

"We can't." She swallowed. "There's a box of your stuff by the door. Did you want to get it, since Shona's giving me a lift in tomorrow? If not, I can bring it with me tomorrow and transfer it to your car at the dig."

He nodded, drawing up next to her flat. Her stomach knotted, and she shifted in her seat to look at him. He pointedly turned his head to his side window and opened his door. Tears filled her eyes, and she fumbled for her bag, blinking to clear her vision. She scrambled out of the car, determined not to let him see she was crying.

He stood on the path to her flat, his posture rigid. She ducked inside, levered up the box and thrust it into his arms.

"There you go. Let me know if anything's missing."

She finally met his eye, and her heart missed a beat to see his tears welling.

"Georgie…" he started, his voice cracking. "Can we talk? Please?"

"No." She forced the word out before her nerve broke, her emotions pinwheeling.

He tipped his head up, biting his lips together, then nodded to himself. "I guess Pappa was right. If you'd ever really loved me, you'd support me and go with me. I should stop being a fool, chasing after someone who doesn't care about me. I'll see you at work."

With that, he turned on his heel, threw the box on to the back seat of his car, and drove off.

She stared after him, wishing that her heart would get the memo about him not being worth it.

50

Friday rolled around. The weather had finally broken, and each day it had either mizzled steadily all day, or there had been brief spells of sunshine interspersed with huge downpours that sent all the team scrambling for the tents. The musty smell from the canvas that had abated significantly with the sunshine was back with a vengeance, permeating into Georgie's clothes over the day and making her need to strip and shower as soon as she got home.

Anders kept trying to talk to her. She kept rebuffing every advance. If it wasn't about work, she wasn't going to listen. He'd *had* his chance to talk to her about the jobs in Norway, and he hadn't taken it. After a few days of her giving him a shoulder so cold it had frost forming on it, he'd largely given up, though she still caught him giving her the puppy-dog-that's-been-kicked face when she happened to glance in his direction. On the Tuesday, she'd found a new puzzle purse on her desk, made from exquisite origami paper with razor sharp creases. Curiosity had won in the end, and she'd opened it. Inside was written: *I love you. Forgive me?* She'd crumpled it up and left it on his desk as her answer. He hadn't left another.

Every downpour in the week had seen Sophie needing to take shelter by his desk, and she'd chattered at him, flirting outrageously, every time. Anders hadn't appreciated it, going as far as putting headphones in one day while she was still talking to him. That had earned him a scowl and a flounce, but it hadn't actually stopped her from sheltering next to his desk again when the next shower arrived. He'd still had his headphones in.

He'd just finished doing the weekly wrap-up on the Friday, and Georgia skulked near to the back of the tent. As usual, everyone was heading to the pub for a drink, but Georgia wasn't sure she wanted to go. Shona sidled up to her.

"Coming?"

Georgia wrinkled her nose. "Dunno. Maybe not."

Across the tent, Anders glanced at her, and she turned away. Maybe she *should* go. Why should the fact they'd broken up stop her from having a fun evening out with the team?

"Yeah, okay," she said, looking back at Shona. "Just make sure I'm not sitting next to him or Sophie."

"Well, Sophie will be as close to Anders as it's possible to be, so it'll be easy to avoid them both." Shona cocked her head. "He's really not interested in her. He's still pining for you."

"I thought he was pining for the fjords," Georgia quipped, making Shona laugh.

* * *

When she got to the pub, Sophie was, as predicted, jammed in next to Anders, with Patrick on her other side. Shona sat at the opposite end of the table and moved her bag off a seat so that Georgia could sit down.

"Get you a drink?" offered Anders, brows raised.

She shook her head. "I'm fine, thanks." She turned to Shona. "What can I get you?"

"Gin and tonic? Thanks."

She hurried to the bar to get the drinks. Just as she put her order in, Anders came to stand next to her.

"Georgie, *please,* will you talk to me? I can't bear you hating me."

She looked up at him. Dark shadows collected under his eyes, and his irises were bright blue with emotion. A very far cry from how he'd looked when he'd blown on her nose at the bar, and she'd thought he was about to kiss her.

"Is there anything to say? I didn't want to go to Norway, but I would have tried to make it work. I would have tried to learn more Norwegian. But I wasn't ready yet. And you knew that."

The barman slid her drinks on to the bar in front of her, and she tapped her card to pay. Anders opened his mouth to speak to her, but she cut across him.

"I hope it works out for you, Anders. I hope it was all worth it in the end."

She moved away, before he could see the hurt in her face, and made her way back to the table. Shona shot her a concerned look, but she shook her head. She sipped her orange juice, avoiding looking at Anders as he sat again. Sophie grinned at him, thanking him for the drink, but his eyes were on Georgia. She wondered how quickly she could just neck her drink and go. Far from enjoying a night out with colleagues, she was regretting not being at home with Becky, watching something on the telly.

She bore it for about twenty minutes, at which point she didn't think she could feel more miserable. She should have sat at the side, rather than head-on to Anders. Every time she raised her head, he was looking at her, always with the kicked-puppy look. She flashed a weak smile at Shona and gathered her things together.

"I'm going to head off. See you on Monday. Have a good weekend."

Shona nodded sympathetically.

Anders gazed down the table at her. "Are you going? Shall I walk you back?"

"Yeah, I'm going, but you're fine, thanks. It's not far, and it's not dark."

With that, she shrugged into her jacket, and made a beeline for the door, trying not to think about the first time he'd walked her back, all those weeks ago.

* * *

"There you go, sir."

The barber brushed the cut hair from Anders's neck and shoulders, then whisked the protective cape away, allowing his chopped curls to tumble to the floor. Anders stared at his reflection. The short-back-and-sides felt alien to him, and the fact he hadn't shaved in such a long time made it look worse, somehow.

"Thank you."

He levered himself up, paid, and headed out, automatically running a hand through his hair, then instantly regretting its shortness.

He strolled home, his brain as busy as ever. After Georgie had crumpled up the puzzle purse he'd made, he'd applied for the other job in Norway that had looked great. Not long after that, he'd had an email inviting him to interview for the post with Professor Gunderson. At first, he'd thought he would have to fly to Norway for it, but they'd agreed to interview him over the internet. Clearly, Professor Gunderson had spoken to his father, because the same evening, Haakon had called to tell him he'd been singing his praises, and that he was probably a shoe-in for the job. Anders would have preferred to get the post off his own merits, not because of any 'old-boy network' or favours between his father and his potential new boss. Still, a job was a job.

He reached his house and went in, kicking off his shoes in the hallway. Perhaps he should bite the bullet and sort out the facial hair; give any tan lines time to fade before the interview. Mind you, given the lack of sun, maybe they wouldn't fade in time and would still look peculiar.

He headed up to the bathroom, found a suitable pair of scissors, and trimmed his beard back as closely as he could. Maybe he should have got himself an electric razor at some point, but he never had.

The beard trimmed back as tight to his skin as he could manage, he lathered his chin and worked his razor over it, filling the sink with long stubble. It took him two passes before he was truly clean-shaven, and he did indeed have a tan line around where his beard had been. His skin flared red and blotchy with razor burn. Hopefully that would fade soon, too.

He dried his face, then dealt with all the hair in the sink, already hating what he looked like.

"Fresh start," he told his reflection. "Remember?"

51

Another week passed, and the dig began to wind up. The rain had made sporadic reappearances, helping no one's temper as the digging got harder and the footing more treacherous. The tents stank of damp and mustiness, and a leak had developed above where Anders had had his desk, meaning that he was now immediately behind Georgia. Close enough that she could hear his breathing. Thankfully, he'd angled his desk so that they couldn't see each other.

On Monday, Anders had arrived on site clean-shaven, with a short-back-and-sides. Georgia didn't ask him why, but Shona winkled out of him that he had a job interview coming up. The job in Norway.

"Good luck to him," Georgia had muttered when she was told, but it still felt as if someone had twisted a knife in her chest.

On the Friday, she loitered at the back of the tent while Anders did the wrap-up meeting for the week, desperate to go home.

"Blacksmith's Arms, seven?" Anders asked the group as he finished.

He shot a look in her direction, and she shook her head, not in the humour. Relief washed through his face before a forced smile settled.

Most of the rest of the group said they would be there. Sophie seemed especially keen. Georgia packed her things together and joined Shona in her car.

"Not coming to the pub?" Shona asked.

"No." Georgia fastened her seat belt. "I'm not sure how much more I can take of Sophie draping herself all over Anders."

"You can't be jealous if you don't want him."

Georgia sighed. "I know. It's more the gleeful look she has about it all."

Shona pulled away, nosing the car out of the field. "He's not interested in her."

They drove to Georgia's, chatting about the finds. Shona parked at the kerb outside Georgia's flat, then looked across at her.

"Not much longer. The dig's nearly finished. Once you've had your input into the site report, you won't have to deal with him."

Georgia shrugged. "He might go to Norway soon. That's what he wants. Thanks for the lift. Have fun at the pub."

Shona nodded, giving her a sympathetic look, and Georgia headed in.

She'd just made herself a cup of tea when Becky came bursting in to the flat.

"Georgie? Georgie!" she bellowed.

"Yeah, in here. Where's the fire?"

Becky barrelled into the lounge, clutching a sheaf of papers. "I've finally finished processing the geophysics survey of the woods."

Georgia sat up. "I didn't even know you'd done it. I thought you were waiting for Anders to sign off on it, and that wasn't going to happen."

Becky shrugged, flopping down on the chair. "I know. But, I talked to Steve… I didn't tell him about all your weird visions. He thinks you're strange enough as it is. I said that some of the finds had suggested that there might be something there, but that you and Anders had split up, and he was being an arse about listening to your theories." She pulled a face. "I mean, that's not entirely untrue. You *have* split up, and he *was* being difficult about your theories. Anyway, I said that you wanted to prove a point. Long story short, much as Steve liked Anders, he likes you more, and it turned out Dig For It still had permissions, and he didn't technically need Anders to sign off, so he agreed he could do it last weekend. And he did."

Excitement fizzed in Georgia's belly. Becky wouldn't be telling her all this if the survey had found nothing, surely?

"And?" she chivvied.

Becky handed over the papers with a flourish. "*And*… it looks like there's *something* there."

Georgia scoured the print-outs, her heart racing. Exactly where she believed the burial to be were shadows and markings on the survey. She closed her eyes, re-living the dream she'd had of the burial procession and then the burial. Einar had been buried with his sword and axe, as well as a whole heap of other grave goods. This could be the find of a lifetime!

"What are you going to do with them?" Becky jutted her chin towards the papers. "I mean, technically, you need to send them to Anders."

"Oh, I'm sending them to Anders, don't worry. He has an interview for that shiny new job in Norway coming up. Maybe if he finds something here, he can piss off out of the UK, and I'll never have to see him again. Have you got these in electronic form?"

Becky had and had already sent them to Georgia's personal email address. Georgia opened up her laptop and found the email, then clicked on 'forward' and typed in Anders's work email. After a moment's thought, she added in his personal email address too, then drafted out the message: *Anders, Dig For It still had permission to survey the wooded area. Please find attached the results. Looks like I was right. Test-pit there on Monday?*

She clicked on 'send' before she changed her mind.

* * *

Anders was more than ready to leave the pub. Never the most sociable person at the best of times, he just wanted to go home and relax. He'd sat so that Sophie wasn't next to him for once, which was a relief as she really could win an Olympic gold in non-stop wittering. He rubbed a palm over his jawline, his gaze settling on his drink in front of him. The razor burn had faded over the week, but his face still felt alien to him. Was he doing the right thing, going for the job? Or was Georgie right, and he was chasing something that wasn't ultimately going to make him happy?

He missed her. He missed being able to talk to her. Part of him still hoped that they might resolve things; that he could patch everything up; that she could forgive him. Even if he got the job in Norway, he didn't have to accept it. He wouldn't, if it meant he could be with her again.

He rubbed his brow, trying to beat down his father's voice at him even *contemplating* turning a job like that down. It didn't work.

"You threw away an opportunity of a lifetime? Over a woman who doesn't love you enough to make it work? You are a fool!"

Sighing, he downed the whisky he'd been nursing, and stood up. "Night all. I need to get home. See you on Monday."

The team nodded and waved at him. He shrugged his jacket on, picked his way between the chairs, and headed for home.

Just as he turned on to his street, his phone pinged, indicating he had a new email. He pulled his phone out of his pocket and stared at the message screen, wondering who was emailing him on a Friday evening. His eyes widened. Georgie? What on earth was she emailing him about? It was from her personal email, so it wasn't about work, and she'd barely said one non-work-related word to him in two weeks. Did she finally want to talk? Was there a way back?

His hopes rising, he opened the message as he walked.

"Anders, Dig For It still had permission to survey the wooded area. Please find attached the results. Looks like I was right. Test-pit there on Monday?"

He opened the attachment, but his phone screen was too small to view the files properly. He dashed home, hurried to the lounge, and booted up his laptop. While his computer warmed up, he squinted at the images on his phone again, his heart rate picking up. Was she right? *Was* there something there?

Impatient, he opened the file on his laptop. The grainy picture filled the screen, and he caught his breath.

He clicked on 'reply' and typed rapidly: *It looks like you were right, Georgie. This looks like a burial!*

He sent the message, then stared at the survey results again, excitement bubbling.

A moment later, his phone pinged again. Another message from Georgie: *Maybe if you find a Viking burial under there, you can get all the plaudits and the shiny new job you've been craving.*

His excitement vanished in a heartbeat. She wasn't wanting to talk. There wasn't a way back. She clearly wanted him gone.

He sighed. Better to have found out that she didn't love him enough now, rather than have waited and missed out on the job. She was right: if he could tell them at the interview that he'd found a Viking burial, he'd improve his chances of getting the job enormously. And then he could start again in Norway and forget about her.

52

On Monday morning, Anders prowled close to the middle of the tent, his nerves bubbling. The team had shrunk back down to only the university people and the group from Dig For It. All of the volunteers had finished helping out now, and the dig was into its last few days. He scanned the group, working out who to steal for the test-pit in the wooded area. Sam was an obvious first choice, not least because he was quite burly, and there was probably undergrowth that would need clearing.

His gaze settled on the shock of bright blonde hair only a few feet from him. He should ask her. It *was* Georgie who had pushed for the survey. He swallowed. Did he really want to spend the next few days in such close proximity to her, when she evidently wanted him out of her life? That could be torture.

Courtesy won in the end.

He cleared his throat, catching everyone's attention. "Okay, listen up."

The group looked expectantly at him, and his stomach churned.

"I know we're close to the end of the dig, but I want to put a test-pit in, in the small wooded area over there." He gestured loosely with his hand in the direction he meant. "Sam? Georgia? Can I steal both of you to help?"

Georgie's head shot up, and she locked eyes with him. "Me? Why me?"

She'd moved and now stood close enough for him to be able to whisper to her. "Because you found it."

Sam was also close by. "It? What do you think we'll find, boss?"

Anders shook his head. "I don't want to say at this point." He raised his head. "Shona, can I leave you to process finds, since I'm stealing Georgia? Thanks. Okay. Everyone happy with what they're doing today? Excellent."

He, Sam, and Georgia grabbed kneelers and tools and made their way to the wooded area. A print-out of the survey results poked out of the back pocket of Anders's trousers, and when they reached the area, he pulled it out to study it, checking the GPS against his phone.

Georgie hung back a little, staring at her boots. Was she finding it as difficult to be working together so closely as he was? His gaze flicked between the scan and the undergrowth. Ideally, he didn't want to have to do major tree-surgery, but he thought that the main area of interest avoided the majority of saplings. He wanted a second opinion before starting. Sam was about as good at interpreting scans as he was, but Georgie excelled at it.

"Georgie? Test-pit here?" he said, pointing to an area on the page.

She raised her head, then picked her way over to him. He held the scan out, and she peered at the paper, the scent of her shampoo filling his nose and making his heart lurch. She frowned, glancing between the paper and the ground.

"Um. Maybe a little further over? Here?" She pointed to the scan, then examined the ground. "Which I would make just over there." She nodded to the ground, then looked up at him, shrugging. "That would have the added bonus of not needing to shift that log. Well, not yet."

He laughed. "I think Sam and I might manage it between us."

The area in front of them was a tangle of small saplings between larger trees, though a relatively clear area lay in the middle of the thicket. Only relatively clear. It was still covered in ivy and other plants, with a couple of fallen tree trunks. Their first task would be to clear enough of the space to put the test-pit in. Anders marked out an area larger than the test-pit, and the three of them set about clearing the plants away and exposing the soil. They stood shoulder to shoulder, Anders in the middle, and started to dig across the area.

"You won't give me any hints about what you think is under here?" asked Sam, pushing his hair out of his eyes and leaving a grimy streak across his face.

Anders shook his head, and Sam leaned forward to see Georgia, a brow cocked. She laughed, pulling her hair into a bandana to keep it off her face. "Nope. If Anders is keeping it to himself, I'm not about to say anything."

Anders smiled over at her, then caught himself and turned back to the digging.

The ivy grew in a thick tangle, making the task difficult. Georgie jammed her fork in, then levered it back, trying to get a knot of roots out.

"Need a hand?" he offered.

She shook her head, muttering, "I can manage. Don't patronise me."

He breathed carefully. "I wasn't. You're significantly smaller than me, and that root looks tough to get out, that's all."

She heaved at the root again. It snapped, throwing her completely off balance, and she toppled into him. Anders caught her neatly around the waist, while Sam laughed.

She scowled up at him, gritting her teeth, and he chuckled, keeping hold of her. "You were saying?"

Her scowl deepened, and she shook him off. "Fine. Yes, oh mighty man, could you help me with this root, please?"

He nodded, his mirth gone. In another era, they would have joshed each other. Those days seemed dead and buried. He drove his fork into the ground and manoeuvred the root out, tossing it on to the growing pile of discarded undergrowth.

"Thank you," she ground out, before moving to the next section to be cleared.

It took them all morning to expose the soil and mark out the test-pit. They broke for lunch together, choosing to sit as a three close to the wooded area, rather than joining the rest of the team.

"Still not going to say what you think is down there, boss?" asked Sam, cracking open his lunchbox.

Georgie sat on his other side, nibbling at a sandwich, her face giving nothing away.

"Um. It could be something big," Anders said.

"Can I at least look at the geophysics results, if you won't tell me what you reckon we'll find?"

Anders passed them across, and Sam rested them on his knee to pore over them. Next to him, Georgie leaned around him to look at Sam. She had a smear of grime on her cheekbone, and he yearned to brush it off.

Sam glanced up from the pages, a smile tweaking his lips, his eyes locking on Georgia's. "The boss said you found this. What made you look here?"

"Just a hunch," she said.

Sam looked at him. "You don't normally work off hunches, so what gives?"

"Oh. She ignored me completely and got the survey done without my knowledge or permission." He caught her eye, smiling. "And I'm glad she did."

She smiled back, making the crack in his heart widen. Sam passed the survey results back to him, breaking the moment. When he looked back at Georgie, she'd shifted her focus to the site and had a faraway look in her eyes.

Lunch over, they finished clearing the ivy and other plants from the site of the test-pit, then began the slower job of excavating. By the end of the day, they had worked their way down through hundreds of years of soil with no artefacts or finds in it at all. Whatever it was under here that was showing up on the scans, it had lain undisturbed for a long time. Anders's brain freewheeled. If it *was* a burial, it wasn't an enormous surprise that no one had built on top of it while the site was occupied. He still believed that the whole site had been abandoned not long after the Norman Conquest, and had had no further occupation. His heart fluttered. If there *was* a Viking burial here, it could be intact.

Anders checked his watch. "Okay. Let's call it a day and get a tarp over it. It's scheduled to pour tonight."

Sam offered to get a tarp from the main site, leaving Anders alone with Georgie. She squatted back on her heels, looking at him.

"It's down here. I know it is," she said.

"I believe you."

He stood up, stretching his aching back, then held a hand out to her. She hesitated, then took it, and he pulled her to her feet.

A jolt of electricity pulsed through his arm. From her reaction, it had affected her, too. He held on to her fingers for a moment, wishing that everything was different between them.

"I'm sorry," he whispered.

She pulled her hand free and stepped back. Sam jogged up, clutching a tarp, and the moment vanished.

Between them, they covered the pit, then joined the main group down at the refreshments tent.

"Did you find what you were looking for?" asked Sophie, beaming at him.

"Not yet. Early days," he replied.

"Come here. You have a big smudge on your face."

She reached up and brushed his cheek with her thumb in a way that suggested far more intimacy between them than there was, and he stepped away smartly. His eyes sought Georgie, hoping that she hadn't read anything into Sophie's actions. She looked as if she'd just been punched in the guts, then she turned away.

"Okay, everyone. See you all tomorrow," he said, wishing that Georgie would look at him and see that Sophie's actions had not been welcomed.

She didn't. She followed Shona out of the tent without looking back.

* * *

In the car, Georgia stared out of the windscreen, her thoughts in turmoil. Surely, it was just Sophie being Sophie. Wasn't it?

What if it wasn't?

Her guts knotted, and she felt sick.

"Do you know if there's something going on between Anders and Sophie?" she blurted out as Shona drove out of the field and turned on to the road.

Shona spluttered a laugh. "Only in Sophie's dreams! Why?"

"Oh, just the way she brushed that dirt off his face. It seemed… intimate. Like they were close."

Shona glanced over at her. "As I say, in Sophie's head, maybe. Anders reacted like she'd burned him. And immediately looked at you, absolutely stricken." She changed gear. "Anyway, what do you care? You gave him the heave-ho."

"I know."

Her eyes flicked back and forth as she tracked the trees lining the road. Why *did* she care? He was a free man. He could do whatever he wanted, with whomever he wanted. Including Sophie.

Given that, why was she so relieved to hear that he'd reacted like a scalded cat?

Because when he'd grabbed her around the waist, when that root gave way, it had felt so right. And when he'd helped her up, electricity had poured up her arm at his touch, and her heart had gone into triple-time.

She'd tried to hate him, but she just couldn't. It didn't matter how many times her brain told her heart to kick him out and move on, it wouldn't. He'd taken up residence in there and wouldn't be dislodged.

"If you've changed your mind, he'd have you back," said Shona. "In a heartbeat."

She watched the scenery. "I think that ship has sailed."

Shona harrumphed, but said nothing.

Could they get back together? Every now and then, they both seemed to forget that it had all fallen apart, and there were glimpses of how amazing things had been. She breathed steadily. They were only ever glimpses.

Neither of them spoke again until Shona pulled up at her door.

"Think about it," she said. "You both seem as miserable as sin at the moment. Doesn't that tell you something?"

Georgia shook her head. "Thanks for the lift. See you tomorrow."

Inside, she poured herself a cold drink and took it out to the tiny square of garden at the back of the flats. Although she stared at the small border of cheerful flowers, her mind saw Sophie brushing at his face, and knots of jealousy cramped her stomach. Should she try to patch things up with him? She folded her arms on the table and rested her head on them, her heart full.

Stop even thinking about him. He doesn't love you enough.

A bee buzzed close to her head, startling her. She sat up again, feeling wretched, images of his wide, easy smile dancing through her brain.

He chose his career and Norway. It's not to be. Move on.
Her heart was having none of it.

53

The following morning found Anders back in the small copse with Sam and Georgie. They slowly peeled back the tarp, draining the accumulated puddle from the overnight rain, then settled into position next to one another. Anders found himself in the middle again, with Sam on his left and Georgie on his right. The overnight rain had left the copse smelling earthy, though the trench had remained dry enough, thankfully. Around them, the trees and shrubs were filled with small birds who popped their heads out, cheeping incessantly as if giving a running commentary on their work.

Space was tight, and Georgie was so close to him they bumped shoulders at times. He could smell her vanilla body wash and the coconut from her hair. He glanced sideways at her, wondering if his proximity was having the same effect on her as hers was on him. Her face had a pinched look, as if she hadn't slept well, and she looked paler than normal. He wanted to ask how she was, but didn't think he should. They worked in silence for a few minutes, but then Anders couldn't bear it any longer.

"Georgie? Are you okay?" he asked, his voice soft.

She gave him a wide-eyed look. "I'm fine. Why?"

"You look a little washed out, that's all." He shrugged, half wishing he hadn't said anything.

"Oh. I'm just tired." She switched her focus back to the trench.

Sam arched a brow at him, but he didn't respond. Would there come a day when Anders stopped worrying about her? He didn't think so.

As they worked across the trench, Sam talked about his plans for a brief holiday after the dig. He'd booked a last-minute break in Italy, and was hoping to get to Pompeii. Anders wondered what the temperature would be like. He'd once been to Greece around this time of year. Never again.

Sam suddenly laughed at him. "You look like that would be your idea of hell."

He looked up, rolling a shoulder, chuckling. "Pompeii would be amazing. Italy at this time of the year? I would boil to death! How you'll manage with your colouring is beyond me."

Sam had a shock of red hair and a creamy-pale complexion, already decorated with more than a smattering of freckles from the summer.

"Sunscreen and a hat. I'll be grand."

Anders shook his head and turned back to the soil.

A few minutes later, Sam's trowel paused mid-scrape. "Boss?"

Anders raised his head. Sam's eyes shone with excitement, and Anders peered over to see what he'd found. Georgia leaned forward, her eyes fixed on the area of the test-pit in front of Sam.

"Is that a sword?" she asked, her voice trembling.

She locked eyes with him, grinning widely. He tried to temper his emotions, but failed, his heart thumping so hard he was sure it would leave his chest. Sam brushed a little more soil away, revealing eroded metal that looked exactly like it was indeed a sword.

Sam squatted back on his heels, eyes wide. "Burial? Is *that* what you think is down here?"

"Maybe," said Anders. "Let's not get ahead of ourselves."

"More paperwork for you if there are bones," said Sam.

Anders groaned theatrically, but he didn't really care. He'd take any amount of paperwork if they found a full Viking burial.

Over the rest of the morning, they carefully revealed not just the remains of a sword, but a shield boss lying a little to the side.

"It must have slipped," murmured Georgie, scrutinising it. "It was over his chest."

"Is that what you saw?" he asked in Norwegian.

Sam shot him a perplexed look, but Georgie didn't look up. "Yes."

A shield would have been laid over either the chest or perhaps the feet, given their placements in other burials. But from the way she'd spoken, she sounded as if she'd actually seen it, not just had a daydream. He still didn't buy into the idea that she'd had flashbacks to life in the settlement that were anything more than her extremely active imagination, but he had to accept that her imagination had proved accurate on more than one occasion.

He helped Sam to clear the soil away from both the sword and the shield boss while Georgia worked where the head would be.

"Anders," she breathed, raising her head.

He glanced over at her hands. She'd brushed enough soil away to reveal something that looked remarkably like bone.

"I think you've got a ton of paperwork to do," she said, her eyes bright with excitement. "I think this is a brow ridge."

She brushed a little more, revealing an eye socket.

"I think it's safe to say it's a burial," said Sam, sitting back on his heels, his face wreathed in smiles. "Well done, boss."

"It's Georgia we need to thank. She knew it was here." He rubbed his cheekbone. "I'm sorry. I should have listened to you earlier."

She shrugged. "You listened in the end. I guess we can't keep on digging until you get the paperwork sorted."

"Nope. I have to call the police and the coroner's office and get Lynette in."

Lynette was an osteoarchaeologist. She would assess the bones and decide whether they were old enough not to warrant the police to be involved, plus sign off on the excavation and so on. He knew her fairly well, and she would know that both he and Georgie had experience over excavating human remains. There would be a delay, but not a huge one.

"Okay. Let's get the pit covered up and protected, and then I'll make some calls." He shot them both a stern look. "Not a word. Not even to the team just yet. I don't want this robbed out before we can excavate it."

They both nodded.

The site covered, Sam brushed himself down, then offered to sort drinks out for them all.

"Oh, you star. Yes, please," said Georgie.

Sam grinned and made his way back to the main site.

"I'm sorry I didn't believe you. You were right," Anders said quietly.

She shrugged one shoulder. "I came to you with stories of dreams and visions and no evidence to back them up."

He had to ask. "Did you *really* see it?"

She took a breath. "The burial? I dreamed it. That morning when you found me sitting outside at your place. There should be an axe between his feet, a whetstone in one hand, a comb, his flint, his knife… and a silver cross around his neck."

"A cross?" He could buy the rest of it, but the cross didn't fit.

"Aelfgyth added it. After Einar died." She looked squarely at him, her eyes troubled. "Half of me really, *really* wants all of that to be in here. The other half of me would find that terrifying."

He didn't know what to say.

She pulled her hair free from the bandana, letting it blow around her face. "I am glad you found it. That's what's important."

She didn't look glad. She looked resigned. A brittle smile lifted her lips, then she turned away. "See you in the tent for these drinks."

He nodded, though she wouldn't have seen it.

"Georgie?"

She stopped and looked back at him, her brows raised.

"Thank you," he said softly. "I owe you more than you'll ever know."

She stuck her bottom lip out. "Make your name with it, Anders. It's what you've always wanted."

With that, she turned away and headed down to the main site, leaving him staring after her, heavy-hearted.

54

The police, the coroner, and the osteoarchaeologist, Lynette, were all satisfied that the remains were from the late ninth or early tenth century. The paperwork went through smoothly, and the licence granted swiftly, allowing Sam, Anders, and Georgia to finish working in the wooded area until the burial was fully excavated. Lynette had joined them for a couple of days until the bones had been removed from the grave. The rest of the team was left to wrap up the main site. The burial was exactly as Georgia had seen in the dream. Alongside the sword and shield boss, they found an axe between the feet, a knife near to the waist, several arm-rings, and a small silver cross on a chain. Anders had flashed wide eyes at her when that was discovered. Georgia had just shrugged, but the fact that the grave was identical to her dream left her deeply unsettled.

The remains of a beautifully decorated comb were found close to the head, and the flint and whetstone by the man's hands, exactly where Aelfgyth had placed them. Lynette had confirmed that the bones *were* those of a man. Even though she was no expert, Georgia had guessed that was the case. Einar must have stood as tall as Anders, maybe even a little taller, with strong brow ridges and a square jaw. A brooch that would have fastened his cloak had shifted a little and been found slightly to the side. Georgia had caught her breath when she saw it. It, too, was an exact match to the one she had seen in her dream. She'd thought that she would be excited that her dream was so accurate, but she wasn't. More than anything, she just wanted to talk to Anders about all of it, and let him hold her close and reassure her that she wasn't mad.

On one of the last days of the excavation, Georgia found

herself digging with Anders alone. Sam had gone to get drinks, and then become caught up in a conversation on the main site. Anders was deep in concentration, picking away at the soil, the unruly lock of hair at the front coiling over his brow.

"Have you told your father about finding this?" she asked softly, trying not to startle him.

He still jumped, making her smile. He'd have forgotten anyone else was nearby, he was so focused on what he was doing.

"Sorry. I was miles away." He flashed her a sheepish smile, and her heart did a couple of somersaults. "Er, no. Not yet. I don't want him coming over and barging around. It's my dig. Not his."

She studied him. "When's the interview?"

He blinked at her, his posture tightening. "It was on Friday."

She frowned. He'd been away in the morning, leaving Sam to set up, but he'd been there by lunchtime, helping her and Sam dig the burial. She'd assumed he was at the dentist or a departmental meeting or something. Anders chuckled at her.

"It was over the internet. I didn't need to go over to Norway." He shrugged. "The guys over there know me, so I guess it was less vital that they met me in person in the interview."

"Did you need to give a presentation or anything?"

He shifted his weight, suddenly awkward. "Mm."

"Were you okay with that? Or was it easier via the internet as you weren't actually standing up in front of them?"

"I think it went okay." He sat back on his heels, picking at some soil on his hands. "You're right. It *was* easier that way."

She bent her head and scraped at some more soil, wondering if she should ask the next question.

"Spit it out, Georgie."

Her head shot up. A smile poked into one side of his mouth, and he tilted his head. She laughed, before a pang hit her. He'd always been able to read her too well.

"Okay. Don't be mad at me for asking this, but are you *sure* the job is right for you?"

When Shona told her he had an interview, she'd pulled up the details for the job and put it through Google Translate. From the description of the role, she thought there was far too much desk-based work and too many lectures to give for it to be an ideal job for Anders.

His smile faded. "Why?"

She put her trowel down and mimicked his posture, sitting back on her haunches, then drew a circle in the air around him. "This is what suits you. Being outside, digging. Making sense of sites. Not paper-pushing. Not giving lectures or presentations at conferences. Not chairing departmental meetings or balancing budgets. I mean, you *can* do all of those things." She wrinkled her nose, sure that he was getting annoyed with her. "But it's more what Haakon loves. Not what makes *your* heart sing."

He swallowed, his eyes still fixed on hers. He opened his mouth, then closed it again without saying anything.

She took a long breath, still not finished. "I am genuinely glad that you found this burial. It's the find of a lifetime and will make your name. It might even let you step out from the shadow of your father." She paused before continuing. "I know you've always dreamed of a high-profile academic career. I've just never been convinced that if those dreams came true, they would make you happy."

The muscles in his jaw clenched, and she held her hands up. "All I'm saying is run towards, don't just run away."

"I…" He tailed off as his gaze shifted upwards, over her head.

"Here you go," said Sam, juggling three drinks in his hands. "Coffee for you…" He passed Anders a mug. "Coffee for you…" He handed one to Georgia. "And a tea for me."

He sat down cross-legged at the edge of the trench, oblivious to the tension between Georgia and Anders. Anders sipped his coffee, his eyes locked on Georgia's over the rim of the mug. She bounced the stare back at him.

"Just think about it."

He took a couple of long breaths, then nodded.

She blew on her coffee, watching him. Was she right to think he'd hate the job if he got it? Maybe he saw it as another stepping stone to something that *would* suit him better. She'd never worked in academia. Perhaps you had to 'serve your time' on stuff that you didn't enjoy before you got to do all the things that made you happy. She let her gaze spin out over the rest of the site, trying to divert her brain on to something else.

The team had only partially excavated the site. They'd revealed enough to be sure that there had been a settlement here, with firm evidence it had been abandoned around a thousand years ago. There were also good indications that the site extended beneath the adjacent field. If it did, there would be at least another summer of digging needed to uncover everything, but she had no idea if that would happen. The university would be the ones to decide that, and Dig For It might not be involved. Anders would be gone soon, one way or another. If he didn't get the job in Norway, he'd be somewhere else as soon as Angela came back.

Sudden tears nipped her eyes at the thought, and she buried her nose in her mug, hoping that neither Sam nor Anders would see them. Not soon enough. Anders canted his head at her.

"You okay?"

She smiled wanly. "Just sad that the dig is almost over. I'm sure there's still a ton of stuff to discover. We've only just scratched the surface of what's here, but I don't suppose Dig For It will be involved if there *is* another dig. We rarely get invited in. The academics usually look down their noses at us."

"I never have," he said softly.

"I know. I wasn't including either of you two in that. Or Patrick."

He caught her eye. Had he noticed that she hadn't excluded Sophie? His lips twitched, suggesting he had.

"Well, I guess I won't be digging it either," he said.

She blinked hard and averted her gaze.

"Any news on the job front?" Sam asked.

Anders shook his head, his posture stiffening.

"Well, maybe Angela won't come back, and they'll keep you on," Sam said. "Or you get that job you went for the other day."

"Well, I hope something comes up, or I'm going to have to live with my dad."

He'd said it lightly enough, but Georgia knew how he really felt about that.

Sam visibly shuddered. "Sorry. I know he's your dad and all that, but…"

Anders laughed. "It's okay. I know exactly what you mean."

His smiles faded, and he sipped at his coffee again, troubled. His hand lay close to hers and, without thinking, she brushed the back of it with her knuckles, wanting to comfort him. Anders started, but recovered quickly. Sam was mid slurp of his tea and probably hadn't noticed. Anders held her gaze for a moment, but she couldn't read him.

And then hurt slipped over his face, and anguish settled in his eyes, and she could read him like a book. He blinked, looking down, and her instinct was to lean over and wrap him up in a hug.

She didn't. She drained her mug and plastered a smile to her face.

"Right. Back at it," she said, over-brightly.

Anders kept his head bowed. When he finally raised it, the pain hadn't left his eyes, and her heart cracked wide-open.

55

On Saturday morning, Georgia sat on the edge of her bed, staring at the small plastic device with a sinking heart. But however much she did, it didn't change the result. She closed her eyes, letting out a long, wobbly breath. Her periods had never been stunningly regular, but she'd never gone this long between cycles before. Between that, and the increasing bouts of nausea, an uncomfortable truth had dawned.

"Can I come in?" called Becky through the door.

Georgia toed the door open, and Becky poked her head around the edge. "All done?"

"All done."

Becky sat next to her, making the bed dip. "Well?"

Georgia turned the pregnancy test so that Becky could read the result.

"Oh," said Becky. "I guess you're going to *have* to speak to Anders."

She was right, but Georgia didn't know how to have the conversation.

"I don't want him to feel obliged," she muttered.

"He *is* obliged. It's his baby too."

She knew him. He would stand by her, whatever. But it would kill him not to be able to provide for her and the baby the way he wanted to. His ideal would have been to land the great job, and *then* to think about a family. Not to have an unexpected baby sprung upon him.

Her heart sank. Maybe he *had* landed a great job.

"He had an interview for that job in Norway," she said in a small voice. "He seemed to think it had gone okay."

Becky sucked her teeth. "Would you move to Norway? If he

was offered the post."

Georgia flopped back on the bed, screwing her face up. "I don't know. The idea terrifies me, because I've *not* spent the last few weeks learning Norwegian, the way I would have done if we hadn't broken up. So, if I went now, I'd be jobless, friendless, *and* with a new baby to worry about. But if he's offered the post and I don't go, where would that leave us? And the baby?"

If he *didn't* get the job, her being pregnant would put him into a complete tailspin.

Becky rubbed her arm. "Anders aside, how do you feel about having a baby?"

She screwed a fingernail into the corner of her eye. "It's not exactly ideal, is it? Yeah, I've always wanted children, and in a perfect world, they would be with Anders. But this isn't a perfect world. We're not together."

"You still have to tell him. He might be offered the job in Norway. He may already have got it. You need to think about what you'll do if he has. What you'll both do."

Georgia swallowed. She didn't want to bring any baby up alone. Which left them patching things up and both moving to Norway as the most likely scenario, if he got the job. Her stomach filled with rocks at the idea.

"What if I tell him, we get back together, and then it falls apart?" she said. "His parents' marriage didn't work out, because Haakon was too focused on his career." Tears prickled her eyes. "I wanted him to *choose* me. I don't want him to get back with me because he feels *obliged* to."

"Georgie, talk to him. I think he would choose you over everything if you just gave him a chance. Call him. See if he wants to get back together."

"And what if I do that and he doesn't? I *then* spring it on him and tell him about the baby? He'd feel trapped."

Becky sighed heavily next to her. "You're going to have to tell him at some point. And the two of you will *have* to have a proper conversation about the future. Is it together? In the UK? Or in Norway?"

"I know."

She stared at the ceiling. Whichever way she looked at it, *one* of them would be miserable. If he'd got the job, she would go to Norway with him and hope for the best. If he hadn't got the job, he would do anything to provide for her and the baby. She knew that. Even if it ruined his career. Would he end up resenting her?

She dried her eyes and started to rehearse how on earth she was going to tell him.

* * *

Anders sat on his sofa, his laptop open on the coffee table in front of him, a feeling of dread creeping into his body. He re-read the start of the email, his fingertips tracing a crease in his brow.

Dear Dr Mortensen,

We are delighted to offer you the post of…

He closed his eyes. This was the third time he'd read it, and he still didn't know how he felt about getting the job.

He reflected on the interview. At the time, he'd felt it had gone well, and he'd even managed to control his nerves for the presentation. He already knew most of the people on the interview panel and got on well with them. And, of course, his father would have been bending Professor Gunderson's ear for the last few weeks. Deep down, he was proud to have been selected but, did he *want* the post?

Georgie's words about running towards something, rather than merely running away, rang in his brain. Hand on heart, he knew he was running away. From Georgie; from the fear of having no job.

He rang his sister, Katya.

"Hey. How are things?" he said when she answered.

"Same old, same old. What's up?"

He leaned back in his seat, closing his eyes, his guts still churning. "I got the job."

"Hey, fantastic! When do you start?"

He didn't reply. Even the *thought* of starting made him feel queasy. That should tell him something, surely?

"Anders?"

He let out a long breath. "I don't know if I want it. But I'm too scared to turn it down."

"Why don't you want it?"

He swallowed. "I'm not sure if it's really what *I* want. I think it might be more what Pappa wants me to have."

There was silence on the line, but he knew it was only because Katya was thinking.

"Would it be a good stepping stone to something else?" she asked at last.

"Yes. But do I want what it would be a stepping stone *to*?"

"What do you mean?"

He scraped his hand through his hair, then ran his palm over the back of his neck, trying to organise his thoughts. "It would be a fantastic bridge to a senior academic position. I mean, really amazing. It's a permanent post. With the publications I'll get from the dig, I could probably get a professorship in the next few years. Challenge Pappa."

He half laughed at the idea, then tailed off.

"I'm not hearing a negative yet, so what gives?" asked Katya.

"I don't know if that's *me*. I mean, I know I could do it all. I'm just not sure if it's what I really want."

Another long silence from his sister.

"How much is this all tied up with Georgie?"

He screwed his face up. "Some of it. She said to me the other day that I should make sure I wasn't just running away, and I think I am. If I took it, I'd be running away from being near her."

"You think you two will ever get back together?"

"No… I don't know." He thought about her brushing his hand the day before, but she'd almost immediately withdrawn from him, so it had probably just been habit and nothing more. "I don't think so."

She laughed at him. "Well, there was a bit of a selection-box there, but none of them were even as positive as 'maybe', so might I suggest you don't make any decision based on whether it will ruin any future with her?"

The idea of never getting back with Georgie left him wanting to howl.

"Okay, let's run through options. You either accept the offer or you don't. Let's say you accept it. Tell me what will be good about it; tell me what would be bad."

Katya clearly had her practical-head on. She could be as

focused and clinical as their father, and he shuffled in his seat, getting his argument straight. "It's a great university. I know most of the people in the department and like them. I think I'd be able to get promoted reasonably easily. There's a chance I might even make professor in a few years." He ground to a halt.

"And the negatives?"

"There's a lot of desk-work. A lot of admin. I don't know how much fieldwork I'd be able to do. And I'd have to give a lot of presentations and lectures."

His stomach knotted at the thought of how many he might have to do on a regular basis.

"And the promotions. Would they take you closer to what your ideal is?"

He considered it for a moment. "I don't know. I don't think so."

"Would the job allow you to move diagonally? Upwards but also sideways into something you'd enjoy more?"

"Maybe." He shrugged to himself, even though she wouldn't see him.

Katya made a small humming sound. "And if you turned it down?"

His nerves jangled. "I have nothing else, and nothing seems to be coming up. I could be out of a job altogether when Angela comes back, and I don't even know where I'd live if that happened."

His sister let out a long whistle. "Okay. Those all sound like pretty major negatives. And I didn't hear a positive. Are there any?"

He swallowed. "No."

"I think you have your answer, then. It's always easier to get another job when you already have one, and at least you'd be making some money while you waited for something more suitable to come up."

"It would just reinforce what Georgie thinks about me, though."

Katya sighed hard. "If she isn't in the picture, it doesn't matter what she thinks of you. Take the job and keep looking for what you *really* want."

He knew she was right, but accepting the job still didn't feel as if it was the right thing to do, and he couldn't put his finger on why that was.

"Alright. Thanks, Katya. Talk again soon."

They finished the call, and Anders fiddled with his phone. He had to talk to Georgie. At least tell her he'd been offered the job and see what she said.

He called her, not expecting her to pick up.

"Hi, Anders."

"Georgie. Hi." His rehearsed words scattered to the four winds.

"Anders, I need to talk to you about something," she said abruptly, making him blink.

"Um. Yeah. Okay..."

"Not on the phone?"

Her words made him frown. "Er... sure. Where?"

There was a pause before she spoke. "Can I come over?"

"Yeah. Of course. Is everything okay?"

There was a long, shaky breath from her before she replied. "I just need to talk to you about something... Why were you calling me?"

"Oh. I'll tell you when I see you."

Another ragged breath. "Can I come over now?"

"Er, sure... Yes, of course. I'll put the kettle on."

"Thanks."

They rang off, and he stared around the room, perplexed. What did she need to talk about? She sounded so upset, like she had to tell him something he wouldn't want to hear.

Oh, god. Was it to tell him she'd found someone new?

His stomach went into free-fall, and he couldn't breathe.

56

He'd almost paced a hole in the floor by the time she arrived. When the doorbell rang, his heart skittered wildly, and he wiped his palms on his thighs before hurrying to the door. Georgie stood on the doorstep, biting her lips together, her skin pale.

"Hey," she said, fixing a smile to her face that didn't convince him of its authenticity.

"Hi. Come in." He stood back, nausea bubbling in the back of his throat, convinced she was here to tell him there was someone else in her life. "Coffee?"

"Um. Do you have decaff?"

He blinked. Since when had Georgie started drinking decaff?

"Er, no. Sorry."

"Okay. I'll just have a glass of water then. Thanks."

In the kitchen, Georgie rested her hips against the worktop, her head down. He reached up to get a glass from a cupboard, desperately trying to read her. If she wasn't here to tell him she'd started seeing someone, what *did* she need to talk to him about? From her face, nothing happy, anyway.

"Why were you calling me?" she asked, frowning up at him.

"Oh. Um… They offered me the job. In Norway." His eyes sought hers, his nerves fraying. If she'd found someone else, she'd be relieved at his news.

She nodded, then lowered her head again. "Congratulations."

He couldn't figure out her emotion. She seemed conflicted. He passed a glass of water to her, and she sipped at it, taking tiny mouthfuls as if she was feeling sick.

"You okay?" he asked. "You're very pale."

She didn't reply. He spooned ground coffee into a cafetiere, still watching her.

"When do you start?" Her voice came out small and uncertain.

"As soon as this job finishes. If I take it."

Her head jerked up. "*If*?" Anger flared in her eyes. "You threw away what we had, and now it's only an *if*?"

She put her water down abruptly and brought her hand up to her mouth, then rushed out of the room to the downstairs bathroom.

"Georgie?"

He hurried after her, but the bathroom door slammed on him, and he heard retching from the other side. He tapped on the door.

"Hey. Are you okay?"

The toilet flushed, then the taps ran. Georgie emerged even paler than before, with tears in her eyes, along with fury.

"Are you alright?" he said.

She flapped a hand, dismissing his question. He stared at her. If he took the job, he would lose her forever. Why would he risk that for a job he wasn't even sure was right for him?

"You misunderstood me," he said, stress making his stomach cramp. "I miss you. I miss *us*. I *love* you. More than I have ever loved anyone, and I can't bear the thought of you not being in my life. I don't want to take the job if it means I could never rebuild things with you. If you want me to stay here and keep looking for another job, I will."

"Oh."

She blinked away her tears, and his heart plummeted. His vision swam a little, and he put his hand out to the wall.

"Georgie?" he said, his voice shaky. Had he just declared undying love for her, and she was going to tell him she'd met someone else?

She indicated behind him. "Did you want to make your coffee? Then we can sit in the lounge. I need to tell you something."

Sweat dampened his skin, and his breath caught in his throat. She *had* found somebody else. She'd come over to tell him that there was no way back.

The kettle had boiled by the time they reached the kitchen, and he poured the hot water over the coffee. She perched against the worktop, still ashen, and he arched a brow at her.

"Are you sure you don't want a cup?"

Her colour shifted towards green, and she shook her head rapidly. He eased the plunger down in the cafetiere, and poured out a mug of strong coffee, adding a dash of milk. He flicked his head towards the lounge, and she nodded.

There, she sat on the sofa opposite him, plaiting her fingers together, not looking at him.

"You should take the job," she said, almost inaudibly.

His vision tunnelled. "Georgie, have you found someone else?"

The words were out before he could stop them, and her head shot up, her eyes wide. "No."

"But you want me to go to Norway."

She dipped her head again, fingering her brow. "Oh, god, this is coming out all wrong. I'd rehearsed what I was going to say on the way over, and now it's all scrambled." She looked up, her face contorting. "Just let me talk? Don't interrupt. Please?"

"Okay."

She took a breath and set her shoulders. "Take the job, Anders, and I'll come to Norway with you. If you want me to."

His heart sang at her words, before questions crowded his head.

"What about you not knowing enough Norwegian and feeling isolated?" he cut in. "What about your job here? *Your* career?"

She half laughed. "Which bit of 'don't interrupt' did you not understand?"

"Sorry. Sorry." He clamped his mouth shut, locking his eyes on hers.

Her smiles faded, and she twisted her fingers together again, her face suddenly falling. She tipped her head up, her breathing tight. "I miss you. I've tried to hate you. Tried to imagine my life without you in it, and I just can't. I love you. Take the job, Anders, and I'll come with you. If you want me to."

She still loved him! His spirits soared. "Georgie, I just want to be with you. You don't have to come to Norway. I'll stay here. Unemployed, if that's what happens."

She let out a long, shaky breath, then met his eye. "Anders, I'm pregnant." She swallowed, making a hiccupy sound. "I don't want to have it alone, but I don't want you to feel trapped."

He stared at her, a million thoughts tumbling through his mind. They were having a baby! Oh, god, how would he provide for her if they stayed in the UK and nothing came up? Did she really want to have the baby in Norway? He would have to take the job and make the best of it.

"Oh, jeez, Anders, say something?" she gasped, tears trickling down her face.

He snatched his attention back to her, then shifted seats to sit next to her, wrapping an arm around her shoulders. She peered up at him, her face filled with fear and apprehension, and she swiped at her tears. More replaced them almost immediately, breaking his heart.

"You don't want the baby, do you?" she whispered, weeping.

"What? Of course I do! Oh, Georgie, come here." He held her tight against his chest, kissing the side of her head. "*Elskling*, of *course* I want the baby!"

She burrowed in against him, pressing her forehead against his neck. "I guess you need to teach me more Norwegian."

He stroked her back, rocking her. "Do you really want to move to Norway?"

She didn't reply for a moment, telling him everything he needed to know. Eventually, she raised her head, pushing her hair back.

"Hand on heart, no… I'd rather stay here, but that's not practical, is it? You've been offered an amazing job. It would give you the step up in your career that you've wanted for years. My career would be on hold while I had the baby anyway, so it might as well be on hold in Norway. Maybe in the future we would move back here. Or maybe I'll fall in love with Norway."

Her hair sprang up again to tickle his face, and he smoothed it down, his brain whirring. Although the post was permanent, he didn't have to stay in it forever. He could move diagonally. He could make this work. She was making enormous sacrifices to move to Norway; the least he could do was ensure she and their child were well provided for.

And yet, his stomach clenched at the thought of accepting the job.

Georgie met his eye, hers full of uncertainty. "We can make this work, can't we?" she asked in a small voice.

He plastered a smile on his face. "Yeah. We can make this work… Oh, Georgie, I love you so much."

He touched a soft kiss to her lips, and she kissed him back, threading her fingers into his hair.

He would make things work. He had to.

57

Georgia tucked her face back into his shoulder, his top soft against her skin. He'd reacted exactly as she'd thought he would: initial shock, then a determination to do things right by her and the baby, even though he'd *just* said he would turn the job down. She wanted to cry. She'd put him in a horrible position. Was he going to end up resenting her for making him take a job he didn't want? Was *she* going to resent being in Norway? If she wasn't pregnant, everything would be different. He'd said he would stay with her in the UK and look for something else. Instead, both of them would have to relocate to Norway, and neither of them was ecstatic at the prospect.

She slipped her arm around his middle, and he kissed the top of her head.

"How pregnant are you?" he asked. "How many weeks?"

She rubbed her cheekbone on the seam of his top. "I don't really know. My cycles can be all over the place at the best of times. The test said over three weeks, but I knew *that.* It's more than that since we split up." She sighed. "I thought we'd been careful."

He stroked her hair, saying nothing for a moment. Was he doing what she'd already done, and fast-forwarded nine months in his head? They would be in Norway by then.

"When do you have to tell them about the job?" she said.

"By the end of next week."

There was a miserable edge to his tone, breaking her heart. "You don't really want to take it, do you?"

He didn't reply for a moment, and her spirits plummeted further.

"I don't know. It's still a great job on many levels, and if it isn't brilliant, I can move sideways or diagonally, I guess. It's not forever." He let out a long breath. "I know you don't want to move, either. I wish I wasn't making you do that. Maybe we both just have to suck it up for a year or so. See what else might come along. I should get some good publications out of the dig. That will help."

Tears made her vision blur, and her nose prickled. "I'm sorry I put you in this position. I didn't mean to."

He tipped her backwards so that he could see her face. "Hey. It takes two to make a baby! Surely I've put you in this position just as much?"

"I know. It's just that things would be a lot easier if we *hadn't* made a baby, right?"

A smile lifted one side of his mouth. "Oh, Georgie, I've wanted to have a kid with you almost since I met you. Is the timing ever right for these things?" He shrugged one shoulder. "It is what it is. We'll figure things out."

She stared at him, full of uncertainty. "You don't feel trapped, do you?"

His brow creased briefly. "Why on earth would I feel trapped? I love you, and I want to be with you. I want to have kids with you. I have all of those things. Why would you think I would feel trapped?" His face suddenly fell a mile. "Do *you* feel trapped? Do you feel like we're only together because of this?"

She scrunched up her face. "Well, we *are* a bit! Yesterday we weren't together. Today we are."

He studied her, uncertainty clouding his features. "If you *weren't* pregnant, and I'd told you I would turn down the job to be with you, what would you have said?"

She rushed to soothe him. "I'd have been delighted. And if you'd told me you'd been offered the job and were going to take it, I'd have said I would come too. I missed you. I hated us not being together. The idea of you going back to Norway and not seeing you again… I thought that was what I wanted, but when push came to shove, I knew it would break my heart."

His expression softened, then he bunched his lips. "When I called you, and you said you needed to tell me something… I was convinced you were coming over to tell me there was someone else."

She laughed. "Well… there is, technically… the baby."

He smiled. "You know what I mean." He blinked slowly. "I was devastated at the thought."

She thought of how seeing Sophie flirting with him, or brushing grime off his cheek, had made her feel, and nodded.

"I kept wondering if you'd finally succumbed to Sophie's advances."

He snorted a laugh. "Credit me with some taste!" He shook his head. "How could you possibly think I would date *Sophie*?"

"I dunno. Rebound?" she offered, a smile creeping over her lips.

"No. Come here." He drew her closer, kissing her tenderly, his breath dusting her cheek, his light stubble a little raspy. "Oh, I love you. How was I ever stupid enough to lose you?"

She arched a brow. "Twice!" Her face fell. "Don't ever do it again."

"Never. I swear." He drew a cross over his heart, his eyes lively, then rubbed the end of her nose with his.

She pressed a kiss to his lips, then cuddled in against him, her fears bubbling up.

"Anders, I'm scared," she whispered, burrowing closer.

He stroked her hair, his touch soothing. "What of, *elskling*?"

She half smiled to herself at how reassuring and practical he sounded. *Tell me what you're scared of, and I'll sort it out.* That's how he made her feel.

"All of it. The baby; moving to Norway…"

"It'll be fine." He crooked his finger under her chin and raised her face. "It'll be fine."

She gazed into his eyes, her heart singing. He loved her; she loved him. She smiled. Everything *would* be fine.

58

Anders dragged his eyes away from the window and back to his computer screen, a leaden lump squatting in his stomach. The dig had officially finished the day before, and he was now back in his office, suited and booted, and resenting the fact that it was a glorious day outside and he was indoors.

His gaze drifted over the framed photo on his desk. Taken in Orkney, it was of him and Georgie sitting on a beach together. The ever-present wind had blown her hair about so much that day, she'd wanted to shave it all off. Instead, he'd braided it for her, badly, and the whole thing was as crooked as a question mark. His shoulder sat at an odd angle from him holding his phone out to take the picture, and his nose was red from the sun, but the two of them radiated happiness. A soft smile crept over his lips. He loved that picture of them.

He shifted his attention back to the letter of acceptance on his computer. His heart wasn't in it. He still desperately hoped that something in the UK would come up. He closed his eyes, massaging his temples. Even if it did, there was no guarantee of him getting it. He had to accept the job in Norway, so he should just suck it up and send the letter.

Someone tapped on his office door. He opened his eyes to see his secretary, Carol, standing in the doorway, her eyebrows raised.

"Um, you're meant to be going to the research meeting," she said. "It starts in ten minutes. Room 5b."

He grimaced. He'd forgotten about it.

"Okay. Thanks. I don't suppose you have the agenda handy?" He screwed his face up.

She smiled brightly. "Here. And the papers."

He smiled, relieved. He wasn't sure why he even needed to go to the meeting. It was about future developments that would happen long after Angela had returned, and he would be in Norway. He didn't feel that he could commit Angela to something in her absence. All he could do was listen to the suggestions made by the key researchers in the department and give his feedback on them, but given that he wouldn't be there to see any of them implemented, they were entirely free to ignore him.

He saved the acceptance letter and screen-locked his computer, then scraped himself up from behind his desk.

"It's the Dean chairing it, remember," said Carol. "You might want to run a comb through your hair."

The Dean was cut from the same cloth as his father, and Anders's heart sank. He turned back to his desk, rummaged through a drawer, and found a comb. He didn't have a mirror, so he guessed where the parting in his hair should be, and straightened it all as best as he could, then peered at Carol.

"Good enough?"

She gave him an unconvinced look and shrugged. "You'll do. He hates tardiness even more than scruffiness, so don't antagonise him on *both* fronts."

Anders laughed, taking the papers from her. "Thank you."

He hurried to the meeting room and found a chair as far from where the Dean would sit as possible. The meeting hadn't started, and a low hum of chatter circulated. The room was stuffy, and he gazed greedily at the sunshine outside.

The Dean swirled in, florid-faced with a drinker's nose, a pair of thick-rimmed glasses dominating his face.

"Oh, let's get those blinds closed. It's dazzling in here!" he barked.

Someone fiddled with the blind cords, extinguishing the sun, and Anders shuffled through the papers he'd brought, already resenting being there.

"Right. Let's get started. Lot to cover."

The meeting required little of his attention, leaving Anders to think about other things. His mind drifted over the slew of other meetings that filled his diary, and he studied his fingers. Despite copious scrubbing, he still had a small patch of grime embedded in the edge of his index finger.

He was going to be a father. The idea thrilled him and terrified him in equal measure. What if he *was* like Pappa? He genuinely couldn't imagine abandoning Georgie and any child to spend more time at work, but if he took the job in Norway, he might end up doing exactly that. Even in the short time he had left in his current role, he was probably going to be working late most evenings, just to get on top of things he hadn't done while the dig was on.

He zoned back into the meeting to give his two penn'orth on a proposal, then zoned back out again. Seriously, all of this could have been covered in an email, but academia loved their meetings. Well, strictly speaking, *the Dean* loved his meetings. Anders was pretty sure almost everyone else in the room would be happier somewhere else right then.

How much would Georgie hate moving to Norway? What could he do to make it better for her? One of his friends there had also just become a father. Maybe Georgie would get on well with his wife?

An image of a tiny baby with mad spiralling hair popped into his head, and he almost laughed out loud, only just catching himself in time. If the baby was a girl, the curls would look amazing, like they did on Georgie. On a boy? He wasn't so sure they would, then wondered if that was sexist of him.

Would the baby have blue eyes like him, or hazel like Georgie's? Or maybe another colour altogether? Surely the baby would be blonde-haired.

He doodled on the edge of his papers, willing the meeting to be over. His phone vibrated in his pocket, and he surreptitiously slid it on to his knee. The screen indicated a new message from Georgie, and he opened it as discreetly as he could.

Have you accepted the job yet?

He sent back: *no. Why?*

Just wondered

He glanced at the Dean, who scowled at him. He'd have to focus on the rest of the meeting. Reluctantly, he turned his phone off and tucked it back in his pocket.

As soon as the meeting finished, he switched his mobile back on, wanting to talk to Georgie on his way back to his office, just to hear her voice. His email pinged. Top of the list was a message from Josh Holmes, the experimental archaeologist they'd met at the re-enactment day. Anders had chatted to him a few times since then, and there had been talk of the four of them meeting up at some point, though nothing had been arranged. The email had been sent with a covering note of: *Wondered if you would be interested in this. Hopefully catch up soon. Josh*

He scanned the rest of the message, his spirits soaring, a grin splitting his face.

59

After the meeting, Anders headed outside to the sunshine rather than back to his desk, and found a bench in a corner of the gardens outside the department, where he could read the job outline again. With every line he read, his spirits rose. The job could be perfect for him.

He called Georgie. "Hey. Can you talk, or are you in the middle of something?"

"I can talk. What's up?"

A couple of students passed, nodding to him. He smiled back, waiting until they were out of earshot before telling her. "Josh sent me the details of a job."

"Yeah? Any good?"

"Yeah." He paused, taking a breath. "Georgie, I think it could be perfect for me."

"Really? What is it?"

He sat back, letting the sunshine warm his face. "It's at the place he works. You know they've opened up a second site next to the main one? Well, the surveys and the test-pits they've dug show that there's a huge, late-Anglo-Saxon settlement there. Probably Anglo-Scandinavian. They want someone to be the academic lead on excavating it, plus developing it as an experimental archaeology centre."

"Academic lead? Associated with which university?"

"None. They don't actually describe it as an academic post, but reading between the lines, that's what they need. They need someone who will make sense of the site, manage the excavation, and be able to write it up after it's been dug. I think they could also get an amazing joint project with one of the universities with the experimental archaeology they're doing. An academic would know exactly how to pitch that and get it off the ground." He leaned on his knees again. "Are you coming over tonight? We need to talk about it."

"Are you cooking?"

He laughed. "Yeah, I'm cooking, if you want." Although Georgie was a far better cook than him, she always preferred him to make dinner.

"Why didn't this job come up a month ago?" she said.

"I know."

It would have saved both of them a great deal of heartache if it had. He pushed his hair back, acknowledging one of his colleagues as they crossed the gardens. It seemed everyone wanted a slice of the sunshine today.

"I'm going to have to go," Georgie said. "See you tonight. Send me the details?"

"Will do. See you tonight."

She rang off, and he watched the scurry of people moving from one building to another, no doubt heading to and from an interminable series of meetings. He read the job description again. It would be perfect for him, but that didn't mean he would get it.

His phone rang. Carol.

"Has your research meeting finished?" she asked.

"Yes. A few minutes ago. Why?"

"You're meant to be seeing Dr Longstaff about the lectures he wants you to give."

He groaned, fingering his brow. "Yep. On my way."

He took a last lingering look at the gardens and made his way back to his office.

* * *

That evening, Georgie arrived at his place only minutes after he got home. She found him in the kitchen, staring into the fridge, trying to figure out what to make for dinner.

"Hey!" she said, pulling her hair out of the band that tamed it, and letting it tumble around her face.

He closed the fridge and hugged her, planting a kiss on her lips. "Hi. Good day?"

She locked her hands at the small of his back. "I'm still

working on everything from the dig, so it was a great day. You?"

He pulled a face. "A meeting about research. One about giving some lectures. A meeting about a meeting… I know… Only in academia, right? Budget stuff. And working on writing up the dig."

She twisted her mouth to one side. "Did you get outside at all?"

"I was outside when I rang you, but then I got dragged back in to talk about giving some lectures to the Honours students just before I go, and how the students would be assessed on them since I won't be here for the exams."

"That sounds…" she trailed off, scrunching her face up.

"Dull?" he cut in. "Mm, hm."

She squeezed him, then stepped back, fluffing her hair out. She was about to tie it back again, but he stopped her.

"Leave it loose. I love its madness."

She snapped the band around her wrist, looking at him with her head on one side. "Did you want to sit outside if you've been cooped up all day?"

A smile crept over his lips. She knew him too well. "Yeah."

They sat at the cast iron table in the garden, Anders moving his seat into the shade. Georgie stayed in the sun, though she put her back to it. Her hair glowed around her head like a mad halo, making him smile.

"So… the job advert Josh sent," she said, stretching out her legs towards him.

"It's perfect, isn't it? Enough academic stuff, but a lot of outside work, and a bit of management. I don't know if I could have designed a better job for me if I'd had free rein."

She studied him, resting her chin on her hand. "It's not as much money as you're on now. And *certainly* not as much as you'd be on in Norway."

"I know." He gazed out at the sunshine, feeling the breeze tickle his face. "But it's enough." He'd spent a free ten minutes in the afternoon between meetings trying to work out if it would be enough for them and a baby.

"It's not academia," she added.

"I know that, too. But it has a lot of academic stuff in it."

"What about the job in Norway? What will you do about that?"

He blew his cheeks out. "Well… I can't accept it, then immediately apply for the job at Josh's place. What if I got it?"

"What if you didn't?" she said softly.

"I know." He closed his eyes, leaning back in his seat. His guts churned. "Georgie, I don't want to accept the job in Norway."

"I know. And being totally truthful, I'd rather we stayed in the UK. But what if you turned down the job in Norway and didn't get this other one?"

They'd be risking having a baby on one income. Or potentially no income once Georgie's maternity pay ran out, unless she went back to work. That idea didn't sit well with him, but he recognised he was being sexist, railing against not being the main provider. He rubbed the back of his neck. All that was months away, though. He'd been pretty good at landing jobs so far. Even if he didn't get the job at Josh's place, something else would surely come up. He'd do *any* job to support her and the baby.

He opened his eyes. "Did you want me to take the job in Norway?"

She didn't answer for a moment, and his guts clenched again.

"I don't know," she said eventually. "I didn't think you would be happy in it, even before this other role came up. But now you've read about that one, I think you'd resent taking the one in Norway, and be constantly thinking 'what if?'. But I know you, Anders. If you turned it down, and then *didn't* get this other one, you'd berate yourself incessantly over us having a baby and you not having a job."

Anxiety prickled through him. She was spot on. He closed his eyes again.

"Do you hate me for getting pregnant?" she asked in a small voice.

His eyes snapped open. "Of course I don't! How on earth could you think that?"

"Because it would all be easy if I wasn't. You could turn down Norway, and it wouldn't matter so much if you didn't get this other job. You could just move in with me and Becky until you found something. But, with the baby…"

He reached across the table and pressed his hand over hers, desperate to soothe her. "Shh. I am *so* happy about the baby. If I don't get this job, and nothing else comes up, I'll find something. We'll be okay. I promise."

"Are you going to turn down the Norway job, then?"

He chewed his lower lip. "Only if you're okay about that. Georgie, I would do *anything* if it meant I was with you. If you'd rather I took it, say, and I'll make the best of it."

She shook her head, smiling softly. "No. I never thought it was a great fit for you. The thing Josh sent would be perfect." She pursed her lips. "Your father's going to go ballistic, though."

He didn't care. All that mattered was that he was with Georgie. He gazed at her, so full of love that he thought he would burst. He would make it work, whatever happened.

60

Georgia eyed the racks of clothes in the store. The shop was much more Becky's kind of place than hers. Like Anders, Georgia was happier in walking trousers and a fleece top. She suffered wearing either a dress or a smart trouser suit for work, but it wouldn't be her choice otherwise. Becky, however, revelled in pretty clothes and owned more skirts and dresses than she did anything else. They'd come to get Becky an outfit for a wedding she was going to later in the year. Despite the bulging wardrobe at home, Becky had been insistent that she needed something new. Georgia sneaked a glance at her friend. Her eyes shone as she scanned the clothes, like a kid in a sweet shop.

A perky woman of a similar age to them emerged from a corner of the shop where she had been tidying clothes. She was immaculately dressed in clothes that the shop sold and looked fabulous.

"Good morning, ladies. My name is Tilda. How can I help you today?"

Becky smiled brightly. "Morning! I booked a personal shopper. I'm looking for an outfit for a wedding."

Tilda beamed at them and pointed to a small sofa. "Take a seat. Let me see what I might have for you. Are you thinking more dress, or trouser suit?"

Georgia and Becky sat on the over-stuffed pastel-coloured sofa. Using a personal shopper was also far more Becky's kind of thing than Georgia's. Georgia would have been happier looking through the rails on her own, but Becky loved the fuss.

"Oh, dress," Becky said, as if the idea of a trouser suit horrified her.

The assistant appraised her. "Size ten?"

Becky wrinkled her nose. "Much as I would like to say yes, I'm probably more of a twelve."

"Super. Let me see what we might have."

She scurried away, and Becky settled back in her seat, glancing over at her. "How's everything going?"

After she'd told Anders about the baby, Georgia had spent most evenings and nights at his place, and the two women had hardly seen each other for several days.

"He turned down the job in Norway." She leaned forward, resting her elbows on her knees.

"Really? Do you think he'll get the other one?"

Georgia shrugged. "I don't know. He's really well qualified for it." She pulled a wry face. "Maybe *too* qualified. It's a step down in salary. Not that he cares."

"They'd be mad to turn him down."

She laughed. "Yeah. I think that too, but you just never know with these things."

Becky crossed her ankles. "How's Anders about the baby?"

"Oh, he's delighted. Probably more delighted to be a father than I am to be a mother, and that's saying something."

"But?" Becky cocked her head, studying her.

A long breath trickled out between her lips. "I just hope he's done the right thing in turning down the job. I know how much he'll beat himself up if he doesn't get this other one."

"But you never thought the Norway thing was right for him."

She acknowledged the point with a shrug. "True. And he was ready to turn it down before I told him I was pregnant. He said that was because he would rather be with me, and that if he took the job, there wasn't much chance of us getting back together, but I think it was just as much that he'd realised it was more what Haakon would want for him, than what he truly wanted for himself. But it was a job, and babies are expensive."

Tilda returned with a handful of clothes on hangers. "Here we go. Now, I think with your colouring, that pastel might wash you out, but I have brought a couple of paler things. Personally, I wonder whether this might not suit you better, though. I realise it might be a little bold for a wedding, but…"

She held up a dress that made Becky grin. Georgia smiled to

herself. Maybe a personal shopper *was* the right way to go, because the dress she held up was perfect for Becky, with its bolder colours and striking cut.

Becky stood and took the proffered items, including the paler ones.

"There's a changing room just here, and there's another sofa through there, too, if you wanted to go with your friend?" Tilda glanced at Georgia, who nodded.

The changing area was empty apart from them, so the two friends continued their conversation through the curtain while Becky tried on the clothes. Tilda said she was going to find a couple more things and would be back in a few minutes.

"And how do you feel about him turning down the job?" Becky asked from the cubicle.

"Okay, I guess. I mean, I would hate for him to get stuck in a job that wasn't right for him, and this other thing would be perfect."

Becky emerged from behind the curtain, wearing the bolder dress. It fitted her perfectly, and Tilda was right. It flattered her colouring.

"That looks amazing. Very you," said Georgia.

Becky studied her reflection. "My backside doesn't look massive, does it?"

"No. It's not massive to start with, and that cut is great on you."

Becky grinned, then disappeared back behind the curtain.

"So, what gives?" she called through to Georgia. "You still sound like there's a big 'but' at the end of that sentence."

"What if he doesn't get this other job? He'll hate himself for turning down something that would have guaranteed he could provide for us. However much he says he's a modern man, that 'provide for your family' streak runs right through him. And Haakon's being a complete pain about it all, which doesn't help."

"Oh, ignore Haakon. He wouldn't be happy whatever Anders did!"

Becky emerged from the cubicle in a dainty pastel dress, and Georgia shook her head vehemently. "Not that. You look like a vampire has sucked out all your blood."

Becky laughed and returned to the cubicle.

"When's the closing date for the new thing?"

"Tomorrow."

"And how has Oslo been about him turning them down?"

Georgia ran her tongue around her teeth. "Oh, okay, I guess. They offered him more money initially, but he still turned them down. He's finding it all horribly stressful, though."

Becky came out in another pale-coloured dress, and Georgia wrinkled her nose. "I still like the first one the best."

"Mm. Me too. Okay, last one." She headed back into the changing room. "Have you talked to Anders about all of it?"

"Yeah. He's struggling a bit."

That was an understatement. He hadn't said anything directly, but after another bruising call with his father the day before, he'd said he needed to go for a run. He'd been gone for almost two hours, and *still* seemed stressed after it, and Georgia was at a loss as to how to ease him.

Tilda returned with another dress just as Becky came out of the cubicle. She held it up to her.

"There's this, but I don't know… I think the colour's right, but I'm not sure the style is. Did you want to try it on?"

Becky eyed the dress, her lips twisted to one side, then she shook her head. "No, I think I'll stick with this one, thanks." She held up the first dress she'd tried on.

Tilda nodded, smiling brightly, and took all the hangers from Becky. "I'll wrap this for you."

She scurried away. Becky tilted her head at Georgia, then hugged her. "It'll work out. Anders has an amazing CV. They'll probably bite his hand off to have him."

"I hope so. He's just terrified that he'll have nothing when the baby comes."

Becky clicked her tongue. "That's months away. Stress about that if he doesn't get the job at Josh's. I mean, you'll know about that one way or the other, *way* before the baby comes." She hugged her again. "It'll be fine."

Georgia smiled weakly. She hoped Becky was right.

61

Anders rummaged in the top drawer of his desk at work, hunting for some painkillers. He'd been stuck in an interminable meeting for an hour, in a stuffy room, while various members of staff argued back and forth over something so trivial he thought he would explode. In the end, he'd upset everyone by snapping, but it had brought things to a head, and a decision had been made.

He found a strip of painkillers and washed two tablets down with the dregs of a cold cup of coffee, grimacing. In all honesty, it was less that the people had been irritating, and more that he hadn't heard back about the job Josh had told him about. The closing date had been a week ago, and his anxiety was spiking. Another difficult phone call with his father the evening before hadn't helped. It was rare for Haakon to raise his voice – he tended to opt for quiet disdain and criticism – but the call last night had resulted in both of them losing their tempers and shouting at each other. He'd hung up on his father while Haakon was in mid-rant and not picked up when he'd rung again.

The problem was, everything Haakon had said was true. He'd berated him for turning down a well-paid job with excellent prospects, when he had nothing else on the cards. With a child on the way, he should be accepting his responsibilities, not yearning for an inferior position with less kudos and fewer opportunities. It hadn't helped that Haakon had sung his praises to Professor Gunderson so much. Some of Haakon's wrath was undoubtedly because he'd lost face.

At least Georgie was being a rock. She must be as anxious as he was that he'd turned the job down when he had no guarantee of anything else. He hoped he wasn't about to let her down. His father was right. He *was* being irresponsible. His headache flared, making him wince.

He leaned back in his seat and stared out of the window. He should really be working on one of the papers about the dig, but his brain was on anything but that. Reluctantly, he turned back to his computer and ran a job search. Nothing new came up. He studied the jobs that were listed. None of them were all that close to what he wanted, but he could do them if he had to.

His email pinged, and a torrent of new messages arrived. He scanned down them, groaning internally. More admin. More meetings, no doubt. And then his eye snagged on the sender's name he'd been hoping for. He swallowed and clicked on it, praying it wasn't a 'thanks, but no thanks' message.

It wasn't. He almost yelled with delight. It was an invitation to an interview. He scanned through it, checked the attachments, then yanked out his phone and called Georgie.

"Hi! You able to talk?" he said, his words coming out in a rush.

"Sure. What's up?"

He lowered his voice, aware that his office door stood wide-open. "I've got an interview."

"Oh, brilliant! When?"

"Two weeks."

"Ooh, that soon? What do you need to prepare?"

He read from the email. "A brief presentation on what I see as the future of the company, and how I would be the ideal person to make it happen."

"Okay. Call Josh tonight? See if you can get any insider knowledge on what the guys are thinking about?"

"Yep."

"Oh, Anders, I'm so pleased for you. You'd be brilliant for the job."

He breathed steadily. He wasn't always brilliant at presentations.

"You're going to be sick of hearing my pitch by the time we get there. I'm going to need to practise it a million times."

She chuckled. "I know. You'll be fine."

He hoped so.

He stared at the other emails crowding his in-box, his heart sinking. "Ugh. I really ought to be doing something else, however much I just want to chat with you. Love you. See you tonight."

"Love you too."

They rang off. Almost immediately, his email pinged again, and he braced himself for more tedious admin, only to be pleasantly surprised to see it was from Josh.

Hey Anders, Congratulations on the interview, and good luck with it. You in tonight? Happy to talk about the company if you want. I really hope you get the job.

Anders hit 'reply': *Hi! Yep, in tonight. A chat would be brilliant. Thanks.*

He sent the reply, then swivelled back to gaze out of the window, his brain planning the presentation. He grabbed a pen and a clean sheet of paper and jotted out notes, flagging what he wanted to check with Josh, and adding stars next to the areas he thought he shone at.

The notes made, a smile settled on his lips. Maybe everything would work out, after all.

63

"Thank you, Dr Mortensen. That was an excellent presentation, and you've given us much to consider."

Chris Walker, the chair of the interview panel, smiled kindly at him, indicating for him to take a seat. Anders closed down his presentation and sat in the seat facing the interview panel.

Alongside Chris Walker – the manager of the project and a man in his early fifties with a reassuring number of smile-lines around his eyes – were Cheryl Lewis, from Human Resources, and Beth Hall, who ran the experimental archaeology part of the company. Cheryl Lewis had largely sat and listened, whereas Beth Hall, with whom he assumed he would end up working closely if he got the job, had made copious notes during his presentation. From what he'd seen of her, and what Josh had said, he thought he would get on well with her. She seemed meticulous and focused, but she also had short nails and chapped hands, so clearly wasn't only involved on paper.

Anders took a steadying breath, surreptitiously wiping his palms on his thighs, and smiled, trying to relax.

"So, Dr Mortensen, in your presentation, you suggested that your academic background would give you invaluable insight on how to take the project forward. Could you tell us a little more about that, please?"

"Certainly."

For the next half hour, he answered their questions and expanded on his presentation. As far as he could tell, everything he said landed well. The chat with Josh the week before, giving him inside knowledge about the potential developments in the company, had provided a fantastic springboard for his presentation, and most of the interview had focused on that area.

By the end of the half hour, he thought he'd convinced them that his academic standing would bring authority and recognition to the work they were doing, and his practical experience would be invaluable in the actual dig. His current role as head of department ticked the boxes for 'management', though privately, he hoped he would be far more involved in the actual digging of the site and the associated experimental archaeology. Although Cheryl Lewis had maintained an inscrutable poker-face throughout, the other two had smiled and nodded encouragingly, settling his nerves.

And then came the sticking point. Cheryl Lewis opened a small notebook in her hand and met his eye.

"Dr Mortensen, I see from your application that your current salary is significantly higher than the upper end of the range available for this post."

He nodded.

"I have to stress to you that, if we were to offer you the post, we absolutely could not go higher than the advertised range."

"I understand that."

Chris Walker raised a brow. "You would be prepared to take such a cut in earnings? If you remained in academia, you'd be able to command much more."

He took a moment before answering. "I know, but to be perfectly frank with you, I care more about whether the job will make me happy than the salary. Academia has its moments and its benefits, I can't deny that, but I'm ready for a change." He laughed self-consciously. "I'm realising that my heart doesn't really lie behind a desk."

All three of them seemed satisfied with his answer, allowing his anxiety to drop a little.

After another couple of questions, Chris Walker smiled. "Well, I think that's everything. We are hoping to make our decision today, but I can't make any promises."

They all shook hands with him, and Beth Hall showed him back out, still smiling widely.

Outside, the sun peeped out from behind the clouds, and the brief showers from the morning had disappeared. He took off his tie and stuffed it in a pocket, then undid a couple of buttons on his shirt. The day was still cool, so he left his suit jacket on while he walked to his car. He'd parked in the company car park, but didn't want to drive back home just yet. He didn't really know the town well, so he moved the car to one of the short-stay car parks and explored. Maybe he would find something for Georgie in one of the shops.

He checked his watch, wanting to talk to her, then sighed. She was scheduled to be in a meeting that afternoon, and wouldn't be out of it yet. He meandered around the town centre, checking out house prices and rental prices at the estate agents and letting agents, and trying to get a feel for the place. The town had a pleasant blend of big-store names and small independent shops, along with a well-stocked bookshop. Apparently, there was a market in the square twice a week, and the town was an attractive mix of traditional stone buildings and more modern suburbs. There were also several parks with play-areas. As he walked around, he'd been relieved at the lack of graffiti, and pleased at the general upkeep. It would be a fantastic place to bring up a child.

Just as he was running out of town to explore, Georgie rang him, and he grinned.

"Hey. My meeting finished early. How did it go? Any news?" she asked.

He ducked down a side-street and stood in a quiet doorway. "It went as well as it could, and everyone seemed very positive. They liked the presentation. They grilled me a bit on some of my ideas, especially about liaising with a university over the experimental archaeology stuff, but I think I convinced them. If I don't get it, I don't think I could have done any more. They may let me know today, but couldn't make any promises. I'm just wandering around the town at the moment."

"What's that like?"

He paused, his gaze drifting over the attractive shop-fronts on the main street just visible at the end of the alleyway. "It's lovely, actually. Nice mix. House prices aren't bad."

If he got the job, the town would be close enough for Georgie to commute to work. It would be a longer journey than she currently had, but it wasn't horrendous. And it wouldn't be for long before she was on maternity leave.

"What's your gut feeling? Do you think you've got it?"

He rested his back against the wall next to the doorway. "I don't know. I hope so. It felt like it went well, but I don't want to get my hopes up and then them call me and say no."

"Okay. I'm keeping everything crossed for you!"

He laughed. "Thank you. How's your day going?"

"Same old, same old. But it's what I love, so that's fine. I ought to get back to it, but I wanted to see how things had gone."

"I'll let you get on. See you later."

They ended the call, and he drew in a long breath, wanting the job more than ever.

He walked back to the main shopping area, dawdling as he checked out the shops. He stopped outside a jewellers, looking at the window display, his heart rate picking up as he looked at one particular object. It would be perfect.

While he was still admiring it, his phone rang.

"Dr Mortensen?"

His heart raced even more. "Yes. Speaking."

"Hi there. This is Chris Walker. I'm calling to let you know about the job."

He tried to control his breathing.

"We would be delighted to have you on board, Dr Mortensen. You were top of our list before the interviews and only confirmed that position today."

He let his breath go in a rush. "Thank you."

"We'll write to you formally, but I just wanted to call you in person, to let you know." There was an apologetic cough on the line. "We genuinely can't match your current salary. I do hope that won't be an issue."

"No issue. I really am looking forward to working with you."

They exchanged a few more words, then rang off. Anders wanted to punch the air and bellow at the top of his lungs. He settled for calling Georgie back.

"Have you heard?" she said, her words almost garbled with her rush.

"Yes. I got it!"

He held the phone away from his ear as she squealed with

delight.

"I knew it! I knew you would! Oh, you amazing man! Well done!"

He laughed. "Thank you. Okay, I'm heading back home. See you soon. I just wanted to let you know."

"Oh, I am so pleased for you! Mwah!"

She blew an enormous kiss down the phone at him, making him laugh again. "Save those for when I see you."

The call over, he took a last look at the object in the jeweller's window, then pushed the door open, making the bell above it jangle.

* * *

Georgia could hardly contain herself when Anders got back later that afternoon. As soon as she heard the front door opening, she rushed to meet him, wrapping herself around him in a tight hug and knocking the breath out of him.

"You got it! Oh, I am so proud of you!"

His face shone, a broad grin creeping across his face. She squealed with delight, and he swung her off her feet, kissing her soundly.

"Thank you. Oh, god, I am *so* relieved!"

She kissed him, then scruffed his hair up, making him laugh.

"Come into the garden. I have something for you." She drew out of his arms and caught his hand, towing him towards the garden. "As soon as you called and told me you'd got the job, I went and got it."

"Got what?" he asked, half laughing.

They emerged into the garden at the back of his house. On the small table there, a bottle of champagne sat in a bucket of iced water, next to two flutes that she'd found in the back of one of his cupboards. She let go of his hand so that she could retrieve the champagne for him to open.

"Georgie," he said, his voice a little weird.

"What?" She pulled the bottle out of the bucket of melting ice and squeegeed the water off the sides with her hands, shaking them out to dry them a little.

Anders cleared his throat. "Georgie?"

She turned, the still dripping bottle clutched in her hand. "What?"

His head wasn't where she expected it to be, and her gaze dropped. Her heart suddenly raced. Anders had one knee on the ground, and was looking up at her with a small box in his hands, more nervous than she'd ever seen him before. He opened the box, holding it up towards her, his hands shaking.

"Georgie, I love you. With every single cell in my body. I have done since the day I met you and I should have asked you this a long time ago. Marry me? I never want to be without you. Ever."

Love and happiness bubbled up in her, overwhelming her, and she couldn't speak for a moment.

"Georgie?" A stricken note entered his voice, and his sky-blue eyes filled with fear.

She rushed to reassure him. "Anders, yes! Oh, a hundred times, yes!"

"Well, hopefully just the once." Relief flooded his face, and his breathing eased.

Georgia looked at the wet bottle in her hands and put it down on the table, then turned back to him.

"Get up! You're ruining your suit!" she said, laughing.

He stood, still holding the box towards her, and she took it, peering inside at the ring. A beautiful diamond flanked by emeralds sparkled in the late sun.

"It's gorgeous," she whispered, smiling up at him.

He took the ring out of the box and threaded it on to her finger, his hands still trembling.

"I should have asked you a long time ago." He nibbled at his bottom lip. "I didn't, because I didn't have a job lined up, and I wanted to be able to give you stability, and security, and—"

She kissed him, cutting him off. "None of that matters, Anders. As long as I'm with you, I have everything I need."

He gazed at her, his eyes full of love, slipping his arms around her waist. "You've made me the happiest man ever. Shall we open that champagne?"

18 months later

Anders shifted his son in his arms. It was easier to carry him today than have him in a pushchair. Tomas peered at him with blue eyes that matched his own, making soft babbling sounds. Georgie reached across to tickle him under his chin.

"Yes, Pappa's famous," she said, grinning.

Anders rolled his eyes.

"I still can't believe that was the best picture of me," he muttered.

They stood near to a glass case displaying the objects found in the burial. The whole burial was laid out exactly as they had found it, with the only exception being that the skeleton was a 3D printed replica of the original. Behind the display case was the photo he was grumbling about. Georgie had taken it of him one day on the dig, and in it, his hair was blowing around his face, he had a straggly beard, and mud all over his top. He was also beaming out joy, which was why Georgie had taken it in the first place, and why she had suggested it was the one used in the exhibition.

The three of them had come to the opening of a major exhibition on the dig. As well as the main centrepiece of the burial, there were exhibits of the other finds, including the small hoard that had been one of the main reasons the dig had been extended, and the beautiful brooches and buckles. The doors to the museum hadn't opened yet, but Anders and Georgie had been allowed in early. Both of them had been involved with organising the exhibition, but this was the first time either of them had seen the final arrangements.

Georgie beamed up at him. "It all looks amazing. Especially *that*."

She pointed to a nearby table bearing a stack of books with his name on the front. A small thrill went through him as he glanced over at them.

The museum director, Maggie Denton, a neat woman in her early forties, approached them. They both knew her by sight, but hadn't spent a great deal of time with her. She smiled warmly.

"Dr Mortensen, Mrs Mortensen."

Anders flapped a hand. "Anders and Georgia, please."

"And who is this little angel?" Maggie smiled down at Tomas, who immediately went shy and buried his face in his father's neck.

"Tomas," said Georgie. "Who is being uncharacteristically quiet right now."

"I *love* his ringlets."

Tomas had not only inherited his mother's hair colour, but also some of its madness. Anders still wasn't convinced that ringlets on a boy would be anything Tomas would thank them for later, but it was what it was.

"Your father has arrived," said Maggie, losing some of her animation as she said it. "Shall I let him in?"

He nodded, resigned. Georgie moved a little closer to him, and rubbed his back, her hand making soft circles between his shoulder blades. Maggie smiled, thin-lipped, and moved away.

Once the excavation had finished, there had been a big news item about the dig, and there was talk about a documentary, though Anders wasn't sure he wanted to be in front of the camera at any point. The discovery of a full Viking burial in Yorkshire had fired the imagination of people far beyond the world of academia, making Anders almost a household name, and leading to the glossy book currently on the table. Haakon had said nothing about any of it.

A few minutes later, Haakon strode into the museum, and Anders's guts tightened.

"Anders. Georgia. Oh, and little Tomas." Haakon reached over to smooth a hand over Tomas's hair, tutting at the curls. "This is all getting a little long." He straightened, looking past Anders to the exhibition. "So, this is it?"

Anders gritted his teeth. "Yes. This is it. Did you want me to sign a copy of my book for you?"

Haakon's eyes narrowed, and he went over to the table and leafed through a copy. "Are you happy with how it's all turned out?"

Anders raised his chin. "I am, Pappa. I think this is one of the most important finds in recent history, and I think the museum has done a fantastic job with the exhibition."

"And your book?" Haakon let the cover close again.

"I'm really proud of the book." He swallowed, squaring his shoulders. "I'm really proud of *all* of it, Pappa."

Haakon stalked around the exhibits, peering through his wire-rimmed glasses at everything, before returning to the display of the grave. Anders shifted Tomas in his arms, waiting for some excoriating dismissal of his achievements.

Haakon stood in front of him, his hands clasped behind his back, nodding slightly.

"Well done, Anders. Excellent work. I'm proud of you."

Tears burned his eyes. "Thank you, Pappa."

Haakon smiled. "You still need a haircut."

He laughed.

The doors to the exhibition had clearly been opened, because a flurry of people entered the room. Anders glanced over to Georgie, hoping that she wanted to leave, too. She gave him a slow blink, and the two of them moved towards the exit.

As they did, Georgie's head suddenly shot up, and she stopped in her tracks, staring across the room. Tomas shifted in his arms, waving madly at the same area. Anders turned to see what had snared their attention.

Across the room, two ghostly figures had appeared, standing next to the display of the grave, and Anders caught his breath. A young woman with long, wavy hair, wearing a full-length woollen dress, held the hand of a small boy with bright ringlets. The boy wore a woollen tunic over woollen trousers and was waving back at Tomas, a carved wooden horse in his fist.

"Do you see them?" Georgie asked Tomas. "Do you see Einar and Magnus?"

"*I* see someone," Anders said, making Georgie's head whip around to him.

"Really?"

"Yes… But I think I see *Aelfgyth* and Magnus, not Einar."

Excitement flooded Georgie's face. "Really? I've never seen her. I only ever saw what she saw. What does she look like?"

He studied the woman, then smiled down at Georgie, his heart full of love. "You. She looks like you."

If you enjoyed reading Anders and Georgie's story, I would be enormously grateful if you would leave a review – on Amazon or Goodreads or wherever – to help other readers find them. Maybe talk about them on social media? Or perhaps have this as your next book-group book?

Thank you!

Out of Time

A wronged man. A race against time. Can she change history and save the man she loves?

Ellie's life is on the brink of ruin - her business is failing and her dreams of expansion are fading away. When she inherits a house, it seems like all her hopes could come true.

But the house has a dark history. According to local legend, the blacksmith who lived there in the 1760s brutally murdered a local girl. And the past is bleeding into the present. The house shifts; rooms disappear; Ellie keeps seeing the ghost of a young man.

When Ellie is catapulted through time to 1762, she comes face to face with the blacksmith, Kit. Far from the violent thug the stories would have him be, he seems kind and honourable.

As Ellie and Kit get closer, they know that history is against them. If they don't discover what really happened to the murdered girl, time will run out for Kit.

Has history wronged an innocent man? If so, can Ellie save him before he's killed for a crime he didn't commit?

Buy Out of Time now and lose yourself in Amanda M Fleet's gripping timeslip mystery romance.

What readers are saying…

★★★★★ Loved it. Loved it. Loved it.
What a fantastic story. I was torn between getting to the end to know what happened, and not wanting it to finish. I read a lot of time slip stories, but this tops them all. XXX

★★★★★ Absolutely captivating storyline
A wonderful tale of true love, spanning over two hundred+ years.

Full of suspense, twists and turns and incredible imagery. I really hope Amanda writes more books, especially time-slip ones. It was just perfect!

★★★★★ Excellent read!!!

My favorite are time travel romance novels and this book "Out of Time" is truly one of the BEST I have ever read! You will not want to put it down! Very engaging! You will not be disappointed!

The Guardians of The Realm series

Book 1: Aegyir Rises

She's living her perfect life until a demon mistakes her for the warrior that imprisoned him. Now he's set on revenge.

Can she stop him before everyone she loves is slaughtered?

Reagan just wants to land her dream job and live quietly with her boyfriend, but her happiness is shattered when an accident releases an ancient creature who believes Reagan is someone else entirely.

All of her life, she's been plagued by dreams of being a warrior in a different world. Can these dreams really be memories of another realm?

When people all around her start dying mysteriously, Reagan realises she needs to figure out who she really is.

Because if she doesn't, no one will survive.

Aegyir Rises is the first book in the thrilling new-adult contemporary fantasy series The Guardians of The Realm.

Buy **Aegyir Rises** now, and lose yourself in a world of soul-stealing demons, warriors, and the fight of good versus evil.

★★★★★ "There's nothing out there as intriguing, tense and unputdownable in the urban fantasy genre that I've come across in a very long time."

★★★★★ "Oh my god! I have cried and been on the edge of my seat!"

About the Author

Amanda Fleet is a physiologist by training and a writer at heart. She spent almost 20 years teaching science and medicine undergraduates at university, but now writes full-time.

Amanda lives in Scotland with her husband and her cat. She can be found writing, walking and running.

Acknowledgements

There are a lot of people who helped me cope with all the blood, sweat, and tears during the writing of this, and I apologise profusely to anyone I miss out here. First and foremost, I need to thank Owain and Nela Scholma-Mason, who gave me invaluable advice over the archaeology, and information about how a site would be run. Any errors in the book are entirely mine.

I am also blessed to have a fantastic circle of writing friends, who have held me together and supported me when things have been difficult, and who have been there to celebrate the successes. There are too many of you to list all of you individually, but I need to thank Angela Moss and Gail Williams in particular, for reading the manuscript and giving me such helpful feedback. You're both stars.

I must also thank my running buddy, Michael Caplis, who had to listen to so much rubbish from me out on our runs, but who was a great sounding board, and who also gave me fantastic information about army tents. I also need to thank my writing buddy, Stuart Lennon, for keeping me supplied with notebooks.

Thank you to my wonderful beta-readers, especially Daisy Ship and Leanne Caplis; your words of encouragement kept me going. My thanks also to GetCovers, who did such a great job with the cover.

And last but most certainly not least, my love, and thanks to my husband, Colin, without whom none of my books would have happened.

Printed in Dunstable, United Kingdom

68431258R00191